PUCKING ROAD TRIP

ROSEMARY A JOHNS

BEING PUCKED © copyright 2024 Rosemary A Johns

www.rosemaryajohns.com

Copyright notice: All rights reserved under the International and Pan-American Copyright Conventions. No part of this book may be reproduced or transmitted in any form or by any means, electronic or mechanical, including photocopying, recording, or by any information storage and retrieval system, without permission in writing from the publisher.

This is a work of fiction. Names, places, characters and incidents are either the product of the author's imagination or are used fictitiously, and any resemblance to any actual persons, living or dead, organizations, events or locales is entirely coincidental.

Warning: the unauthorized reproduction or distribution of this copyrighted work is illegal. Criminal copyright infringement, including infringement without monetary gain, is investigated by the FBI and is punishable by up to 5 years in prison and a fine of $250,000.

Fantasy Rebel Limited

❦ Created with Vellum

BAY REBELS

Three NHL hockey players. One second chance. And a PR nightmare.

Word to the wise, never go on a road trip with your forbidden lovers. Especially when they lose everything, if they don't win the season. Doubly, when you're the coach's daughter.

Why did I? Because I'm their live-in PR.

I'm also madly in love with these men who have bodies like gods. And they're obsessed with me.

The tall, dark, and grumpy captain. The star forward with spellbinding gray eyes and golden retriever energy. And his tattooed, protective PA twin.

Forced to share a tour bus and hotel rooms, the tension is as explosive off the ice as on it. Will we survive, however, when a dangerous secret from our past catches up with us?

On this pucking road trip, I may not be able to wear

my men's jerseys to games but I'm desperate to be forever theirs.

BOOKS IN THE REBEL VERSE

ALL BOOKS ARE STANDALONE SERIES

PACK BONDS OMEGAVERSE

REBEL & HER KNIGHTS
EMBER & HER MARSHALS
ANGEL & HER CHAMPIONS
JEWEL & HER KINGS
PUCK & HER BLADES
MERCY & HER DEVILS
CANDY & HER SAINTS
JULIET & HER ROMEOS

CONTEMPORARY STANDALONE

DARLING MADNESS, LOST BOYS OF NEVER
ELITE
ONE SECRET RULE

BAY REBELS, ICE HOCKEY ROMANCE

BEING PUCKED
SECRETLY PUCKING
PUCKING ROAD TRIP
PUCKING OBSESSED

REBEL ACADEMY -WICKEDLY CHARMED COMPLETE SERIES

COMPLETE BOX SET
CRAVE
CRUSH
CURSE

REBEL WEREWOLVES - COMPLETE SERIES

COMPLETE BOX SET
ONLY PERFECT OMEGAS
ONLY PRETTY BETAS
ONLY PROTECTOR ALPHAS

REBEL: HOUSE OF FAE - COMPLETE

HOUSE OF FAE

REBEL GODS - COMPLETE SERIES

BAD LOKI
BAD HADES
BAD RA

REBEL DEMONS - COMPLETE SERIES

MY DEMON OF FIRE
MY DEMON OF AIR
MY DEMON OF EARTH
MY DEMON OF WATER

REBEL ANGELS - COMPLETE SERIES

COMPLETE SERIES BOX SET BOOKS 1-5
VAMPIRE HUNTRESS
VAMPIRE PRINCESS
VAMPIRE DEVIL
VAMPIRE MAGE
VAMPIRE GOD

REBEL VAMPIRES - COMPLETE SERIES

COMPLETE SERIES BOX SET BOOKS 1-3
BLOOD DRAGONS
BLOOD SHACKLES
BLOOD RENEGADES
STANDALONE: BLOOD GODS

THE SHADOWMATES SERIES - COMPLETE

WOLF TRIALS
WOLF FATES

AUDIO BOOKS

LISTEN HERE...

BOOKS IN THE OXFORD VERSE

RECOMMENDED READING ORDER

OXFORD MAGIC KITTEN MYSTERIES
COMPLETE SERIES

A FAMILIAR MURDER
A FAMILIAR CURSE
A FAMILIAR HEX
A FAMILIAR BREW
A FAMILIAR GHOST
A FAMILIAR SPELL
A FAMILIAR YULE
A FAMILIAR BRIDE

OXFORD PARANORMAL BOOK CLUB
COMPLETE SERIES

BITING MR. DARCY
HEXING MERLIN

MERCHANDISE, SIGNED BOOKS, AND LIMITED EDITIONS

A GUIDE TO LOVING HOCKEY PLAYERS

Robyn's Number One Rule: Learn to love hockey players by remembering three essential things...

1. *They're gods on the ice but are more devoted to you than their sticks.*
2. *They'll burn down the world to protect you against your dark past.*
3. *The Prince twins*

.

But never forget it all began with D'Angelo...

CHAPTER ONE

Captain's Hall, Freedom

obyn

"Are all hockey players obsessed with their sticks?" I stretch out on the bed, aching deliciously after my wild night. I push my wavy, flame-red hair out of my emerald eyes. "Do you two need some alone time?"

I struggle to keep my face straight.

The dominant, gorgeous man who's sprawled next to me, cradling his hockey stick on his lap and stroking it like this is how players jerk off, shoots me an icy glare.

Of course he does because he's Jude fucking D'Angelo.

A grumpy dick.

Also, the man who is every dream and hope that I have.

I try to look innocent.

But it's hard, when I'm naked with smudged mascara, puffy eyes from allergies, and a hickey on my neck.

I don't regret the hickey.

Allergies, however, suck.

Robyn McKenna, twenty-seven, independent businesswoman and PR Director of the Bay Rebels, and *hot mess*.

I pull the glimmering covers closer around myself.

I glance under my eyelashes at D'Angelo, as he rubs his thumb in a way that's far too suggestive over the toe of the stick.

I swallow.

That has to be deliberate, right?

Now, I wish that I could be a fly on the wall in the Bay Rebels locker room, if this is how the whole team act.

D'Angelo is captain of the Bay Rebels NHL hockey team, my best friend from college, and the man who I'm desperately in love with.

Unlike me, he's dressed in an immaculate designer navy suit and waistcoat with the sleeves rolled back to reveal his strong forearms.

Does he get up half an hour early just to be certain that he's dressed smartly, before I am?

It'd be the sort of thing that he would do.

D'Angelo is six foot three with olive skin and piercing ice blue eyes that are so frosty they make me shiver.

Raven curls frame his strong face, as he tips his head forward to finish retaping the stick heel-to-toe.

D'Angelo's bedroom is large and overlooks the pasture at the back of Captain's Hall ranch. The drapes are open. Soft morning light cascades over D'Angelo's antique silver bed. The room is as elegant as the man himself.

The floors are carpeted and white like the walls. The entire far wall is a mirrored walk-in closet.

Scissors, tape, and stick wax lie on the nightstand.

D'Angelo smooths down the tape compulsively three times.

"Are you jealous? I find your possessiveness cute, principessa," D'Angelo replies, coolly.

"Jealous?" When I sit up, the covers fall off me. "We're already in a polyamorous relationship with the Prince twins. Fine, I'm open to discussing dating your stick as well."

"You'll like her. She helps me think of you, during every game that I play. I score more pucks by feeling that I'm touching you, even on the ice. She's called Robyn."

"You've named *your* stick after me?"

D'Angelo looks affronted. "You make it sound like I named my dick."

"Well, have you?" I blush.

D'Angelo's lips twitch, as he leisurely scans over my naked body; my skin goosebumps. "What if it's Lady Godiva's Horse?"

I definitely am okay with riding him.

Except, it so isn't.

If D'Angelo wants to play this game, then I'm down

with it. After all, our love language is banter.

"Moby Dick?" I quirk my brow. "Mount Vesuvius? *Little Guy?*"

I can't help it.

D'Angelo's eyes darken. He growls, placing his stick down and leaning it against the bed.

Whoops, I've poked the bear.

D'Angelo twists to lean over me. His silky curls brush my face.

I can feel his hard cock through his pants against my hip.

It's definitely not *Little Guy*.

"Would my cock receive its own VIP invitation to clubs?" D'Angelo claims my lips in a kiss that's far too brief. "My cock is not a separate identity to me. So, it doesn't need its own name. I'm not insecure or narcissistic enough for that. But *little…?*"

"Wilder named his dick," I say to distract him.

Wilder Talon is my ex-husband who abused, stalked, and cheated on me. A star 'golden boy' of the NHL, as well as D'Angelo's rival, Wilder lied to both D'Angelo and me to keep us apart for years.

And D'Angelo's right, Wilder is a narcissist, one who wrecked our relationship.

This is our second chance.

Plus, Wilder is the jerk who liked to get creative with his stick in the kinkiest ways. If I could wipe my brain of my ex being butt naked with his own hockey stick *up* that butt, then I'd be eternally happy.

Or at least, would need less therapy.

I could also do without the memory of how he'd fart like he was trying to compose a hit record, each morning as he woke up.

D'Angelo's eyes light with amusement. "Please tell me that Talon's is named Little Guy."

"Sorry. It's Thor."

"Talon looks like a Viking turned dark. If I was naming mine, it would be Lucifer."

Of course.

D'Angelo is a beautiful fallen angel.

He straddles the line between devil and angel. Right now, he's definitely on the wicked side of that line.

I reach up, tracing the scruff of stubble on D'Angelo's chin. His gaze softens.

He kisses me again, and this time, his plush lips linger.

D'Angelo's fresh, masculine scent wraps around me. I reach out, carding my fingers through his hair. His strong hand rests on my thigh, stroking circles.

D'Angelo deepens the kiss, dominating it.

I melt into it, but he draws back with a final nibble over my bottom lip.

"Are you okay, principessa?" He asks.

"I'm good. Better than." I smile. "Last night, celebrating your victory on the ice and our victory over the journalist who's been trying to destroy us, was incredible. Melanie has bullied my brother and me since high school. Seeing her get the justice that she's always escaped was everything. Plus, being able to show Shay that he could be bound in ropes but also held safe by them, after what he suffered at the hands of his abusive domme, felt healing. I know that it's only the first step in a hard journey, but we can take it together. We have each other, right?"

D'Angelo nods.

He scans me, assessing.

He does this.

He's good at aftercare.

He doesn't only check up during a scene or after it. He'll check in for at least the day after. If something has been intense, then he'll keep a close eye for the next week.

D'Angelo is a trained dom and he's the most protective — and possessive — man who I've ever met.

Even though I'm in a polyamorous relationship, D'Angelo needs to snatch these quiet moments together, when it's just the two of us.

My eyes widen. Panic floods through me. My heartbeat races.

Wildly, I look around myself. "Where are the twins? Where did we put them?"

D'Angelo scrunches up his nose. "They're not pets. What am I saying? Shay is our pet. Our good boy."

My cheeks pink.

Our good boy.

Those words pull at something deep inside me.

Shay Prince is loved by both D'Angelo and me. He wants to be *owned* — fucking possessed — by us.

He's equally part of our relationship. I can't imagine my life without Shay held between us.

Since he arrived from England with his twin, the two brothers have not only been adopted by my small town of Freedom and the Bay Rebels.

They're both in my heart, and I couldn't cut them out without dying.

"I can't help it." I wet my dry lips. "Shouldn't Shay at least still be sleeping wrapped around me like a limpet?"

I love the way that Shay tangles his legs around mine, while his golden hair falls over my cheeks, as he sleeps.

He's a sleep cuddler.

"An adorable one," D'Angelo says. "Don't tell him I said that. I'll deny it."

"I get the same panicky feeling as when I don't know where my iPhone is."

D'Angelo snorts. "It's not surprising. Shay is a walking disaster. He has the same klutzy charm as you, although he falls over less often. I should take out insurance for both of you. The puppy has broken two vases, a picture frame, and the mirror in the bathroom with an impressive high kick. And that's not to mention the window at the back of Captain's Hall, when he was playing football. The equipment manager, Kay, despairs because somehow Shay breaks his stick almost every game."

"Plus, he's lost *his* iPhone—"

"Every day. But Eden always finds it for him."

We both chuckle.

Eden cares for all of us. He has an equal place in our lives.

Eden was a hockey player, until an injury knocked him out of the NHL. Yet he doesn't resent that his brother shines as one of the best players still. He supports Shay.

That takes strength.

Now, Eden works as D'Angelo's PA, despite his social

anxiety, while he recovers from severe post-concussion symptoms.

He was attacked on the ice, during a game. His injuries ended his career. He'd already received too many blows to his head as a kid to make receiving any more the same as playing Russian roullete with his life.

Now, he's receiving treatment from the hospital and my brother, Cody.

Cody's Director of Physical Therapy at the Bay Rebels.

Eden never complains.

It worries me that he doesn't think he deserves to.

I fucking adore him.

I've woken up each morning for the last few weeks thankful for these three men who each meet a different need in me in the same way that I do for them.

Since I was trapped in a marriage to Wilder, I never expected to experience this type of love.

These men have opened my eyes to what's possible.

This relationship is liberating and empowering. *I've never felt so seen.*

Warmth and contentment curls through me.

This is my found family. My home. My new life.

D'Angelo shifts to sit next to me with his back against the headboard. He crosses his long legs at the ankles, smoothing out his suit.

"Take a deep breath," D'Angelo drawls. "What can you smell?"

When I wrinkle my nose, I'm instantly flooded by the delicious aroma of fragrant, aromatic tea and smoky bacon.

My mouth waters. "Tea and bacon. Eden promised to bring it up to bed this morning. He's the best boyfriend."

D'Angelo looks close to pouting. I pretend not to notice.

"All I can offer is being a millionaire star player who gives debauchery a PR facelift, while looking beautiful draped over a piano or with a riding crop in my hand."

"And having no ego at all."

"None whatsoever." D'Angelo smirks. "You know, Atlas tapes his stick at the arena before games. The guy owns four dogs. He's worried about their fur messing it up."

"Isn't it me who normally rambles with non sequiturs?"

"If I offer to adopt a cat for Eden, I'd have to tape my stick at the arena." D'Angelo's expression has become thoughtful.

My eyes widen. "You're serious."

He nods.

D'Angelo pretends to be a grumpy dick. Sometimes, he is.

But I can see behind the mask.

I grasp D'Angelo's hand, entwining our fingers. "Eden loves animals. He walks in the woods because he finds it easier to be around them than humans. He told me that when he was young, he wanted to be a vet. He'd officially adopt a squirrel, if he could."

D'Angelo's eyes crease at the edges, as he smiles. "To save us from the fate of finding nuts in our shoes or pants, then I'd better offer to adopt a cat from a shelter. How about after the season ends?"

"That makes sense. Eden's never had a girlfriend before. I'm all his firsts. This new family for him is overwhelming. He doesn't understand friendship like we do. It will prove to Eden that you truly mean this isn't a short term set up but that you see a future together."

"It's Shay who needs to be reassured about that."

He's right.

Shay is haunted by fears that D'Angelo only sees this as a hookup. He can't understand that he's worthy of being loved or a true relationship. He's never had one before. He's been abused and used for sex like he's a toy simply because he's a submissive.

D'Angelo and I are both going to prove to him that he's a man first.

"Is Shay with his brother?" I ask.

D'Angelo shakes his head. "After I carried you into bed last night, I gave Shay aftercare for a couple of hours."

I flush at the memory of being manhandled over D'Angelo's shoulder.

Also, how's he able to make me wet simply with a memory?

D'Angelo's sultry, half-hooded look, which he's now giving me, should be illegal.

"Wasn't my massage effective?" I ask.

When D'Angelo winces, I narrow my eyes.

Don't people like my massages?

Huh.

"I'm sure that it was *something*," D'Angelo replies. "I ran

Shay a hot bath with scented oils and allowed him a long soak. He was half-asleep by the end. Then I gave him the praise and petting that he needs. I didn't want his insomnia to keep him up. Not that coach's phone call of doom helped."

D'Angelo's piercing gaze meets mine.

I cringe.

Dad rang late last night with his brand of hard-ass parental concern. He warned of the upcoming road trip for the away games, which I had been looking forward to.

Except, now dread coils through me about them.

...And this road trip...hell, the shit is going to hit the fan. I can't protect you. All the dark secrets of our family are going to be exposed...

"Dark secrets, huh?" D'Angelo quirks his brow. "What did coach mean?"

I cross my arms over my chest. "Who doesn't have those?"

D'Angelo's expression is inscrutable. "No one."

Unsettled, I shift on the bed.

Suddenly, my hip knocks against something hard underneath the covers.

Unless D'Angelo's cock has grown in size over night and now is tail length (I've been reading far too many monster romances, even if demons have beautiful possibilities with *their* tails), then there's something else in bed with us.

Confused, I slip my hand underneath the covers.

"Hmm," D'Angelo grips me by the chin, "a little higher."

"I'm not trying to stroke your *stick*," I squeak.

D'Angelo's brow furrows, and his hand drops from my chin.

Hurriedly, my hand closes on the item, and I pull it out from underneath the covers with a flourish.

I wriggle closer to D'Angelo, squinting against the light at the thin, pretty book.

So, not a devil's tail.

Disappointing.

At first glance, it looks like a hockey strategy book in arctic blue and white with lines, arrows, and arcs on the front.

There's also a crude puck and hockey stick.

I drew those.

I also wrote the scrawled words, which are along the top:

A GUIDE TO ~~**AVOID**~~ **DATING HOCKEY PLAYERS**

The **AVOID** is scratched out with silver pen.

During my yearlong nightmare divorce proceedings with Wilder, I created it as a guide with rules to keep me on the path to never, *ever* date a hockey player again.

Obviously, I fell off that path…spectacularly.

Three times.

And that's when I scratched out the **AVOID**.

The Guide includes photographs and press clippings.

There's an entire chapter on D'Angelo, including photographs of him pole dancing, being spitroasted over tables at kinky clubs, and wearing a horse riding outfit complete with riding crop that makes him look like Darcy meets Christian Grey.

Actually, I should have changed therapists. Is it any

wonder that I remained obsessed with my first love?

At least I listed his negative characteristics.

Okay, bullet pointed, numbered, and written in different colors.

Using glitter pens.

Yet that only made D'Angelo look like the bad boy in an inevitable enemies-to-lovers romance with the best hate sex.

"Hey, where's my hate sex?" I wave the Guide at D'Angelo.

D'Angelo blinks. "How could we have that, when I love you more than life itself, cara mia? Or is that one of your fantasy role plays? Then add it to your list."

Of course, the fantasy lists.

D'Angelo has turned the Guide onto its head as the reasons that we should be dating with tips, positions, and our desires.

It's now the Hockey Kamasutra.

We all contribute to it.

A journal on our explorations, kinks, and fantasies is exactly the type of thing that I'd imagine D'Angelo would think up.

Anticipation thrums through me, as I sneakily turn to the back.

I run my finger over the lists of our fantasies. They're stamped with one word **CONFIDENTIAL**, and have been stapled into the Guide.

D'Angelo made the rule, when we negotiated our contracts, boundaries, and limits that we couldn't see the lists yet.

I had fun writing down my innermost desires.

I lick over my lips, itching to find out what the men's fantasies are.

Why are secret, forbidden things so much more tempting?

D'Angelo tuts, gently drawing away my hand.

"Do you want to know one of the reasons that Shay loves orgasm denial?" D'Angelo leans closer, pushing my hair back from my face. Then he kisses behind my ear, just where I'm most sensitive. My back arches, and I whine embarrassingly loudly. I feel D'Angelo's mouth smile against my skin. "The anticipation. The buildup of arousal, so that when the pleasure finally hits…" He kisses me again, and my knuckles whiten around the Guide. "It's mind blowing. Understand?"

"Uh-huh." I carefully turn over the page away from the folded lists of fantasies.

In approval, D'Angelo licks across the shell of my ear, and my eyelashes flutter. "Good girl."

I melt.

Shit, *those two words*.

D'Angelo pulls back but lays his arm comfortably around my shoulders. Our hips are touching. His warmth seeps through my naked skin.

I burrow even closer, resting my head on his shoulder.

He turns and presses a kiss to the top of my head.

I flick through the Guide, smiling at the list of kinks that Shay has added that he wants to explore. He's included complex ratings out of ten, which look like football scores. I also study the smutty stick men illustrations that D'Angelo added, then the romantic but heartbreaking Ten Reasons I Love Robyn, which Eden wrote and signed like a marriage contract.

I flip to the final page.

Last night, I added something new myself.

I wrote in blue pen on the top of a fresh page:

A GUIDE TO LOVING HOCKEY PLAYERS.

Because I do...love these three men.

I wanted them to understand that this guide should no longer be about dating but loving.

Eden needed to know that no longer playing hockey didn't mean that hockey wasn't in his blood or part of his voice.

It will always be his identity, even if his journey is now to find out how to live *after* hockey.

To my surprise, someone has already written something beneath it.

Having lived next to D'Angelo in dorms at college and spent many late nights trying to drag him away from his work, I'd know his handwriting anywhere.

A G<small>UIDE</small> to Loving Hockey Players

Robyn's Number One Rule: Learn to love hockey players by remembering three essential things...

1. *They're gods on the ice but are more devoted to you than their sticks.*
2. *They'll burn down the world to protect you against your dark past.*

3. *The Prince twins*

.

But never forget it all began with D'Angelo...

"You wrote it in glitter pen," I point out.

"They're your favorite."

"At least you own the stick obsession."

"Don't kink shame."

"What's this about *learning to love* you?" I close the book, leaning to place it on the nightstand. "I already love you. Haven't I made that clear enough? I know that I screwed up by believing Wilder's lies and manipulations. I hurt you by rejecting and abandoning you. But I'll give everything to make this work. I fucking love you."

D'Angelo hesitates, before clasping my hands between his.

He looks like he's thinking hard about how to put this into words.

My heart is beating too hard. Adrenaline spikes through me.

What the hell is he going to say?

"We only have a week until the California road trip." D'Angelo tightens his grip on my hands. "They're the most brutal away games. This week is our chance to truly get to know each other without (please Christ), stalkers or crazy journalists. I adore you, principessa. But Eden is only at the start of exploring his first relationship and his dominance. Shay has been abused or used in every relationship that he's been in. He doesn't know what it means to *be* loved. We need to show him. I've known that I've loved you since college, just like I've been openly bisexual for years. Our Shay's only just started his journey, however, discovering about his sexuality. See, we know that we love each other but not *how* this will work."

"You're a good man, Jude D'Angelo."

He scrunches up his nose. "No need for insults."

I can tell by the flush that's staining his cheeks, however, that he's pleased.

"You're our goddess, cara mia." D'Angelo's cold voice becomes rumbling and warm in a way that makes my core throb. I push my thighs together. "And we're going to learn how to worship you. I suggest to do that, we each spend a full day this week with you, separately."

"Three day long dates…?" I grin. "I can get behind that. Plus, you have a point. We need to connect both as a group and individually."

"I'll take Shay on a second date as well." D'Angelo's lips curl up at one side. "He'll probably be flustered about being included. But under no circumstances am I letting the ball of sunshine who is also a horror fanatic choose the movie this time."

"Did you have nightmares?" I ask, sympathetically.

D'Angelo was freaked out in college by watching *Labyrinth* with me.

I realized that it was love, when on his first date with Shay, he suffered through *Hellraiser*.

"*Oh, it's just a touching love story*, he said," D'Angelo

mutters. "*A classic*. Yeah, I'm not trusting that English freaky horror fan again. He'd probably choose *The Ring* and convince me that it's only a thriller about videotapes."

Poor D'Angelo.

"If you watch that," I can't stop myself, "I'll definitely call you mid film and see which of you is brave enough to pick up the phone."

"Since we're watching my choice of comedy this time," D'Angelo replies, "the answer is irrelevant."

It would definitely be Shay.

He'd probably answer cheerily, even if he was talking to a vengeful ghost calling to warn him of his death.

Unexpectedly, D'Angelo shifts on the bed to kneel in front of me.

I stare at him in surprise.

He slips his hand into his pocket and pulls out a small, luxurious velvet box. It's bound with a silk blue ribbon that matches his eyes. The ribbon is tied in a bow.

D'Angelo holds the box on the palm of his hand like an offering. "I got you a gift."

"It's not my birthday," I blurt.

"I'm aware," D'Angelo replies. "It's also not Christmas, Easter, or the one year anniversary of when we first fucked." I flush. "I had this commissioned for you, a couple of days after we first met up again, during the pre-season. But with everything going on…"

"Like my stalker ex, the intense press scrutiny, and the start of the most important season of your life?"

"There didn't seem to be an appropriate moment."

I stare down at the curves of my naked breasts,

sticky skin, and tangled hair. "And you thought that me sitting in a messy bed with smudged mascara and dried cum like a necklace (blame your kink for marking me as yours), would make the perfect romantic moment…?"

"You're beautiful."

Butterflies swarm in my stomach.

D'Angelo really is looking at me like I'm the most beautiful woman who he's ever seen.

No matter if I'm surrounded by models or billionaires in perfect dresses, rather than creased clothes that I haven't had the time to iron, D'Angelo doesn't notice anyone else because all his attention is on me.

It's the best feeling in the world, after having been married to a man like Wilder who made me feel undesirable in and out of bed.

When I found out about Wilder's multiple affairs, it broke me for a while because it felt like the proof that I wasn't enough.

Except, I am for D'Angelo.

I am for the twins.

They show me that every day.

I bite my lip. "I haven't bought you anything."

"*You're* the gift."

"Smooth."

"I try."

When D'Angelo significantly looks down at the velvet box, I take it from his hand.

Excitement rushes through me.

What's inside?

I pull off the ribbon, which is as elegant as D'Angelo is himself. I toss the thick ribbon onto the bed.

Then I hold out the box in front of me.

I take a slow breath, before I open it.

"I'm sorry it's not diamonds," D'Angelo apologizes, when I don't immediately say anything. He taps out a rhythm of three on his knee, anxiously. "I'll buy you those next time. But this is special to me."

"It's perfect." I trace over the silver 22 design, which appears to have been sunk into a gold signet ring. "Twenty-two is my favorite number. You remembered."

"I remember everything about you, principessa." D'Angelo gently takes out the ring, while I drop the box to the side. I shiver at the intensity in his gaze. "It's why I chose it for my jersey number."

My eyes widen.

"So, all those years, when we were apart…" I whisper.

D'Angelo caresses his fingers up my neck, before burying his hand in my hair and tightening his hold. "I was thinking of you. The silver twenty-two in this ring was a lucky charm that I carried in my pocket. Like my jersey, it was a way that I could feel close to you during my games. I had it made into a ring for you. Then you can think about me, while you wear it."

I suck in a sharp breath.

D'Angelo's love is all-encompassing.

It's a fucking obsession.

In nine years, while we weren't together, he had casual sex but never dated *because he was in love with me*, even though he thought that he'd lost me forever.

Wilder damaged both of us.

We do need to learn to love each other.

"Can I put it on you?" D'Angelo murmurs.

I hear the yearning in his voice. I know how much this means to him. But his hand is steady.

In answer, I hold out my right hand.

It's never going to be my left one.

All my men are equal, and as much as it feels that we're married in our hearts, there's no way for us to make this type of relationship official.

I won't marry just one of them.

Why do I need that label anyway, when our relationship is deeper, more real, and loving than my marriage ever was to Wilder?

When D'Angelo slips the ring onto my finger with a self-satisfied look like he's been imagining this exact moment for weeks (and I bet that he has, although did it include me with a hickey and puffy eyes?), I lean forward and kiss him.

"Don't think that this means I'm promising to love, honor, and obey you."

D'Angelo's expression becomes wicked. "But you've already signed a contract agreeing to *obey* me."

Damn, never make a deal with the devil.

D'Angelo raises my hand to his lips, kissing the ring like he's sealing the deal.

All of a sudden, I hear fast footfalls out in the corridor. Then a gasp.

"You proposed to her," Shay's shocked voice comes from the open doorway.

CHAPTER TWO

Captain's Hall, Freedom

obyn

"Oh, fuck." I snatch my hand back from D'Angelo, hugging it to my chest.

Shay is leaning in the doorway, looking impossibly gorgeous.

And naked.

Shay has an aversion to wearing clothes, especially in the mornings or after showers.

I'm hundred percent not going to break him of that habit.

Sue me.

I wet my dry lips, studying Shay's muscled chest and toned abs. He's athletic with broad shoulders. His skin is ice-white but it's not unmarked.

Last night was about grounding Shay in this relationship.

Grounding all of us.

Shay's body is marked with claiming scratch marks and bites, which will be hidden under clothes, since our relationship needs to be kept secret from the press.

They'd tear it apart — tear *us* apart.

Yet *we'll* know that those marks are there. And Shay will feel them, which he'll love.

Except, now he thinks that he's walked in on D'Angelo proposing to only *me*.

Shay is six foot, which means that he's shorter than most hockey players. He's prettier too. Shay's spun golden hair tumbles over his sharp cheekbones.

He's only twenty-one and is normally the most sunny person I've met. Apart from when he's working out his anger issues on the ice, of course.

He's one of my three beautiful PR nightmares, who Dad, Austin McKenna, the coach of the Bay Rebels, has made me responsible for twenty-four seven here in Captain's Hall.

Because of his traumatic past, Shay has a philosophy of seizing every opportunity in life.

Shay puts a positive spin on his hellish training with the Assistant Coach, Colton, claiming that it gives him the chance to *learn from the best*.

He's even positive about my habit of sleeping like a starfish and stealing the covers.

He doesn't have D'Angelo's patented jaded look.

But now, there's a hurt that he's trying to hide in his large, winter gray eyes.

My chest is tight.

"Congratulations." Shay attempts to flash a smile. "Shall we open the champagne?"

D'Angelo appears to be struggling to contain his anger.

He pushes his curls back from his face, before snatching my hand from my chest and holding it up. "Is this her right or left hand? Perhaps, English astrophysicists truly do get their degrees by sending away for them online."

Shay straightens, looking insulted. "Hey, I worked bloody hard for my degree. And that's her right hand."

"Uh-huh?" D'Angelo strokes over hand, before dropping it with an expectant expression.

When realization dawns on Shay, it's like the sun coming out from behind a cloud to see his face brighten. "Fuck, you scared me."

"Why, cucciolo?" D'Angelo says with a dangerous softness.

I try to shake my head at Shay, but risky thrill seeker that he is, he ignores me.

Shay rocks on his heels. "I've been expecting it, darlin'. It's okay. You have everything to offer our Robyn, and what do I have? I look like trash next to you. I *am* trash. If you ever need to do this to get the press off our backs, then I get it. I just want to be allowed some place in your lives. I love you both. You wouldn't leave Eden and me behind, if you married, right?"

My heart clenches.

Shit, has this been his fear from the start?

Eden's?

My eyes burn with tears. I feel sick.

D'Angelo growls, pulling himself off the bed.

Called it.

He's pissed.

Really pissed.

D'Angelo stalks toward Shay, who flattens himself against the doorframe.

D'Angelo cages him.

I clench the covers, darting glances between the two men. I can never tell whether they're going to fight or hate fuck in these moments.

I don't know whether they know either.

Shay often dances the line between daring D'Angelo to both spank and kiss him at the same time.

Yet I don't think that he's bratting now.

He meant what he said. And that makes my heart hurt.

I'm going to think up a way to show both the twins that they're equals in this relationship and that I want them forever — I'll never abandon them.

It'll be a long process, however, because they've been abandoned too many times before.

D'Angelo towers over Shay. "Say. That. Again."

Shay slips his hands behind himself like he's wisely protecting his ass. "Hard pass."

D'Angelo shoves Shay against the wall with an arm

across his neck. "Eden and you are fucking family. My brothers. I don't have my own family. Robyn and you are my everything. I may be competitive on the ice but I'm not off it. I'd never leave you behind."

Shay's eyes widen, before he relaxes into D'Angelo's hold. "Your everything?"

D'Angelo leans closer, until their lips are brushing. "Are you trying to get me to compliment you?"

Shay's lips quirk. "Is it working?"

D'Angelo smirks, before skirting his hand down Shay's front, not quite touching his cock, which hardened to half-mast the moment that D'Angelo pressed him against the wall.

Shay sucks in his breath. His pupils dilate.

He attempts to hump his hips. But D'Angelo stills him by pressing his arm harder against his neck.

"A compliment…?" D'Angelo tilts his head, as if appearing to think hard. "How about that your lips look incredible stretched around my thick cock? Or the way that you break apart, when I deny you permission to come, makes me fucking hard? Or how your submission is a precious gift that I will always treasure?"

"That's three," Shay pants.

"Is it?" D'Angelo kisses Shay, passionately.

I watch the two men. It's fucking hot. And they're both mine.

D'Angelo pulls back from Shay.

He only releases Shay from his hold for a moment, however, before sliding his hand to the back of his neck in a hold that borders on the edge of being too harsh.

But it makes Shay melt.

D'Angelo drags Shay to the bed, before throwing him onto it.

Shay bounces with a delighted grin. "Beast."

"Beauty." D'Angelo smooths down his sleeves.

Shay crawls up to greet me with a kiss that's slow, gentle, and fucking perfect.

I push Shay's golden hair out of his beautiful eyes.

I need him to listen and understand this.

"Eden and you truly are equals to everyone else in this relationship," I promise. "You won't be abandoned again. You say you understand that but then, something like this morning happens, and I know that in your heart, you don't get it yet."

Shay nods. "I hated therapy in the past, love. But my brother has convinced me that I should try it again. I see why I need it." Then his face lights up, and he bounces up onto his knees. "Does this mean that Eden and I get to buy you a ring as well? It's like your jersey pendant that we bought you together. You could wear them secretly all the time. It'd be like our commitment to each other, but no one would know."

D'Angelo looks conflicted.

I can tell that this ring was something special that he wanted to share with me.

But who can say no to Shay's hopeful face?

Who can crush him twice in one day?

Please, don't crush him...

D'Angelo marches stiffly to the bed.

"Precisely," D'Angelo says like it'd been his idea all

along.

I meet D'Angelo's eye over Shay's head, shooting him a grateful smile.

This proves that D'Angelo loves Shay as much as I do.

Shay studies the ring, smoothing his finger over it; his nails are painted with chipped metallic gray nail varnish. "Jude's jersey number. Great idea. Wait, isn't that the lucky charm you carry in your pocket to games and kiss three times, before…?"

"Enough." D'Angelo reddens, diving to the bed and slamming his palm over Shay's mouth. Shay's laugh is muffled. "Do you have a lucky charm?"

He pulls his hand back from Shay's mouth.

Shay wraps his strong arm around me. "You're my lucky charm, love."

My lips quirk. "Will you kiss me three times before every game?"

"Definitely." Then Shay's expression clouds. "But I haven't received my first paycheck yet. Do you mind if my ring isn't as fancy as Jude's?"

I tip up Shay's chin, kissing away the whisper of sadness and shame on his lips. "I wouldn't care if it was neon pink plastic or a bottle cap."

"Good because with Eden, it's likely to be a cat ring." D'Angelo chuckles.

Fuck, he's right.

Or a squirrel one.

Possibly a cat hugging a squirrel.

Before Shay can freak out about money again, D'Angelo slips out his phone and turns in on. "I'm advancing

Eden his PA pay. I can't have him unable to buy the best kitty ring that money can buy." He swipes on the phone, before closing it. "Done."

Then he slips his phone back into his pocket.

Shay reaches out to clasp D'Angelo's hand. "You're the best boss."

D'Angelo's expression becomes devilish, as he rumbles, "I believe that you've made big promises in the past that you'd happily wake up to using your mouth on Robyn or me every morning." He reaches to trace over Shay's petal soft lips, and Shay allows his lower lip to be dragged open. "Don't you think that this pretty mouth should be put to good use?"

My cheeks heat.

When I try to close my thighs, D'Angelo tuts.

"I don't think so, principessa." D'Angelo's eyes are frosty. "Lie down and spread your legs. Let our pet see what he'll be ravishing."

Desire pulses through me at his words.

I take a deep breath, before rearranging myself on my back.

My legs splay open.

It turns me on to be this exposed before the men who I love.

Shay grins. "It's a bloody perfect breakfast, love. I can't wait to worship your gorgeous clit."

"Tell me your safe words," D'Angelo orders.

"Red, yellow, and green," I reply.

"And what are you now?"

"Green." Shay's eyes are already glassy.

"Seriously green," I reply.

"Call me Sir," D'Angelo commands.

"Seriously green, *Sir*."

D'Angelo's breathing speeds up.

I forget the power that I have over him with that single word.

Shay crawls to lie over me. His hard, naked body presses against my sweaty skin.

I can't resist reaching out and running my fingers along his pecs, feeling the muscles jump at my touch.

His breath hitches.

I ease my other hand over his shoulder.

Shay leans down to kiss me, and his hair brushes over my face.

His skin is soft but taut over corded muscle.

All of a sudden, D'Angelo snatches Shay by the hair and drags him down the bed to lie between my thighs.

Shay lets out a pained hiss, but I don't miss the way that his cock has now fully hardened.

D'Angelo's expression is commanding. He wrenches Shay's head closer to my pussy.

D'Angelo's gaze settles on me. "Don't move. Let our toy do the work."

Shay looks up at me through his thick lashes. He smiles, kissing my sensitive inner thighs, first one and then the other, reverently.

He adores my curves like I'm a goddess and not a hot mess.

He always does.

I'm already wet and throbbing to come, seeing this model-like man between my thighs.

Except, it's the strength of his adoration that pushes me to the edge, before his lips are even touching me.

D'Angelo's expression softens just for a moment, when his gaze meets mine like he knows how I'm feeling. Then it hardens again, as he pushes Shay's face firmly against my pussy.

Shay's nose grazes my clit, and I whine.

When Shay kisses my pussy, I wring the sheets between my hands.

Then he licks down the center of my pussy, and I arch off the sheets.

Pleasure is winding through me, higher and higher.

My pleasure is what's getting Shay off.

He's humping the sheets, and I don't even think that he realizes it.

"That's it, good boy." D'Angelo directs Shay's head where he wants it to go, up and down in maddening patterns over my pussy and clit. "Tongue Robyn's pussy. Make us proud. Make her come. And if you don't manage that before your brother brings us breakfast…" D'Angelo tightens his hand in Shay's golden hair. My startled gaze meets D'Angelo's. The twinkle in his eye doesn't reassure me. "Then you won't be coming for the rest of the day."

Shay lets out a shocked whimper against my pussy that almost makes me come from the vibrations alone.

He starts tonguing me with renewed, desperate fervor.

D'Angelo pushes Shay's face so hard against me that I don't think he can breathe.

Shay doesn't appear to care because he's devotedly dedicated to making me come.

I moan. "Fuck, Shay, that's…"

Incredible. Perfect. Overwhelming.

My orgasm is rushing toward me.

I can feel it, building up faster than normal.

Shay grips my hips harder to keep me in place.

"This is where you belong." D'Angelo lays his strong hand on the back of Shay's neck and squeezes. "Where you will *always* belong, pet. Do you understand that? You may have stress on the rink, with the press, or the upcoming road trip. But between us, you can shed all of that. Because this is what you crave. To be covered in my bites and marks, owned and claimed with your tongue buried in Robyn's pussy. Your mouth will be filled with her taste for the rest of the day. Make her come. And admit that you're our pet. Because this is where you belong — between Robyn and me — *forever.*"

Shay is shaking.

When I glance down, his eyelashes are trembling with tears.

But he doesn't stop trying to make me come.

He's sucking hard on my clit.

I'm shaking apart.

"Fuck, fuck, fuck." My toes curl. "I'm going to…"

"Tea," a deep, rumbling English voice says from the doorway.

CHAPTER THREE

Captain's Hall, Freedom

obyn

Tea...

That one word, as if I have a kink for English butlers (and maybe I do), tips me over the edge.

"That's right, just like that Shay." I throw back my head, closing my eyes. "Fucking, yes…"

A wave of pleasure hits me.

My back arches. My hips lift off the bed. I thump the sheets, once and then again.

I'm shivering, as a second wave of pleasure hits me. I struggle to ride it out.

D'Angelo caresses my stomach. Shay strokes my hip.

I take deep, gasping breaths, before laughing.

I can't help it.

That was fucking intense.

I glance down at Shay.

D'Angelo finally lets go of Shay's hair, sprawling back indolently like he hasn't just masterminded some of the best sex of my life.

I reach down to card my fingers through Shay's hair to soothe the tremors that are running through him. "You're such a perfect man. Gorgeous and good for me."

Shay stops sucking, although his heavenly lips are still sealed around my clit.

I don't blame him, since the one word, *tea*, which sent me crashing over the edge into orgasm, means something very different to him.

It means that he'll be aching with frustration for the rest of the day. Of course from our negotiations and contract, I also know that he'll love that, as much as he hates it.

Plus, the orgasm that he has tomorrow will more than make up for it.

D'Angelo knows that too, which is why he's playing this game.

"What is it with people leaning in my bedroom doorway this morning?" D'Angelo demands. "I'm going to start to learn to close doors because obviously, I was raised in a barn, or else buy you bells to wear around your necks by pretty ribbons like you're kittens."

Eden doesn't look guilty but he does appear to be insulted by that image. "Kitten abuse."

"But sweet."

"Is my brother in trouble?" Eden demands.

I glance at Eden.

I'm lying in a sweaty heap on the bed, dazed and debauched. Eden's twin looks even more of a hot mess than I do, laid between my thighs.

Eden, however, is calm and put together.

He has golden hair like Shay, but it's slicked back from his face. This makes his cheekbones look sharper than his brother's. His right eyebrow is pierced, making him seem edgier too.

Eden is dressed in a gray t-shirt and black leather trousers. He's holding a serving tray that's decorated with cartoon cats in top hats and monocles.

Happiness winds through me at the sight of the steaming blue mugs of tea and piles of bacon rolls.

My mouth waters.

Eden's balancing the tray on one hand. It's impressive. The muscles on his arm bulge.

His other arm is in a sling.

I can see by the way that he's shifting that his cracked ribs must be hurting him.

I bet that he won't say anything. He never complains.

Eden has gorgeous tattoos on his arms. The ink is in stark contrast to the ice white of his skin.

Black roses wind up both of his forearms with spiky thorns like he's fighting his way through them.

I was privileged for him to tell me what his tattoos

mean. I'm the first woman who he's been able to talk to about them.

The twins were literally sold by their addict biological parents, when they were kids.

They both have different ways of coping with that trauma, some of it healthy and some of it not.

Eden's ink is a way of taking back control over his life and body. Black roses symbolize that he's endured pain but he's still bloomed.

And Eden *has* bloomed.

Eden's brother may be the star athlete who shines on the ice, but Eden is the fucking heart of our relationship. He may be quieter than his extrovert brother but he holds us together with his caring dominance.

When he's not making sure that we eat by slipping sandwiches and snacks in front of us, he's ironing my clothes for important meetings, or even managing to out dom D'Angelo to make sure that he rests.

I just wish that he would realize he's worthy of the same care.

Shay gives my clit one final kiss, before resting his head on my thigh with a sigh. "Am I in trouble? Let me put it this way, I don't get to come for the rest of the day because I didn't get Robyn to come in time, that's all."

Eden's gaze slides to D'Angelo like two dominants checking in with each other. "Fair."

"Traitor." Shay looks outraged. "So much for the Circle of Twins."

"Work harder to please our Robyn next time." Eden

advises with the same tough attitude that he uses to coach his brother on the ice.

It's effective.

When Shay looks at me for sympathy, despite knowing that it's for show, I can't help urging him up to rest against my stomach.

When I pet Shay's hair, he happily hugs his arms around me.

"That was amazing," he murmurs. "Thanks, love."

I smile. "Let's sit up and have some real breakfast."

"I only need you."

"You won't be saying that, when I've eaten all of your brother's bacon rolls."

"And she can do it," D'Angelo warns.

"I can," I say, proudly. "They're my favorite."

Shay reluctantly lets go of my legs.

Together we sit up next to each other on the bed. Shay pulls me into a slow, lingering kiss.

When we draw apart, Shay kisses down my jaw. I shiver at the electric sensation that makes my skin tingle.

He sits as close to me as he can. He needs this closeness after a scene.

I wince, when I see how painfully hard he is. His gorgeous cock curves up against his stomach.

It's difficult to resist licking it.

Shay looks hopefully at D'Angelo. "Darlin', you wouldn't let me just…?"

He gestures down at his cock, before making the universal jerking off gesture.

D'Angelo's eyes become icy. "Not a chance, cucciolo."

"Good try." I nudge Shay's shoulder.

D'Angelo pushes off the bed and strolls to Eden. "Let me help."

"I can manage," Eden replies. "I'm not weak."

"I know that." D'Angelo huffs. "Asking for help or allowing yourself to be helped, however, doesn't mean you're not strong. It took me years to work that out."

After a long moment, Eden holds out the tray to him, and D'Angelo takes it.

Together the two men stroll to the bed. They sit down, as on other mornings, opposite Shay and me.

Although, I'm not sure that there have been other mornings, when Shay and I have both been naked, and Shay's cock has been like a steel pole.

Shay doesn't appear self-conscious, ignoring his dick now or at least making a good impression that he is.

I grimace.

Shay is more accident prone than I am.

I really hope that he doesn't spill his tea...

When Eden passes me a porcelain mug, I scrunch up my nose at the softly aromatic and fragrant scent.

I meet Eden's stormy gray eyes. "Do you have an endless supply of Earl Grey?"

Eden's expression is serious. "I don't run out of essentials. I always have an emergency supply."

I suppose English people don't run out of essentials like stiff upper lips, chat about the weather, or sarcasm.

Eden gives me a piercing look, before nudging the plate of bacon rolls toward me.

The bacon rolls are large, buttery, with thick bacon hanging temptingly out of the sides.

My eyes light up. My stomach rumbles.

I grab a bacon roll, which is soft and warm. When I take a bite of the smoky, meaty roll, I moan in delight.

"Hmm," I mumble.

Suddenly, I realize that the three men on the bed are watching me with wide eyes.

"Respect." Shay's fixated on my mouth. "You could have your own OnlyFans site, love. It would just be you eating food. I bet that you could make millions."

"How about a site with me spanking your ass?" D'Angelo growls.

Shay tilts his head. "It depends. How much do you think we could make?"

I swallow as fast as I can. "Hey, vetoed. All vetoed. As PR Director, I'm saying stay focused on your current careers. We have enough secrets that the press could use against us."

"They have no right to." D'Angelo's lips pinch. "Our relationship should be personal. We may be public figures, but I don't know why I deserve to be punched in the dick by that public for everything that I do in my private life…or simply for being *who I am*. But the press have already ripped me apart for being a *playboy* for six years, as well as for my bisexuality. I don't want any of you to go through that. We need to protect ourselves. So, Shay shouldn't be outed. Nobody should be pressured to reveal their sexuality, gender identity, or whether they are submissive or dominant. I'm going to do *everything* to shield you from that."

"And that's my job too as your PR Director." I place down the bacon roll and warm my hands on the mug. "I know that it's been a tough start to the season. I swear, however, that I've been messaging every contact I have in the media to change your images, along with the narrative around the team. I'm curating a list of friendly journalists and influencers. You'll be the darlings of the press soon."

D'Angelo chuckles. "Truly devil to angel."

"I can see your halo already."

"I can't." Shay gestures at his dick. "This is the work of the devil."

D'Angelo smirks. "But you took Robyn to heaven."

Eden picks up a mug and passes it to D'Angelo, before passing another one to Shay.

"Thanks, bro." Shay takes a swig. "That's good."

Eden looks pleased but he's studying the ring on my hand.

He doesn't say anything.

I exchange a glance with D'Angelo.

"I gave her the ring," D'Angelo explains. "It's my jersey number. Shay has suggested that you each buy her a ring too. It's a good idea. I've advanced you this month's salary, if you'd like to get her something today. You can use my connections to have it ordered and delivered. There are some perks to being a millionaire. I don't often use them but well…"

Eden clenches his hands for a moment but he looks thoughtful.

"You don't have to," I say, worried. "It was just—"

"Are we getting engaged?" Eden asks.

I stare at him in shock.

D'Angelo closes his eyes for a moment.

Shay leans forward, until his forehead is touching his brother's.

I don't intervene because this feels important.

Eden doesn't speak much. When he does, it's imperative to listen.

"Is that what you want?" Shay asks, quietly. The twins' golden hair mingles. "You know that it can't be official, right? Sadly, the press and sponsors won't be accepting of our poly set up. At least, not yet. Plus, we don't need anything traditional like that because our love is just as precious without it. We have other ways to show our commitment. These rings are like a secret promise between us. You've known from the start that I'm bloody obsessed with the woman. I want to show her that I'm in this forever, if she'll have my overactive, accident prone self. But you don't have to be at the same stage that I am. You can take your time and just see how things go. There's no pressure."

I hold my breath.

Eden grips the sides of the tray. He closes his eyes for a moment, thinking hard.

When he opens his eyes again, they're steely with determination. "I want you to be happy, Shay. Being engaged to someone who loves you would make you feel safe and wanted. I dreamed of that happening one day. But I'm not sure that I'm ready."

"Then you don't need to be," I say, hurriedly. "Eden, we can all take this at our own pace. We've known each other for varying lengths of time. We're different people, with different pasts and needs. There's no right way to love. Simply having you in my life right now makes *me* happy, right?"

Pink tinges Eden's cheeks.

"Hear that, bro?" Shay pulls back from Eden, nudging his shoulder. "You're enough for our Robyn."

"This is why we need to learn to love," D'Angelo points out. "We should spend a day alone together on dates."

Shay's expression brightens. "Mine's going to be the best."

"Not competitive, remember?"

Shay leaps off the bed, as if the excitement of the date has made him forget about his hard cock and aching balls, and begins pacing.

He also appears to have forgotten that he's holding a mug of tea.

When the hot liquid splashes Shay's naked abs, he flinches. "Whoops, I'll just put this down, before I scald something important to me."

"Important to Robyn and me too," D'Angelo points out.

Shay places the mug on the nightstand, before returning to his pacing.

"So, we have an entire day with Robyn...?" Shay twirls, waving his hands around for emphasis. "Wow, love, I'm going to plan such amazing things for you."

I grin. "I can't wait."

Eden gathers the bacon rolls onto a porcelain plate, which is decorated with cats playing hockey, and places it next to me. Then he places the tray onto the floor.

He avoids meeting my gaze. "I have to work."

D'Angelo shrugs. "You don't. I've spoken to your boss."

"You're my boss."

"Exactly. He seems like a good guy. I liked him. Anyway, when I spoke to myself, I agreed that you could have Monday off to spend it taking Robyn on the first date."

Eden's lips twitch into an almost smile. "Thank you." Then he finally raises his gaze to mine, holding out his hand. I take it, squeezing. "I'll do my best."

"However we spend our day, I'll love it because I'm with you," I promise.

Eden's lips twitch again, which is as close to a smile as he usually gives.

Apart from the first time that we had sex.

Until then, he was a virgin.

When he smiled, I treasured it.

I treasure Eden.

Shay crawls onto the bed, scrambling across to kneel in front of D'Angelo.

"Would you go on a date with me too next week?" He asks in a small voice like he's expecting to be rejected.

I hold my breath.

Is this the first time that Shay's asked out a man before?

D'Angelo has allowed Shay to go on his bi-awakening

journey himself and at his own pace. Shay is the one who told us that he was in love with us both.

When he went on a first date with D'Angelo, however, it was because D'Angelo offered and arranged it. He wanted Shay to realize that they weren't a casual hookup and that it wasn't only about sex.

But this is different.

D'Angelo studies Shay over the lip of his mug, as he takes a sip of tea. "Did you think that I hadn't planned to spend one of the days with you as well?"

Shay sits back on his heels in shock. "You did?"

D'Angelo's expression gentles. "Of course I did, cucciolo."

"Oh." Shay looks shell-shocked.

D'Angelo's eyes flash like he wishes that he could hurt everyone who has ever made Shay doubt himself. "And yes, I would love to go on a date with you. Let me make this clear, however, as this is our second date, *I* get to choose the food and movie. I will not be burning my mouth on another curry or having nightmares about Pinhead."

Shay looks smug.

He pats D'Angelo's leg. "Don't worry, darlin', we'll eat Italian and watch a comedy, if that's what you want. Don't feel bad. Not everybody can handle hot foods or scary movies."

Shay truly doesn't want to come any time soon...

"Brat," D'Angelo mutters.

Shay's eyes dance.

"Don't forget your scheduled practice sessions this

week with Colton," Eden points out like the perfect PA that he is.

D'Angelo finishes his tea with a flourish, placing the empty mug on the nightstand. "It had to be with that hard-ass."

Shay perks up. "I love the way that Colton pushes us to be the best that we can be."

See, Shay's my Little *Mr.* Sunshine.

"I'll remind you of that next time you're puking up your guts from skating laps," D'Angelo mutters.

"Then we'll also have to prepare and pack for the California road trip," I say.

D'Angelo shudders dramatically. "How about not mentioning it by name? Don't jinx it."

"Superstitious." Eden pulls back from me to cross his arms.

All of a sudden, I sit bolt upright, almost spilling the remainder of my tea in my lap (and naked that truly would've made me howl). "Dad!"

Eden gives me a long, considering look.

"She does that," D'Angelo drawls, "yells out *Dad* in bed. It's not surprising with her mammoth sized daddy issues."

Asshole.

I blush.

"No…yes…not like that…sort of…but not in the kinky…" I take a deep breath to stop my desperate rambling, especially when I see how amused Shay is looking. "We can prepare as much as we like, but nothing changes that Dad told us that shit is going to hit the fan on the away games and that our *dark secrets* will be exposed. What's the mystery? We'll have to try to find out before we go, or I'll fail at my job of shielding you. You'll be caught in some kind of PR nightmare, when we're far from home without the support of our town and most of our home fans. If…whatever this is…blows up in our faces on the road trip, then we're fucked."

Suddenly, D'Angelo's phone vibrates on the nightstand, making me jump.

"Sorry." D'Angelo reaches to answer it, before scowling. He glances at me in surprise. "Are you able to summon your dad by mentioning his name? I've often wondered if he was a demon."

"It's Dad?" I hiss.

Eden and Shay both sit up straighter like Dad can see them through the phone.

Wildly, I can't stop myself glancing around the room.

Please don't let Dad have bugged this room.

If he has, then he deserves the trauma of hearing D'Angelo say this morning *lie down and spread your legs*.

But possibly not the therapy that he'll need to recover from hearing D'Angelo say last night *you look so pretty, when you're choking on my cock*.

I blame the parental third eye again.

D'Angelo holds the phone to his ear and answers the call.

"Coach," D'Angelo says with a false calm like he isn't sprawled in bed next to the man's naked daughter, "any reason that you're calling me so early on a Sunday morning?"

D'Angelo winces, and I can hear the tinny voice of Dad no doubt yelling at him.

Anxiety spikes through me.

D'Angelo pales, as he always does when faced with my dad who is both a parental and an authority figure. He also holds D'Angelo's career and future in his hands.

Dad has too much power.

D'Angelo has a troubled past with his own asshole parents but he'll still stand up against mine.

I admire him for that.

"Your daughter doesn't need to be leashed to her phone," D'Angelo snaps. "I thought we'd already established that. So, you're playing the game of calling all of us again to get to her, are you?"

I bite my lip.

I should remember that Dad expects me to be available twenty-four seven.

D'Angelo arches his brow at me, which I know means, *do you want to take this?*

I definitely don't.

I shake my head, hugging my arms around myself.

Eden rests his hand on my knee.

D'Angelo straightens his shoulders. "She's gone out. Running."

Okay, not the most believable lie.

That tinny yelling again.

D'Angelo grimaces.

"Oh, give it here." I hold out my hand. D'Angelo hesitates for a moment, before passing over the phone. "Morning, Dad."

"That was a short run. You returned to the house miraculously fast." Dad's gruff voice harrumphs.

"That's me — a miracle."

"You're a *PR Director*," Dad barks. "I warned you that starting today you'd need to be on top of the crazy press scrutiny after the whole opening to the season that included a blackmailer journalist."

"I didn't know that today had started yet." I mime looking at my watch, despite being naked. I'm not certain whose benefit it's for, since Dad can't see me. But it makes me feel better. "It's not even seven a.m. yet."

"The early bird gets the worm and the lazy assed bird gets eaten by the cat," Dad warns.

"Wow, that's a harsher saying than I thought it was."

"It's my version. So, get out of bed…" I start to splutter, but Dad cuts me off. "Don't try and deny it. Jude could never lie to me, and I know him too well. Then get your ass down to Rebel Arena. We need to talk."

CHAPTER FOUR

Rebel Arena, Freedom

"Jude couldn't have thought of a better lie than a run at dawn to cover your ass?" Dad demands.

He's carrying a stack of papers. They're emblazoned with the team's logo, which is a puck flaming with arctic blue fire.

The papers look official.

"I'm sure that he simply got me confused with Shay." I struggle to keep up with Dad's fast strides alongside the rink without slipping. "I'm surprised that he didn't tell you that I was thrill seeking on my Harley or rock climbing."

Dad stops to turn to scowl at me. "Don't tell me that Shay is still doing those, even though the season has started?"

"No…?" I try but am not convincing.

Shay needs at least ten times the adrenaline that most people do.

Probably a hundred times as much as me.

I'd prefer to relax with a glass of wine. Eden would choose a good book.

D'Angelo would rather lounge over a piano with a cocktail in his hand, rather than dangle off a mountain.

Dad grits his teeth. "Have fun telling our insurance."

Dad once had the same red hair as me but now, looks like a silver fox. He's tall with a neat beard and twinkling, emerald eyes, which means that there's still no missing that he's my dad.

He's dressed in a sharp charcoal suit with a green shirt and tie.

He always wears suits like D'Angelo does.

Since he's been D'Angelo's mentor from the beginning, kicking his ass if he doesn't present himself as immaculate at all times, I'm beginning to wonder whether that's part of the reason why D'Angelo always dresses up in the same way as him.

Dad is old school.

It gets him results but it causes fucking psychological damage, even though Dad is one of the few coaches who'll take players who have been rejected by the rest of the NHL because of their mental health or physical needs.

Dad will give second chances to those who've screwed up like D'Angelo and Shay.

Dad took up coaching the Bay Rebel's new team to redeem himself and offer the same chance to his team of misfits.

Ironic, huh?

Dad fucked up his own career in a scandal where he injured a player on the ice. It was sensational because they were both star players who'd won the Stanley Cup.

It was such a big deal that it tarnished the entire sport for years.

The press intrusion that followed tore apart his life and haunted my childhood.

When Mom died from cancer, Dad retreated into himself, abandoning my brother, Cody, and me.

It's taken years to process that.

In many ways, he remained a good dad…to me.

But he hurt Cody, over, and over, *and fucking over again*.

It's why I'm so protective of my brother.

I hope that Dad can repair his relationship with Cody but that's on Dad.

Dad starts walking again, faster this time, and I struggle to keep up. We pass the cold metal benches that line the vast ice rink.

A rush of excitement washes over me.

Damn, I love this sport.

I wrinkle my nose at the smell of the arena, which is as

familiar as coming home: the bite of cold air mixed with sweat and rubber.

I'm dressed in a woolen green dress and sturdy boots. You can't wear heels at the rink.

Shivering, I stuff my gloved hands into the pockets of my pea-green coat.

Eden wrapped his gray scarf around my neck this morning to hide the hickey.

I insisted that Eden not come with me, after checking whether he had any symptoms from his concussion.

When Eden grudgingly admitted that he was suffering at pain level three (a system that my brother put in place as part of Eden's physical therapy to help him to recognize and then voice his pain), I suggested that he rest quietly this morning.

Eden would never have made that choice himself.

But he'd do it because I asked him to. I'm beginning to realize that.

I'm going to be careful with that power.

I turn my head to take a deep, sniff of his sweet, vanilla scent on the scarf.

"Did you have to make them practice just because they came down here to support me?" I hunch my shoulders, wandering close to the boards. "They were being good boyfriends."

The lights are dim, apart from the spotlights that are directed onto the rink and its red and blue markings.

I stare through the glass at Shay and D'Angelo. They're dressed in Bay Rebels jerseys.

D'Angelo is slouching. He's trying to make it look

casual, as if he's not exhausted. I can see the way that his curls are plastered to his forehead, however, and the sheen of sweat on his skin.

I lean against the glass.

I can't resist trying to get closer.

Unlike D'Angelo, Shay is skating.

He's mesmerizing.

Every time that I see him skating it's like it's the first time.

He's a virtuoso of the ice hockey world. The way that he handles his skates is like the way D'Angelo turns the piano into something spellbinding.

Sublime.

My breath hitches. Shay skates past me.

He's faster than anyone in the NHL.

Faster than anyone alive.

How is this possible?

Do the other teams know what they missed out on by not signing Shay?

What potential he has?

Shay could be the best player in the NHL. Possibly, with the right coaching and mentoring, who has *ever* played.

I know that Dad feels it too.

Shay is the reason that the Bay Rebels have a shot at the playoffs for the first time, despite being the newest and poorest team.

Yet that type of responsibility and pressure on the shoulders of such a young athlete is a hell of a lot. He's only just moved from his English college team, and now, he's at the center of making the impossible possible.

If Dad pushes him too hard, then I'll kick his ass.

Although right now, it's the Assistant Coach, Colton, who's doing that.

I glower at Colton.

Now in his mid-thirties, Colton played junior ice hockey, and he has the type of sour face that makes me feel that he never got over failing to make the selection in tryouts to the NHL.

He definitely puts the players through hell in training camp.

It's earned him the nickname Stick No Carrot.

He's proud of that.

He's taller than Shay and much broader. His arms are crossed over his barrel chest, as he watches Shay skate laps with a self-satisfied look.

He has neat white blond hair and a mustache that looks like a fuzzy caterpillar that's crept on there and died.

"Can't he stop now? You're pushing him past his limits," I hear D'Angelo call. "Isn't it my turn now?

Concerned, I notice that Shay is looking green around the gills.

Perhaps, D'Angelo hadn't been exaggerating about the risk of Shay puking on the ice.

"You always try to take the control," Colton replies with a dismissive sneer. "You never remember that on the ice you may be captain but *I'm* the coach. I didn't ask for your opinion. Keep going, Prince. Faster."

I gasp.

Jerk.

Impossibly, Shay looks determined, before pushing himself even faster.

"See, Colton's effective." Dad watches Shay with an air of hawk-eyed possession. "He can put Jude in his place, when most can't deal with his cocky behavior. He can—"

"Make players collapse from exhaustion?" I hiss. "Does he always drive them like this in practice? Colton's a hard-ass."

Dad chuckles. "Yes, but he's *my* hard-ass."

"Dad, come on, even for you this is—"

Dad taps sharply on top of the pile of papers. "Do you know what I have here? A damn nightmare, is what. Almost every board member and senior manager calling for my head — or yours — after your stunt with that journalist. It doesn't matter that Melanie Helt is the criminal. It's about scandals being attached to this team. We need to pull something seriously out of our ass on the next games, or we're screwed."

My heart speeds up.

I clench my hands in my pockets. "What's this got to do with you forcing my men to skate to their limits?"

Dad's smile is dangerous. "If they insist on acting like overprotective assholes, then I'll make them skate laps in order to get this meeting alone with you. It's too important. And I'll do it every time that I need to as well."

My eyes widen.

Shit.

"Is that a warning?"

"More like a threat."

I twirl away from the glass to face Dad. "So, you're saying the faster that we sort this out, then the faster they can stop practice, right? Shit, why didn't you say anything? What do you want to talk about? Hit me."

Dad quirks his brow. "Slow down. If you talk at the speed of light, Robyn, I won't be unable to understand you."

Then his gaze settles on my neck, and his expression darkens.

Confused, I reach to trace my neck, then shiver when my fingers press on the hickey.

I redden.

Hell, it wasn't as well covered by the scarf as I thought it was.

I tug at the scarf, trying to cover the hickey.

Dad shakes his head, uncomfortable. "This is part of what we need to talk about. You being...*careful*."

I freeze.

Oh no.

It can't be.

Seriously, can't be.

This isn't Dad's very...very...way too late...sex education talk, right?

He's the type of Dad who was awesome about having tampons delivered every month to the house without once mentioning the fact to me as a teenager.

But he preferred to pretend that even his married daughter wasn't having sex.

Cody got away with a stern look and a packet of condoms dropped onto his lap.

"I am." I drag my hands out of my pockets and wave them about like that'll convince him.

"It doesn't seem like it," Dad says. "You need to be more discrete. Keep it professional in public. If you can cope with watching Colton kicking other players' asses, then cope with him kicking your special projects' asses too. Don't show favoritism. Hockey's a tough sport. Would you care if Atlas puked?"

"Yes." I arch my brow. "Atlas is cute."

Dad points his finger at me. "Stay away from my other players. They're not here for you to catch and collect them all. They're not Pokemon."

I grin. "Of course not, I wouldn't fuc—"

"Robyn," Dad barks.

"What do you want to talk about?" I look over his shoulder at the rink. Shay is beginning to slow down, as exhaustion catches up on him. He's looking rough. My guts churn. He's going to need an ice bath and then massage after this. His muscles will ache for the rest of the day. This had better be worth it. "I get it. We'll keep the relationship secret. And we're taking this road trip seriously."

Dad's gaze skitters away from me.

He's not telling me something important.

He has a nervous energy about him, which isn't normal for him.

What's the true reason behind why it's important that the road trip doesn't go wrong?

Dad rubs his beard. "The Bay Rebels have never started a season so strongly. We've never made the playoffs before. Until the last few matches, nobody was expecting anything from us. But now, they are. That's dangerous. It's the reason that Eden was targeted. Once you're a threat, someone will find a way to take you down. We're not prepared for that like other teams are because we only have a fraction of the sponsorships, backing, and staff. Perhaps, if this season goes well, then that can change. We're playing with the big boys now but without their support or finances. We're at a turning point. Everything rests on this."

"I understand."

"Then you'll understand why I took an important decision." Dad fixes me with a hard stare. My hands feel clammy. "This isn't called the California Death March for nothing. It's the most brutal of the road trips. It may be unfair, but the pressure will be on D'Angelo as the captain and Shay as our chief scorer and star player. They'll have to suck that up. The likelihood is they'll relapse, however, under the pressure into their bad old ways and destructive patterns of behavior."

I cross my arms. "Like what?"

"Well," Dad's eyes twinkle, "last time with Jude it was partying, drinking, and being found sleeping in a fountain wearing nothing but a pair of bunny ears and the team's official bow tie."

I choke on my tongue.

Oh, fuck.

Flustered, I swallow. "But this time, they have me."

When Dad gives a slow smile that flashes his canines, I know that I've walked straight into his trap.

Wily old fox.

"I'm glad that you agree with my decision." Dad looks smug. "This time, I can't risk *that* happening. Or Shay transforming from a cuddly golden retriever into a pit bull on the ice. D'Angelo has also insisted that he needs his PA by his side. So, I won't have any of you traveling with the other players and staff on the road trip. Instead, I'm arranging for you to drive there separately together. You'll stay in your own hotel. Robyn, you'll be responsible twenty-four seven for keeping my misfits leashed and away from the press. Nothing must go wrong."

CHAPTER FIVE

Captain's Hall, Freedom

hay

EVERY TIME that I think I can't become more obsessed with Robyn, I fall harder.

The way that she watched me yesterday on the ice, as if I was both a god but also the man who she'd die to protect, shook me.

But then, I'd do anything for her.

Fucking anything.

And that's lucky, since it turns out we'll be traveling and living together on this road trip, because apparently, D'Angelo and I are still a risk, *blah, blah.*

I didn't really listen to that part.

The important thing is that this is going to be a brilliant road trip.

I have no bloody clue why the others are concerned about it.

Twenty-four seven Robyn and D'Angelo…? What's not to love about that hot combo?

I groan, stretching out.

All my muscles ache after the intense training session with Colton yesterday, even after the ice bath followed by Eden's massage.

Stick No Carrot is a bastard.

He pushes me harder than anyone, even Robyn's dad. On the other hand, he clearly wants me to achieve my best. He just has harsh methods.

I'll work hard and prove myself to him. I won't lose this opportunity to learn. I'm so fucking lucky to have this place on the Bay Rebels.

Nowhere has truly felt like home before. It's overwhelming to have that now.

I knew that playing in the NHL would be tough.

If I want to succeed here, I'll need to suck it up.

And I will.

It was the same at college, especially being the shortest on the team along with my brother.

You learn to deal.

Now, I'm the newbie.

When you're bottom of the ladder, you accept your place and the ass kickings.

I love that D'Angelo's a glowering over-protective

captain, however, who tries to shield me from the worst of it.

But I don't think that he really gets it about my brother and me.

I don't blame him because it's hard to talk to anyone outside therapy about the full details of our past.

It's too private.

When your early memories include hearing your twin brother being beaten, while you're locked next door and banging and screaming until you lose your voice to get to him, then a coach's words can't hurt you.

I refuse to let the monsters from my past devour me in the present.

If that means taking shit from Colton and turning it into learning points that improve my career, then that's what I'll do.

It's early morning, but I'm already dressed in a red t-shirt and jeans. I'm too excited about the news of the road trip to sleep.

I squirm on my messy, unmade bed on the bottom bunk. I link my hands behind my head.

My bedroom with Eden is the smallest in the mansion.

I chose it because of the metal framed bunk beds, which meant that I could share with Eden. They also reminded me of our beds in dorms at college.

The luxury and size of Captain's Hall makes me uncomfortable.

I've never even visited anywhere this large before. Eden has at least cleaned wealthy homes in his college job as a cleaner.

It makes me antsy living here sometimes.

I can't help feeling D'Angelo is going to realize that I'm trash dirtying up the place and kick me out.

But I can relax in this small room with its bunk beds.

There's a closet and mirrored chest of drawers and wardrobe against one wall.

My gaze darts to the open door out to the corridor.

Eden and I never close it.

Being in rooms with closed doors with no escape is triggering for both of us.

On the far side of the room is a large, arched window with gray drapes.

Pale morning light shines through over Eden. He's standing next to the top bunk, tidying it with military precision.

He's only dressed in black leather trousers.

The light from the window streams over his bare chest, gleaming on his silver nipple piercings. It lights the flames of the stunning phoenix tattoo on his back.

"Mum can't believe that we're going to be driving across America." I grin.

Eden glances at me out of the corner of his eye. "When did she call?"

"Yesterday, when you were in your physiotherapy session with Cody. Sorry, Dee, do you want me to get you next time?"

Eden thinks for a moment and then shakes his head.

I kick him lightly with my foot, and he stares down at me. "Mum and Dad say hi. They asked loads of questions about you. Don't worry. I kept the Twin Code and fielded."

"I'm fine."

"Sure. That's what I told them."

He's not fine.

After all, Eden's standing there in a sling with cracked ribs and an expression that's more shuttered than normal.

Plus, he's still struggling to find his feet after his hockey career ended.

I'm proud of him, however, for working hard for D'Angelo, facing his social anxiety, and finding his voice more than ever before.

I bite my lip. "Just think though, Mum and Dad have never been outside their county, let alone on a plane. But now we're in America and are about to go on this big adventure. It's my dream come true."

"I'm sending my first paycheck to them." Eden looks fierce. "I want them to go on holiday. Like we are."

Our adoptive parents have worked hard all their lives to afford to take us into their home, even paying for us to skate at the rink, when they realized what good therapy it was for us in different ways. They then helped support us through college alongside my scholarship, despite having almost nothing themselves.

They deserve the world.

"I think that the words used about this road trip are *brutal*, *nightmare*, and *death*. Definitely not holiday. But yeah, let's both send as much as we can of our first month's salary back to them. I'll tell Mum that it's for a holiday because otherwise, you know them, they'll spend it on something sensible."

"By plane," Eden adds. "Abroad."

"You're right. They'll be too sensible about where they choose to go as well." I push up on my elbows. "It should be somewhere hot, relaxing, with those drinks that have little umbrellas in them."

Then I kick Eden with my foot again because otherwise he'll add other clauses like to an island *with cats*.

Eden glances down at me. "What?"

"We'll have enough between us soon for everything that they need. They won't have to work two jobs or worry about rent." I settle back with a happy sigh. "What's the first thing that you'll buy for yourself?"

Eden never thinks of himself.

He never has.

Eden looks startled like the thought hasn't crossed his mind.

He fiddles with a leather bookmark, which is marking the place on an open book that lies on top of his covers. "Myself?"

"And no cheating by saying a new kitten t-shirt that you then give to our Robyn to wear at night."

Eden's gaze scans across the room for a moment longingly, before he answers, "A bookcase for in here."

Fuck, I should have thought of that.

D'Angelo gives me any stupid shit that I ask for.

Seriously, I said that it was boring waiting for toast in silence. The next day, D'Angelo had a toaster installed that was also a radio.

I even asked D'Angelo for a bunch of quiet sex toys for us to take on the road trip and like the cut x-rated sex toy buying scene out of *Pretty Woman*, he went on a buying spree for everything my kinky heart desired.

Yet Eden has never asked for anything.

My heart clenches. "You could ask—"

"No," Eden says, sharply. "I want it to be mine."

He slams shut the book, hugging it to his chest.

"Is that another of Robyn's book club recommendations?" I ask.

Eden's stormy gaze settles on the cover. "It's *The Count of Monte Cristo* by Alexandre Dumas."

I wrinkle my nose. "Romance, right? Boring shit."

Eden's lips twitch. "Actually, a dark adventure about suffering, false imprisonment, and revenge."

My eyes widen.

I can see why Eden would be drawn to that.

He's darker than I am.

I swallow. "It doesn't include burning anything down, right?"

"Sadly not." Eden drops the book onto the bed. "Anyway, revenge does more damage to the avenger than the avenged."

I perk up. "You really think that?"

Eden snatches his gray t-shirt from the end of the bed and drags it over his head. "Of course not. That's a line from the book."

I settle back onto the bed with a pout. "So much for learning from literature."

Then I notice that Eden is squinting against the light.

I leap out of bed and rush to the drapes, yanking them closed. "What pain level are you?"

Eden rubs his hand across his temple. "Three."

"Dee," I limp back to Eden, as my muscles protest, resting my hand on his shoulder for a moment, "you know that Cody's rule is that you mustn't go over level four. How about I get you some pain meds?"

"I'll get them myself in a minute." Eden peers closely at me. "You were limping. Pain level?"

"Three." I smirk. "Circle of Twins. We're identical, after all."

Eden scowls. "I could burn Colton."

See, it's always burning with my brother.

"How about subscription bombing instead? The fun kind of petty revenge. We sign Stick No Carrot up to every newsletter that we can think of. Scientology, penis enlargement, and Martha Stewart."

"Do it." Eden gives me a long look. "Is he hurting you?"

I flinch back. "He's *pushing* me. I'll survive."

"We always do."

Eden cards his fingers through his slicked back hair. It's only one gesture, but I can tell that he's nervous.

Today is important to him.

He's never spent an entire day by himself with a girlfriend.

I know how much Robyn means to him. Yet these emotions are new and frightening to Eden.

"You look good, bro," I reassure him. "So, you're the

lucky bastard who gets to spend the first day with our Robyn. What have you planned?"

"Secret."

I rock on my heels. "Whatever you do, she'll love it. She just wants to spend time with you and truly get to know you."

Eden's brow furrows. "But why?"

There's so much beneath that question.

I reply, softly, "Because you're worth getting to know."

Eden doesn't reply.

Suddenly, there's the sound of water turning on in the bathroom, which is next to our bedroom.

My face lights up, "She's showering."

And that's not voyeuristic since it's through a wall, sort of.

"Hmm," Eden replies, dreamily.

Then like most mornings, our little mermaid breaks into an off-key version of Justin Timberlake's *SexyBack*.

Time to break out the dance routine, hoping that this morning it'll make Eden laugh.

I have spent my life as the class clown because you're less likely to be rejected or bullied that way.

It hid the fact that both Eden and I were genius level smart. Few teachers believed it anyway.

Charm with a dash of comedy and a smile.

It's the magic formula that I discovered would stop kids, teachers, and other adults from wanting to abandon, reject, or hurt Eden and me, since Eden couldn't talk until he was twelve.

I had to talk twice as fast and loudly to make up for my twin.

I've spent my life hoping that if I can draw the attention onto myself, then I'm the one who'll be beaten and Eden never will be again.

In high school and college, it worked.

Seeing Eden with his arm in a sling, however, I hate that it failed when we thought that we'd found our lucky break together.

If I clown now, however, it also gets Eden to laugh.

I've always done anything to get him to do that.

I lip sync along to the song.

Then I break into the dance routine, which I've perfected over the weeks. I give a slink of my hips, adding in over the top stripper moves.

I ignore the protesting scream of my muscles, sliding into the splits because I'm insanely flexible (I hope to show Robyn the advantages of that).

As I leap to my feet, grinding and wriggling my ass, I have a happy day dream that Robyn can see me.

That she's in her shower right now, having a daydream of *me*, dancing for her.

And that she's as obsessed with me, as I am with her.

I'm obsessed with her curves, flame red hair, and beautiful green eyes.

That my dance is making her so hot that she beckons for me to join her in the shower.

Her dancing boy.

The water cascades down her gorgeous curves, clinging to her pretty tits that I long to lick, and kiss, and suck.

Instead, she passes me a soapy sponge, and I wash her — *serve her.*

My red-haired goddess.

I worship her.

Robyn's singing breaks off.

Sadly, I'm back in the bedroom with only my hard cock pressing against my jeans as a reminder of my fantasy.

I collapse to the floor, panting.

Show over.

Eden rolls his eyes, but they're twinkling with amusement.

Robyn does need a thorough education in *real* music. Then I can dance to something decent.

I'll lend her my Arctic Monkeys albums.

Maybe I should start a music club with her. Eden shouldn't have all the fun with his book club.

We could sit around on the couch making music recommendations like The Strokes. We could listen to the same iPod, which I've always wanted to do with someone. Then we could have a chat about who we think the next big thing will be and what our favorite gigs have been.

I give a small smile.

I'm definitely suggesting that.

I take a deep breath in and then out to slow my heart rate and catch my breath.

Unfortunately, it doesn't make my cock get the message. It's still uncomfortably pressing against my zip.

Today wasn't the day to go commando.

I lean forward to massage down my thighs, working out the knots with a grimace.

Then my stomach grumbles.

Instantly, Eden looks grim. "Breakfast. I should have been cooking already. I won't let you be hungry, Shay. I swear, no one in this family will starve or live in fear. You're safe from the monsters now."

CHAPTER SIX

Captain's Hall, Freedom

den

"You handle that knife like you're a solider." Robyn sprawls in our nest in a distracting way, watching me slice the strawberries on a small board. "Or an assassin. You'd make a good assassin. You know, with your stealthy sneaking in the shadows ways. You make D'Angelo jump at least once a day by lurking somewhere and then saying something when he doesn't think you're in the room."

I straighten my shoulders. I do that.

You notice more from the shadows.

It's my brother who likes the spotlight.

Robyn and I are lying on the floor in the lounge next to each other so close that our thighs touch.

Her heat feels like a brand. I love that we can touch like this.

She makes it feel casual and easy.

It's not to me.

It's overwhelming.

I wish that we could be like this in public.

My head is throbbing. But I'm not telling Robyn that and ruining our day.

I can handle my own shit.

Pain is nothing. *My* pain is nothing.

I'll deal with it.

I always have.

The bright noon sunlight streams through the windows over the lounge's heavy, purple and black furniture. A gilt mirror gleams above the fireplace. The black Steinway grand piano sits across the room.

Shay's always wanted to learn an instrument. But he didn't think that it was the type of thing men like us did.

Yet D'Angelo has started to give my brother lessons on the Steinway.

D'Angelo didn't ask anything in return for the lessons.

Is that what friendship means?

D'Angelo also offered to allow me this first day with Robyn.

I'm beginning to trust that D'Angelo's my friend as well as my boss.

"I've always wanted to role play fucking a soldier." Robyn waggles her eyebrows.

She wriggles closer to me, hugging a cushion to her chest with a happy sigh.

She's dressed in relaxed green joggers and a t-shirt.

Luckily, I don't cut off my finger in surprise.

I'm too trained. But I wasn't in the army.

I'd have made a good soldier though.

They're emotionless like me. Focused. But I bet that they don't get hard-ons in their pants like I am now.

Maybe they do.

It'd take real discipline to march with cocks like steel and aching balls.

I should remember not to wear such tight leather pants around Robyn. I try to shift into a more comfortable position so that she won't notice.

I built a nest out of blankets, bedding, and pillows from my bedroom at the base of the in-built bookcases, which are my favorite part of the room.

They're heaven.

I haven't seen so many books outside of a library.

I run my fingers over the spines each evening. It's a reassuring ritual.

They feel like friends too.

Would Robyn laugh at me, if I told her that?

I don't think so. She loves books almost as much as I do. She treats them like babies. This is why I've built her a nest.

I'm learning that you can get dating tips from books. Robyn loves omegaverse romance.

See, *nests*.

Robyn's as cuddly as any omega.

Men should read romance books more for tips. Only, not dark romance, unless they want to end up in jail.

I finish cutting the strawberries and tip them into a blue ceramic bowl.

I didn't speak until I was twelve. It was safer in my silent world.

Now, it's still hard to force out words. They burn my throat.

I don't understand why people would suffer that for *small talk.*

Words are painful — important.

I fix Robyn with an intense gaze. "I'm *your* soldier. I'd die and kill for this family. You're my war."

Robyn meets my gaze and doesn't look away. "Fuck."

She dives up and tumbles against me, wrapping her arms around my neck.

I wince, as the movement jostles my arm in the sling.

I stifle my gasp but I drop the knife.

Robyn misses her target, kissing me on the corner of my lips.

My eyes widen. "Careful."

"Sorry." Robyn glances down. "Whoops, almost accidental knife play."

My brow furrows. "You should never play with knives."

She laughs. "Ask your brother about that one. From his kink list, he'd disagree."

I wrap my free arm around Robyn's middle, carefully lifting her onto my lap. She adjusts herself so that she's not leaning on my injured arm.

My ribs are aching. I shutter my expression to mask it.

I won't let my shit ruin the mood.

When I kiss Robyn, she deepens it. Our tongues twine.

The feel of her soft arse against my cock is hell and heaven all at the same time. I need to feel more of her. I stroke through her hair, and she slides her hands down my chest.

When she pulls back, she studies me.

For a long moment, neither of us say anything.

There's this feeling in my chest. It feels too big.

Once, I was numb.

Hollow.

I didn't feel anything and that was safe.

But now, I'm feeling *everything.* This is how it's always been for Shay.

This is dangerous.

The more that I experience this spark, however, the greedier I am for more, and more, *and fucking more.*

I can't give this up.

Is this what true love feels like?

It hurts.

But I've hurt all my life. I can take this, if it means that I get to live with these incredible people.

I adjust the tray in front of us. "I didn't learn cooking in the army. I worked kitchen jobs to pay my way through college. I picked up useful skills."

Robyn plays with my hair. "Did you enjoy it or was it just work? It must have been tough to need to work that hard on top of your studying and skating."

No one has ever asked me that.

"I liked it more than the shop work that Shay did. I hated that when I tried it," I reply. "And my brother had it harder than me because he needed to keep up with his scholarship at the same time. He never complained. He had so much energy. But I couldn't deal with the customers in the shop. People talking to me and shit. In the kitchens though, they set me up in one corner, taught me one type of food prep, then left me to it. The chef didn't make me talk."

"You're an amazing cook and baker." Robyn licks her lips, as she scans the BLT sandwiches, bowls of fruit, and freshly baked blueberry muffins and pastries. "This is a feast. But then, so was breakfast." Her voice becomes cautious. "You do like doing this for us, right? It's not work for you."

Confused, I blink. "You need to eat."

"I can manage to stick two slices of bread together with some cheese in between. As much as I don't want to deny myself your delicious treats, I don't want you to feel obliged to—"

"Care for you?" I pick up a strawberry and handfeed it to her. When she groans, my gaze flicks between her fluttering eyelashes and tongue, which darts out to lick the juices off my thumb. "None of you will be hungry."

Man and Woman, our parents, were addicts.

We never called them anything else.

They dumped Shay and me in squats, abandoned cars, and alleyways, and we scavenged for our own food.

I remember the cold and the clawing hunger.

When either of us were ill, we'd feed each other what we'd found for ourselves, even if we were starving.

Food meant life.

Food meant care.

Food meant love.

I pick up another strawberry and feed it to Robyn. She doesn't look away from me, as she nibbles on it, before licking it into her mouth.

She gives an orgasmic moan as she chews. "Thanks."

I kiss her forehead. "Welcome to my love nest."

Robyn chuckles.

"Where's your brother?" She squirms to get comfortable on my lap. "It's been suspiciously quiet for hours."

"When we were walking in the forest earlier, I received a text from Jude. It said that he'd taken Shay out to the rink to give us space. At least, I think that's what it said. It included some emojis that I didn't understand. It may have meant that he was being taken for a spanking."

Now that's definitely an act of friendship.

I'm becoming better at recognizing them.

"Remind me to kiss D'Angelo tonight for that," Robyn says. "I loved our walk through the wood this morning. It was perfect."

I paused at my favorite trees on the trail, pushing Robyn against them.

Then I kissed her, passionately.

Kissed her because then I didn't need to struggle to explain my feelings.

Kissed her because actions are easier than words.

I quirk my brow. "It's important to practice."

"Hmm," Robyn arches her brow, "that's what you said. I suppose that this is new to you. I am the only woman who you've kissed. So, what else do you need to practice…?"

She says it innocently. But she's flirting, right?

I find these cues hard to work out without my brother's support.

My pupils darken. "Everything."

She cups my cheek. "I want that too. And we have time to practice everything that you want but we'll be careful because of your injuries." She gives me a sultry look, however, reaching into her pocket and pulling out a shiny condom packet. "Practice makes perfect, right?"

I knew that she was flirting.

To my surprise, however, she drops the condom packet next to the bowl of strawberries, before primly sitting back. "But first, this is our book club. We're meant to be discussing what to read next week."

I gaze longingly at the little packet that she dropped.

My cock throbs.

Fuck, I never thought that I'd be angry at my beloved books.

"I don't know," I growl.

Robyn gives me a teasing smile. "Should we read a hockey romance? I mean, I seem to have a thing for players."

I snort. "Not if it's one of those fictional heroes who act like psychos, bullies, or stalkers."

Robyn snatches a sandwich and holds it to my mouth.

I want to eat something delicious today. But it's not food.

I wrinkle my nose, unsure about this reversal of the handfeeding, but take a bite.

"To be fair, they sound realistic to some of the players who I've known," Robyn replies. "I wonder if those authors have met my ex?"

My expression darkens. "Talon was the villain."

"Good point. Although, after his suspension and the investigation into his bad behavior, Wilder's pretty much the comic relief now."

"Good."

I can still kill the comic relief.

It'd be a mercy killing.

Robyn absentmindedly feeds me the remainder of the sandwich. "How about Aldous Huxley's *Brave New World*?"

I cock my head. "You want dystopian?"

"Well, we're living in a dystopian world right now. It feels fitting." Robyn sighs. Fleeting worry flits across her face. "Since I took my PhD and trained in PR, things have moved at such a pace that it's hard to keep up with how to protect Bay Rebels. The dark arts of the press, trolling, and AI on social media is moving at such a fast pace. It's like fighting fires."

"And not the good kind," I mutter.

Robyn side-eyes me. "You used to only have to fight fake smear stories but now you have to fight fake ones that *look* real. Did you see the fake AI video of D'Angelo fucking himself with his own stick that's been circulating?"

I stiffen, shaking my head.

Who would do that?

Bastards.

Robyn puffs out a breath in relief. "Then hopefully he hasn't. It really did look like him. I mean, he does have a genuine sex tape circulating somewhere. I had to watch the AI video at least ten times to work out that it wasn't old footage of him. Really, that's the only reason I rewatched it. Anyway, I thought *Brave New World* could act like a kick up our asses that we need to rebel against—"

"Those who are making videos of D'Angelo shoving a stick up his arse?" I quirk my brow.

Robyn nods. "And not blindly allow ourselves to be conditioned by technology or to accept that it has the right to our images."

I look down, flushing.

The words are stuck in my throat, but I force them out. "Are there videos like that of Shay and me?"

The way that Robyn quickly looks away gives me the answer.

There are.

I feel too hot. My skin is too tight.

I feel owned again.

I promised Shay that this would never happen to either of us in America.

Promised.

I can't be touched right now.

I gently maneuver Robyn onto the pile of blankets and pillows next to me, edging to sit next to her.

She stares up at me, surprised.

Her red hair is splayed around her head like a flaming halo.

Then Robyn's expression softens like she understands without me saying anything. "Would it have been better, if I hadn't told you?"

I don't know.

Is it worse to be owned and not to know it?

I shrug.

"I try and get them taken down," Robyn rushes to explain. "Shay's popular. These recent wins have brought him global attention. But technology means that people can then imagine him any way that they want, naked or—"

"They don't own us." I clench my fist.

"I know."

"We're not slaves."

"*I know*." More gently, this time.

"They can't touch us," I whisper.

"Eden, I'm shielding you as much as possible from this."

I look at her. I believe her. But this isn't her battle alone.

"I need to shield you all too," I reply. "*Shield my brother.* Show me this week how to protect Jude. I already keep him away from the trolling and death threats as his PA. I need to face this alongside you."

Robyn studies me, looking thoughtful. "It's a good idea. You're also the official photographer on this road trip. You're talented. My idea is that we focus on some on and off the ice photos, which show them as men, you know, *real people*. We take back control of their image, and at the same time, let people connect with them. That way, hopefully they'll understand that it's harmful to objectify them."

"That's a good plan." My shoulders relax. "Let's read *Brave New World*. Books are powerful."

Robyn stretches in a way that makes me suck in my breath. I can see her peaked nipples through her thin t-shirt.

"Will we be able to convince your brother of that?" She asks.

I shake my head.

I find it hard to talk about these things. But Shay has been encouraging me to share more with Robyn. She wants to use these dates to know more about us and our pasts.

I'm trying.

"He doesn't have the attention for reading," I force myself to reply, despite how uncomfortable I feel. I grit my teeth. *I can do this.* Only with Robyn, but I can for her. "We'd never even picked up a book, until we were five. I learned fast and caught up, but Shay didn't. We had a teacher in primary school who gave my brother shit in front of the rest of the class. Shay is a genius, but everything he knows is stored in his head. He struggles to put it down on paper. He looks at books as his enemy now."

"What a bitch." Robyn looks outraged. "I wish that I could kick her ass."

That was easy.

I stare at Robyn in surprise.

How does she make everything feel like she's part of the Circle of Twins?

Unexpectedly, her expression becomes half-hooded. She bites her lip in a way that goes straight to my cock, before sliding her bare foot up and down my thigh.

How is it possible for someone's foot to be the sexiest thing about them?

"I've tormented you enough." Robyn gives me a teasing look. "I call this book club to an end. Time for our sex club. We have some important practicing to do."

"Sex club?" My eyes become stormy, as I lean over Robyn. Her breathing picks up. "That sounds like a D'Angelo activity."

"With our pet, Shay, on our leash at our feet."

I never knew humans could be pets. But apparently, my brother is Robyn's.

Her gaze is fixed hard on my lips. So, I kiss her.

Robyn tastes sweetly of strawberries.

I could steal an infinity of her kisses.

When I draw back, she reaches for the condom packet next to the bowl. "Ah ha!"

"Wait." I reach for something equally important myself, which I've hidden under a fluffy cushion next to her head.

Something more important.

D'Angelo giving me an advance on my salary proves what a good boss he is.

A good friend.

I think.

I was able to order my Robyn a ring.

I want to send most of my money back to my adoptive parents, but if I'm frugal with my own expenses for the remainder of the month, then I have enough.

I've been frugal my entire life. I can manage it.

I was tempted by a pretty silver cat ring. I've never spent so much on a single item.

But then, I found something even better.

Maybe I can buy the cat one for Robyn's birthday.

Unexpectedly shy, I push the red velvet box into Robyn's hands.

Enthusiastically, she sits up, and our foreheads bang together.

"Two," I blurt, before I can stop myself.

"Ouch, sorry." Robyn gives a rueful smile, rubbing my forehead and then her own. "See how excited I am? How are you doing? Is this too much? Should we take a break?"

"No," I say, as quickly as I can.

If we wait any longer, my cock could burst

Robyn gives me a knowing look, then eagerly turns back to the box.

It makes an unexpected warmth fill that hollowness inside me to see her so happy to receive a gift from me.

I've only had Shay and my parents to buy for, and mostly, I made them something or baked for them because money was tight.

I'm not a real person.

I've known that my entire life.

The people at school and college recognized that.

Robyn doesn't.

To my biological parents, I was livestock to be sold.

I've tried to tell Robyn. But it hurts too much to take away how she looks at me…sees me…values me.

She's studying my gift like it's *valuable*.

Does that mean I am?

"Are you sure that you're ready to give me this?" Robyn caresses the top of the box. "You don't need to feel like you have to. I can wait."

My gaze rests on the stunning signet ring that D'Angelo gave Robyn. It's sturdy. Gleaming. It bands her finger in a silver **22** design, which is sunk in gold.

"I can talk to you," I struggle to explain. "Bake, run, read books with you. I feel like I exist when I'm with you. Today has been fucking perfect."

"It has. And it's not over yet." Robyn flips open the box. Then she gives a soft gasp, lifting out the ring. "Hell, this is beautiful."

"You are."

The gold ring gleams in the light. It's a flaming phoenix with amber eyes.

"Your tattoo," Robyn breathes.

I slip the ring onto Robyn's middle finger next to D'Angelo's. "It's not an engagement ring…" Frustrated, I break off. How to put this feeling into words? She's staring down at the ring on her hand with a delighted expression. "The phoenix is me. Now, you'll always have part of my soul. We burn together."

Robyn's breath hitches. "I fucking love it. Thank you."

She pushes up to steal a kiss, then drags me down by my t-shirt to lie side by side next to her on the blanket.

Her pupils are dilated.

Huh, gifts turn women on.

This is the type of shit that Shay should have taught me.

Robyn wriggles out of her joggers as fast she can, kicking them out of our nest. "Practice. Right. Fucking. Now."

I'm not arguing.

I slide my leather trousers and underwear below my hips. I grit my teeth, as my cock springs free against my stomach.

Robyn's gaze is hungry, as she scans over my cock and balls.

She scoots closer to me, before she wraps her small hand around my dick and begins to slowly stroke.

I hiss, when she adds in a clever twist that I'd fucking die for.

Then she rubs over the head of my cock. She teases the sensitive glans at the same time with her thumb, and finally, I can't lie still. My back arches, as I hump into her touch.

The pain in my ribs is worth having her attention on me like this.

Yet isn't this about *me* practicing?

I intend to show her pleasure.

The other two men have been fucking women for years.

Plus, I didn't even recognize most of the things that were listed on our yes-no-maybe list of kinks. There was a box for experience, yes or no, and one for willingness from zero to five, zero being a definite no and five being a definite yes.

Shay's was a sea of yeses and five.

Mine was a sea of no and mostly, the annotated note: **DON'T KNOW WHAT IT IS.**

D'Angelo said that was fine. He's going to teach me. I can adapt the form, change my mind, and see how I feel.

He said there's no wrong answer.

Am I safe with these people to risk believing that?

My first time with Robyn — with anyone — she explored my body to show me how pleasurable sex could be.

Now, I want to show *her* pleasure.

I pull her down into a kiss.

As my tongue tangles with hers, I hear her ripping the condom packet, then her light fingers sheathing my cock.

I draw back, licking across the seam of her lips, then explore down her neck with my tongue, lips, and teeth.

She's panting. Her cheeks are flushed.

"I fucking adore you, Robyn McKenna," I murmur.

Her breathing picks up. Her eyes are blown wide.

I lift her hand away from my cock. It does something to me that she's been giving me a hand job with the one that's wearing my ring.

I stare at the gleaming gold phoenix, entwining our fingers, before kissing the ring like this is a holy rite.

"I'm the one who needs practice." I look determined.

Robyn nods with a smile.

I place her hand down, before we turn on our sides to face each other.

In this position, it takes any strain off my arm and ribs, but I can still be face to face with her.

I need that connection.

I thumb across Robyn's breast, intently watching the pleasure play across her face.

Her nipple pebbles, and I circle it. Then I flick it lightly. She moans, shivering.

Our foreheads touch.

We're lying so close that our thighs brush against each other, as we spoon. Her skin is damp against mine.

It's the most intimate thing that I've done.

When our gazes meet, it's electric.

Neither of us look away.

I drag my fingers down Robyn's side, leaving goosebumps in their wake. I rest my hand on her hip, experimentally tracing circles.

She pushes against me like she's trying to get even closer.

I never knew what it felt like to want to climb into someone's skin before and become part of them.

I slip my hand between us, rubbing along her pussy.

She's already wet.

"Yes, Eden, please…" She gasps.

I slip one finger between her folds, in and out.

Robyn rocks against me, encouraging.

I add a second finger, never looking away from her beautifully expressive face.

I take my time.

She lets me.

It's my turn to explore her now.

Caught in this moment — this quiet — there's no need for words.

Yet we're talking louder than we have before. We're holding a conversation with our bodies.

I slip my fingers from Robyn's pussy to her clit, tracing circles over it.

Her breath hitches.

My fingers are soaking.

"Fuck me," Robyn whispers.

I stare deep into her soul. "I want to learn to make love to you."

Robyn's breath hitches like she understands exactly what I truly mean.

To learn to love.

Instantly, she lifts her top leg like she's showing me how.

My eyes widen in awe, then I thrust into her slow and deep.

Her warmth is incredible. The rush is intense.

I'm beginning to understand why Shay loves this.

Except, I'd only want this with Robyn. It makes me too vulnerable and exposed.

She clutches onto my shoulders and wraps her leg around my waist, urging me on, deeper.

Her breath is hot against my neck, as mine is against hers.

I've never been this close to anyone.

I thrust into her over and over again.

"I love you," Robyn chants. "Love you, love you, love you…"

My balls tighten at her words. My heart pounds.

Then I'm groaning and coming.

At the same time, Robyn claws at my back, coming with a scream.

Then against Robyn's shoulder, where no one can see, I smile and smile, and *fucking smile*.

CHAPTER SEVEN

Rebel Arena, Freedom

'Angelo

I LEAN against the rink's boards in Rebel Arena, crossing my arms.

The lights are dim. The cold cuts across my cheeks.

I take a breath of the scent of rubber and sweat.

I run my hand through my curls, watching as Shay skates past me. He's slower than normal.

I smile, smugly

It's my fault.

He catches my look and ruefully rubs his ass. "Beast."

"Problem, cucciolo?" I arch my brow, examining my palm.

Shay narrows his eyes, before determinedly forcing himself to skate faster.

I chuckle.

It's been exactly three hours and twenty-two minutes, since I calmed Shay down in the bathroom at Captain's Hall with a spanking.

Shay' ass, wet, hot, and red over my lap, looked so beautiful that I had to bite it.

Had to.

Hard.

It's been three hours and seven minutes, since Shay was so turned on by that spanking that he kneeled flushed, naked, and gorgeous in front of me.

He was also the most relaxed and pliant that I've seen him.

I could have promised him anything in that moment.

He has so much power, when he offers me his willing submission.

I love that he's beginning to realize how much power he has, when he's on his knees.

On the other hand, I was born dominant in the same way that I was born bisexual.

Figuring this stuff out about myself and learning about communication and trust has helped me. My power exchange relationships have been the most healthy and positive part of my life.

Also, the most fun.

In the bathroom, I laughed, running my fingers through Shay's hair.

"If I knew that the switch to slow you down was on your ass," I said, "I'd have swatted you earlier."

I promised to buy this man two yachts.

I'd give him the world, if I could.

Then Shay nuzzled at my crotch, before giving me an inexperienced but eager blow job.

I'll buy him *three* yachts.

Four, if I can teach him to deepthroat.

I didn't let him come, however, because I'm not that generous.

It's been two hours and forty-two minutes, since I dragged Shay with me to the rink for extra practice.

I wanted to give Eden as much space with Robyn as possible.

Eden's a caregiver dom who doesn't yet understand his dominant side. He's hasn't been in a relationship before. Add his traumatic past, and he needs to spend as much time as possible with Robyn.

And possibly adopt some animals.

I'll probably own a mansion, a dozen yachts, and a menagerie by the time that my family is complete.

I smile.

Family.

I clench my hands.

When my parents had me abducted in the middle of the night to be taken to a brutal private boarding college for troubled teens simply because I kissed a boy, I never thought that I'd have a family again.

Family meant being beaten by my brother until I tasted blood.

Family meant my parents standing with cold faces, while I screamed for them to *save me* — except, they didn't.

Family meant being rejected.

Yet Robyn and the twins accept me, even though they know that I'm a grumpy asshole.

I sent Eden a text to tell him where we were going with emojis that explained about the spanking and the rink.

He may not understand. He does appear to have emoji blindness.

"Why are you smiling?" Shay calls, glancing around the rink to check that we're alone. "Thinking of my tight ass, darlin'?"

"Skate." I fix my icy glare on him. "And only how soon it can go over my lap again."

"Promise?" Shay grins. "That was bloody brilliant. My ass is warm like your hands are still on me. It makes me feel safe. Sort of like I need to sleep though."

"Do you want to stop?" I check in. My expression softens with concern. "What do you need?"

Shay never wants to sleep. He has terrible insomnia.

Perhaps, he needs more aftercare.

Shay has to be closer to me than normal after a scene.

He follows me around like an adorable puppy.

I can get used to that.

It's good practice for after the season ends, when I adopt a cat for Eden.

Shay skates up to me, slamming into the boards with enough force to make me wince. "Can I tell you what I like…?"

"Always."

"The way that this morning after you'd turned my arse red, you wrapped me in a towel, then cuddled me on your lap. Then you took another towel and dried my hair for me." Shay's cheeks flush.

"I noticed. I trust that you'll tell me what works and what doesn't both in a scene but also, in the aftercare. It's just as important."

Shay looks down.

I wish that I could kick the ass of the abusive domme at his college who has made him look like this.

"Yeah well, I didn't even know what aftercare was before." Shay looks up and meets my gaze. His beautiful winter gray eyes are large. I feel like I can see myself reflected back in them but as Shay sees me — as a hero. *His hero.* I need to live up to that. *Fuck, that's hard.* "But you've shown me that I can talk to you. That things can feel different. *Be different.* I won't be used and kicked out to deal with everything on my own."

"Never," I reply, firmly.

Shay fiddles with the tape on his stick. "At college, I'd feel shit for days after a scene. Cold, exhausted, and depressed. I'd have to skate, feeling like I was going to burst into bloody tears every time the coach tore into me. It was a fucking nightmare trying to skate, not knowing back then that I was actually suffering from subdrop."

"I could find that woman, Blythe. She was a fake domme. She abused you." My expression is dark. "Let me."

Shay looks at me, startled. "You sound like Eden. You're going to be talking about killing her next."

"There are many ways to kill someone. What if she's still pretending to be a domme? She could be doing this to another sub."

Shay pales. He looks like he may be sick.

He shakes his head. "I can't think about this now."

I'll get my PI friend, Garcia, working on it.

Garcia's in the same BDSM community as me. We're tight-knit.

If Bythe's in England's community, then I can get her blacklisted from every BDSM club, munch, and event.

Being wealthy and powerful needs to have some perks.

I can make sure that warnings are spread about her in online forums and chat rooms.

It's a start.

Shay presses close enough to me that our hips are touching. "She trained me to think that I wasn't allowed to take pleasure, only give it to others. You're this bloody amazing pleasure dom, however, and I love everything that you do to me."

Dominance surges through me in a rush of adrenaline.

Protectiveness rises up as well.

Shay is mine to wreck but also, to put back together. And only because he consents to this.

I lean over Shay, caging him against the boards. I press one arm across his throat.

If anyone enters the arena rink side, it'll look like I'm kicking his ass.

Hockey players are physical with each other.

Just not always in the way that Shay and I are.

Usually.

Shay sucks in a breath.

"*Everything?*" I growl.

I ghost my hand down his hip and then to his ass.

"Everything," Shay repeats in a challenging whisper, before tacking on like he knows the impact that it'll have on me, "Sir."

He's fucking perfect.

I push my arm tighter against his throat.

"When I get you home," I promise, or possibly threaten, "I'm going to start stretching out your pussy."

Shay shivers on the *pussy* like I knew he would. "You're going to train me...?"

I love the thrilled anticipation in his voice on the *train*. Between us, it's being transformed into something precious and beautiful.

Something that he deserves to enjoy and claim back as his own.

"The hole is a muscle," my voice is low and rumbling. Shay melts. "I need to transform you into my perfect fleshlight. I'll use butt plugs of increasing size. I can do the same thing each morning. I'll leave one out for you to put in every time that you wake up. You'll wear them because *I* want you to. But then, you'll feel nice and filled. You'll spark with tormenting pleasure every step that you take. Your pussy will never feel empty."

I know that this type of talk turns Shay on from our negotiations.

"Fuck, darlin'." Shay's voice is raspy with desire. He lets his head *thunk* against the glass. His long throat is deliciously tempting. I wish that I could sink my teeth into it. "Exercise is good. I'm dedicated."

He's as sunny about training his ass, as he is about training on the ice.

It's hard for me to drop my mask and simply smile with happiness at seeing how playful he can be about something Blythe tried to destroy.

Instead, I press harder against his throat, when what I want to do is kiss him and never stop.

I've found the perfect submissive for me.

All of a sudden, however, I glimpse movement out of the corner of my eye.

Reluctantly, I pull away from Shay, trying to make the move look casual.

"Are you okay for a couple more laps, then we'll get changed?" I say evenly, as if I haven't just been dirty talking about sticking stuff up Shay's spanked ass. "Despite me giving him the day off, your brother still made us a freshly made packed lunch. We can eat that here to give Robyn and him more time together."

I should give that man a raise.

They don't make PAs like Eden. He's even made my filing more efficient.

He knows my schedules better than I do.

And the things that he can do with Post-it notes are probably illegal in some states.

Shay straightens. "Do you think that they're doing okay?"

"Eden has food, books, and Robyn. He'll be in heaven."

Shay nods, before forcing himself to skate another lap. His eyes look dazed, however, and his movements are off.

I watch him, concerned.

I'm taking him off the rink as soon as I can for a massage and as much aftercare as I can give him.

And cuddles. He likes those.

Shit, when did I become the type of man who gives cuddles?

A short but athletic man with tanned skin and rich, amber eyes ambles down the side of the rink. He has a wild tumble of golden curls. He nervously glances at me. He's only twenty-one but he's dressed in the medical staff nurse uniform with Bay Rebels logo.

"Hey, Noah." I turn to face the nurse.

Noah's face brightens. "Hey, sir."

He has to hide that he's a submissive because his family would never accept him, if they found out. They're poor and from the rough side of Freedom. They're distant cousins of Silas Anderson, the finance manager.

Anderson is a prejudiced asshole. He'd fire Noah, simply for his dynamic.

It's frightening to have to mask who you are.

Noah's as trapped in a secret life, as I am.

He stays with his abusive family for the sake of his brothers, who he protects.

I understand.

I only spent one night with Noah, when we were

paired at a fetish ball in a demonstration as lion tamer and his lion.

It was a mind-blowing demonstration. Noah is beautiful underneath a whip.

I feel a sense of responsibility toward everyone within our small BDSM community in Freedom. Noah is part of it, and I wish that he'd take up my offer to move into my mansion.

To be safe.

My brow furrows at the anxious way that he's shifting from foot to foot.

Perhaps, I can introduce him to some of my inner circle of friends. I don't trust easily, but these people have earned it. Noah needs a support system, and they offered that to me when I most needed it.

Once we're back from the road trip, I hope to introduce my friends to my new found family too.

"What's wrong?" I quirk my brow. "Is it your dad?"

Noah shoots me a shy glance; he hero worships me as much as Shay does. "When isn't it my dad? I just wanted to thank you for the offer to stay at your place. I'm still thinking about it. It's hard…"

"You don't need to explain. The offer's not going anywhere. Take your time."

I wish that I could tell Noah what I suffered with my family. I know what it's like to be beaten and mocked because of my bisexuality.

Simply because Noah doesn't fit his family's outdated idea of masculinity, he turns up to work bruised and limping. And they don't even know the truth yet.

If they did, Noah's whole life would crash around his ears.

I tap my fingers on my thigh in a rhythm of three.

If I don't, then the sick feeling spreads through me that something bad is going to happen.

It's the same OCD feeling that I've been struggling with for the last decade.

The men are going to come, break in tonight, then…

It's an intrusive thought. It's not real. It won't happen.

I shove it away.

Noah pushes his wild curls behind his ears. "I also wanted to tell you that I'm coming on the California road trip. I'll be traveling with the staff and Cody."

He gives a small smile.

I fight to smile back, hoping that it looks natural but feeling stretched too thin. "Cody, huh? Is he a friend?"

A hesitant nod.

I'm not surprised. Cody could befriend a nervous hedgehog.

"Unlike my grumpy ass," I reply, "Cody's good at this friendship business. You should stick with him."

"You're good at it too," Noah replies loyally or possibly stupidly. He's bad at judging people's characters. That's dangerous. I blame him being dazzled by the memory of that ring master's outfit. I did look particularly handsome in it. And my ass was at its best. "You're not grumpy, you're…" Noah appears to be struggling for a word. "Broody."

I arch my brow in a broody way.

"Don't you have work to do?" Colton's voice sneers

from behind Noah. "I know that you're not a real nurse, or a real man for being a nurse, but you must be needed for something."

Asshole.

Colton steps up to the boards, towering over Noah. His white hair and mustache are bright points in the shadows.

Colton's not on the schedules to be in work today. It's his day off, which is the reason that I brought Shay here, despite his muscles having been overworked yesterday by Colton.

Shay is in no state to be put through that again.

Noah's shoulders slump.

I start to open my mouth to tear Colton apart, AC or not, on his behalf, but Noah casts me a pleading look and shakes his head.

I close my mouth with a snap, gritting my teeth.

I'm telling coach though. I can at least be a snitch.

Colton can bully the team because hockey is a tough sport. Players are paid millions, plus we need to be pushed to perform.

But bullying the staff — punching downward and abusing his position of power — is fucking unacceptable.

The staff shouldn't be treated with anything but respect.

I'm the captain. I'm not fucking having it on my team.

Noah hangs his head, and his curls hide his face. "Yes, sir." He shoots me a glance out of the corner of his eye. "See you on the road."

"Bye, Noah." I wave, as Noah scurries past Colton and down the side of the rink.

Colton watches Noah, shaking his head in contempt.

"You shouldn't have said that to him." I can't hold it in any longer.

Colton snorts. "The little snowflake needs to toughen up. He won't survive on the staff of a team like this otherwise. I'm doing him a favor. It was just a joke, or can't you take those either, captain? Your tantrums in the press and every time that players throw chirps at you suggest that *you're* the one who needs to toughen up."

My eyes flash with ice-cold rage at the same time that my cheeks flame with humiliation.

I slowly turn to face Colton.

He must see something in my expression because he straightens his broad shoulders. "Something you want to say?"

Robyn's calm, steadying voice and hours of media training rushes through my mind: *no comment, no comment, no comment...*

See what a good influence she is.

"No comment," I reply.

Colton gives a self-satisfied smile. "That's what I thought."

He crosses his arms over his barrel chest, before swaggering to the glass. He watches Shay's slow skating critically.

Dread churns in my guts.

Shay's in the stage that he needs me to take him to the

locker room, massage him, and when we're alone, whisper *good boys* in his ear.

Then afterward at home, wrap him in blankets and hold him tight to my chest.

He needs slow kisses and reassurance.

He doesn't need an ass kicking from Stick No Carrot.

"Faster," Colton yells. "What the hell do you call this? I wouldn't accept this level of skating from a high schooler. *I said faster.* Are you sick? You look sick."

Shay's eyes widen, and he only stops himself from falling over with a flail of his arms.

"He's past his limit," I bark. "This isn't official practice. We're stopping now."

"I'm the AC. You stop when I say so." Colton's gaze is hard. "Get your ass over here, Prince."

Shay skates over to join us. I hate that his smile dims the moment that he sees Colton's thunderous expression.

"Coach, I'm sorry." Shay's painfully earnest. It hurts my heart. "I'll try harder."

"You'll be useless to us on the road trip, if this is all you have to offer," Colton snaps.

Shay flinches.

"That's not fair," I snarl.

"I'm just being honest," Colton replies. "I don't sugar-coat. You should take the criticism and use it as motivation to do better."

Thank Christ this fucking gas lighter isn't a dom.

Unfortunately, Shay isn't in the right head space to know not to listen to this shit.

He looks determined. "I will. I'll do better."

"Damn straight you will, Prince."

"He's in pain from practice yesterday." I clench my jaw. "We need to take it easier today."

Colton raises his eyebrow. "Are you?"

Shay looks uncomfortable. "I overworked—"

"It's not that bad." Colton waves his hand dismissively. "You're not used to the NHL, kid, but that's what it's like. Pain is part of the deal. I know men who have played games with broken legs, torn groin muscles, and punctured lungs. You suck it up."

"I know how to suck up pain." Shay's expression is now worryingly flat.

Fuck.

"Then deal with it. You should be grateful for this opportunity. I'll offer you every bit of advice that I can. But I don't like whiners, understand?"

Shay looks shattered. "Yes, coach."

"Stop talking to my teammates like that," I burst out. Fuck the *no comment* rule. Robyn is going to be pissed. "He's not a whiner, he's a..." *Good boy.* My gaze meets Shay's. My fingers brush his, and just for a moment, his curl against mine. I hope that he knows what I'm thinking. By the way that light sparks in his eyes again, I think that he does. "...dedicated, hardworking player. Our top scorer. And like every other member, he's my brother. So back the fuck off."

Silence.

Shit, I don't normally talk back to coaches like that.

You don't.

Mustn't.

Robyn's dad would hand me my ass, if I ever did. He probably will for talking to Colton like that.

I don't care.

Shay is looking at me like I hang the moon, and no matter what, Shay's done for the day on the ice.

It's what he needs, and I'm always going to make sure that he gets that.

I swore that I'd protect him. I don't break my promises.

"Congratulations on volunteering to take the laps for your *brother*." Colton leans against the glass, until he'd be touching me if it wasn't there. "I'm going to make you skate them, captain, until you puke. It's for your own good. Captain or not, you need to remember who's in charge the moment that you step into this arena. And it's not you. You're arrogant enough to forget the hierarchy. Players are only just above Seal, our mascot, in my eyes. You come and you go. You may be McKenna's favorite now but you're not *the board's* favorite. So, one wrong step, D'Angelo, and I'll see you kicked to the minor leagues."

CHAPTER EIGHT

Tide Cottage, Freedom

*obyn*

"Then that jerk threatened to send D'Angelo back to the minor leagues." I flick my wine glass, imagining that it's Colton's ass.

Satisfying.

The glass *clinks*, and the red wine sloshes dangerously close to the rim.

My brother, Cody, rushes across his kitchen in Tide Cottage to steady my glass.

"Let's not take out a coach's assholery on my kitchen,

Ryn," Cody pleads. "I need to remind myself of that rule most days."

I bet.

I smile sheepishly, clutching the wine to my chest. It's too precious to spill.

This is one of those rare nights, when my men are exhausted enough to collapse into bed without needing me as a stuffie to hug between them.

I need a quiet evening with my brother in his cottage on the coast to unwind.

My beautiful rebels can't get up to too much trouble, while they're asleep, right?

Everybody loves an optimist.

When Cody pulls me into a quick hug, he's the one who almost spills my wine, this time down the front of my comfy One Direction sweater and joggers.

"Code," I protest with a laugh.

Cody pulls back, laughing as well. "Whoops. You're drinking too slowly. You need to catch up with me. I've already opened the second bottle. It feels like a second bottle night."

"A *three* bottle night."

Cody is two years younger than me. He's so athletic and sun blushed, however, by his time spent surfing that he could still be a college student.

He's handsome with neat brunette hair, freckles across the bridge of his nose, and russet eyes. He's dressed in a pastel blue sweater and matching boardshorts.

I've always been close to my brother.

Until he married his husband, Michael, Cody had no one to stand with him and love him unconditionally.

Dad fucking didn't.

David Bowie's glam rock "The Man Who Sold the World" is playing on repeat.

Cody loves David Bowie so much that he has one of his songs as his ringtone.

I settle myself more comfortably on the window seat.

I glance out of the window.

The beach is remote with sea stacks, which rise from the swelling waves.

Above, the cold moon plays across the sands like silver water.

Being close to nature like this, as well as being surrounded by my brother's easy love and affection, is why I come here.

Cody and I share a past and childhood that connects us in a different way to anyone else.

I regret every day that my ex, Wilder, kept me apart from Cody. I won't let that happen again.

The kitchen is cozy with exposed beams and wide-planked wooden floors. The walls and open shelves are painted sky blue.

Cody's surfboards are stacked against the far wall, and the tangy brine smell wars with the sweet scent of fresh bread.

I raise my wine in a salute to Cody, before draining it. "This is me draining Colton."

Equally satisfying.

"*Lost Boys* style vampiric draining. Awesome revenge."

Cody wanders back to the butcher block countertop at the back of the kitchen.

He has a cheese platter laid out with freshly baked bread and cake.

My brother's famous for his baking skills.

The cheese platter is probably Michael's influence. It's the type of thing that he'd like, since he's into classical music, hummus, and golf.

D'Angelo is the only one who can casually deal with what my best friend, Neve, calls Michael's *boring old guy* shit.

Of course, Michael is also hot and a perfect husband for my brother.

He takes Cody, who's a bundle of energy, out to bars to dance and sing, despite the fact that he doesn't enjoy singing or dancing himself.

He may be exhausted after a twelve hour shift at work but he still makes time for Cody.

Michael works in ER at Freedom Heart hospital, where he's a doctor.

Both men are lucky to have each other.

Cody snatches up the almost empty wine bottle, playing the waiter.

He strolls to me. "Madam?"

I hold out my glass. "Go on then."

I'm catching a taxi home. I deserve one night of letting down my hair, before things get serious.

Unfortunately, I have a feeling that they may already have become serious.

Cody pours the wine with a flourish and doesn't stop,

until the wine is at the brim of the glass and the bottle is empty.

He winks. "Look at that, we need to open the second bottle."

"How'd that happen?" I take a sip of the fruity wine. Then I sigh, and the tension bleeds from my shoulders. "It was D'Angelo and Shay who looked like they'd been drained, when they came back from the rink earlier. Perhaps, Colton's the vampire."

Cody's eyes widen. "Fuck, that'd be a scary horror movie."

"Ice hockey vampire romance. Quick, make us some garlic pizza to protect us from that mashup genre being discovered."

"Will French garlic cheese work?"

I lick my lips, glancing at the cheese platter on the side. "How about we try it, Code? For the sake of our lives?"

"See, my food saves lives the same as my husband does."

I hope that he doesn't actually say that to Michael.

Unfortunately, I'm not exaggerating about the state that D'Angelo and Shay returned from the arena in the late afternoon.

D'Angelo could barely walk. He was shaky and pale.

Shay pulled Eden and me aside.

"Jude won't tell you this." Shay looked guilty. I didn't understand why. "He stood up for me to Colton. Back talked him. The bloody bastard made Jude skate laps, until his legs buckled. He puked four times."

I could have kneed Colton in the balls.

Eden and I nodded at each other, agreeing to end our day and take care of our family.

We spent hours giving both D'Angelo and Shay baths, massages (Eden insisted on doing this one-handed, instead of me; I don't know why), and wrapping them in blankets, despite D'Angelo's constant insistence that it *wasn't necessary for him*.

D'Angelo needs to learn that he deserves to be cared for too.

He's good at doing it for others. But he sucks at accepting care for himself.

Eden cooked one of D'Angelo's favorite meals, spaghetti Bolognese, as his offering to make him feel better without needing to say anything.

Then before I came out tonight, Eden decided that D'Angelo and Shay's aching muscles was an excuse for payback.

After he collapsed because of his concussion, Eden was under doctor's orders for no strenuous exercise, including sex.

D'Angelo set up a scene, where Eden needed to watch, while D'Angelo fucked me.

Of course, Eden still jerked himself and got off.

I love Eden's growing confidence because it was him who insisted that D'Angelo and his brother weren't well enough to join in and needed to rest…on doctor's orders.

He pointed at the antique chair in D'Angelo's bedroom.

Bristling like a cat, D'Angelo settled in it, before pulling Shay onto his lap. Then he deftly undid Shay's pants and pulled Shay's dick into his hand. He held it like a toy without stroking it.

Eden shared a nod with D'Angelo.

Then Eden fucked me harder and faster than he has before.

It was the perfect end to our day together.

It was made more intense by knowing that the other two men were willingly sitting — unmoving — in the chair.

Watching me.

I was putting on an exhibitionist performance to drive my lovers wild.

D'Angelo's jaw was clenched. His gaze was firmly fixed on me, burning and feverish.

Eden's eyes were dark.

He kissed and stroked every inch of me, while his twin was unable to touch me, whining like he was in pain.

Shay was flushed. His hands tightened on his lap.

His cock was hard in D'Angelo's fist.

When Shay tried to look away, D'Angelo grabbed him hard by the jaw and forced his head back.

"Eyes on your goddess," D'Angelo commanded.

At last, D'Angelo's hand began to move on Shay's cock in time with his brother's thrusts into me.

Fast and hard.

Shay's desperate, longing gaze never left mine, as he was worked to a hard, painful orgasm that seemed to tear his soul from him as well as a scream.

Can it be called payback, however, when we all derived such pleasure out of it?

If so, I've decided that I love revenge of the kinky kind.

Now, Cody crosses the kitchen and picks up the wooden tray with its crusty, buttered rolls, peanut rum cake, and selection of cheese. "Time for my lifesaving cheese."

My stomach growls. "And bread."

"I charge extra for the bread." Cody waggles his eyebrows.

Cody bakes everything from scratch. I've never tasted *anything* as delicious as his fresh bread and pastries.

"Are you exchanging recipes with Eden yet?" I ask. "He'd love it. And he's too isolated. He's an incredible baker like you are. So, he'd probably have some good tricks."

Cody's eyes light up. "Yep, we set up that Bakers of Bay Rebels online Whatsapp chat like you suggested. It's been a good way to get to know him as a friend. Plus, steal his English recipes because I'm jealous of his buns."

"Is that a euphemism?"

"Yes and no."

"Does he...?" This is hard to say. "Do you think he understands that you're his friend?"

Cody's brow furrows. "He *is* my friend, Ryn. That's what matters."

Cody strolls across the kitchen, sitting on the window seat next to me.

He places the tray on the floor between us.

The scent of fresh bread and garlic cheese wraps around me. It's warm and as easily relaxing as my brother is.

My mouth waters, as I select a roll, before using a knife to smear on some of the strong cheese.

When I take a bite, I can't hold back the moan.

"Good?" Cody asks.

"Vampire ice hockey coach repellent good," I mumble around my mouthful.

I have freshly baked bread in one hand and good wine in the other.

I'd be happier with a beer and chocolate. But this is Michael's idea of heaven, and I'm coming around to it.

Cody reaches down and snags himself a roll as well. "You know that you can drop around here any time, Ryn. It's no problem. Michael and I love seeing you. When things are stressful, it's good to have somewhere that you're safe to go. I wish you'd known that with Wilder. But I won't make that mistake twice."

My eyes smart. "Thanks, Code. I hope you know that it goes both ways."

Cody takes a bite of his roll. "Last time I did that, I saw a naked butler in your kitchen who threatened me with a spatula."

I choke, and Cody pats me on the back.

To be fair, D'Angelo had been wearing an apron and he'd been polite enough to invite Cody to stay for breakfast.

Cody smirks. "But what an ass he had. I asked Mike for my own naked butler, but he growled in a possessive way that no one was allowed to be naked in front of me but him. Then he demonstrated, which was fun."

"Why are you talking about naked butlers again?"

Michael says, dryly, as he walks through the lounge door. "I thought that we'd established I'm too possessive for us to get one."

"Shame. I'd look pretty in an apron." Cody stuffs the last of the roll in his mouth, before jumping up.

He bounds to Michael. "Are you just back from Freedom Heart?"

Michael nods.

Michael is in his late thirties. He's hot but stern with ebony skin and salt and pepper hair. He's dressed in a casual tan suit that's open at the neck.

Michael slings his arm around Cody's shoulders. Cody relaxes against his chest, happy and secure.

I smile seeing them together.

"I'm sorry that I missed dinner again." Michael sighs. "I couldn't drag myself away from all the—"

"Saving lives?" Cody quirks his brow.

"Blood, vomit, and in one unfortunate case, explosive diarrhea."

I scrunch up my nose. "That's why I didn't become a doctor. Along with the whole being shit at science."

Cody levels his stare at me. "You could have become anything that you wanted. I was the screw up in the family. I worked my ass off to achieve my first job in Bay Rebels. I don't think dad ever expected me to be anything but a dropout."

Michael's expression is grim.

He tightens his hold on Cody. "Then he's a fool not to see your talents. My husband is also achieving his dreams. You're a remarkable physiotherapist."

Cody flushes with pride. "You don't say that when I need to practice my physiotherapy on you, Mike."

"God, no. But then, I don't come home after a long day and give you an enema or stick you full of needles."

Cody gives him a coy look. "Well, outside of a scene…"

I flush. "TMI, Code."

I knew that Michael was Doctor Kink.

Michael gives my brother his patented stern look, which is enough to take him gently in hand.

Cody leads Michael to the window seat.

"What were you two gossiping about, apart from naked butlers?" Michael asks.

"Vampires," I reply, eating the last bite of my cheese smeared roll.

The guys are already asleep, so I don't care about garlic breath.

That's a tomorrow morning concern.

"If you'd have said zombies, then I'd have been worried." Michael settles himself next to me, and Cody kneels in front of him. "But with vampires, I have a whole blood bank at the hospital to appease them with. I'm safe."

Sometimes, Michael says thinks so dryly, it's hard to know when he's joking.

Cody carefully cuts a large piece of peanut rum cake onto a cheerful plate with **I'VE GOT A LOT OF ~~PATIENCE~~ PATIENTS** written on it and passes it with a dessert fork to Michael.

Their hands brush.

Of course, Michael would be one to insist to eat with a dessert fork.

"My extremely hungry stomach thanks you, Code." Michael smiles at Cody, who beams back. "This smells delicious."

And it does. I can smell it from here.

It's nutty but also fruity with a hint of rum. It weirdly reminds me of happy Christmases before Cody and I lost Mom.

When I lean over a little too close to get an extra sniff of nostalgia, Michael arches his brow. "Shall I simply pass mine over now?"

Cody laughs. "I made enough for us all. I'll cut you a slice, Ryn."

I flush, sitting back. "In actual fact, we were sitting here complaining."

"And now we're sitting here eating cake." Cody passes me a slice.

This time without a fork.

See, that's called sis knowledge.

We smirk at each other.

Michael stabs at his cake with his fork. "Complaining and eating cake. It sounds like just before the French Revolution."

My eyes light up. "I'm up for that. Join us in the rebellion."

"Vive la revolution!" Cody cries, bouncing on his knees.

"Hmm," Michael hums, considering. "That depends. Who are we guillotining? Who is losing their head?"

I take a large bite of my cake.

My eyes flutter closed at the delicious taste, which

somehow manages to pull off the *exact* memory from Cody and my childhood, before everything went to hell.

My chest feels tight.

Can you have a taste memory?

It's faint. But it's there.

This must be one of Mom's recipes.

Mom didn't bake often.

My brother would have been too young to remember much of that time because she grew sick and then stopped baking for much of his childhood.

I tried to shield Cody, as much as I raised him after Mom's death.

Dad preferred to pretend that my brother didn't exist, if he wasn't punishing him, but I wonder now…

Perhaps, Cody remembers more than I think.

I don't know if that's a good thing.

I drop the sticky cake back onto the plate and lick my fingers. "Colton."

"Who's that?" Michael asks.

"The Assistant Coach at Bay Rebels," Cody explains. "As much as we really were complaining, this asshole called Shay a *whiner*. Then he put Shay and D'Angelo through hell on the rink today."

Michael snorts. "Shay doesn't whine. He's as bad as his twin. Those two could have their legs hanging off but still insist that they're fine and just need to walk it off."

Cody holds up his hand. "I vote: off with his head."

I raise my glass. "Seconded. Off with his head!"

"Wait a moment." Michael grips Cody gently by the chin, directing his attention back to him. "This man isn't bullying you as well, is he? He's staff, right? The hospital consultants can be hard for me to handle sometimes. They certainly don't hold back, if someone makes a mistake. Last week, they made one of the nurses cry for a simple error that was easily fixed. These are high pressure environments, and staff often get the brunt of that."

"Stick No Carrot, as he's known, isn't bullying me." Why does Cody look uncomfortable? "But he is giving Noah a hard time. Noah is a nurse and a fucking good one. But Colton is a jerk to most of the staff. I didn't think that it could be worse to be singled out for praise at how well I'm doing my job, straight after he's ripped the person next to you to shreds for being shit at theirs."

I narrow my eyes. "You *are* great at your job. But it's probably a tactic to make the others feel worse and divide the staff."

Michael sweeps his fingers up from Cody's chin to his cheek in comfort.

He doesn't like public PDA, but the gesture is still achingly tender.

Cody leans into his touch.

"Luckily," Cody gives an easy grin, "most people still like me because I bring the fun. I've promised to as well on the staff bus. Plus, the drinks and the donuts."

"Cody," Michael says, warningly.

It's usually all he needs to say to rein in my brother.

Cody pouts. "I'll behave."

He squirms around to sit next to Michael's feet, leaning his head against his thigh. Michael rests his hand lightly on Cody's head.

"Of course you won't." Michael's eyes dance.

"I'll miss you." Cody turns his head to kiss Michael's knee.

"I'll phone between shifts. You can always contact me, even at the hospital." Michael looks pained. This will be the first time that they'll be apart since the wedding. "And you'll be with your sister."

"I'm traveling separately with D'Angelo, Shay, and Eden," I point out. "Dad wants me to keep them in line and away from the press, twenty-four seven."

"Poor guys, under house arrest even on a road trip." Cody pulls a fake sad face.

"I know. It's so challenging for them to be handled by me. A serious hardship."

Eden was *handled* by me in bed earlier, and all of the guys were seriously *hard*.

"You'll need quiet toys to pack with you," Michael points out. "I've advised Cody on what to take, while I can't be with him. If you don't already have them, make sure to go with the best quality, with silicone covers and ones that have built in dampening technology. Also, order lube that has noise-dampening particles. Plus, you could go for suction clitoral vibrators or vibrating anal beads."

I should have guessed that Michael would have researched the science.

Noise-dampening technology and lube exists?

It would have saved me from hiding under blankets to muffle the noise, playing the radio loudly, and blaming the sound of my vibrator on my razor in my teenage years.

"Okay, Doctor Kink." I take another bite of cake.

Did I just say that out loud?

I called my brother's husband Doctor Kink to his face.

It's true, but still...

Can I blame the wine?

Cody smothers his laughter on Michael's knee.

Michael turns his stern face on me.

Shit.

"I'm honored to have earned a new doctorate." Michael's eyes twinkle. "Although, I'd have thought that it was D'Angelo who was Professor Kink."

"Touché." I take a sip of wine, before realizing that my head may be swimming just a little.

My loose tongue is definitely the fault of this being a two bottle night.

Pissed Robyn can't be responsible for what she says.

That's fair, right?

Cody's expression becomes devilish.

I swallow.

I forget how dangerous he can be.

"How about a bet?" He leaps to his feet, excitedly. "Your Professor Kink vs my Doctor Kink? I bet—"

"Code," Michael shakes his head, "no bets, when you're both pretty drunk. I can tell, I'm a doctor."

"Yep, it's a doctor superpower." Cody crosses his arms. "But most of our bets have been when we're pissed."

Michael chuckles. "And you've won all of them. I'm standing up for sober Robyn, who'll wake up tomorrow with a sore head and serious regret if she takes your bet."

"It would have been an awesome bet."

Not for me.

I usually end up dressed in a tutu and dancing on tables singing ABBA as a forfeit.

"This road trip isn't going to be all vibrators and anal beads. Sadly." I scrunch up my nose. "Although, the plane with the players may be. It's going to be more like frat bros on tour, when Grayson and Lucas get together. But Dad's been working hard to make it sound like the trip of doom. He's got this antsy energy about him like there's a huge mystery. I can't work it out. But I have this feeling that if I don't, then it's going to seriously bite me in the ass."

Cody looks concerned. "That's not like Dad."

"He's worried about some dark secret from our pasts, which is connected to the trip."

Michael holds out his hand, and Cody clasps it.

I love seeing the easy way that Michael takes his husband's hand.

Dad would often summon Cody to his study after Mom's death.

Cody was younger than me, and the one thing in my life that I could cling to and protect. I never wanted him to go to the study because I knew that his being summoned meant punishment.

A punishment that was way out of proportion to whatever chore he'd forgotten to do.

I'd be flooded with fear. Cody would tremble.

We'd clutch each other's hands.

Yet Dad would bark, "Be a man."

Despite the fact that Cody was still a kid.

Then he'd yank us apart, before dragging Cody inside the study by the ear. I'd be left outside.

I'm haunted by the sound of the study door slamming.

It's the sound of my failure to protect my brother. The sensation of being torn apart from him. *Of letting go of his hand.*

Of knowing…yet not knowing…what happened to him in that study.

As often as I can now, I hold Shay's hand to prove that I can.

It causes a joy, which makes my eyes burn with tears, to swell through me that Cody's married someone who frequently and easily holds his hand with pride.

And it doesn't make either of them less of a *man*.

It makes them *better* men.

Suddenly, Cody pales. "Fuck, I should have realized."

Michael looks alarmed.

Anxiety spikes through me, sobering me up. "What?"

"The three teams that you're playing. They're the Los Angeles Kings, San Jose Sharks—"

"And the Anaheim Ducks," I finish. "What? As a surfer are you scared of the sharks? Don't worry, on a rink, the water's iced over."

"I'm more scared of the ducks." Cody wrinkles his nose. "Huh, that sounds like I have a quacking phobia. I'm actually scared of their coach."

My palms feel sweaty, sliding on the stem of the wine glass. I carefully place the glass on the floor, wiping my hands on my jeggings.

"Who's the coach?" My heart speeds up.

"Larry Gibbs." Cody bites his lip. "He took over last year. I never lost track of where he was because…"

He trails off, ducking his head.

Yet I understand. And it shatters my heart.

Larry Gibbs is the man at the middle of the scandal that haunted our childhoods.

We were innocent but the press never cared about that.

I spent too many hours wondering what Dad would have been like, if he hadn't lost his temper on the ice and attacked Gibbs.

Dad owns what he did.

On the other hand, he's labeled Cody a troublemaker for standing up to my bullies in high school, who beat the hell out of him for months, because he was scared that Cody would wreck his life like he did.

Dad's also worried that Shay is similar to him with his anger issues on the ice. It's why he's tough on him.

Sometimes, it feels like he's kicking his *own* ass.

When Gibbs was still a huge star, and Dad was a player who'd just beaten him in the Stanley Cup, Dad made the biggest mistake of his career.

Gibbs talked shit on the ice about Mom.

Dad lost it.

He did a head shot that would be illegal today, and it gave the other player concussion.

It could have killed Gibbs.

Dad's lucky that it didn't.

Dad has been making up for that ever since.

It ended both their careers in a blaze of publicity. And

in many ways, it screwed up my life along with my brother's.

I become ashen. "This will be the first time that Dad's team will be playing Gibb's. Have they spoken since that incident?"

Cody shakes his head.

Michael tightens his hold on Cody's hand.

I bang my head against the window's glass, as the joy of the evening is sucked from me. "*Fuck*. It's not only Dad. He's turning up with a team that includes his son and daughter. More than that, he's doing it in a year where he's a triumphant underdog, riding to victory against the big boys…like Anaheim. Talking about provoking the man. Gibbs is going to want to fucking slaughter us. And the press will be buzzing with the rematch rivalry. It's gold dust for them. They'll dig up our pasts, every ghost, and destroy us publicly."

CHAPTER NINE

Captain's Hall, Freedom

hay

It's Tuesday and my chance to spend an entire twelve hours with my beautiful Robyn all by myself.

It's my dream come true. And I'm not wasting a bloody minute.

Of course, on the back of my red and black beast of a Harley, I don't need to because life is much faster seen from the back of a motorcycle.

I whoop.

My heart is pounding. My pulse is frantic.

I pull back onto the driveway through the tall trees

that line the manicured lawn. The bright morning sun glints off the windows of the ranch style Captain's Hall in the distance like a beacon.

The drive by the coast this morning with Robyn clutching around my waist for dear life has been thrilling.

I'd never stop driving, if it meant her always holding me this close.

I grin and then can't stop.

It's like flying.

It's the same adrenaline shot as I get from skating, faster and faster, around the rink.

I'd spend hours as a kid, pushing myself to skate faster than anyone else.

Because this…on skates or a bike…*is freedom*.

Does Robyn understand?

Does she know what it means that I'm sharing this side of myself with her?

I haven't with anyone else, even my twin.

I never feel as alive as I do when facing down death on a motorcycle.

Unless it's riding one with Robyn.

I'm dressed in biker gear: dark waxed jeans, battered black boots, and my favorite leather jacket, which Eden gave to me on my twenty-first birthday.

He saved for an entire year to afford it.

As we draw closer to the house, I begin to slow the Harley.

All of a sudden, Robyn's hot breath is on my ear.

"When we're home," Robyn whispers, "I'm going to ride you as hard as you've been riding this Harley."

"Fuck." I shiver.

I can feel Robyn smile against the sensitive skin of my neck. Then I stiffen in anticipation, as her hand wanders from my waist, along my hip, then to my cock.

I suck in a sharp breath.

Robyn rubs her palm against my dick through my jeans.

My breathing becomes labored. Then she firmly grips me.

Does she think that my cock is a joystick?

Beautiful tormentor.

I skid the Harley to a stop, steadying it.

"Look, we're here." Robyn sounds like she's trying not to laugh. "I'm getting used to these controls now."

She squeezes my cock for emphasis.

"You'd better let up now, love, unless you want the controls to explode in your little hand," I gasp.

She gives me a final squeeze, before releasing me.

I puff out a breath half in relief, half in disappointment.

My dick twitches, trapped in my tight jeans.

Then I jerkily pull off my helmet, throwing it down.

Behind me, Robyn pulls off her own helmet, placing it behind her. She stretches her muscles with a happy sigh.

I twist to her. "Tease."

"You love it."

"You know me so well, love."

I curl my hand into Robyn's gorgeous flame hair.

I'm wearing black leather gloves, which look fantastic contrasted to the red of her hair.

I love the sensation as well.

I'm discovering that I have a serious leather kink.

Then I drag Robyn into a deep kiss like I've been desperate to the entire ride.

It's slow and drugging.

When I draw back, her pupils are dilated. She looks dazed.

I stroke my leather-encased thumb down Robyn's cheek, and she takes a deep breath like she's breathing in the glove's scent. "You look fucking edible in that outfit. But I can't wait to get you out of it."

Robyn's wearing jeans, boots, and a tan motorcycle leather jacket.

Like this, she feels uniquely like she's *mine*.

Energized, I pull back. Then I climb off the bike.

I hold out my hand to Robyn and help her off the motorcycle as well.

I begin to run, dragging Robyn after me. "Promises have been made. Sexy ones. How about a ride now, huh?"

I push open the front door. Then I yank Robyn after me up the wide stairs.

She laughs, stumbling to keep up with me. "Who could say no to a romantic offer like that?"

I miss a step, twisting my ankle.

I grimace.

Does she want romance D'Angelo style? I can do that.

I was *planning* to do that tonight. I've bought her a ring.

But I'm not the same as D'Angelo. I can't compete with

the years of shared experiences that they have between them.

He's her first love.

What am I? A one night stand who she's decided to allow to stay in her life?

A kinky fuck?

A pet? A toy?

A man who she truly could love one day?

Because I fucking love her.

"Shit, are you okay?" Robyn drops my hand and kneels to check my ankle. "That's horny karma for you."

"It's nothing." I hop up and down on my foot to check it out. It's not injured. "Do you want to do something more romantic? Should I be carrying you bridal style or something?"

Robyn stares at me. "I was joking. And you should keep pressure off your ankle. These legs are valuable. They're what will carry you to victory on the ice."

"Have you enjoyed today so far?" I ask, trying not to show how much her response matters to me.

Her face lights up in a way that can't be put on.

"It's been fucking amazing." Robyn's the one who's gently tugging me up the final steps now and down the corridor. "Waking up warm in your arms, then getting to chill in bed with you, while your brother went to the study to work and D'Angelo left for the rink. Then showering with you, before being hand fed breakfast like a princess. Finally, our ride out by the coast. It's been perfect. Are you listening, Shay? *Perfect*."

"Like you are, love." Then I look around myself in confusion. "Hey, this is your room."

"Fancy that."

I love Robyn's bedroom.

It's happy and welcoming like she is.

The walls are painted a soft blue. Couches, wardrobe, and a chest of drawers are surrounded by waves of books and abandoned chocolate wrappers.

Above me, the ceiling fan spins slowly. Light streams into the bedroom through the floor length window.

In the middle of the room is a large bed with a violet quilt and a wooden headboard that's brilliant for bondage.

When I turn my gaze back to Robyn, she smiles.

"This day is just as special to me, as it is to you." Robyn playfully circles me, trailing her hand across my ass in a distracting way. "I want you all to myself. Aren't you excited to remember the first time that we met? Make it feel like this love is ours?"

Perhaps, I am the man who *she* fucking loves too.

My lips quirk. "Madam Kidnapper up to her old tricks again. Am I your prisoner?" I enthusiastically hold my wrists up like they're tied by rope. "How cruel."

This is one of my favorite role plays, especially with Robyn.

It's hard to stop smiling.

A prisoner should really not be smiling.

Robyn rolls her eyes. "You don't look unhappy about it."

Whoops.

I work hard to look more like a kicked puppy.

Robyn strokes down my cheek. "Aww, poor puppy. How sad and pitiful. But I can be kind."

Okay, that must have worked.

My gaze flicks downwards. "I'm told that I have a talented tongue. I could kneel and earn your mercy."

Please.

I try not to look like on my knees with my head buried between her thighs is exactly where I'm longing to be.

By the smirk on her face, she knows.

Robyn cards her fingers through my hair, and I lean into her touch. "Don't you think you should earn that honor?"

She's checking in.

I furrow my brow. "What if I told you that I'm a foreign prince in disguise and I deliberately allowed myself to be taken prisoner, so that I could earn it?"

"I'd say that it's a fucking *good* disguise."

Our gazes meet.

Then we both break character and burst out laughing at the same time.

"A foreign ice prince?" Robyn kisses me lightly on the mouth. "An English one, huh? I'm honored that my pussy is worth throwing away your kingdom for."

"It's worth dying for."

"What a gentleman." Robyn tightens her hand in my hair, wrenching back my head. I hiss. "I need you, more than you know right now. Make me forget about this upcoming road trip, Gibbs, the press, my past…everything but us."

My eyes widen.

Then my expression steels. I can give her this.

I mime breaking free of the ropes, before wrapping my arms around Robyn's shoulders and dragging her into a tight embrace.

She lets out a shocked gasp, as I claim her mouth in a hard, passionate kiss.

Robyn's hold on my hair loosens.

Our tongues entwine, as I fuck her mouth with my tongue. Then I pull back, licking across the seam of her lips.

"I'll make you forget everything but how much you're loved." I kiss Robyn again, across her jaw and down her neck.

She trembles like a bird in my arms.

I'd give her anything.

Everything.

Sometimes, it feels like D'Angelo and Robyn hollow me out and fill me up again with their souls. I don't know if that's healthy, but it's better than never being loved and only being used.

I haven't experienced it before.

This love is large and messy and scary.

But I never want to stop feeling it.

Robyn's voice becomes haughty again. "On your knees then, prince. Your tongue has a job. Prisoners must behave or they're punished."

How is tonguing her not a *reward*?

I try to look chastened, even if I'm bouncing with excitement inside.

I kiss Robyn's neck one final time in supplication.

She shoots me a smile.

Then I drop to my knees.

I slowly undo her boots one at a time.

I draw off my gloves and drop them to the side. I want to slide my hands over the boots, feeling their leather.

My cock is achingly hard.

Robyn's breathing is ragged already, as I duck my head over her boots, low enough to ghost my lips over them. I pull off the right one and then repeat the ritual with the left one.

I remove her socks.

Then I deliberately glance up at her through my eyelashes, as I place a kiss on each of her feet in turn.

My lips graze the softness of her skin.

It's worship.

My eyelashes flutter. I fight not to moan.

Robyn is worth sacrificing a kingdom to kiss her feet or her pussy.

When I glance up at her, she's frozen.

Robyn's cheekbones are suffused with pink.

She doesn't look away, as I kneel up.

Then I open the buttons of her jeans, before working the jeans down her hips.

She doesn't help me, only watching with a hungry look.

I carefully work the jeans off, one leg at a time. Then I fold them with a lot more care than I know Robyn ever does her clothes, placing them onto the end of the bed.

Robyn's hands are clenching like she's battling not to grab my hair.

I smirk.

I lean forward like I'm intending to pull down her panties. Instead, I mouth at her crotch through the silk material.

"Fuck." Robyn stiffens.

I smile around her white panties.

I rest my hands on Robyn's thighs and redouble my efforts. I suck the damp material into my mouth. I can taste Robyn on it.

She's already wet.

Was she excited by the anticipation on the bike ride with her teasing?

Kissing me?

By seeing me kneel?

My kissing her feet?

She's wet now, and it's like fucking nectar.

I mouth at her hungrily.

Unable to resist, she rests her hands on my head.

"Good boy," Robyn murmurs.

Warmth soaks through me at her praise.

I fucking love those two words.

In response, I take pity.

I may be the prisoner on my knees but I have the power here. I'm setting the pace.

I know that wearing leather gloves will make the sensation more intense for Robyn, when I push her panties to the side. I stroke down her pussy with my fingers.

I rub her at the same time as licking and sucking across her clit, enthusiastically.

I show her my adoration.

I make her forget.

"Yes, fucking y-y-yes." Robyn tightens her hold on my hair, moving me now where she wants me to go.

She pushes me harder against her pussy.

I can't breathe but I don't need to right now.

I only need the taste and smell of this gorgeous woman.

My mind becomes fuzzy, and I let myself sink down.

Contentment and calm washes over me.

This is where I need to be, *exactly* where I've always fantasized of being: between the thighs of a woman who wants me.

To whom I can being pleasure.

I don't even reach to touch my cock.

Its painful throb is background noise to the drive to make Robyn come.

My hands tighten on her thighs. I know that I can tap her three times to make her release me, if I need oxygen.

I'm lightheaded.

But that doesn't seem important, while sucking on Robyn's clit is.

Robyn's shaking.

"I'm going to..." Robyn throws her head side to side. "Shay..."

Then as my vision begins to gray, she comes.

And this?

Is everything.

Robyn loosens her hold on my hair. I pull back, turning my face to the side.

I rest my head on Robyn's thigh, taking desperate gasps of air. My lungs burn, but I'm smiling.

My lips are still wet. I lick them, happily.

"That was amazing," Robyn pants. "Are you okay?"

She caresses her fingers through my hair and down my neck.

"Bloody fantastic, love." I peer up at her.

She's flushed and smiling too.

"Well, I don't break my promises." Robyn urges me to stand up. "I did say something about riding."

My smile widens. "I'm better than any bike."

Eagerly, I drag my trousers down to my ankles, and my hard cock springs up.

I wince.

"You're going commando?" Robyn doesn't sound disappointed by that.

"Always be prepared." I bounce excitedly onto the far side of the bed, sprawling back dramatically with my arms above myself like I'm a damsel in a romance novel. "Even to be taken prison by Madam Kidnapper. Now, are you going to have your way with me, love?"

My cock is waving its enthusiastic consent.

Should I add a wink to make it even clearer?

Robyn does it for me, winking as she strolls to the nightstand. "Always be prepared, huh? That's my motto too, which is why I have condoms in here now."

She opens the bottom drawer with a flourish.

I turn my head to peer down into the drawer.

Then I chuckle. "So, that's where you keep your

monster fucker appreciation dildos. I love the tentacle one. It's the sexy suckers."

"I forgot that I put that there. Can you forget now as well? Isn't that what we're meant to be doing? Collective amnesia. I'm sure that's a thing." Robyn reddens. "The damn dildo is haunting me. I should bury it or something but I'm worried that it'd come back in some kind of *Pet Cemetery the Sex Toy Sequel* way."

"Now there's a horror movie that I'd queue to see."

Robyn picks up the intimidating tentacle dildo and waves it at me. "How about we try this one out on you?"

My mouth drops open in mock shock. "Help! Help! I'm being threatened with a tentacle arse probing."

Robyn chucks the vibrator back into the drawer and plucks out a condom packet instead.

She hushes me, leaping onto the bed and slamming her palm across my mouth.

I give her hand a slow lick.

Robyn's nose wrinkles, and she pulls back her wet hand.

But she's trying not to chuckle. "Shut up, unless you want your overprotective brother to come thundering in here."

I give a sunny smile at the thought. "Then he finds me with my trousers down, a drawer full of monster peens, and my mean kidnapper—"

"About to gag you," Robyn blurts.

Yes, please.

Robyn appears to have spoken without truly thinking about the words, but they go straight to my cock.

I moan. My pupils are blown wide. My tongue darts out to wet my lips.

Robyn lies next to me, studying me closely. "I may really need to *gag* this smart mouth of yours."

When she traces her soft finger over my lips, they tingle.

She's testing out the thought and checking in with me. She's giving me time to back out.

No chance.

I can't help being eager. I've wanked to this fantasy at least ten times already.

"Yes, please, love." I capture her finger, licking and sucking it like earlier I worshiped her pussy.

Her breath hitches.

But then, Robyn looks around herself unsure. "I don't know… I haven't got anything…"

This is where experience counts.

What D'Angelo has been showing me is that I can still communicate and be listened to within a scene. It's not wrong for me to give input and do it in a teasing way because that suits Robyn and my dynamic.

I've never felt as relaxed as I do when I'm in bed with her. It's been like that since the night we met.

"Oh no." I clutch my hands together as if in prayer above myself. "Please don't take off your pretty soaked panties and stuff them in my mouth to stop me screaming out."

I bite my lip and give her a heated look just in case she misses the heavy, *heavy* hint that I'm encouraging her to do just that.

Panties make the perfect instant gag.

Robyn gapes at me like I've short circuited her mind.

Then a mischievous smile steals across her face. "Bad English ice princes who make too much noise earn exactly that."

Even as she says it, it sounds like a *good boy* wrapped up in a reward.

Robyn kisses my mouth like she's going to miss it, before she slips off her panties. She's in such a rush that she doesn't make a show it.

There's no hiding that this idea is turning her on.

Her cheeks are flushed.

"Open wide, prince." Robyn taps my cheek.

Then she stuffs her panties into my mouth, until I can't close it.

I moan.

Fucking heaven.

"Wicked woman," I try to sass, but my words are muffled.

"What was that?" Robyn says, sounding satisfied with her handiwork. "I can't hear you. There seems to be something in your mouth."

When I arch my brow, she kisses my nose.

I suck on the panties.

They taste like nectar.

Like Robyn.

Like love.

I'll take having panties stuffed in my mouth, if I'm denied a pussy.

Robyn stares down at me for a long moment like she can't believe I'm real.

I hold myself still.

She runs her hand along my stretched arms, neck, across my leather jacket, then finally rests just above my straining cock.

I can hardly breathe.

Fucking touch me.

Robyn draws back, however, and my thighs quiver with the strain of not moving or humping my hips.

I hear the foil packet being opened, then my hips jerk, as Robyn slowly sheathes my cock.

She pumps me once, then again.

It's torture.

When Robyn kneels over me, she guides my cock to her pussy. Then she reaches to grab one of my hands and encourages me to rub across her clitoris.

I gasp at the sensation of pleasuring her at the same time that she does.

Our fingers tangle together.

Our gazes meet, as she sinks onto my cock. I struggle not to come at once.

It feels like I've needed to for hours now.

I'm desperate to tell Robyn how fucking incredible she feels but I can't because of the gag in my mouth, and knowing that makes desire pulse through me faster.

I don't move my second hand, even though Robyn rides me as fast and hard as she promised on the bike, until she grasps it and urges it to rest on the gorgeous curve of her breast.

My back arches.

I gently squeeze Robyn's breast. When her breathing becomes ragged, I circle her nipple, before flicking across it rhythmically.

She doesn't speak. She could. But her gaze is firmly fixed on my gag, and it's like she's sharing the experience with me.

Everywhere that Robyn's touching me — her kisses to the corners of my mouth and throat, how one hand claws at my shoulder, and the other brushes against mine as she rubs her clit, and the tight warmth of her pussy as she fucks me hard — feels much more intense in this silence.

I could spit the gag out of my mouth at any moment.

I'm in control here.

With Robyn, I always am.

Yet I bite down hard on the makeshift gag to stop myself.

Robyn gave it to me not as a punishment but as a reward.

This silence is a gift.

Robyn doesn't need me to perform for her.

I'm enough.

Normally, I can't stop myself from bantering and joking.

I need to talk to fill the silence, which scares me.

The quiet means being thrown back into a past of dark, imprisonment, and pain.

You can cover up a lot with laughter, chatter, and smiles.

If you never stop talking, you never have to think.

Eden has tried to tell me that. But he's spent too much of his life in silence. I'm been terrified of what would happen, if I became like him.

I don't have his strength.

Today, however, I'm willingly giving up my safety net. Robyn has taken my voice.

Meeting her gaze, however, as she doesn't look away from me once, she's showing me that even like this, *I still have one*.

She kisses over my open lips.

My heart clenches. I didn't expect to feel like this.

My eyes smart with unexpected tears.

Can she feel how much she means to me? How much she's proving to me in this moment?

I'm not thrown into a bloody flashback.

In Robyn's kisses, taste of her in my mouth, and emerald gaze, I'm held in the present with the woman who I'm fucking obsessed with.

When Robyn's fingers claw into my shoulder, it pushes me over the edge.

I bite hard into the gag.

Yet I'm not silenced.

Because I know in my bones that even though Robyn can't hear my scream as I come with a toe curling, shuddering rush, and she tumbles after me, I'm safe.

Robyn will only make me scream in pleasure and not pain.

The world outside our love wants to hurt us, but we'll never hurt each other.

CHAPTER TEN

Captain's Hall, Freedom

hay

THIS HAS BEEN the best bloody day of my life. And it's not over yet.

The night's cold. I rub my hands together to warm them up. Then I pull the violet blanket more snugly around Robyn's shoulders.

We're surrounded by a nest of purple cushions that I borrowed…stole…from the lounge. I'm learning about Robyn's love of comfy nests.

Is that a Robyn or a girlfriend thing?

Eden's reading in the lounge. D'Angelo's playing on the piano. He tends to play in the evenings. I think that he does it to perform a mini concert for us, but he never admits it.

Eden enjoys the music.

Again, he doesn't admit it.

Those two say more in their silences than in words.

The opposite of me, really.

Robyn's sitting next to me on the tartan blanket, which I've laid out for her on the flat roof of Captain's Hall.

I'm coming to see this as *our spot*.

I first found this flat section of roof, when I was restless during training camp in my first few weeks in America. I clambered through a skylight and explored this new world.

It made me feel at peace.

The stars are an escape for me. They have been since I was a kid.

It's free to study the sky. I became good at finding ways to keep myself busy that didn't cost anything.

Somehow, your own problems never feel as large or frightening, when you realize now large the universe is.

Connecting with the vastness of the night sky helps me to hold faith, even when people feel small and cruel.

Eden busted my balls for taking the risk of breaking my neck the next morning.

I didn't care. Having a refuge on the roof was too important to me.

D'Angelo's such a brilliant friend that he paid for a

ladder to be installed to make coming up here safer for me.

It often feels that he has a kind of money wand that he can wave.

I'll never get used to that.

D'Angelo saved me both from a broken neck and another ball busting.

He's been saving me from the moment that I met him.

I didn't think that I'd be able to share my refuge with anyone. At college, I had a spot that was private to me.

I never took any woman there.

Blythe punished me so hard that I was bruised for days because I wouldn't take her stargazing.

It's one of the rare times that I refused to submit.

Even though I thought that Blythe was my girlfriend and domme (and am now beginning to realize in a way that's shaken me to my core that she was actually my abuser), my stars were a safe space.

And that meant being alone.

For the first time, however, I'm comfortable to share both my nighttime refuge and stars with Robyn.

Except, if she abandons or hurts me as well, then she'd do more than destroy me.

She'd take away the only thing that's ever belonged to me.

The only thing that's stopped me from breaking completely.

But she's worth taking that risk.

I stare up at the sky.

Unfortunately, clouds are streaming like rags across the moon.

The moon and stars are obscured.

I glance across at the telescope that I set up on the far side of the blanket.

It's gleaming bronze.

Beautiful.

I've been frugal with my money in order to be able to afford it, as well as a ring. I've been desperate for a proper telescope like this my entire life.

I itch to look through the telescope but I know that it's no good tonight. It's far too cloudy.

"So, this is meant to be the romantic section of the date." I wince. "The weather appears to be my enemy."

"You English, always talking about the weather." Robyn's lips curl up at the side.

"I could throw in a joke about the Royal family."

"How about you tell me what you love about the stars?" Robyn snuggles closer against my side. I fucking love the way that she tucks her head against my shoulder. "Being up here with you *is* romantic. Plus, you're hot as hell, when you're smart as shit about your astrophysics stuff. You hide that side of yourself a lot. But I'm into your expert side."

"Do you mean the theories like the Big Bang, dark matter, cosmic inflation, or the fundamental theories of physics?"

I struggle to keep a straight face.

"Keep talking, scientist man, I'm so wet right now."

Then we both laugh.

"You mean my passion for the stars, love?" I kiss the top of Robyn's head. Her hair is soft. "No one but you is interested. Well, Mum is, and Dee was into the myths. I love that you want to share this with me."

Robyn entangles our hands. "At college, I spent more time partying, than I did studying. I saw how hard D'Angelo worked but I didn't *see* it. I didn't realize how much pressure he was under, even though he was my best friend. I should have done. Sometimes, I'd take him out and treat him to ice cream or a meal to make him take a break. But I was in my own bubble, with friends and then a boyfriend. I believed lies about him that fucking wrecked him. I don't want to make the same mistake again."

I nod.

My heart aches for both Robyn and D'Angelo.

I want to give this to her, the truth.

She's been honest with me, and that couldn't have been easy to admit.

I steel myself.

"My adoptive parents had no money. They still don't." I tighten my grip on her hand. "My brother and I were still in heaven because it was more than we'd had before: a roof, food, and clothes. I was terrified, however, that we were going to lose it at any moment. I never lost that feeling. It's why I can't sleep. I have this creeping sensation that the moment I close my eyes, everything will truly vanish. When I wake up, I'll discover that this life is a dream, and I'll be back there, with my biological parents or trapped in that dark room. Dee and I never escaped our real life."

"Shay," Robyn whispers, sounding broken hearted.

Eden knows why I have insomnia.

As a kid, I'd climb into his bed and lie with my head resting on his chest. Hearing his heartbeat and knowing that at least he was alive could be one way for me to fall asleep.

The second way was to run outside, as long as Dad didn't catch me, and wait on the doorstep for Mum to return from her late shift.

She was never angry. She understood.

Mum would look exhausted with deep bags underneath her eyes. But she'd take the time to sit on the step with me. Sometimes, she'd pull me onto her lap. That was the first time that she started pointing out the stars and constellations to me.

It was magical.

It was also the first special time alone with Mum. It was rare because she worked so hard.

Usually, I'd fall asleep that way, while I stared at the stars.

It became the only way that I felt safe I'd wake up to freedom the next day.

"It's okay." I shrug. "Now, I wake up to you each morning. And it's brilliant because every day I'm a little bit more sure that I will again."

Robyn lifts her head from my shoulder and kisses me.

It's tender and slow.

She sucks on my lower lip, before deepening the kiss again. I reach to cup the back of her head.

She slows the kiss like she wants me to feel every moment of it and remember that she's here.

That she always will be.

I believe her.

The thought shocks me.

I pull back from Robyn, and she chases after my lips.

I smile, when she pouts. "Stars were an escape to a new world for me. Somewhere bigger and brighter. They seemed the opposite of how I felt: strong *and bright*. They shone, and everybody saw them. I wanted so bloody much to be like them."

"You are now." Robyn tugs me down to lie next to her on the blanket. "You're an actual star."

I pillow my head on my arms. "Mum said that my brother was a star. It's why she read him stories about them. Well, especially about a constellation: Perseus. It's probably what got him into the myths. He dragged Dad to the library for more books on them whenever he could. Dad was a sucker for Dee's big eyed hopeful look."

"I can imagine." Robyn wriggles even closer. "So, who's this Perseus guy?"

"A hero." I smile at the memory. "Mum pointed out the constellation for me one night, when Dee was up as well, trailing after me down the stairs. Sometimes he did that. He checked up that I was okay even then. Perseus was the son of Zeus, who was cast into the sea by his Mum and grew up without his parents. He was tricked by a king into killing a snake-haired monster, Medusa. Then on the way home, he also saved Princess Andromeda from a sea monster."

"A man without parents who slew monsters."

"A hero who *saved* people," I add. "Mum simply said, *you saved your brother*. And Dee did."

"Our Perseus." Robyn stares up at the suffused light of the moon.

I roll my eyes. "Please don't call him that, love. He had Mum tell him that story every night for months. Then he had me act it out with our stuffies—"

"You had stuffies?" Robyn squeals looking way too excited. "What were they called?"

"I'm not giving you *that* ammunition." I laugh. "Our stuffies played Medusa and the sea monster. And I had to play…" Shit, I'm going to give her this ammunition though, aren't I? "…the princess."

Robyn looks like she's stopped breathing for a moment.

Then she turns to me looking even more delighted. "Fuck, we have to role play that. You'd look amazing dressed up as a Greek princess."

My eyes widen.

That didn't go in the direction that I was expecting.

"I bet that I could pull it off," I declare. "I do have great legs. D'Angelo would make a hot as hell sea monster. Hmm, I'm just imagining you with snakes in your hair…"

"Hey." Robyn rolls on top of me, laughing as she pins me down.

"Scary, you're getting into the role already." I reach up and claim a quick kiss. "Your hair is trailing all over me like red snakes. Oh, your eyes are flashing now with fury too. Wait, they're turning me to stone and…"

I pretend to freeze like I've been turned to stone.

"Serves you right." Robyn sits up on me in triumph. "Medusa claims another male victim. Win for women everywhere." Then she frowns. "Has your cock grown?"

I'm almost startled enough to sit up.

Robyn wriggles backward to sit on my thighs. When her hand reaches into the pocket of my jeans, I realize what she's found.

I remain petrified to stone, but my heart is still beating.

It's hammering in my chest.

She pulls out a small silver box.

Robyn glances at me. "I wish that you weren't stone."

I remain still.

It's a curse.

But I watch Robyn closely.

"I'll take that as a yes." Robyn opens the box, then a smile spreads across her face.

She gently lifts the ring from the box.

It's a simple ring. It's silver with four stars, one to represent each of us in this relationship.

It's not as valuable or sentimental as the other two rings from D'Angelo and Eden, which are glistening right now on her hand.

But I thought about what would mean the most to me.

It feels easier now to lie still and pretend that I'm stone and Robyn's reaction can't shatter me.

But it can.

"Shay, I love it." Robyn traces over each star in turn.

"These are meant to be each of us, right? Our family of stars because we're your escape now. We're…"

When she breaks off, I'm shocked to see tears in her eyes.

When one chases down her cheek, I break free of the curse and sit up.

"Look at that, your tears freed me. That's some fairy tale shit." I wipe away Robyn's tears with the back of my hand. "Eat your heart out Jude, I can bring the romance too."

Robyn gives a type of sobbing laugh. "I get it. This ring means a fucking lot. After Wilder, I could never have guessed that I'd find three people who'd really love me. Family and home were no longer safe ideas. I doubted myself. I thought that love meant being owned and controlled. But you've shown me that it doesn't need to. I'd have been scared of accepting a gift like this before. But with you, this is like accepting freedom."

Now my eyes are burning too.

"Stop it, love, you're making me blush." Gently, I guide her to place the ring on her thumb. I stroke across each of the rings in turn. "You look fantastic in these. I'd capture the stars from the sky and bottle them for you, if I could."

"I should get you guys a ring too," Robyn says, determinedly. "You've given me these things, so that I can think of you. But I want you to be able to secretly think about me, when I'm not with you."

"That'd be amazing. Although, I have to admit to still thinking about you every five seconds anyway."

"Isn't that meant to be sex?"

"Sexist."

"I didn't say that *I* didn't think about it just as frequently," Robyn replies. "I want to take my time and make the right choice of rings, once we're back from this road trip. I'm excited to be spending this time with you, but knowing that the guy who Dad gave the concussion to is now the Anaheim's coach is fucking with my head."

"Eden's too." I shift, uncomfortable. "He's still wrestling with losing his career because of being attacked on the ice and being concussed. Now, there's this whole thing with the same setup from coach's past. Jude's already being ridden hard enough by Colton. It triggered severe OCD today. Jude spent over an hour folding and refolding clothes in his room. He tried to go to coach about Colton again, but coach is too preoccupied with Gibbs threat."

"Dad owns what he did to Gibbs. He feels remorse. But the press are going to have a field day over it. And Cody and I, as Dad's kids, were always caught in the crossfire. It won't be different on this trip." Robyn's shoulders hunch.

I drag Robyn into a hug. "Hey, we're going to be together. *Four stars shining in the night.* This road trip will be fine. You're smart at the press stuff, and Eden will hold it together. He's our Perseus, remember? D'Angelo and I will have everything on the ice covered."

Except, I know that the pressure on the ice will be on *me*.

I'm the top scorer.

Coach has made it clear that he expects me to lead the team to win, even if D'Angelo is the captain.

Coach will kick my ass, if I don't. And that's fair. I owe it to everyone to do my job and score.

Only, I don't care about having my balls busted.

What I care about is not letting down Robyn and D'Angelo, these incredible people who have let my twin and me into their lives.

CHAPTER ELEVEN

D'Angelo's Beach House, Freedom

'Angelo

THE MOON and stars shine down on the crashing waves and winding path, which leads over the sand dunes of my private beach.

Who gives a fuck about the night sky, however, when I have the woman who I love lying with her head in my lap?

I'll leave the stargazing to Shay. All I want to gaze on is my Robyn's face.

Or that face sucking my cock.

Robyn's lips look amazing stretched around my large

cock, while she stares up at me with eyes that have haunted my dreams for years.

She looks even more gorgeous, when she valiantly attempts to deepthroat me.

She's always been ambitious.

It's Shay, however, who looks incredible gagging on my cock, while his eyes glisten with tears.

Making Shay cry is becoming my new favorite hobby, especially when it's from pleasure.

Robyn appears too comfortable to disturb, however, lying curled resting on me, even for the sake of a blow job.

I don't normally believe in orgasm denial (for myself), but this time, I'm happy to stick with the romance of the moment…for now.

An open box of luxury chocolates rest on the arm of the couch.

I'm wearing a navy suit and tie but I've thrown my jacket over the back of the couch, which is on the back porch overlooking the sea.

Robyn looks beautiful in a light green off the shoulder dress with a flower embroidered pattern. She's pushed off her sandals. Her bare feet rest on a cushion.

I bought this beach house, when I was dizzy with my new wealth and wanting to invest in something.

Property, businesses, and charities.

But then, I discovered that it's lonely to drive out to a beach house by yourself.

There's nothing more certain to make you feel like a loser than vacationing for the weekend in an empty mansion by the sea.

When I woke up this morning, after missing Robyn all of yesterday while she was off with Shay, I couldn't wait to have her to myself.

So, I'm possessive.

Is it wrong to wish that you could tattoo your name over your loved one's ass?

Actually, I'll probably have more luck tattooing it onto Shay's cock.

Something to think about.

Robyn peers up at me. "What are you scheming? You have a devilish look."

"Do I, *principessa*?"

Robyn presses a kiss to my thigh. "Yep, it's kind of hot."

I stroke her hair, and she cuddles down onto the couch. "Wouldn't you like to know."

"I have a feeling that I wouldn't," she replies. "Now, hush. We're missing the very end of the movie."

"What a shame."

It's not.

This is the *second* time that Robyn's watched *Finding Nemo*, her favorite Disney movie, since we arrived today.

And the second time that I've suffered through it with her.

I truly must be a good man.

We're sitting out on the back porch of my wood paneled beach house, which is painted white like the wooden decking.

It's filled with tall vases of orange roses. There are so many that it's like being surrounded by a rose garden.

I ordered the roses specially for today because they're Robyn's favorite.

When she saw them, her eyes opened with surprise, then a breathless joy.

And that was the first moment I truly realized this is what our life could be like.

I could have this.

Robyn and I could vacation here at weekends.

I don't need to be alone anymore.

After this season, I could live in my mansion in town with Robyn and the twins and then vacation here with them.

Eden would love the wildlife.

Shay would love skinny dipping on our private beach like Robyn and I did this afternoon.

We just need to survive this season.

A television is set up across from us, along with a sound system. Golden lanterns cast puddles of light at the corners of the porch. At the far side is a grand dining table and chairs.

Also, a globe that contains alcohol.

I needed to have a drink to get through this movie.

The other thing that's helped me to get through this rewatch has been the feel of Robyn in my lap, along with her happy narrative, as she talks along to the movie like I don't know what's coming next.

Only she could make it charming to say the lines of dialogue, before the characters do.

See, that's the power of love.

It's the memory of the many, *many* times that we did

just this at college as friends, before things became complicated because of Wilder, which makes warmth flood through me.

I think that Robyn wants to recreate that time too.

For six years, I never thought that I'd have this with her again.

I'm not going to fuck up my second chance with Robyn.

I push a curl of hair behind Robyn's ear, studying her face.

She's focused on the movie.

I force myself to look away from her and back at the screen.

Then I let out a relieved sigh. "The end credits. Thank Christ. This is my favorite part of the movie."

"You like Robbie William's swing cover of "Beyond the Sea"? It is very you."

Robyn turns her head to nip my thigh in retaliation.

"No biting, she-devil." My dick twitches. I can't be blamed when Robyn's so close to cock sucking territory. "I meant that the movie is finally ending. Although, the song playing over the credits is a good one. I could drink a cocktail to it and imagine that I'm in a smoky jazz lounge."

"Why would you want to," Robyn waves in the direction of the crashing waves, "when we're somewhere amazing like this? We're fucking lucky. Thank you for today. I can't wait to bring the others here too. It's going to blow Shay's mind."

I chuckle. "He'll bound around the beach excitably and probably break half my stuff."

"But he'll be lit up like the sun. So, it'll be worth it."

I smile, softly. "Yes, it will. Plus, it'll give me the excuse to punish him in enjoyable ways."

"Harsh."

"But fair."

"And if it makes Eden smile, then—"

"It'll be even more worth it."

I pluck a heart shaped chocolate out of the box, and Robyn opens her mouth like a baby bird for me to feed it to her. Then she takes it from me, licking across my fingers.

"Hmm, strawberry cream." She munches with a moan that makes my cock harden.

Fuck, I wish that Robyn would turn her head and nuzzle at me through my trousers.

If she was Shay, I'd simply grab her hair and guide her head where I wanted her to go. But we have a different dynamic.

Patience is hard.

"Don't trick me and feed me a yucky coffee cream" Robyn attempts to look cutely stern.

"I wouldn't dare."

"Do you remember how we'd curl up together like this and watch *Finding Nemo* at college? Of course, without the handfeeding and licking."

"I remember everything, cara mia."

My heart beats quicker. My cheeks flush.

Robyn twists to look up at me. "Jude…?"

Damn, it does something to me when she uses my first name, especially whispered in that hushed voice.

It sounds like a prayer.

"Being with you at college on those movie nights with snacks, laughter, and deep chats about the meaning of the universe and other bullshit until the early hours..." I admit, my piercing gaze meeting hers. "They're most special memories that I have. You were my best friend. You still are. Back then, spending time in your room granted me the greatest stability that I'd had in years. It was like having a home again for the first time since the day I kissed a boy and lost everything. Since my family beat the shit out of me and threw me into hell."

"I didn't know." Robyn's voice is raspy with tears. "You were my best friend too. But I could never read you. I treasure every moment that I spent with you. I wish that you'd felt able to tell me what you were going through then."

"I wasn't able to talk about it with anyone, even my sister. Plus, I was a dumbass. I was too proud. I was already a scholarship student who couldn't afford new clothes or to eat some days. I became infamous for my Halloween costume, but it was the only way that I could go to the party."

Robyn's brow furrows. "You mean when you turned up as the horny devil, naked with only a pair of horns on your head...?"

"I couldn't afford an actual costume. But I've learned to be creative, principessa. Naked is effective, when you don't have anything to wear."

"Shit."

I shrug. "Luckily, I also learned to love being naked. I had so many rules at the discipline school that once I was out of there, I was desperate to break as many as possible. I didn't want you to look at me and also see someone who was damaged."

"I never would have." Robyn's eyes flash.

"You wouldn't now." I look away. "Back then, I couldn't trust anyone. So, I guess that I've grown up too."

"You're right." Robyn reaches to stroke down the front of my shirt over my abs, and I shiver. "You only need to tell me things when you're ready."

"At that point, I was still learning what it was like to function as an actual person, an individual who'd survived the tyranny of that school. Finally, I had the freedom to smile, look at who I wanted, even watch a movie without punishment."

"You're serious?"

"I wish that I wasn't. If you lost attention even for a moment, or glanced out of a window to see the sky, then you'd be put in solitary confinement. It would have fucking destroyed Shay." I take a deep breath, tapping my arm three times to control my spiraling anxiety. I can't think of my cucciolo being sent somewhere like that just because he realized that he was bisexual. I'd never let anyone do that to him. *Never.* "Once, I tried to stand up for this new kid who was only in his early teens. He was sweet, terrified, and in tears. It was a mistake."

Robyn's eyes are sad. "What happened?"

"They made sure that I never stepped in again." I run

my hand through my curls, unable to stop myself checking that they're still there. "They shaved off my hair."

It should have been a small thing compared to everything else.

But it wasn't.

It fucking wasn't.

I was stripped and tied to a chair, while two women forcibly shaved my head. Watching my black curls fall to the dirty floor was like watching the last of my old life being cut away from me.

I didn't recover from that.

Immediately, Robyn sits up.

She kneels next to me and wraps her arms around my neck.

I can't look at her.

"Abusive pieces of shit. I wish that I could kick their fucking asses for you," she growls.

She sounds dangerous.

I like that she's fierce on my behalf.

"You don't need to do that." I run my hand through my hair, compulsively. "At college, you were the one who taught me to relax again, how to breathe, and how to *live*. I started to believe that I'd recover. You pulled me out of a dark place in my life, principessa. Well, that and a lot of therapy."

"And Disney films." Robyn kisses my cheek.

I chuckle. "You invented a whole new style of therapy."

When she tugs at me, I get the message. I twist to face

her. Then I sprawl back against the couch, as she holds onto me tightly.

"What's your favorite one?" Robyn asks, hopefully. "We'll watch it next time."

I love the way that she assumes driving here in my Alfa Romeo is going to become a regular thing now, as if my abandoned beach house has truly been brought to life by her presence.

"Lucky me." I roll my eyes. "Nothing with talking fish, cars, or…" I hesitate. "I am rather fond of a certain talking fox, however, an English one. Maybe that's why I find Shay so sexy."

Robyn perks up. "You want to give him a fox's tail. There are butt plugs like that."

Fuck, yeah.

Also, I've played like that with other submissives. Shay would look fucking hot as a cute fox.

"Cara mia, you have the best ideas. Our pet would look adorable with a tail swinging from his tight little ass and ears on his sweet head. I can just imagine that brat as a mischievous fox." The image makes my cock even harder. I narrow my eyes dominantly at Robyn. I can imagine her right next to him. For now, I settle for adding, "Of course, Shay's also English. Do you remember the animated Robin Hood film, which is set in England? Robin Hood is a gorgeous fox with fuck me eyes and a voice like melted caramel?"

Robyn flushes. "Sort of, but also, we have to watch that now because *you* certainly do. And the fox does sound like Shay."

"Let's just say that the fuckable fox in that movie kick-started my bi-awakening at a young age." I wrinkle my nose. "And also confused me about foxes for a long time."

Robyn laughs.

Predatory now, I push her back on the couch. She lets out a surprise gasp. Her breathing picks up.

I lie over her, caging her. I push my hips against her.

My pupils dilate at the sensation of my hard cock in my pants, as it rubs against her thigh. I grind against her, letting myself ride on the waves of pleasure.

I entwine my hand with hers. The three rings gleam in the golden light.

Why am I not surprised that Shay gave her stars?

Robyn's eyelashes flutter. Her dress rides up.

"Of course," I murmur close to her ear, "there was that time you became obsessed with *Frozen* and watched it four times in a row."

"F-f-five," she manages to force out.

I arch my brow. "I rest my case. I'm the best friend in the world."

Robyn's laugh vibrates through me. It feels incredible.

"Is this…" She gestures between us, as I continue to pin and dry hump against her, "…your revenge for that? Because if it is, please don't stop making me pay."

I speed up my thrusts, struggling to hold back my orgasm. I let go of her hand, working it between us instead.

I push up her dress to give more friction against her thin, lacy panties.

She's trembling. Her eyes are wide.

She's never looked more beautiful.

Taking her apart drives me wild.

"If I was," I say, "then I'd discipline you with a spanking because I had that song, *Let It Go*, as an earworm for months. But this…" I move one hand to Robyn's throat, caressing the dip of her collarbone, before tightening my hold just enough to make her eyes widen further with pleasure. "…is my way of telling you a fantasy that I had of the movie but couldn't admit at the time."

She wets her lips. "Don't tell me that you have a thing for snowmen as well as foxes?"

I tighten my hand around her throat, even though I laugh.

Robyn grins, before opening her lips to beg for a kiss.

I answer her request, ducking my head to capture those delicious lips.

She relaxes into the kiss, before I pull back.

Our lips still graze each other on each word that I say. "Want to know my fantasy? Poor Prince Hans. Mistreated by his family. A villain…but one who only needs to be taken in hand — by me — with a long, hard spanking. Then an even harder fucking."

"You were seriously sitting there plotting through the four…five…screenings of the movie about fucking Prince Hans? Imagining him over your lap?" Robyn sounds scandalized.

Why is she surprised?

Naïve.

Plus, if I had to watch a movie that included comedy

snowmen, then I could at least indulge in fantasies about taming wicked princes.

It's only fair.

I didn't understand that side to myself back then.

Yet I always had a dominant side. It's a fundamental part of who I am.

I simply needed to find a community who could help me to express it in the safest and healthiest way with consent and boundaries.

My grin becomes as wicked as Hans'. "Not only Hans. I planned to seduce the two sisters as well. Then together, we could keep Hans, our bad boy, in line."

I nibble on Robyn's bottom lip, before looking up at her through my long eyelashes.

Robyn's breathing has become rapid and uneven. Her hands clutch at my shoulders, even though she's attempting to look outraged.

"I don't believe you were thinking that. You told me that the film was boring." Robyn's hands open and close, as she humps up and down against me.

She's close to coming, I can tell.

She doesn't know that I won't let her come. Not yet. I have plans.

Foreplay, however, is all about the buildup and the anticipation.

Her orgasm will be much more intense this way.

Pleasure is as much about our minds as our bodies. That's one of the things that I learned, when I trained as a dom.

There's more power in words than any flashy sex toy, expensive kink dungeon, or super-sized cock.

There's even more power in planting a story or image in someone's head, then letting them do the work of making themselves wet.

Robyn's breathing hard.

Her panties are already soaked through.

"Did I?" I quirk my brow. "I jerked off to that fantasy in the college showers that night. Then I imagined what it would be like if *you* were the one over my knee."

It's true.

I don't need to make anything up.

"Fuck." Robyn leans up and steals a kiss, unable to resist.

I'm not expecting her hunger and passion. She grabs my hair, yanking me even closer.

My hand slides from her throat.

My hair covers her face like we're in a world entirely by ourselves under the glow of the lanterns and the moon.

The movie has ended, and there's nothing but the sound of the waves.

I could live here with her forever.

Except, I have another fantasy to fulfill for Robyn tonight.

I draw back from the kiss.

She's looking at me with a depth of love that I've never experienced before.

I love the hell out of this woman who wears my lucky charm ring on her finger.

Robyn, my lucky twenty-two.

My intent gaze holds hers. "We need to drive back to Captain's Hall in a couple of hours. But now, I'm going to take you to my bedroom, and we'll christen it. Christen this entire house as ours. Then I'll mark you as mine with a fantasy from the list that you made, which I marked confidential in the Guide. I promise, cara mia, these upcoming weeks may be tough, but you're never going to forget tonight."

CHAPTER TWELVE

D'Angelo's Beach House, Freedom

'Angelo

INSIDE ROBYN'S Guide is an entire chapter on me, including photographs clipped from newspapers and printed out from social media.

In some, I'm pole dancing or being fucked wearing nothing but a leather harness.

Robyn told me about her favorite photograph on our first date.

In it, I'm dressed in a horse riding outfit. Robyn said that it made me look like a cross between Darcy and Christian Grey.

Horrifying.

Still, I remember the outfit. I wore it to a Bridgerton styled fetish ball, which I attended in Freedom.

When I read the fantasy that Robyn wrote into the Guide with me dressed up like a dominant Duke, how could I resist giving her that role play?

Only, without the toxic assholery that is Christian *fake dom* Grey.

The riding breeches are so tight that the bulge of my hard cock is outlined.

Did Darcy have the same problem?

I bet that he did when he walked out of that lake. The shirt clung to his chest in a way that definitely made me desperate to bend him over and fuck him *hard*.

I'm wearing high leather boots, a designer show shirt, and a blue riding jacket that matches my eyes.

I'm gripping a wide tipped riding crop against my thigh.

It's my one of my favorite implements. It fits supply into my hand, comfortable and familiar.

I stand with a wide stance in the center of my beach house bedroom.

The silver drapes are open. The only light is from the star bright nighttime sky.

The windows are floor to ceiling along one side of the bedroom. The wardrobe and nightstands are carved from driftwood. The giant bed stands in the center of the room with crisp, white bedding.

The room is all white in fact with views over the moon drenched ocean.

Orange rose petals are strewn over the bedding. They also lead in a path on the floor to the bed like a wedding aisle.

Robyn stands in the doorway.

She's staring at me, mesmerized. "I thought that you no longer owned that outfit."

"I bought a new one for tonight."

"Just for me?" Robyn sounds bewildered, as if she's still unsure that she has a right to her own needs being met.

Her ex is a fucking jerk.

I wish that I could knee him in the balls as part of my daily routine.

"Isn't this what you've been dreaming about?" I tap the crop on my thigh, and her fascinated gaze tracks the movements. "The kiss of my crop?"

Robyn swallows. Her cheeks flush.

Then she nods. "I want to please you. Can you show me how?"

She looks shy all of a sudden.

It's cute.

It also makes my back straighten and adrenaline rush through me.

I live for moments like this. Submission offered with such belief makes me fall into domspace.

I'm already feeling high from the trust that Robyn's placing in me.

"Obey me and you'll please me, cara mia." I feel at ease, hyperfocused on Robyn.

I'm in control.

I'm going to guide her through this.

Robyn's breathing picks up like I knew it would.

She nods.

"Words," I say, sharply.

"Yes, Sir."

Robyn's also falling into the right headspace.

We have a tough couple of weeks ahead. We need to let go, feeling only sensation, pain, and pleasure.

I point with my crop to a point on the carpet in front of me. "Come here, principessa."

Robyn follows the aisle of petals towards me. She runs her hand down the embroidered flower on her dress. She looks half wrecked already.

Excellent.

She stands in front of me. Her toes curl nervously into the thick carpet.

She can't look away from the crop, as I tap three times on the floor.

"Kneel," I command, coldly.

It's less elegant and more like her knees have buckled. But I've still never seen anything as beautiful as the way that Robyn falls to her knees in front of me.

Robyn's hair flows in tangled waves around her shoulders. She looks up at me with wide, dilated eyes.

She's spellbound.

The power is a fucking rush.

"Tell me your safe words." I arch my brow.

"Red for stop, yellow for slow down or I need a break, and green for *I consent to continue, more please, more.*"

I can't stop myself smiling. "Are you going to be my good girl?"

I stroke down Robyn's cheek.

She leans into my touch. "Yes, Sir. And I'm green."

I wind my fingers through Robyn's long hair, before wrenching back her neck.

She gasps.

I lean over Robyn, whispering into her ear, "Good because I'm going to have you stretched out and naked, writhing in ecstasy under my crop. I'll leave beautiful marks under its kiss. Do you want that?"

I need to check in with her one final time.

A sense of rightness — fulfillment — floods through me, when she nods.

Then she forces herself to be a good girl for me and verbally answer as well. "So fucking much."

Her chest is rising and falling rapidly. A pink blush spreads down her neck.

I don't miss Robyn's physical cues. She's falling into subspace.

She's fantasized about this for weeks.

I have a sense that she's actually touched herself to thoughts of it for years, ever since she discovered that photograph of me from the ball.

I straighten, towering over her.

My expression shutters. "Then beg for it."

Robyn looks unsure for a moment, before licking her lips. "Please punish me."

Instantly, I let go of her hair.

My expression softens. "No, cara mia, I won't. This isn't a punishment. This is a reward. It's for your pleasure because I love you. Do you understand?"

Because I love Robyn more than I thought it was possible to love anyone.

I'm obsessed.

Does she have any idea of the power that *she* has over *me*?

She always has.

Robyn reaches up to caress my thigh, and I hiss in a breath.

My cock tries to get impossibly harder in the confines of my tight breeches.

"I understand." Robyn looks at me with a tender expression. "You're an amazing man, Jude D'Angelo. May I please be kissed?"

This woman is smart.

Who could say no to a plea like that?

Not me.

I grab Robyn by the shoulders and pull her to her feet. Then I kiss her, hard and claiming.

She's mine, and I prove it with every sweep of my tongue and savage bite to her lips.

Then I rip at her dress. "Off."

Robyn tries to strip, but I'm animated with a dominant energy that needs an outlet and her dress is getting in the way between me and her gorgeous pale canvas of skin.

I drag her dress over her head, batting her hands out of the way.

Robyn stares at me with startled eyes.

I rip her panties off and throw them across the room.

When I trace my finger over Robyn's pussy, however, she's wet.

Her nipples are peaked.

I raise the crop between us in reverent ritual.

"Kiss it." My voice is low and rumbling.

Robyn lowers her head and kisses the crop.

She shivers, but it's not from the cold.

"Do you like this?" I ask. "Being stripped bare in front of me? Kissing the implement that's going to spank you, marking you as mine?"

"I love it." When Robyn's gaze meets mine, I'm shocked by the depth of emotion in her eyes. It shakes me. "Just like I love you, Jude."

That does it.

I can't hold back.

I growl, tossing the crop onto the bed. Then I slip my arms underneath Robyn, *my everything*, and pick her up into a bridal carry.

She yelps in shock.

Then I toss *her* onto the bed as well.

She lands amongst the petals and soft white cushions like a princess about to be ravished.

Robyn's limbs splay out like her hair.

She's how Disney princesses *should* be: curvy, red-haired, and independent.

Also, klutzy.

Endlessly kind.

A real woman.

And the only one who I'll ever want in my life.

"Lie on your stomach close to the edge of the bed," I order.

Robyn blinks at me.

"Did I stutter?" I ask, icily.

Robyn scrambles to turn over onto her front, clutching a cushion to her face.

I swagger around to the side of the bed.

I study the delicious curve of Robyn's back and the even more delicious curve of her ass.

The skin is pale and unmarked.

But not for long.

I pick up the riding crop again.

I bought it several years ago from an equestrian sports shop. I preferred that than buying from a BDSM site because it simply felt more genuine. I could also feel how it swung in my hand.

Plus, the scent of leather in equestrian shops is drugging. I'm fucking hard from the moment that I step inside, let alone run my fingers over the crops and dressage whips.

I'm sure that the assistants know that I'm not intending to use the implements on a horse. They shoot each other flustered and knowing looks.

And that's a thrill too.

I tighten my hold on the crop.

Yet I allow myself the indulgence of running my hand along Robyn's back and down over her gorgeous ass.

Her skin is soft.

She jumps and then settles, arching up into my touch. It will sensitize her skin and make her feel the spanking more.

It will also add to the *pleasurepain* of the experience.

I know that she's going to love both sides.

I straighten, before gently swinging the crop. It lands softly on her ass.

Robyn gasps, but I think it's more from surprise at the snapping sound than the light sting.

There's no mark.

"Okay?" I ask

"Green," Robyn replies. "More."

I start out light.

I need to test what she can take. She's moving up towards the crop, however, pushing her ass up like it's begging for more spanking.

Who am I to deny such a pretty ass?

I swing a little harder, urging Robyn's legs apart to smack her lower buttocks and thighs, which gets more of a reaction.

She moans, but still, doesn't pull away.

Her ass is now a rosy color like a blushing peach.

It's fucking gorgeous.

"What are you?" I demand.

"Yours," Robyn gasps.

I can't hold back my own moan. "Turn over."

I have to see her face.

Slowly, she turns over onto her back.

Robyn's cheeks are flushed. Her eyes are bright.

She looks energized, wildly turned on.

In turn, that makes me want to throw aside the crop and leap onto the bed, driving my cock into her drenched pussy.

Ravish her like she deserves…*desires*.

But this isn't about my pleasure.

Robyn needs me to follow through on her fantasy. And tonight, I'm going to give this to her.

"Good girl, being obedient for me. Don't move." When I rest the tip of the leather crop on her cheek, her breath stutters.

She holds herself still.

Perfect. I have her attention.

Teasingly slowly, I draw the crop from Robyn's cheek, over her throat, between her breasts, down her stomach, then leave it tauntingly close to her pussy.

"I'm nowhere near done with you yet." I smack the crop harder than I have before onto her thigh.

Robyn gasps.

Immediately, I lower my head.

My hair trails over Robyn's pussy, but I skirt it. Instead, I kiss over the mark that's left on her thigh, soothing it.

At the same time, I slip my fingers to her pussy. I sweep them up and down, as if I'm a tongue, licking.

Robyn's shaking, overwhelmed with the onslaught of different sensations.

She's close to coming. It won't take much to tip her over the edge.

"So wet for me, cara mia." I lick her thigh, imitating my fingers.

Robyn clutches at the bedding. "F-fuck, that's... I can't... It feels incredible. I'm going to..."

"You're soaking my fingers," I murmur against her crimson skin. Skin that I've marked as mine. "What has you so drenched? My tongue? My fingers? My crop?"

"All of them." Robyn wails. "Please, *please*..."

She's passed the point of knowing what she's begging for. But she's still capable of — almost — coherent speech.

I can't have that.

If she wants all of it, then she'll get it.

She did ask for it.

I straighten.

I don't take my hand away from her pussy, however, instead fucking her with one finger, then two.

I rub across her clit with my thumb.

Robyn whines, thrashing her head from side to side.

I glide the crop from her stomach up to her breasts. Slowly, I circle them.

She opens and shuts her mouth like she wants to talk but can't.

This is more like it.

When I tap the leather tip gently in time to my fingering across her left nipple, she writhes in ecstasy.

Commandingly, I rest one knee on the bed, leaning over her. "Look at me."

It takes a moment for Robyn to obey me, although she can't stop her body from twisting in pleasure still.

When I raise the crop above her nipple, her pupils become blown.

She knows what I'm about to do.

"You have my fingers and now I'm going to give you the crop." I hold her gaze. "Color?"

It's a buzz to see how hard she's struggling to answer.

I'm patient.

"Green," Robyn finally whispers.

The moment that she does, I snap the crop down gently onto her nipple.

"One," I whisper against her lips.

I force her to keep looking at me.

I'm with her in this experience.

We're together.

I hope, forever.

I finger her faster. She's become even wetter.

"Again." She's flushed with excitement.

I snap down the crop, and this time her cry sounds more like someone cresting on the edge of orgasm.

"Two," I murmur.

She's panting.

Her hips hump against my hand.

She's trembling. Falling apart.

I've never experienced anything better in life, than bringing someone to this intense level of sensation and then seeing them break…*only to fly.*

I lower my lips, so that they're hot against her ear.

Then I snap the crop down harder again. "Three, my wife."

My wife.

I don't know where the words come from.

They're darkly possessive.

But they're as right as being in this beach house with Robyn is.

As right as giving her the ring with my lucky twenty-two charm.

As right as spending my life together with Robyn.

Robyn screams.

But she's screaming because she's coming.

I drop the crop, resting my forehead against hers.

I close my eyes.

Robyn's coming apart beneath me, shaking and shuddering. I work her through it with my fingers, one orgasm and then a second immediately after.

It's the most intense orgasm that I've given her so far.

Then she raises her arms to grab onto me and pull me even closer.

"My husband," Robyn whispers.

I meet her fervent gaze.

"Wife," I repeat.

"Husband," she replies like an oath.

My heart both sings and shatters.

Because I wish that this wasn't only a fantasy.

CHAPTER THIRTEEN

Captain's Hall, Freedom

obyn

"Wife," I whisper to myself. I can't stop smiling. "Husband."

It was only a fantasy, while D'Angelo and I were caught in our dream in the beach house. It's never going to be possible because I love all my men equally but in different ways. I won't choose one of them to become my official husband, while keeping the others in the shadows.

A dirty secret.

No matter that this would get the press off our backs or that society would approve of us living in that way.

Yet last night, I realized that D'Angelo *is* my husband in my heart.

I don't need a piece of paper or a ceremony to make that true.

Does he know that it wasn't merely pretend to me?

Last night, after the most intense sex of my life, D'Angelo wrapped me in blankets and massaged each inch of my body. He fed me chocolate and orange juice, while murmuring praises and kissing me, softly.

His aftercare is like a drug.

Afterwards, he ran me a rose scented oil bath.

Then we both dressed.

I was disappointed, however, that D'Angelo chose his suit and not the riding outfit.

D'Angelo drove us both back in his classic Alfa Romeo through the silent, nighttime mountain roads to Captain's Hall.

I miss the beach house already.

Yet returning to Captain's Hall felt like coming home.

I missed Shay and Eden intensely, even though I was only away from them for a day.

Eden is already up and working. He's the most dedicated PA in America.

I glance behind me at his warm, snoring, and naked twin.

Shay is spooning me with his arm slung around me. He always sleeps as close to me as he can. His legs are tangled with mine, and his cheek is pressed to my shoulder.

If he's not pressed close to one of us, he can't sleep.

It's like Shay is terrified that something will happen to one of us, or that otherwise, he won't wake up here.

He waited up last night for D'Angelo and me, bounding to greet us at the door with eager questions about our day.

It was hours, before he'd sleep. It's no wonder that he's not awake now.

I turn my head back to D'Angelo, who's lying on the other side of me.

Sleeping in the middle of these men is my happy place.

I study the outline of D'Angelo's sharp cheekbones. His long lashes fan out, as thick as raven's feathers.

I can't help being jealous. The guy doesn't even need to get lash extensions to look that good.

I'm naked, but D'Angelo is dressed in black silk pajamas, which are unbuttoned, revealing his powerful chest. The pajamas look decadent next to his olive skin and the silver bedding.

The warm morning light streams through the open drapes.

It's rare for me to be able to watch D'Angelo sleep.

I don't mind if that sounds stalkerish because D'Angelo's already admitted that he watches *me* sleep.

He's almost always up and dressed in a smart suit, before I'm awake.

But yesterday must have worn him out.

I press a kiss to his cheek. "I love you, Jude."

I'm shocked how easy it'd felt yesterday to slip back into the familiar friendship that I'd enjoyed at college with D'Angelo.

For a short while, it'd been like the shit with Wilder didn't happen.

Except, it did.

I can't go back. In some ways, I don't want to.

I'm a different person now. So is D'Angelo.

I'm a better person. At least, I'm trying to be.

I didn't understand D'Angelo back then but I'm starting to now.

Behind me, Shay stirs.

He snuffles at my neck, tightening his hold around my waist.

"Morning, love," Shay says, sleepily.

I love when he's half-awake like this. It's the only time, when he's not vibrating with an uncontrollable energy that feels like it's close to tearing him apart.

Well, the only time apart from immediately after sex.

I wriggle around in Shay's hold to face him. Then I card my fingers through his golden, mussed hair, trying to tame it.

Unsuccessfully.

"Morning." I kiss Shay, lightly. "We've slept in late, even D'Angelo. It's your day with him. Are you looking forward to it?"

"After some of the things you two got up to...?" He grins. "Too fucking right. Plus, Jude said that this is *his* date. So, I don't know what he's planned."

"You'll be in for a treat. And I didn't tell you *everything*."

Shay's eyes light up. "Spill."

I slip my hand to his ass, and he bites his lip.

I slide my fingers up and down his crease. "We made wicked plans to turn you into our fox."

"I am your pet, love." Shay pats his head. "I'd look cute with ears."

In turn, I pat his ass. "And a tail."

"Kinky."

When Shay glances over my shoulder at D'Angelo, his expression softens with affection. "Do you remember that I said I'd happily wake up to using my mouth on D'Angelo or you each morning?"

I flush at the memory. "How could I forget?"

"Don't you think that I should start this date right?"

I nod.

Shay presses a quick kiss to my lips. "Watch me...?"

I nod again.

Shay's putting on a performance for me, as much as for D'Angelo.

I lie on my side, ready to enjoy what happens next.

Eagerly, Shay scrambles over me, before straddling the still sleeping D'Angelo.

He doesn't touch him.

Instead, he stares down at D'Angelo in awe.

Shay looks at D'Angelo like he's truly a fallen god who he's lucky enough to be allowed to worship.

Shay's adoration for both D'Angelo and me is overwhelming.

It's intense and precious.

It's also dangerous because Shay's laying his heart on our altars to be sacrificed.

He holds nothing back.

And we could hurt him more than anyone else ever could.

D'Angelo's eyes flutter open. His nose scrunches up in a way that I'd never dare tell him is adorable.

"Darlin'," Shay murmurs, leaning forward and resting his hands either side of D'Angelo's head on the pillow.

D'Angelo is sleepy enough for Shay to have the rare upperhand.

Shay is enjoying making the most of it.

D'Angelo licks over his dry lips. "Hmm, what a nice view."

"May I wake you up with a kiss?" Shay asks.

"That sounds like the perfect start to our day together."

Shay gently lowers his mouth to D'Angelo's.

The kiss is slow and tender.

D'Angelo raises his hand to Shay's lower back, but only rests it there, caressing circles.

When Shay pulls back, however, his eyes dance with mischief. "I have a better way to kiss you awake. Do you want my mouth…?"

He significantly glances down D'Angelo's body at the same time as rubbing his hard cock against D'Angelo's through his silk pajamas.

D'Angelo hisses. "I always want your pretty mouth."

Shay looks delighted, before sliding down D'Angelo's body. Then he grabs D'Angelo's pajama pants and yanks at them.

D'Angelo rolls his eyes at Shay's enthusiasm but raises his hips to allow himself to be stripped.

"Thanks, darlin'." Shay pulls the pants fully off and flings them down the bed.

"You could have folded them," D'Angelo scolds.

I snort with laughter.

D'Angelo quirks his brow at me. He sprawls back, cushioning his head on his arms.

He looks like an arrogant king, waiting to be *worshiped* in an intimate way.

And that's fucking hot.

"No time. I have more important things to do." Shay illustrates this by stroking his hand up and down D'Angelo's hard cock.

D'Angelo clears his throat. "Go ahead."

"Gracious of you, Sir." Shay's amused gaze meets mine, as he settles between D'Angelo's thighs, resting one hand on his hip.

I smile at Shay, encouragingly.

Blow jobs are still new to Shay. But he's growing in confidence.

It's good to see him offering like this and exploring what he enjoys.

Shay fondles D'Angelo's balls.

My lips quirk to see D'Angelo battling not to look affected.

His cool mask cracks, however, when Shay lowers his head and licks D'Angelo's cock from the base to the head.

Then he swirls his tongue around the sensitive tip.

"Fuck, that's good." D'Angelo's jaw clenches. "Do that again."

Shay glows at the praise. "Whatever feels good. This mouth, tongue, and lips, belong to you."

D'Angelo's mask breaks entirely at those words.

He growls, flushing with desire.

Shay swirls his tongue around the head of D'Angelo's cock again.

Then he wraps his hand around the base, before he lowers his mouth onto D'Angelo's shaft and sucks.

D'Angelo's heated gaze watches the way that his large cock spears in and out of Shay's stretched lips.

D'Angelo balls his hands like he's struggling not to lower them into Shay's hair and force him further onto his cock.

Instead, he allows Shay to control the pace.

This is Shay's offering.

I'm happy that D'Angelo is allowing him this.

Shay looks up at D'Angelo from underneath his eyelashes as he sucks harder.

D'Angelo's hips begin to hump, thrusting like he's being driven wild enough that he can no longer play the aloof king.

Shay gags but he doesn't pull back.

Determined, he works harder, despite the tears gleaming in his eyes.

My core throbs.

I lazily slip my hand to my clit, teasing it.

"I'm close," D'Angelo warns.

Shay doesn't back off.

Instead, his brow furrows like it's a challenge.

He takes D'Angelo's cock even deeper. He caresses D'Angelo's tight balls.

D'Angelo moans, and as he comes, he finally lowers his hands and buries them in Shay's hair, holding him in place.

Finally, he releases Shay, who pulls back with a dreamy grin.

Shay licks his lips, swallowing.

His voice is raspy. "We should definitely work that into our morning routine."

"Agreed." I reluctantly pull my hand away from my clit.

I want to snuggle closer to D'Angelo instead.

D'Angelo equally relinquishes his hold on Shay's hair to throw his arm around me.

The BJ was worth it because D'Angelo isn't his normal grumpy morning self. He's relaxed and smiling.

Interesting.

All he needs to be reformed from his grumpy ways is blow job therapy.

It could be a new craze.

"You mean, ambushing your captain?" D'Angelo arches his brow.

Perhaps, not *entirely* redeemed from his grumpy ways.

Shay freezes. "Ehm…"

D'Angelo smiles. "Get up here, good boy."

Shay relaxes and squirms up to lie on top of D'Angelo's chest, as if he's trying to get as close to both him and me as he can at the same time.

Neither of us are complaining.

"I could not have planned a better start to our date," D'Angelo says, and Shay brightens. "I have, however, planned a perfect day for us."

"What?" Shay asks.

"It's a secret."

Shay pouts. "Unfair."

"Whatever it is, it'll be fun." I lean across D'Angelo to poke Shay. "Although, I bet that it won't beat our skinny dipping."

"You went skinny dipping?" Shay's eyes widen. "Please tell me that there are photos."

I laugh.

Shay looks down. "I'd love to… I mean, not now but in the future… Do you think…? Will you ever invite me to your beach house? Just to see it?"

Shay looks hopeful but like the chance is such a far away dream that it hurts me soul.

D'Angelo appears as pained as I am.

He'd better say yes.

"Cucciolo," D'Angelo replies, gently, "after this road trip, I'm going to take all of you for a vacation there. We'll have earned it."

"Yes!" Shay's excitement is infectious. "I've always wanted a holiday."

I freeze.

My stomach churns.

"You've been on vacation before, right?" I ask, tentatively.

Shay shakes his head but he seems unconcerned like he can't see the problem. "We didn't have the money for stuff like that. Any money that we did have went on paying for ice hockey and college. Mom and Dad definitely didn't have any cash to spare, when we were young. They took us to the funfair once though. I loved the candy floss, but you should have seen Eden's face when he tried mine. He looked like a cat who'd sucked a lemon."

Shay's laughter is unrestrained.

He can find joy in a single day spent at a carnival throughout his entire life.

He doesn't complain at what he's missed out on.

"I'm going to take Eden and you to the beach, on vacations, and out of season yachting around the fucking globe," D'Angelo says with an earnestness that isn't like him. "You're going to be spoiled. You won't know how to cope."

Shay's eyes widen. "You don't need to. I'm fine without any of that stuff."

"I know you are." D'Angelo strokes down Shay's cheek. "But I'm not okay. So, let me treat you, for my sake."

"For you." Shay's eyes glimmer with tears. "I wouldn't want you to suffer."

"And I'll take you to a traveling carnival," I promise, pushing Shay's hair away from his face. "One comes to Freedom each year. You can eat candy floss until you're sick. I'll buy Eden a caramel apple. Hopefully, he'll like that better."

"Deal." Shay grabs my hand to shake it. "As long as you promise to go on the rides with me, the big, scary ones."

"Hey, who said anything about that? Then I'll be the one who's sick."

"Seems fair." D'Angelo smirks.

Shay hesitates, before he sits up.

My brow furrows.

Is something wrong?

Shay flings himself to the edge of the bed, before pulling something out of the top drawer and hugging it to his chest.

I see a flash of arctic blue.

Wait, is that my Guide?

"Did you hide something in *my* bedroom?" D'Angelo demands. "I tend to know where everything is in here. I would suggest that you find better hiding places."

"It worked, didn't it?" Shay scoots closer to us both again, sitting crossed legged. "I put this in there, when you were out yesterday. I wanted to surprise you both with it this morning. I thought that it'd be a brilliant start to the day." His gaze darts to D'Angelo. "I know that you want to be mysterious and shit about our date's details. But I still wanted to offer you something more than my mouth."

Unexpectedly, he looks shy as he drops the Guide on the bed. He's still clutching his iPod.

"More kinky ideas?" D'Angelo asks.

"I know that I have my kinky stuff in here but I also wanted something that had deeper meaning to me." Shay blushes. "It's a playlist of my favorite ten songs. Ones that have meant something special in my life. I'm flaying myself raw here. Nothing is more personal to me than these songs. I've always wanted to care about someone enough to make them a playlist."

"Shay," I whisper, touched. "And you say that you don't do romance."

Shay studies me, as if to be certain that I'm not taking the piss.

Then his expression lightens. "I do my best, love."

D'Angelo sits up with his back against the headboard, dragging me to rest against his chest. "And I've always wanted someone who cared enough about me to *make* me a playlist.

"Then it looks like we're the perfect fit," Shay replies.

"It looks that way."

Shay flips open the Guide, past D'Angelo's written section under my scrawled:

A GUIDE TO LOVING HOCKEY PLAYERS

"Perhaps, we can all listen to the songs," Shay says. "Plus, we could each add our favorites into the Guide. Ones that make us feel alive. Then add them to Spotify."

"I love that idea," I breathe.

Shay passes over the Guide, and D'Angelo and I hold it between us to read:

Shay's Ten Favorite Songs Playlist

The Strokes — "You Only Live Once"
White Stripes — "Fell in Love With a Girl."
Arctic Monkeys — "R U Mine?"
Kasabian — "Days Are Forgotten"
FOALS — "Mountain at My Gates"
Blur — "Song 2"
The Lumineers — "Ophelia"
Yeah, Yeah, Yeahs — "Maps"
The Smiths — "Heaven Knows I'm Miserable Now"
Pulp — "Common People"

. . .

THE PLAYLIST IS UNIQUELY SHAY. I can't wait to listen to it.

I also can't wait to find out why the songs are important to him.

"Not a Justin Bieber song in sight." I shake my head in mock sadness. "I guess that I'll have to settle for badass indie rock bands instead."

Shay laughs. "They're ones that have this…vibe. They speak to your heart, bones, and balls, you know?"

"Yeah, apart from the balls."

Shay passes the iPod to me, but his gaze flicks to D'Angelo as well. "I uploaded the playlist onto here."

"It means a lot that you're sharing this with me." D'Angelo grips tightly to the sides of the Guide.

Shay's shoulders relax with relief.

Thrilled, I unwind the earbuds, slipping one in and then pushing D'Angelo's curls aside to slip the other into his ear.

When I press the iPod on, The Strokes start playing in a burst of upbeat guitars and drums with raspy vocals.

Instantly, I'm wearing the same sunny smile as Shay.

I can see why this is Shay's favorite song.

"I used to listen to this on loop at college, when I was having a tough time. Drove Dee mad." Shay edges even closer, resting his hand on D'Angelo's knee. "Music gigs were my best nights out."

"Who did you see?" I ask.

"Nobody that you'd know. I couldn't afford to see anyone famous, just local bands. There was this small pub in Guildford, which was like a cellar. It hosted up and coming bands. It had a tiny stage. But it was fantastic because that meant you were up close and intimate. When I could manage it, I'd take a break from my work on Friday nights to watch these aspiring bands play. I didn't know anyone there, but it didn't matter because we were united, drinking and dancing up and down to the glorious music. It was a bloody escape from our lives. Fuck, I wished that I could play guitar like them. It would have been incredible to have been up on that stage, singing and rocking out."

He looks painfully wistful.

"I'm teaching you piano." D'Angelo rests his hand on the back of Shay's neck. "And you *can* sing."

Shay has an amazing voice.

He clearly doesn't believe that by the way that he shrugs.

"Don't you think that it would be brilliant though to have all those people watching you, admiring, and loving you?"

"They do," I point out. "Every time that you play a game for the Bay Rebels, thousands of people in the rink are looking at you like that. Plus, millions at home. You're the literal star of the team."

Shay appears sheepish, as if he's never thought of it that way.

And that's why I fucking love him so much.

Shay ducks his head. "It's going to take a while to sink in. Only a couple of months ago, I was the bloke watching the bands on stage and seeing a glimpse of a world that I could never touch. I haven't yet become used to the fact that *I'm* now the bloke on the ice stage."

"Well, get used to it," D'Angelo growls. "Because you're as talented as those guitarists. You're a fucking prodigy on the ice. I don't know why your college coach was too much of a dumbass to see it, or why Colton gets his kicks by putting you down. But I'll say it, if no one else will. You're one of the best in the NHL right now. But here's what's important: nobody needs to be the best at everything. Being skilled at one thing in life is enough to set you amongst the stars. And you shine, Shay."

Shay looks flustered, unable to know what to say to so much praise.

I rescue him by promising. "After this road trip, I'll go to a gig with you. We can find somewhere small like that place in England."

Shay smiles. "I'd like that, love."

"And talking of the road trip," I sigh, pulling the iPod out of my ear and swinging myself to the edge of the bed, "I need to get dressed and then start packing for it."

"You mean grabbing things that are currently stuffed without being ironed at the back of your closet and then throwing them into your suitcase." D'Angelo crosses his ankles. "Oh, along with a ton of books, shoes, and sex toys."

Asshole...who happens to be right.

"I feel called out." I sniff.

"What's the plan tomorrow?" Shay settles next to D'Angelo against the headboard.

"I'm driving us there," D'Angelo replies. "If we drive all day with minimal stops, it should take three days."

"What are we driving?" Shay asks. "Please tell me that it's something cool like—"

"I've sorted it out. You'll find out tomorrow."

I wrinkle my nose. "Why am I worried now?"

"You shouldn't be. Eden's arranged it for me." D'Angelo glows with pride. "He's been on top of hiring what we need, the timings, and our itineraries. I imagine that he's already working on the last minute details now. He's even packing for me."

Shay gasps. "His arm is in a sling."

"That man can do more with one arm than I can do with two."

I flush.

Isn't that the truth?

By D'Angelo's knowing look, he can tell what I'm thinking.

Damn.

I swing my legs. "So, I could get Eden to pack for me?"

D'Angelo looks smug. "Definitely not. He's not *your* PA."

Touche.

I wonder what Eden has hired for us to drive? What are the plans for the long journey?

I could simply work on Eden to tell me...

I try to hide my scheming face, but this time, D'Angelo catches it.

D'Angelo wags his finger at me. "And no pleading, puppy dog eyes, or tricking of my PA to tell you the details. You'll find out everything en route. If coach insists that we're *handled* twenty-four seven like our house arrest goes on tour, then we may as well enjoy it. So, *enjoy* the surprise."

I pretend to laugh, holding my sides. But there's no going against the wagging finger combined with dom face.

They're deadly.

Suddenly, D'Angelo's phone vibrates on the nightstand.

Shit, not Dad again.

D'Angelo sighs, pulling out the earbud with an apologetic glance at Shay. He leans over him to pick up the phone.

Then D'Angelo frowns. "I don't recognize the number."

D'Angelo's sudden tension unsettles me. "Who could be phoning you?"

"I don't know." D'Angelo's expression is tight. "For security purposes after everything that's happened since the start of pre-season, only a couple of people know this number. The security team have made certain of that. This shouldn't be possible."

Anxiety spikes through me.

"Don't answer it," I urge. D'Angelo's finger hovers over the phone. "Please."

Finally, he nods.

"We'll need to tell security." I wrap my arms around my middle.

All of a sudden, the phone vibrates.

I jump.

"It's a text." D'Angelo's expression is grim.

"What does it say?" Shay peers over D'Angelo's shoulder.

"It says," D'Angelo voice is low, "*truth or dare.*"

CHAPTER FOURTEEN

Garden of Eden Restaurant, Freedom

'Angelo

"D<small>ID</small> you just steal a spoonful of my tiramisu?" I stare at Shay in shock.

Shay leans back to his side of the table, shamelessly licking the last of *my* dessert off the spoon.

Thief.

I stare at him over the tiny table in the booth at the back of the luxurious Italian restaurant, the Garden of Eden.

The restaurant's walls and roof are draped in velvet

crimson and golds. A chandelier that looks like a tree, dripping crystal leaves, hangs above us.

On the far wall is a cocktail bar.

The wall is bright with bottles of spirits, gleaming with a gold counter and stools.

The restaurant is empty, however, apart from the waiters who are bustling around at a distance, occasionally checking on us or adding more wine to our table.

The owner is the co-founder of my business with me. It's why I know that he'll be discrete. I've been discrete when he needs often enough.

It's his new venture, and I also want it to succeed.

I'm loyal to my close friends.

I bought the restaurant out for tonight. This second date with Shay is important to me.

I promised Shay that I'd wine and dine him.

I don't remember promising to share my dessert.

"Hmm," Shay sighs. "It tastes of coffee and chocolate. Yummy."

I tap the handle of my fork against the thick tablecloth three times. "Are you my royal food taster?"

Shay sprawls further on the crimson leather. "I'm not poisoned, Your Majesty. It's safe for you to continue."

"You're too kind," I deadpan.

Shay is wearing a punky, scarlet silk shirt and tight, black pants.

He looks more edible than anything that's been on the menu tonight.

I subtly adjust myself.

Shay can make me hard with a single smile.

It's becoming a Pavlovian response at this point.

I'm dressed in a black tuxedo, which made Shay trip down the final step of the stairs at Captain's Hall, when he caught sight of me.

I plan to train Shay, as much as I'm being trained to seek his happiness.

Shay looks sadly at his glass plate, which has been scraped clean. "I've already eaten all of *my* pudding. It was bloody delicious. I'll say this, I'm a convert to Italian food now. This restaurant is fantastic. The spaghetti dish was a hundred…thousand…times better than the spaghetti meals that Eden and I would cook back in dorms because it was cheap. Don't tell Eden that. And this…"

"Chocolate panna cotta," I supply, as proudly as if I'd cooked the meals tonight myself.

"It's like hot cocoa turned into custard." Shay glances wistfully at his plate again. "I could have eaten three of them."

"So, that's why you've moved onto mine." I slice my fork into my tiramisu and savor a bite.

It's creamy with tangy mascarpone.

Shay bites his lip. "Fuck, this is food porn. Take another bite. More slowly this time…"

I almost spit out my mouthful in shock.

I glare at Shay but then I catch his dancing gaze.

"You're playing with fire, cucciolo." I pick up my wine instead, watching Shay over the rim.

"Don't I always? Anyway, isn't this what people do on these types of dates?" Shay sounds more unsure. I don't like it. I want the playful version of him back. "I've never been taken somewhere like this before. This is new to me. But I'm trying and... This is romantic, right?"

I struggle to keep a straight face, edging my arm protectively around my plate. "It's theft."

"Possessive."

"Always."

When we first arrived at the grand restaurant, Shay looked around himself in awe.

Shay tried to hide his nerves. But he didn't manage it.

I casually slipped my arm around his shoulders, as if I didn't notice his anxiety. I led him to our booth, but he still managed to almost knock over the crystal table lamp as we sat down.

I caught the lamp just in time.

When we opened the menus, Shay's brow furrowed. "There are no prices. Should we tell them that they printed these menus wrong? I don't want to embarrass anyone."

My heart clenched.

Places like this don't include prices.

If you can afford to eat here, then you don't need them.

If they allow you to *book*, then you don't check prices.

I refused to ruin this date by making Shay feel small or like he didn't belong here for not knowing that fact.

I remembered what it was like to be made to feel like trash by Wilder and the rest of the hockey team throughout college.

Shay faces challenges with a positivity that floors me.

I face them like a grumpy asshole.

"I'll tell them later," I promised. "Well spotted."

Shay shielded us with his large, leather menu, before he whispered. "Can I afford this...? I mean, not having the prices on here isn't some kind of trick, right? I wondered why it's so dead in here."

I leaned across the table and placed my hand over his. "It's usually full. People need to book months in advance and can hardly get a table. Well, unless you know the owner personally. And I do. He gave me this table as a favor. I hired the whole place."

Shay choked, then became ashen.

"I'm sorry, I should have said something the moment that we came in here and I saw the chandelier and stuff," Shay whispered urgently, looking sick. "I promised Eden that I'd send most of my salary this month back to our parents. I can't break that. I don't think that I can stretch to hiring half a restaurant. Did we pay a deposit or...?"

I gave a soft smile. "*We* didn't do anything. I am rather wealthy, as I keep reminding you. And I want to spend it on the people who I love, including my boyfriend. This is our second date. You paid for the first one. So, this is my treat."

Shay's eyes widened. "The first one was a homemade curry that burned your mouth and a horror movie that gave you nightmares."

"And that's why I got to choose what we did on this date."

Shay dropped the menu, laughing brightly.

He leaned across the table and kissed me. "You're the best, darlin'."

Now, I pat the side of the booth next to me. "Come here, cucciolo."

Shay narrowed his eyes. "If you're going to spank me for stealing your food, then you'll probably give him..." He nodded at a gray haired waiter with striking amber eyes, who was hovering closest to us, "a coronary."

I couldn't hold back my laugh. "I know him. And he'd enjoy the free show." Shay blushed. "Now, are you going to obey? I'll feed you."

Shay's beautiful eyes light up. "You don't need to tell me twice. Wait, you did, didn't you?"

He scoots around the booth, until he's sitting so close to me that his warm thigh is touching mine.

My cock hardens.

My Shay should always be within touching distance.

It's the only way that I know he's not doing something reckless or impulsive like climbing onto the roof, driving off a beachside road on his motorcycle, or pushing himself in practice to the point of collapse.

Shay opens his mouth like a baby bird, glancing significantly down at my plate.

Fuck, he's like sin.

He's sitting there in public like an invitation to have my cock shoved into his pretty mouth.

Does he know what he's doing?

I struggle against the urge to push Shay to his knees underneath the restaurant table and have him suck me.

I'll finish my dessert myself, while feeding Shay a different type of cream.

It'd serve him right...or reward him.

Possibly, both.

I battle against the temptation.

I settle one hand on Shay's thigh, squeezing, while I lift the full fork to his mouth.

Shay's eyelashes flutter. He moans indecently as he eats.

It's a crime to share your tiramisu.

This must be love.

Yet the noises that Shay is now making mean that the sacrifice is worth it.

I watch the way that he leans back, revealing his long pale throat. I can't wait to kiss and bite it.

I've spent our day together trying to ensure that Shay believes that he deserves dates in the same way that Robyn does.

Shay is struggling to understand that our relationship is real.

Why doesn't he think that he deserves that?

Because he was used by Blythe in college and taught that subs can't be loved? *Are only toys?*

Because he was neglected and literally sold by his biological parents?

I am going to find a way to prove to him that Robyn and I want him for something as meaningful as we have with each other.

Today, Shay and I went on a run together, before Shay had fun teaching me about soccer.

He's a true soccer fan and (unsurprisingly), talented.

He's fast with the ball, can score goals insanely well, and can do mind-blowing trick shots.

He could have tried out for a soccer team, if he didn't play hockey.

Then after lunch, I gave Shay another piano lesson.

My most repeated phrases — *sit still, concentrate, maintain posture* — were needed about half as much as the time before.

So, an improvement.

Shay is working hard. He's serious about learning. It's all I can ask for.

He gives a hundred percent in everything that he sets his mind to. I've never met anyone as dedicated as him, apart from his twin.

I set down the fork and take a drink of my fruity, white wine. "Mom would make tiramisu for us each Sunday. The smell reminds me…"

I set down my glass, adjusting its placement three times.

It's bittersweet.

The aroma contains some of my happiest memories, even if they're lost forever to me.

Did the mom who cooked my favorite meals and worried about me not eating enough, read a story to me each night, wrapped me in scarves and gloves because she obsessed about me being warm enough, truly exist?

The mom who loved me?

Except, it wasn't unconditional.

Perhaps, she existed.

It was *me*, the son who she imagined inside her head, who didn't.

She was the one who built up a son who wasn't real.

She didn't want the real me, only her fantasy of a dream son.

As soon as I no longer fitted into the mold that she'd created the moment I was born, she threw me away.

Erased me.

"Where did you go, darlin'?" Shay says, gently.

I blink. "Nowhere good. I'd rather be here with you."

Shay slips his hand into mine, which is resting on his thigh, firmly.

"You are here, and I've got you." He tightens his hand around mine. "Sundays in my house in Guildford were the only day that my entire family were together and not working. So, they always smelled of this bloody huge English roast dinner for lunch that Mum and Eden would cook together. Mom never had much to spend but she still managed to produce a chicken with gravy and stuffing, these fucking incredible fluffy roast potatoes, and broccoli, carrots, and parsnips. Dad would work overtime to make sure that we could always afford it. Mum was great at making the leftovers stretch in dishes throughout the week. Sunday was my favorite day of the week because I'd have practice at the rink early in the morning, then lunch with my whole family. That smell means being together with them."

"You miss them."

I'm going to find a way to fly the twins' parents out this season.

They shouldn't miss their sons' first season in the NHL.

Eden and Shay's adoptive parents have worked hard to support them since they were kids.

They deserve to see Shay play.

And Shay deserves to have his only family from England watch him.

Shay looks down. "Eden and I knew that leaving them behind was part of moving into the NHL. My parents urged us to follow our dreams. They didn't need to take us into their house. They didn't need to give up any hope of having enough money to live comfortably in order to support us. And they bloody didn't need to then encourage us to move across the Atlantic and away from them. But they did all of that because they're good people and it's what was best for us. If it wasn't for them, then I'd never have learned what loving someone actually means."

My chest is tight.

I learned the opposite from my parents.

What loving someone fucking *doesn't* mean.

I reach to grip Shay's chin, turning his face up to me. "They are good people. I'll be forever grateful that Eden and you had them in your life. I'm also going to make sure that I continue to show you what true love is."

"Now, that's romantic."

"It is." I rub my thumb across Shay's jaw in circles, and his breath hitches. "On the road trip, don't forget to phone your mom and dad. They may not be here, but with all our technology, there's no reason that you can't message them as often as you like."

"Are the phones secure though?" Shay looks worried. "What was that *truth or dare* stuff?"

I draw back from Shay, running my hand through my curls.

What fucking asshole sent that message? Who's trying to mindfuck me now?

My lips thin. "Security are providing us with new phones. They don't know who sent that bullshit. That number is untraceable. Garcia is working on it but he doesn't know how long it will take."

Dread curdles my guts.

I fiddle with my cufflinks compulsively.

Is it Wilder again? One of the journalists who are connected to Melanie Hest? Someone from my own troubled past?

"Have you played truth or dare?" Shay asks.

I relax. "The kinky version."

Shay's eyes become half-hooded. "Of course you have, darlin'. Tell me more."

I lean closer, sliding my hand up Shay's thigh, just shy of where I know that he's aching to be touched.

Shay's breathing speeds up.

"It was the type of game that included dares like stripping naked and acting like a puppy, being spanked over the back of the couch, or crawling around in a collar and leash for the rest of the night," I murmur into Shay's ear, careful to watch his reaction to each dare.

Shay's pupils become more dilated on every word. By the time that I stop talking, he's staring into my eyes, wild and fucking turned on.

Nailed it.

Those three ideas are going in the Guide.

Shay swallows. "Where do I sign up to this game?"

When I palm over Shay's crotch, he only holds back the groan by biting his lip, hard. "You don't. Did you forget that I'm possessive? You're Robyn and my pet, remember? When we have you in a collar and leash, as our spanked puppy, that's just for us."

"Do you mean that?" Shay's gaze is intense.

My heart breaks.

"I really *am* going to tattoo my name on your cock," when I grip Shay's dick through the tight material of his pants, his eyes widen, "if you don't accept how much you're loved and wanted."

"I accept it," Shay replies, quickly.

I stroke over Shay's cock, before releasing it. "Now that's settled, what's been your favorite part of today?"

I want to learn about him.

I lean back in the booth, letting go of his hand. I grab my wine and take another drink.

Sometimes, Shay seems like an open book. But I'm learning that's not always true.

Shay casts me a shy glance. "The comedy movie that we watched together on the couch after the piano lesson. You were just so relaxed. I enjoyed watching you laugh. I mean, you're often like that around Robyn. But you're rarely like that with me."

I startle.

Shit, is he right?

Shay does tend to bring out the cold and commanding side in me. It's the way that he leaves trash out, eats jam from the jar, and is getting his kicks from pranking me.

We're best friends. But guys often want to kick the asses of their best friends, right?

It's our vibe.

Shay's a brat, and I'm a brat tamer.

Perhaps, sometimes he likes to see my softer side.

"Since you love comedy," Shay continues, blithely, "we should watch my favorite one on the next date."

"You're not tricking me again." I wag my finger at him. "You say comedy but what you really mean is…?"

"*Shaun of the Dead*. An English horror comedy with flesh-eating zombies and a pub. What could be better?"

He doesn't mean that ironically, does he?

I narrow my eyes. "A *horror* film, of course. You worry me sometimes."

"Thanks, mate." Shay looks pleased. "I loved the film that you chose. I've never seen it. The rodent thingy was cute."

Is he kidding?

I stare at him. "You've never seen *Groundhog Day*?"

"As a small kid, I never saw any television. Then my adoptive parents weren't big on it. Guess I missed it. I loved the idea in the movie of being caught in a time loop, living the same day over and over again. To me, *that's* a horror movie. I mean, fine if it's a bloody brilliant day like today. But what if it's…?"

Shay's expression darkens.

I deliberately clink my glass three times, and it snaps Shay back to the present with me and not to whatever day he's imagining.

It's not anywhere good.

"I grew up on that movie," I explain. "It played every year. You know that scene where Bill Murray gets to become a virtuoso on the piano? It made me practice even harder at my lessons. Later, when I was at the discipline school, I held onto the idea that you could make a mistake, fuck up, but instead of your whole life being wrecked forever, you could wake up and try again. Everything would be reset, back to normal. Sometimes, I'd open my eyes, as I lay on the hard mattress and wish so fucking hard that I'd be back in my bedroom at home. Wish that it'd be that school morning, before I chose to bring my friend home from the football team. But this time, I wouldn't kiss him."

"I'm glad that your life wasn't reset." Shay's eyes glitter in the dark of the restaurant. "Because what happened wasn't a mistake. It was who you were, right? Your parents and brother were the ones who fucked up, not you. You shouldn't have felt that you needed to change for them. I like who you are now. I wouldn't want to lose that."

Joy surges through me. My hand tightens on my wine glass.

Warmth fills me in a way that makes tears prickle at my eyes.

I blink them away.

I swallow. "*Like* me, huh?"

Shay edges even closer to me, taking the wine glass from me and placing it down.

Then he rests his head on my shoulder, peering up at me through his lashes. "I fucking *love* you, darlin'."

His words shoot through me.

They're electric.

Yet I remain frozen, allowing the feel of Shay, warm and secure against my side, to bleed into me.

He makes himself more comfortable, wrapping his arm around my waist.

This feels right.

It's the perfect end to the perfect date.

Only, it's not over yet.

My lips quirk. "Comfortable?"

Shay squirms around again. "Getting there."

I grab him by his golden tumble of hair and yank his head up to force him to look at me. "I'm so pleased. But don't get too comfortable because this date isn't winding down just yet.

"Fantastic. I could die for an espresso about now."

I chuckle. "I can order you one without it costing your life. But I also have a secret."

"A good one?" Shay asks, eagerly.

"Very." I lean to capture his lips in a tender kiss.

He kisses back more passionately, tightening his hold around my waist. Our tongues twine.

He tastes deliciously sweet, of coffee and chocolate. I can taste my own dessert on his lips.

Reluctantly, I draw back.

"What's the secret?" Shay gazes at me like I'm a god.

My breath stutters.

I'm never going to get tired of Shay looking at me like I hang the fucking moon.

"This restaurant is also a boutique hotel with a small

number of rooms above it. I've hired them all as well. So, we're staying here tonight." My smile becomes devilish. "Robyn cleared it as a reward for our hard work on the rink. Security are outside. We have one night entirely to ourselves. I can keep the promise to tie you to the bed. There's nobody to hear you. So, cucciolo, you can scream as loudly as you like. All. Night. Long."

CHAPTER FIFTEEN

Garden of Eden Hotel, Freedom

'Angelo

I CARRY Shay over my shoulder down the long corridor like a caveman hauling his bride back to his cave.

The soft crimson carpet silences my footfalls.

Shay doesn't appear to mind being manhandled, even if he did mutter *brute*, when I dragged him up from his seat and slung him over my shoulder.

He secretly loves my brutish side.

Plus, the waiters deserved some kind of show along with their thirty percent tip.

I slide my hand over Shay's tight ass. "Have you been

stretching your tight hole each morning like I taught you to? Are you prepared for me?"

I smirk, imagining that Shay is blushing.

I wish that I could see his face but I settle for patting his ass.

"You can't just say things like that." Shay gasps.

"Can't I?"

I can.

I intend to say worse.

"What if someone hears?" Shay whispers.

"Who? Mr. Invisible the Voyeur? We're alone here. I hired every room, remember? I chose the one that I thought you'd like best."

"Now I really want to see it, darlin'. Are we nearly there, or are you carrying me in circles because you like…"

"Dominating you?" I arch my brow. "Of course I do, as much as *you* like me dominating you."

"I can't argue with that."

"And I'm going to show you how much I love it tonight. In fact, I intend to also show you just how fucking obsessed I am with you. You're not only my teammate, friend, and sub, cucciolo. You're the man who I've been searching for my entire life. I'm going to tie you to my bed and never let you go."

I force myself not to stop walking, even though my heart is beating faster.

Was that too much? Too possessive?

It's the truth.

Shay makes my heart flutter in a way that no one has,

apart from Robyn. He fits between Robyn and me like he was always meant to be there.

Robyn feels it too. Shay meets a need in both of us.

It would destroy us, if we lost him.

"You don't need to tie me down to keep me." Shay strokes my back. "I'm just as fucking obsessed."

I let out a relieved breath. "Then we'll use the ropes in the bedroom merely for fun."

I expect Shay to laugh.

Instead, he sounds startlingly earnest and vulnerable; it's unlike his normal playful self, which is why I listen carefully. "Sometimes, I'm scared by how much I need Robyn and you. More than I need to breathe. You're my captain. My boyfriend. *My sex god.* Jude, I've been following the Post-it notes that you've left out for me each morning and night about how to clean myself out, stretch my arse, and whether or not I can fucking touch myself. If anyone else did that…or had ever tried it…I'd punch them in the dick. I'm not going anywhere."

I struggle to speak for a moment, before I clear my throat. "Who said that I would let you anyway?"

"My beast," Shay says, sounding happy again.

My shoulders relax at the bubbling laughter in his tone.

Reaching the sleek door at the end of the corridor, I slip the keycard out of my pocket and use it to open the door. "We're here."

I hope that Shay loves his room as much as I do.

I want this night to be special for Shay.

It's the first that we've spent away together. I get the

feeling that a partner may never have taken Shay away before.

He'll have to get used to being spoiled like this.

The room's light springs on automatically from a chandelier that drips with crystal feathers above us.

I swagger to the four-poster bed in the center of the room.

The silk bedding is crimson velvet with piles of plush cushions. Shimmering gold drapes sway around the bed, matching the ones at the floor to ceiling windows.

Light from the silvery moon washes over the gold-gilt antique furniture and vast mirrors.

I drop Shay in the center of the bed, and he bounces. His golden hair tumbles over his face.

Shay grins up at me. "This is brilliant."

Then he notices the mural on the wall behind me.

I stroll over the nightstand, as Shay pushes himself up onto his elbows, whistling.

I study him out of the corner of my eye. He looks awestruck.

The far wall is decorated in metallic paints by a local artist with a picture of Lucifer fighting an angel in the Garden of Eden.

A giant snake coils around them.

It's extraordinary.

"Shit, it's incredible." Shay's eyes are wide. "And they're both beautiful. Which are you then? The devilish tempter or the angelic warrior swooping down to save me?"

Shay often hides how smart he is.

But I should remember it.

I can't hold back the smile. "Which do you want me to be?"

"Both," Shay says, looking hopeful.

I can manage that.

"Perhaps, it depends whether you're a good boy." I deliberately look away from him.

Instead, I pick up the decanter of whiskey, which has been left on the nightstand.

My friend who owns this place knows me well.

It's why he's also left the other more…specialist… items that I've requested.

I pour myself a glass of whiskey, before opening the top drawer of the nightstand.

Satisfied, I realize that everything is here.

I pull out a large arctic blue velvet box.

When I turn around to Shay, however, he's already taken out his phone.

I narrow my eyes. "Am I boring you already?"

Shay glances up at me. "I'm just sending a message to my brother, so that he's not triggered into overprotective mode. I don't want him worrying, when I don't come home. Eden and I have this system, if the other one is staying out. I only need to send him a single emoji: smirking face."

"Uh-huh." When I point to the spot in front of me on the bed, Shay obediently crawls in front of me, slipping the phone back into his pocket. "You don't think that I may have already told Eden about my sneaky plans for you tonight? As my PA, he knows more about me than I do."

"I hope not *all* your sneaky plans."

I stroke through Shay's hair, pushing it back from his face. "Not all of them. No need to be embarrassed. He's seen you being ridden by Robyn, while I fucked your face. He knows that you're my trainable, pretty little pet."

Shay gives a whole body shiver. "Fuck, keep talking like that, and I'll come in my pants."

I tighten my hand in his hair, tugging hard enough to make him wince. "You don't come, until I give you permission. Or do I need to teach you a lesson first to make sure that you remember?"

"Tempting." Shay's chest is rising and falling fast. His lips look fucking kissable. "Enjoyable as that sounds, I want to know what's in that box."

His gaze darts to what I'm holding.

"Impatient." I toy with the box. "I guess that it *is* for you."

I toss Shay the box, and he catches it.

He clutches it. Light gleams off his gray painted nails.

I let go of Shay's hair, picking up my glass of whiskey and taking a sip.

"For me?" But then, Shay's expression crumples. "But I didn't get you anything. Shit, don't tell me that this is a ring…? Darlin', I'm a bloody bastard. I bought Robyn a star ring. I should have bought you—"

"*You're* the star." My expression becomes darkly dominant. "And you're giving me yourself. I don't need a ring, cucciolo, because I have your cock, balls, ass…submission. You belong to me. I fucking own you. Don't I?"

Shay is staring at me now like I truly am both the devil

and his guardian angel on his shoulder. "You do. You bloody do."

"Then open the box."

Shay pushes open the box's lid as carefully as if it's a relic.

Then his brow furrows. "I don't want to sound ungrateful but I don't think that this will fit my finger."

My lips quirk. "That's because it's not for your finger."

Shay studies the large black silicon ring, which is peeking out from amongst the velvet. "It won't fit my thumb either."

"I would hope not. But it's perfect for your cock."

Shay drops the box in shock. "You bought me a *cock ring*…?"

"You wanted romance." I hide my grin behind my whiskey glass. "Voila."

Shay stares at me and then he bursts out laughing. "You kinky devil."

"It takes one to know one."

"Too right." Shay pulls the black silicon ring, which has a longer piece at the back, out of the box. "What makes me think that this is a present for you as well?"

"For all of us," I reply. "I know from our talks and negotiations that orgasm delay is one of your kinks. What about having your cock turned into a dildo for our Robyn to ride? Wearing that ring, you'll be nothing but a toy for her pleasure."

"Fuck, yeah." Shay licks his dry lips.

I'm beginning to understand my pet.

I fall into a headspace that feels easy and natural with

him. I'm in control, but he's still Shay, even as he worships me.

I've played with hundreds of subs.

But I've never experienced such a connection before.

Shay isn't a sub. He's *my* sub.

I twist away to a switch on the wall. When I press on it, Arctic Monkey's "R U Mine?" booms around the room from hidden speakers.

The hypnotizing vocal with badass guitars and wild drumming makes me want to shove Shay back onto the bed, drag off his clothes, and fuck him like I promised until he screams.

Shay leaps off the bed looking as wild as the song.

He's vibrating with excitement. "You're a legend. This is—"

"Your playlist." I slam down my whiskey glass and catch Shay harshly by the scruff of the neck. He melts into my touch like I'm caressing him, rather than yanking him toward me. "And you *are* mine."

"I am," Shay breathes. "All of me. Every last inch. Do you want to prove it by claiming my cock and balls? I'd take this over a tattoo."

I only just stop myself from pouting.

A tattoo would be permanent.

Shay holds out the cock ring like a squire would a sword to their knight.

I take it from him. "Strip."

"My specialty." Shay eagerly pulls off his t-shirt with one hand.

He's attempting to do it in time with the music.

I struggle to keep my composure, as inch by inch, his gorgeous pale skin, defined chest, and abs are revealed.

Then he shimmies down his jeans.

My breath catches.

He's gone commando tonight.

To be fair, it's harder to get Shay into underwear than out of it.

Like this, with Shay naked, while I haven't even removed my suit jacket or loosened my tie, I feel how much taller I am than him.

It's obvious who is in charge here.

I cross my arms, casually inspecting Shay from head to foot. His dick twitches.

Shay's cheeks flush.

"Put your hands at your side," I say, coldly. "Don't cover yourself. You know what to do." Shay's flush deepens, but he obeys me. "Good boy."

Those two words make Shay's cock curve onto his stomach. A bead of precum glistens on its tip.

I play with the ring in my hand. Shay truly does need it.

But he's going to curse me before he thanks me.

I smile, wickedly

Shay fidgets.

"Stand still." I drop to my knees in front of him.

Shay gasps. Then he moans, when I grab his cock and take it deeply into my mouth.

Shay sounds like he's in heaven.

He tries to buck his hips, but I hold him still firmly by the thighs.

He mustn't get greedy.

"That's good," Shay pants. "Fuck, it's amazing. Where did you learn…? Your mouth is… I can't… I'm…"

He's exactly where I want him to be, teetering on the edge of orgasm.

Before he can come, however, I draw back, giving him a final long lick, from the base to the head of his dick.

Shay looks like he's dying. "W-w-what? Where are you going? Do you want me to beg? I will. *Please…*"

Shay's puppy dog eyes are so good that most people would break at this point.

Most people aren't me.

I pull the cock ring at its opening to widen it, then snap it over the base of Shay's cock to stave off his orgasm.

He wails.

The back of the cock ring rests behind his balls over his sensitive perineum.

When he plays this with Robyn, they are both going to be in for a surprise.

"Mean." Shay's legs are trembling.

When I give Shay's rock hard dick a final stroke, he shudders.

I fluidly stand, rubbing the dust off my suit trousers. "That's mean, *Sir.*"

Shay laughs, shakily. "Where do you want me and my painfully hard cock now, *Sir?*"

"Lying on your back in the middle of the bed with your arms outstretched to the four corners, *pet.*"

Shay's coherent enough to wink (I'll have to change

that). "Now, that's definitely not something you need to tell me twice."

He jumps onto the bed, throwing off cushions onto the floor. I'm not going to tell him how much each of those is worth and reduce his joy.

He exuberantly lies out like a sacrifice.

Fuck, he's beautiful like this.

My black ring around his cock, marking it as mine, is just as beautiful a statement.

Shay's gaze becomes tender, when he notices the direction that I'm looking. He appears to be holding himself unmoving with a great effort.

I reward Shay by not making him wait.

Instead, I crawl onto the bed after him, leaning down to kiss him in reward.

He sighs, happily.

I grip Shay's cock and pump it; he whines. "Oh, look. I like your dick, so I put a ring on it."

"Ha, ha," Shay manages to say, but it's shaky.

I reach above him and pull down a central part of tonight's event, which I had my friend set up for me.

This is why it's good to be friends with people within your local BDSM community, who are happy to set up not only cock rings but also loop your Bay Rebels official arctic ties to the corners of the four-poster bed without questioning it.

Shay's eyes widen. "You're using our ties."

"I've noticed how much you hate wearing them on game nights. I thought that I'd associate them with something more pleasurable. You may enjoy having them around your neck more after tonight."

"Or I'll get hard every game night remembering this. You're the best captain."

Unexpectedly, a cloud skitters across Shay's expression.

"Are you okay?" I stroke my thumb down his sharp cheekbone. "Use red, yellow, and green as safe words. If you need to stop, then I'll always honor it."

"But Blythe didn't." It hurts me to hear the pain in Shay's voice and to know that someone masquerading as a domme has put it there. "I said red over and over, but she just kept on hurting me. She left me tied up for hours. When she told me that she was only disciplining me for my own good…because I deserved it…because it was how I'd learn to become a good sub…I believed her. But it was a lie. I'm coming to terms with that now. Yet I didn't think that I'd be able to trust someone to tie me up again. At least, that if they did, it'd be because I'd earned punishment. But with you…"

"Yes?" My throat is dry.

"With you, it's never for punishment and only for pleasure. I trust you, and believe me, that means more than me saying that I love you. I *fucking trust you*, darlin'."

Joy, relief, and fucking exhilaration hit me at his words.

I know how much it took for him to say them.

I also know how much deeper trust is than love for men like us.

"I'm honored," I reply. "I cherish your trust. I won't take it for granted."

"I know. That's why you have it." Shay squirms like he can't hold still any longer. "Now, can we get to the part where you tie me up and fuck me senseless?"

Brat.

"Keep talking like that, and I may simply order you to lie like this for the rest of the night with neither you…nor me…touching that pretty cock of yours," I threaten.

That's never going to happen.

Shay, however, looks horrified.

"Sorry, Sir." He bats his lashes with possibly the worst attempt at contrition that I've seen.

I roll my eyes. "Lucky that I'm generous."

I bind the first tie around Shay's wrist. I slip my finger underneath the material and his wrist, making sure that it's not too tight in order not to bruise him.

Then I move onto his next wrist, pulling his arm to stretch him out onto the bed.

He's flexible.

This will drop him into the right headspace. Plus, he looks incredible with his shoulders pulled taut and his muscles bulging.

Shay draws in a sharp breath.

He's quivering.

"Are these tied too tightly?" I check. "Do they hurt? Are your hands numb?"

Shay shakes his head.

I smack his hip crisply, enjoying the sight of the crimson handprint that I leave behind. "Words, pet."

"No, Sir."

I lean down and lick across the seam of Shay's lips. He makes a hungry sound, trying to draw me into a deeper kiss. But I don't move closer, and he's too tightly tied down to be able to pull himself up and reach me.

Deliberately, I keep the kiss maddeningly light.

Frustrated, he strains but can't claim my mouth.

He collapses back onto the mattress.

"That's right." I kiss the corner of Shay's mouth, before biting on his lower lip. "You take only what I give you."

Shay's looking dazed now, sinking into submission.

Lazily, I lie over him, kissing him but at my pace.

Shay accepts it, letting me take the lead.

My eyes are dark. "You look good bound in our ties. You'll think of this every game night. Perhaps, one date, I'll have you like this. But instead of impaling you on my cock, I'll use your hockey stick."

"Fuck." Shay's hands clench into fists.

I can feel the fast thud of his heart, as he pushes his naked chest against mine.

He's sweating.

My legs are thrust between his, keeping them apart.

Shay's hard cock rubs against mine through the material of my pants.

My voice lowers to a deep rumble. "I'll put you into predicament bondage, balancing on your toes. Your legs will be spread wide with your own stick, slicked up and dangerously close to your hole, rod-like underneath you. You'll be sweating and using those trained muscles of yours, as you stand on two piles of your brother's books. If you lower from your tip toes…"

"You fiend," Shay half laughs.

"Devil." I glance over my shoulder at the mural. "Do you think calling me names would be wise, pet? Because then, I'd remove those books, one by one. And you…" My lips curl into a decidedly *fiendish* smirk. "You'd inch by inch slide down onto your stick, feeling it fuck you, hard and deep. You'd still be feeling it, when you played the big game the next day. And you'd remember that sensation, of being fucked by your stick while I watched, every time that you picked the stick up to go onto the ice."

Shay is lost in the fantasy. "I can feel it now."

His eyelashes flutter. He throws back his head.

I lay my hand around his throat, which snaps his attention back to me. "Are you ready for me to do everything that I want to you?"

Shay's eyes are blown wide with desire. "Green, bloody green."

My hand tightens at his throat, as I stoke down his trembling body.

I brush over his sensitive nipple, thumbing at it.

His nipple peaks, and he arches up, as much as he can.

I don't order him not to move. I enjoy the way that he struggles and I want him to enjoy that sensation as well.

I flick his nipple more insistently, before tracing lower. I smooth over his abs.

Shay's breathing fast.

I'm hardly holding it together.

Finally, I can't take it anymore.

I let go of Shay's throat and sit back, reaching to undo my trousers and then into my underwear to pull out my hard cock.

Shay watches my movements, licking his lips.

But I don't want his mouth right now.

Instead, I slip my hand into my pocket and pull out a small bottle of water based lube and a condom.

Shay raises his eyebrow.

"Let's simply say," I admit, "I planned for this second date going well. And it's turning out exactly how I'd hoped."

I rip open the condom packet, before sheathing my cock.

Then I maneuver myself between Shay's thighs.

I pop open the lube's lid and dribble some onto the fingers of my right hand. "Spread these legs for me." I slap his inner thigh. "Wider. You can do better than that. Good."

Shay whines but manages it.

I stare down at his hole long enough to make him blush.

When I tease around the edges, he gasps. I know that even these feather light touches are intense.

I want to deepen his blush. He looks beautiful like this.

"Look at your pretty hole." I spread it with my fingers, dribbling more lube down Shay's crack and struggling to hide my smile at his hiss at its coldness. I slide one finger in and then out a couple of times. "So hungry for my touch. You weren't lying about stretching yourself for me and following my instructions. Good boy. You truly are eager to be fucked."

"As eager as you are to fuck me," Shay challenges.

"Do you want me to show you how eager?" I slip two instead of one finger into him this time.

Shay's breath hitches. "Yes…"

He yanks on the ties binding him like he can't stop himself.

"Color?" I demand.

Shay hesitates. "Yellow."

"Slow down?" I check.

He nods.

I return to one finger, and Shay relaxes. This is only the second time that he's been fucked like this.

Sometimes, Shay's mouth doesn't know what his ass can handle.

I make sure to stroke over his prostate, massaging it.

Shay jerks, moaning in pleasure.

Then he relaxes, spreading his legs impossibly wider. "Please…"

I can make this feel incredible for him. I intend to turn him into a puddle of desire, where he's so relaxed that there's no pain and only pleasure.

"Color?" I check again.

"Green, *please…*"

Slowly, I try a second finger.

This time, Shay's open and ready for it. He pushes back against it, welcoming me into him. I rub over the bundle of nerves, which are making his cock weep.

Shay looks close to crying from frustration too.

"May I come?" Shay begs. I didn't think that I'd have him at this level yet. "P-p-please? Sir, can I? P-p-lease, just, *fuck…*"

I add a third finger, slowly stretching him.

Shay whimpers and shudders.

"Not yet." I lean down, enjoying how fast Shay's pulse is fluttering in his neck, as I bite down it gently.

My cock rubs against Shay's, sending sparks jolting through me.

When I look up, Shay's gaze is locked on mine with a tender love that takes away my breath.

"Fuck me," he murmurs. "I'm all yours, darlin'. *Show me.*"

I growl, grabbing his thighs and bringing them upwards to rest on my shoulders.

He's bent in half.

It's good that he's flexible.

Our gazes are locked on each other.

I never want to look away.

Then I trust into him, deep and hard.

I swallow his cry with a kiss.

Caging him, I fuck him, slowly enough to give him time to adjust.

When I draw back, our foreheads touch.

I feel like I'm drowning in him.

"Harder." Shay's lips quirk. "I *dare* you…"

I falter, and he laughs.

What?

He didn't seriously just dare me, when I'm balls deep in him, right?

The man has a death wish.

My curls brush his cheek, as I nip his ear, hard enough to make him yelp.

Then I murmur, "I never back down from a dare."

He asked for this.

If Shay wants to release my devil side, then I'm happy to fall.

I push his legs impossibly higher, as I kneel up, never stopping thrusting into him.

I don't look away, darkly dominant.

Shay's gaze is fixed on me like he's mesmerized.

He doesn't even look away, when I slip my hand between us and pull apart the cock ring to release him from his captivity.

I throw the ring to the side, clamping my hand around the base of his cock. "Not yet. You come when I tell you."

Shay blinks like that means yes.

I don't force him to use words because I don't think that he's capable of them right now.

"Truth to go with your dare." The words flow from me, as I stare down at this gorgeous man who is willingly beneath me, but in so many ways, shines above me. He's the angel in this room. "I've felt like there was a missing part of me my entire life. I've been searching for something…someone. Now, I've found it, and it's you. So, I'm never letting you go."

This truth feels blindingly large.

"Jude…" Shay whispers.

I raise both hands to rest by his head, before I rut into him.

This time, I don't hold back.

There's nothing slow or gentle about it.

It's wild and unrestrained.

Primal.

Shay throws his head from side to side, unable to escape the onslaught. His muscles strain, as he struggles.

He's like a bound god on a stone altar being ravished by a demon.

I bite his throat, needing to hear him scream.

"Come," I command, licking over the bite mark.

I thrust into Shay even harder.

Then Shay screams again like I promised that he would. But this time, it's because he's coming from an orgasm, which is so intense that he passes out.

CHAPTER SIXTEEN

Merchant's Inn, Freedom

obyn

I HOPE that Shay is okay.

Nervously, I chew on my lip, shifting from foot to foot on the sticky floor of Merchant's Inn. I run my hand through my hair, which is damp with sweat in the heat.

I'm wearing an apple green cotton dress and matching heels.

When D'Angelo took Shay out tonight on their second date to the Garden of Eden, he was vibrating with a such a high level of dominance that I'm certain Shay won't be able to either walk or sit down tomorrow.

That doesn't leave Shay many options.

Plus, D'Angelo asked me to drop off two special things for his first overnight with Shay: a mysterious package that he told me not to look at and two Bay Rebels ties.

Remembering my own date with D'Angelo, I don't think that the ties will be for wearing.

I have no idea what the package is.

Mysterious.

Despite the likelihood that Shay is tied onto or over something right now, they both need this time alone together.

Plus, it means that I get this final chance to take a break, before the brutal road trip begins.

It still makes me antsy to leave them alone this close to the away games, especially after that freaky text message.

Truth or dare.

Still, the only danger D'Angelo and Shay are in tonight is of having wild sex followed by cuddles.

I push toward the bar.

My nose scrunches at the scent of smoke and stale beer.

It's quieter tonight, mid-week. Although, it's still busier in Merchant's Inn than anywhere else in town.

Merchant's Inn is a rare safe space in Freedom with the added bonus of cheap beer, loud rock, and a couple of rooms for travelers.

The locals love this old, grungy slice of town with its dance floor and stained wooden walls that are covered with paintings of Emo bands like a shrine.

Freedom is a town with two sides: the wealthy,

including the tourists, and those who are struggling but working hard.

Merchant's Inn is at the heart of the working side of town.

Neve owns Merchant's Inn.

We were best friends in high school. Neve still wears the emerald and silver friendship bracelet that I made for her.

Neve was once treated as an outcast by both haters and her own family who threw her out. But she didn't leave town. Instead, she worked harder than fucking anybody and now she's a success.

I fucking love that about her.

I invited Eden to join me tonight at the bar. With his social anxiety, however, an evening out in Merchant's Inn is his equivalent of being forced to sing karaoke.

And that's hell on It's Raining Men earth.

Instead, Eden shook his head, lifting his copy of *The Count of Monte Cristo*.

He's spending the evening on the couch with a cup of tea and a book that he appears to strongly identify with.

Should that worry me?

Probably, but tonight isn't for worrying about Eden's inner darkness.

Tonight, is for drinking.

Hopefully, for getting pissed.

Tomorrow is realistically for regretting my choices and groaning with a throbbing headache and epic hangover.

Tom, the tiny but feisty bartender at Merchant's Inn, waves when he sees me. "I'll get to you in a minute."

"No hurry."

Tom's hair is even redder than mine. He has beautiful jade eyes.

Tom serves a tray of beers to a rowdy group of women in front of me expertly.

If I'd tried the same move, sliding those glasses across like that, for the very short time that I worked here when I first moved back to Freedom, then I'd have smashed them onto the floor. Alternatively, I'd have sloshed at least half of the alcohol down the women's short, glitzy dresses.

I'm proud of the fact that Neve put up a plaque in the staff bathroom commemorating my record number of broken glasses.

It's better than being commemorated for something boring like an achievement of historical significance, for example, winning a Nobel Prize.

"Hey, don't rush off, baby," the woman at the front of the group slurs. "Why are you ignoring me? How much do we need to tip for a kiss?"

She snatches at Tom's arm, yanking him closer.

He pales, struggling to free himself.

He's smaller than her. She's pulling him painfully into the wooden bar on his side of the counter. He grimaces, as his hip is bruised.

If Neve was here, then she'd rip this woman apart.

She has a zero tolerance policy to anyone touching Tom or any of her staff. She's particularly protective of

Tom, however, although I don't know his story in order to understand why.

"Hey," I yell, edging closer. "Get your fucking hands off him."

The woman's friends are looking uncomfortable. They don't back her up.

She glances around herself, appearing to realize it. She gives a fake laugh, releasing Tom.

Tom shoots me a grateful look, backing away. "Thanks." Then he narrows his eyes at the woman. "Get out. You're barred."

The woman gapes at him. "You can't do that."

"The owner has given me the power, if anyone crosses the line with me. And you just did." Tom's expression shutters. "Do I need to get the owner?"

"Fucking bitch," the woman hisses, turning on her heel.

She stalks to the exit.

Tom flinches.

I stiffen.

Would Tom mind if I kicked this woman's ass?

I arch my eyebrow at her group of friends. "You too."

To my surprise, they mutter variations on *sorry, Tom*, as they leave. They look shamefaced, as they should do.

Tom is liked.

Yet I know that he has to put up with being treated like that much more than he should do.

Tom starts to aggressively wipe down the bar with a cloth.

"Are you okay?" I ask.

He doesn't look at me. "Yeah. The usual?"

"I have a usual?"

He pushes a beer bottle across the counter to me.

Huh, it's exactly what I want. It appears that I do have a usual.

That thought makes me feel all fuzzy like I have not only a local now but a bartender who can automatically give me my usual.

I drop the payment onto the counter, along with a tip.

Tom collects it. "Could you not tell Neve about what happened? Thanks for stepping up for me. But she's having a good night, and I don't want to spoil it. Plus, I need this job. I don't want her thinking that I can't deal with my own...that I can't handle myself. It's part of the role."

I frown. "But it's her role to make sure that you're safe here too."

"Please."

"I don't understand."

Tom wrings his cloth between his hands. "She could hire someone who isn't targeted like I am. Or who doesn't freeze when... Just someone else. And I can't lose this—"

"I get it. It's dealt with. No need to bring down the wrath of Neve, I promise."

Tom shoots me a relieved smile. "You're the best, even if I pray that your klutzy ass never steps near my glasses again."

I laugh. "You and me both."

I snatch up my beer and work my way across the bar.

The fiery sound of The All-American Reject's "Dirty

Little Secret" playing over the music system fills the room with a throbbing, angsty Emo vibe.

I hum along to the song, feeling my mood lightening.

Then I drop my beer onto the chipped oak table in the middle of the leather booth in the corner.

I slide myself onto the seat next to Neve.

Neve snorts. "Did you go all the way to the brewery for that beer?"

I give her the finger.

She gives it back.

Neve sprawls on one side of the booth with her converse trainers resting up on the table.

She's my age with chestnut eyes and spiky midnight hair. She wears large, horn-rimmed glasses. Her rich brown skin glows bronze on her cheeks.

She's dressed in skinny jeans with a studded belt and a black t-shirt with the words **ALL DOWNHILL FROM HERE** written across it in yellow.

It's hard not to tell her about what happened to Tom, but I promised.

Neve appears to notice that something is off because she narrows her eyes. "You suck at hiding shit from me. What's wrong? Do you remember that time in elementary school that you ate my candy, then felt so guilty that you cried and hid in the corner? You were amazed that I guessed it was you, RH."

RH is her nickname for me, Robyn Hood.

I take a deep swig of my beer. "And that's when I figured out that the career of criminal mastermind wasn't for me."

"You just need to know how to bury your conscience." Neve pushes her glasses more firmly onto her nose. "Along with the bodies."

Statements like that should worry me. But I've known Neve long enough that they no longer do.

"Or be best friends with someone who can." I salute Neve.

"As long as D'Angelo remembers that." Her smile is dangerous.

Neve only has a truce with D'Angelo.

D'Angelo should take the shovel talk that Neve gave him both seriously…and literally.

Cody chuckles.

He's sitting on the other side of the booth in a blue t-shirt and jeans. He's nursing his own beer. Michael has his arm slung around him, pulling Cody against his side. He's wearing a tan suit, although it's open at the neck.

I can't help noticing how dark the shadows are underneath Michael's eyes.

Michael raises his brandy and takes a sip. "Talking of bodies, my shift today was grueling."

I grimace. "Why do we always end up talking about bodies and not in the sexy way?"

"Because my work is long and bloody." Michael quirks his brow. "Like a Tarantino movie with a similar number of dismembered limbs but less of the excessive dialogue. The same amount of cussing from the consultants, in private of course."

Cody grabs hold of Michael's hand. "Tough week?"

"Exhausting, but being out with all of you is a good

distraction." Michael glances at his husband. "How has it been preparing for the road trip?"

Cody brightens. "Exciting. The staff are pumped for the first trip away together. They're a great set of people. On the other hand, however, everyone's terrified, which isn't what I was expecting."

Anxiety rushes through me. "*Terrified*, Code?"

"The senior staff and board members are putting pressure on everyone. It's a huge deal that the team performs. No one expects all three games to be won because the odds are stacked against an away team from the beginning. Nobody gets a sweep of three wins. The Ducks, Kings, and Sharks are fucking hard teams, even without their home advantage."

My hand tightens around the bottle. "The media are going one of two ways. They're either writing the Bay Rebels off as *losers* already, or building them up with hype like the new golden team who are going to defeat the old, has-beens. Both narratives are putting intense pressure on the players. If they don't perform, the press are going to tear them apart like wolves."

"Then they better score goals." Neve picks up her bottle and points it at me. "Your dad can kick their asses, and you can fuck them. Use those penis extension sticks of theirs, if they need extra motivation."

I spray my mouthful of beer over the table, spluttering.

"Classy, Ryn." Cody laughs, mopping up the mess with a paper napkin.

"Talking of fucking." I'll take a leaf out of Eden's book

and have my revenge. "How are things going with your hot blond nurse, Lucy?"

"Mind-blowingly. She's a fucking tonguing artist." Neve curls her tongue in illustration, and it's me who pinks and not her.

Why did I forget that nothing makes Neve blush?

"But then," Neve wiggles her fingers, "we're also scissoring prodigies. We're well-matched."

"With how talented you are, it's amazing that you're not famous. How did throwing yourself out of a plane go?"

"Well, I'm not dead." Neve pulls a face.

"Not a fan?"

"Skydiving sucks. But Lucy is into all that athletic, thrill-seeking shit. If she hasn't risked her life three times a week, she isn't happy. So, she was pleased that I'd shared the experience with her and that's what matters."

I never thought that Neve, who's never even been in a plane before, would jump out of one.

I also never thought that she'd care about sharing experiences with someone.

This Lucy is good for her.

"When will we get to meet her?" I ask.

Neve looks startled. "I don't know. Her shifts at the hospital are crazy. We'll see. She wants us to go swimming with sharks in a couple of weeks."

Cody laughs. "I love Lucy already."

"You're kidding." I stare at Neve in amazement. "What if they see that you're an Emo in black and mistake you for a seal? They'll eat you."

"They'll take one bite and realize that I taste too bitter. They'll spit me out." Neve leans closer. "And I haven't forgotten that you're hiding something, RH. Spill."

My mouth dries.

I should have known that Neve wouldn't forget about my shifty behavior.

She never forgets anything, whether it's the embarrassing moment that I tripped and flashed my cat underwear to the entire class in high school (excruciatingly mortifying). Or the time that I stayed over with her and thought her rubber ducky was a cute toy, only to get the shock of my life, when it turned out to be a vibrator.

That was one hell of a quacking fun bath time.

I wipe my mouth on the back of my hand. "Hiding something? If I'm acting freaked, it's because D'Angelo received this weird message on his phone yesterday."

I intended to ask their advice anyway. It's the perfect way to throw Neve off the scent.

Cody sits up straighter, concerned. "What type of message? That asshole Wilder isn't stalking you again, right?"

"I don't know. The number was untraceable."

Neve's eyes flash. "Dismembering body time."

"As tempting as that is," particularly tempting, when it comes to my abusive ex, "the problem is that we don't know who sent the message or why."

"Report it." Michael looks grim. "I know that Austin can be difficult sometimes, but at least the security team need to know."

"I have," I reply. "D'Angelo also has his PI, Garcia, working on this as well."

"Who are these shadowy people who are friends with D'Angelo?" Neve raps the table on each point. "A vintage sports car. Mysterious men connected to the underworld. And an alphahole in a suit. Look at that, D'Angelo *is* Bond."

I grin. "I know you mean that as an insult, Neve, but D'Angelo would fucking dine out on that description."

"But are you safe, Ryn?" Cody looks set to fight the world for me. "What did the text say?"

"Truth or dare."

The other three freeze, and it settles on me, just how ominous those words actually sound spoken aloud like that and not at a party.

"It could be a prank," I say, weakly.

"Maybe." Cody sounds unsure.

"I hate that game." Neve kicks her feet off the table in disgust. "People are fucking sheep. It's about nothing but pride and ego, being unable to back down."

"Or they're simply pissed," I say.

"Pissed, on top of thinking that they'll look weaker backing down from a dare, rather than letting people who are laughing at them duct tape them naked to a football goalpost."

Good point.

"It's the kind of thing that Grayson and Lucas would play." Cody's brow furrows. "Those two are pranksters. Are you sure that it's not them?"

What if it is just players hazing their captain?

If it is, then they'll have their asses handed to them by D'Angelo.

Yet D'Angelo's respected by his team. He treats them like family.

Brothers.

Surely, they wouldn't mindfuck him just before the first road trip.

Right?

I push my beer away from myself, disquieted. "I don't know. I have no idea who'd send it. At the moment, I'm hoping that it's not important. It's just that after being stalked and blackmailed in the first few weeks of the season, I don't want to take any chances. My guys have been through enough."

"So have you," Cody says.

I look down. "We've survived it. We're the strongest that we've been and we're happy. I hate that I don't know what we're facing."

"I'm the King of Bets." Cody cocks his head. "But games like truth or dare are different."

"They're dangerous." Michael curls his arm more protectively around Cody. At the same time, he fixes me with a stern look. "Don't engage with whoever this person is. Even if the game seems innocent to start with. You're hiding too many secrets to be able to tell the *truth*. Yet *dares* are set up to reveal a hidden fantasy or fear and grant you permission to do it publicly. And that could destroy your careers."

CHAPTER SEVENTEEN

Captain's Hall, Freedom

hay

I LUG my tattered scarlet suitcase after me down the steps of Captain's Hall into the dazzling sunshine.

It's so hot that I'm already sweating, despite only wearing a thin crimson t-shirt and jeans.

I'm still in a daze after last night.

D'Angelo drove us back here a couple of hours ago from the Garden of Eden to finish packing up for the road trip.

I've never passed out from pleasure before.

I mean, from starvation, illness, or beatings but not from an earth-shattering orgasm.

D'Angelo could destroy me.

Truly wreck the last, hidden part of me that I've kept safe from the world all these years.

So could Robyn.

But instead, D'Angelo's breaking me down in a way that builds me up stronger afterward.

It works like the best training sessions on the ice do.

How did I get so bloody lucky?

Last night, I came around to find that I'd been untied from the bed. D'Angelo was petting my hair and massaging my wrists like I was precious…*how he normally handles Robyn.*

My breath caught.

I pretended to still be unconscious, simply to feel him continue to be gentle with me for a moment longer.

I'd crawl over broken glass for the aftercare that D'Angelo would offer afterwards.

When D'Angelo finally noticed my change in breathing, he raised a bottle of Gatorade to my lips.

"You were excellent for me," he praised, as I drank. "You took all of that so well. I'm proud. How are you feeling?"

I assessed myself for a moment. "Good."

"How did you find it? Was the cock ring too intense?"

I cuddled closer to D'Angelo, needing the physical contact.

D'Angelo pulled me against his chest at the same time as dragging a blanket around me.

"The cock ring was bloody intense," I replied. "But I loved the way that it held me on the edge but also meant that my orgasm felt fully under your control. You could delay or deny it. Also, it made me feel…" I flushed, glancing away. "Owned. *Wanted* by you. It was almost like a…"

I cut myself off in time from saying a *collar*.

D'Angelo hasn't offered that, and I know that it's too early to be mentioning one.

I should be fucking grateful that Robyn and him are granting me this place between them.

I am.

But what if one day, they did offer me a collar?

It would be like a marriage, right?

I can't let myself hope for that.

But if they did, maybe I'd feel safe that they weren't going to throw Eden and me away.

I attempt to leap down the final step and then regret it, when my arse twinges.

Fuck, D'Angelo has an unfairly large cock.

Millionaire, musician, tall, dom, plus owner of a giant cock…it's selfish of him to hog *everything*.

I squint through the light at the mammoth motorhome that's standing in the driveway.

I whistle.

Shit.

"She's a beast like you." I grin at D'Angelo, who's leaning against the motorhome with the same proprietary air that he saves for his Alfa Romeo or my ass.

D'Angelo's dressed in his favorite navy suit and waistcoat. He's stripped down to his crisp, white shirt with the sleeves rolled back to show his forearms.

His jacket is slung over his arm.

It's so rare to see him casual like this that it feels like we're on holiday already.

D'Angelo pushes open the door to the RV. "Wait until you see inside."

Excitement bursts through me.

I bounce on my toes, before rushing to join D'Angelo in front of our new home for next couple of weeks.

I've never been on a road trip before.

My brother and I haven't been on holiday.

After all the shit that Eden has been through (and is still going through), I'm determined that this feels like a holiday for him, even if it's one with a fuck load of pressure and ice hockey games that could change my life, one way or the other.

I'm going to be on the road and visiting different places in America, however, with the people who I love.

After everything that's happened in my life, that's all that matters.

Seize the day, right?

"How are you now?" D'Angelo stops me by gripping my elbow, concern coloring his words. "Still feeling all right?"

Warmth floods me.

So, this is what it feels like to be truly, properly cared about.

Or would D'Angelo act the same way for any sub?

"Sore in the expected places," I admit. "But I like it, you

know? It's a reminder of last night. And you were careful to check that there wasn't any damage. I won't break from some rough handling."

"I may," D'Angelo lets go of my elbow, "if I ever broke you in a way that I didn't intend. Or if I couldn't put you back together. So, apart from the pleasant type of soreness, are you okay?"

I take a moment to truly think about his question.

I shouldn't have forgotten that these check ins are as much to meet D'Angelo's health and needs, as they are for mine.

"I'm brilliant, darlin'," I reassure him. "I'm more relaxed than I have been in days. The shower that we took together afterward helped my sore muscles. Practice has been challenging, and I don't think that I realized how much I needed to be dropped. But it wasn't only that. The whole day with you…"

How do I explain?

The only person who has taken me to expensive restaurants and treated me as special was Blythe.

I thought that she wanted to be my girlfriend.

Yet the moment that I tried to be her boyfriend, she tied me up and then beat me with a belt for daring to think that I deserved romance or love.

I was nothing but a plaything to her.

Deep down, I was terrified that D'Angelo would date me and then discover the same about me.

That I didn't deserve to be his genuine boyfriend.

But instead, he spent an entire day as my best friend, boyfriend, and lover. He romanced me, before tying me up, and this time, he didn't hurt me for daring to assume that what we had was real.

Instead, he tormented me with pleasure.

And afterward, we kissed, spooned, and slept together alone in the bed like a *real fucking couple*.

I've never had that.

I never dreamed that I could.

Please, don't let me wake up.

D'Angelo's expression gentles, before he kisses me, slow and tender. "Both day and night were perfect. I even appear to have won you over to comedy movie nights."

I scrunch up my nose. "How about comedy horror as a compromise? I bet that you'd love *Army of Darkness*. Bruce Campbell is a legend. In it, he gives the grumpy *get the fuck away from me* vibes that you're so good at, especially in the mornings."

D'Angelo lets go of me with a haughty shove. "Dangerous words and an even more dangerous bet."

"I like to live dangerously."

I glance around, as Eden trudges down the steps with Robyn at his side.

Eden is dressed in relaxed gray joggers and t-shirt. Robyn's poppy floral dress is pretty, flowing to her feet.

Eden is carrying his own gray bag over his shoulder and Robyn's polka dotted suitcase in his hand.

His expression is mask-like, but I still know his expressions of pain well enough to read the thinness of his lips.

He shouldn't be carrying those heavy bags. They must be hurting his cracked ribs.

To my surprise, D'Angelo moves at the same time as I do, bounding up the steps next to me.

Neither of us say anything, as we each take a bag from my twin.

Together, we walk toward the motorhome.

"This is incredible, Jude. It's three times as large as I was imagining." I study the giant white and silver vehicle.

"My remarkable PA here arranged it." D'Angelo nods at Eden. "He's in charge of the entire travel itinerary."

Eden ducks his head. "The equipment manager has our gear. The itineraries have been emailed to you all."

I snort. "*Pfft*, who has time to check…?"

D'Angelo glares at me.

"I mean, I do," I hurriedly add. "As soon as we hit the road. Well done, bro."

"Luckily, we have one person who's super organized." Robyn kisses Eden. "If this was down to me, we'd probably end up in Alaska or Australia."

"Anywhere beginning with 'A' then." D'Angelo chuckles. "I've always wanted to visit both places. Perhaps, we should have put you in charge of this trip."

Robyn shudders. "Hundred percent no."

I trace my finger along the side of the motorhome. "Wasted opportunity here, Dee. Why didn't you make it arctic blue? Wait, I know. What about the Bay Rebels logo? We could graffiti spray on a puck with all those flames. It'd look epic like a racing motorhome."

Robyn strolls to me, before gripping me by the chin. "Incognito. Laying low. *Undercover*. Perhaps, I wasn't clear enough about our PR role here, but it's not to ride a trail through California promoting the Bay Rebels, while we're without security, and possibly being surrounded by screaming fans. By being separated from the other staff and players, we're meant to be avoiding trouble, rather than becoming a beacon for it."

"Got you."

Robyn's brow furrows, before she turns my head to the side. "Did you have fun last night?"

My expression becomes dreamy, as I catch D'Angelo's gaze. "So much, love."

"So much that a vampire bit you?"

Shit, D'Angelo's playing rough moment last night, when he bit my neck.

I shiver.

Eden's stony gaze slides to D'Angelo.

"A gorgeous vampire," I hurriedly clarify, "who swooped over poor me, the innocent beauty who was sleeping." Robyn snorts. Rude. "Then ravished me, sinking his fangs into my neck and drinking my yummy blood. Now, I'm shackled to their will, spell-bound as their blood lover."

My cock hardens.

I need to add that to my fantasy role play list. D'Angelo would look incredible dressed as a vampire.

"I even used a ring to control him," D'Angelo says, coolly.

I flush. "Thanks for adding that detail."

"No problem."

Robyn perks up. "I've been desperate to know what was in that mysterious package. I had a guessing game with Neve and Code last night, which included a squeezable stressticles toy, **HOCKEY HAIR, DON'T CARE** key chain, or a penis leash."

"A penis leash…?" My eyes widen.

And now I'm imagining being led around by my cock, with D'Angelo holding the chain.

Kink unlocked.

"That last one was Neve, wasn't it?" D'Angelo says, frostily. "She better have been planning for Shay to be the one wearing it."

"I wouldn't bet on it." Robyn smirks.

Before D'Angelo can explode, I tell Robyn, "I've packed the ring. How about I show you later?"

Robyn smiles. "I'd love that."

D'Angelo arches his brow. "If you're bound to my will, cucciolo, then get your ass inside. Now."

I roll my eyes. "Vampires, always so grumpy in the sunlight. Shouldn't you be the one worrying about getting inside, before you're turned into a little pile of ash?"

Robyn laughs.

When D'Angelo bares his teeth into a snarl, which is disturbingly (and hotly), convincing as a vampire, I hold my hands up in surrender. "Okay, okay. I know that you're all bite and no bark."

D'Angelo swipes my ass, as I climb up the steps into the motorhome.

I chuckle, hearing the others trail behind me.

Then I stare around myself in amazement.

"Is this the TARDIS?" I drop the bags onto one of the two plush silver couches, which curve around both sides of the vehicle. It even has blue cushions on it. "It's bigger in here than our dorm room was. I mean, it's not much smaller than the ground floor of our parent's house."

I take a deep breath in, then cough. "What's that chemical stench?"

"New RV smell." Eden pushes open a window.

"Huh, like new car smell." I dart around the motorhome, dragging open drawers and peering into lockers. "I've always wanted to know why people rave about that."

The inside is wooden with accents of silver and blue. Behind the curved couches is a table with a bright blue cover on it for meals. Stools that are welded to the floor stand underneath it.

To one side is a gleaming kitchenette.

When I drag open the fridge and poke around, it's fully stocked.

"Beer," I exclaim. "You've thought of everything, Dee."

"What about whiskey?" D'Angelo throws his bags next to mine and then settles behind the huge wheel at the front, adjusting the seat and mirrors.

Of course he's driving. He'd never let up that control to someone else.

Eden shakes his head. "You're driving. But I have tea."

"The sacrifices that I make," D'Angelo mutters, checking over the controls.

Robyn bounces up and down on the couch, as excited as I am. "This is amazing."

When Eden sits next to her, she happily lays her head on his chest.

I explore to the back of the motorhome, sliding open the doors with a satisfying whoosh to discover a tiny shower and bathroom.

I slide the doors open and shut a couple of times, enjoying the sound.

"Shay," Eden scolds behind me.

I hunch my shoulders. "Sorry."

"Let him," Robyn says. "What's the bedroom like?"

I bound the final few steps to the back of the RV.

I throw open the sliding door with a flourish.

Then I stare at the silver room, which is entirely taken up by a vast single bed with luxurious blue bedding that matches Eden and my eyes.

I turn to Robyn with a smile. "Look at that, it's an only one bed situation. Looks like we're going to have to share. The hardship."

"You could take the couch." Eden's lips twitch.

"He can't." Robyn's dancing gaze meets mine. "Who else is going to give me the best morning wake ups in the world?"

I lean in the doorway. "It would be a crime to miss my tongue."

"It would be a crime not to wake up in the arms of the three men who I love." Robyn's gaze is the sun that warms me.

When Robyn looks at me like I'm everything — like just being with me means the fucking world to her — it makes me want to live up to being the man she thinks I am.

I will.

Every goal that I score will be for this new family of mine.

For the team that signed me, when no one else would.

For her dad, the coach who believed in me.

For the town that has adopted me.

And most of all, for the woman who is not only in my heart but *is* my heart.

Eden leans over and kisses Robyn like it's for both of us.

My brother's gaze is dark. I know that he's thinking the same as I am.

We won't be alone again.

Finally, Eden draws back.

Robyn's eyes are glassy. Her chest is rising and falling.

She looks a hot mess. Yet I love seeing her worked up like this from simply a kiss.

"You're getting good at that." Robyn settles back on Eden's chest. He loops his arm around her shoulders. "Kissing."

"Practice makes perfect." Eden's amused gaze slides to mine.

I just about stop myself giving my twin the thumbs up.

I slip my hand into my pocket and send him the emoji thumbs up instead.

"Lots and lots of practice," Robyn agrees. "You need dedication. Multiple times a day."

"That's the ethos I live by. Except, replace kissing with fucking." I stroll to the front of the motorhome, leaning on D'Angelo to watch him as he messes with the controls.

When I reach to touch a particularly exciting looking button, D'Angelo bats away my hand.

"No touching," D'Angelo commands.

I cradle my hand. "But what about…?"

D'Angelo shoots me a warning glare. "No."

My eyes light up, when I notice the music system. "As resident music fanatic, I claim the radio."

I reach for the knob, but with his legendary fast reflexes on the ice, D'Angelo catches my wrist. "Anybody who touches the radio or changes the station will lose their fingers."

He sounds dangerously serious.

"Does that mean that we'll be listening to dead blokes like Mozart the entire way?" I demand.

D'Angelo smiles, smugly. "Prepare yourself for an entire journey of *dead blokes* from Bach to Beethoven."

"Be scared of the alliteration," Eden deadpans.

I glance between them. "I don't know about this *alli* guy, but the others sound boring as hell. Don't worry, I'm sneaky. I'll have you singing along to the *Arctic Monkeys* by the time we arrive."

D'Angelo lets go of my wrist with a caress. "Try it, cucciolo."

Is that an invitation or a threat?

"Music wars aren't the important thing here." Robyn leans forward. "We're traveling apart from the others to keep off the press radar. So, how about you keep your attention on the road and don't crash?"

"*Don't crash,*" D'Angelo repeats. "Why do I think you don't have a high level of expectation?"

"More like I'm tempering expectations to avoid disappointment. We simply need to get through this."

"Are we pulling up somewhere to sleep at night?" I ask. "Jude can't drive day and night for three days, and Eden and I don't have the right license to help."

"And I *would* crash," Robyn adds.

"It's in the itinerary." Eden rubs at his forehead. "A parking lot and a campsite on route. Jude has insisted that he'll drive fourteen hour days. We need to go now to meet our timings."

D'Angelo salutes. "You're the boss. Well, I am, but you're the man with the schedule and that makes you the true boss like most PAs. Now, everyone move to the seats at the front and strap yourselves in." He puts in the ignition key. "This pucking road trip is officially about to begin."

CHAPTER EIGHTEEN

Parking Lot, Arkansas

Shay

I WALK MY FINGERS SLOWLY — sneakily — toward the button that will change the radio station.

Come on, Shay, you can do this.

I glance at D'Angelo out of the corner of my eye.

I'm sitting next to D'Angelo at the front of the RV. He's staring fixedly at the road as he has been for the last three hours without a break.

D'Angelo's scarily focused when he drives.

He's also a music dictator who loves to listen to classical shit at top volume.

I wince.

Somebody has to stand up and rebel.

I should earn a rock medal shaped like a guitar, if I succeed in this mission to change the music to Motorhead rather than Mozart.

I fight to stop my leg jiggling with nerves, as my fingers inch toward the button.

Now, I only need to press it...

"Change that channel," D'Angelo says without glancing away from the road, "and lose your fingers."

How does he do that? *Brat mindreading?*

I snatch my hand away like I've been burned.

Eden snorts with amusement.

I glare over my shoulder at my brother.

Eden is relaxed in the row of seats behind me like a cat, despite the seatbelt.

He's balancing a laptop on his lap, typing one handed on it much faster than I can do with two hands.

Robyn's head rests on Eden's shoulder, where she's slumped snoring in the seat next to him.

It must be love, when I can find her adorable, even with drool at the corner of her mouth.

"You're working too bloody hard, bro," I complain. "This is meant to be a holiday."

"Firstly, it isn't," D'Angelo points out. "Secondly, keep your voice down, our Robyn is taking a nap. And thirdly, *you're* not working. So, it balances things out."

I cross my arms, lowering my voice. "It is a holiday."

I stare out of the window at the night sky.

It appears clearer here, somehow. The moon is brighter.

The mountains are rugged. The beautiful hickory forest lies in shadow on either side, blurring as we pass. The roads are quiet, while occasional cars drive by like ghosts.

When I glance back at D'Angelo, to my surprise, his hands have tightened around the wheel.

"I was wrong," D'Angelo says. "It is a vacation, if we want it to be. But the driver is still in charge of the music."

"Is that a rule?" Eden asks.

D'Angelo hesitates. "It was Dad's rule. My family sometimes hired an RV over summer." He forces his hands to relax on the wheel. "Play anything you like, cucciolo."

My chest is tight.

I hear what he's saying as loudly as what he isn't.

I don't even know my biological dad's name. Eden and I only called him Man.

But it'd kill me, if I thought that I was acting the same as he did.

I'd make sure that Eden kicked my ass the moment that happened.

"It's okay." I shrug. "This classical shit is growing on me."

Sorry, rock gods.

"Well, that was convincing." D'Angelo's lips quirk, before he reaches to turn down the music.

Finally.

I glance out of the window at the forested mountain in

awe, as D'Angelo navigates a bend. "Everywhere feels so much bigger than in England. What state are we in now?"

"Arkansas." Eden looks up from his laptop. "Pull off at the next exit."

I'm proud of the way that although D'Angelo is in charge inside the RV, my brother is in charge of the journey itself.

Eden's really stepped up with directions and planning this trip.

He's finding his voice.

D'Angelo nods. "Thank Christ. It's been a long day."

D'Angelo slowly pulls the motorhome off at the exit. The new rood is smaller and quieter.

A small collection of houses, however, begin to gather on either side.

"Was it too long?" Eden sounds worried. "I can adjust the timings for tomorrow."

"It's better for us to get there," D'Angelo replies. "Shay can give me one of his massages."

"Of course, darlin'." I wiggle my hands. "They're magical, which is why you shouldn't threaten them."

I give D'Angelo a hopeful look.

"Perhaps," D'Angelo arches his brow, "it's why you should be careful not to misbehave."

"Never going to happen. Where are we parking?"

"A store parking lot, where it's legal." Then Eden resignedly adds, "you still haven't read the itinerary."

"I glanced at it over lunch." Shit, why didn't I pay more attention? I blame how mesmerizing Robyn's tits are. I was happily stroking them, while she fed me a chocolate-chip muffin. It was difficult to keep my concentration on my phone. "I'll memorize it tonight, I swear."

"You won't." Eden's gaze darkens. "Everybody needs to relax."

Just for a moment, D'Angelo's expression becomes wicked. "Excellent idea."

I look startled.

What the hell is he thinking about?

"Here." Eden points out of his window.

D'Angelo sweeps the motorhome into a small parking lot, which is in front of a grocery store.

The lights are still on inside the store. It looks open, but there are only a couple of other parked cars.

Eden carefully places his laptop into its bag, which he's decorated with the Bay Rebels logo, as well as a black cat **TALK TO THE PAW** sticker in the corner.

D'Angelo parks the motorhome in a dark corner under a tall oak tree at the far side of the parking lot, away from the other customers.

I sigh with relief, as the engine shuts off.

D'Angelo slips off his belt, stretching and turning his neck from side to side. "That massage sounds good about now."

"Yes, Sir." I grin at the way that D'Angelo's pupils instantly dilate.

I throw off my own seatbelt, before squirming up onto my knees. I reach to massage D'Angelo's shoulders.

D'Angelo groans like he's just come from my touch alone. "I apologize for ever wanting to damage your hands."

"They can do more than massage." I stroke down D'Angelo's chest toward his hard crotch, palming him.

D'Angelo hisses out a sharp breath. "Cucciolo, we're in a public place. Anyone could look in the window and see us."

Fuck, that thought goes straight to my dick.

I swallow. "They could hear us too. So, we'd better keep quiet."

"We?" D'Angelo's voice is dangerously soft now.

Uh-oh.

I don't stop rubbing over his crotch, but he's holding himself still, which makes me on the alert.

My skin tingles. "Ehm…"

D'Angelo's hand snaps out, snatching me by the throat. Taken by surprise, my eyes widen with shock and desire in equal measure. He yanks me closer with the right degree of roughness.

"You're the one who'll need to keep silent, *pet*." D'Angelo's breath is hot against my lips. "Unless you want everyone in Arkansas to know that you're owned by the Bay Rebels' captain and his principessa."

Owned.

It shoots electric sparks through me.

I can't deny it.

"Robyn, who's currently snoring." I hang in D'Angelo's harsh grip but I don't stop stroking over his clothed cock.

D'Angelo's teeth are gritted like he's struggling hard not to show how much he's enjoying it.

We both know that he is.

D'Angelo and Eden exchange a glance.

It's never good when they look like that.

It always means that I'm fucked, both figuratively and sometimes, literally.

Eden slips out of his seatbelt and undoes Robyn's.

Then he stands and gently picks Robyn up, hefting her in his arms in a bridal carry. Her head lolls against his shoulder, and her hair falls like she's burning him up with flames.

I wish that I could sleep as deeply as that.

"Take her to the bed," D'Angelo commands. "Time to relax after my hard work by tormenting those who've been resting all day. Perhaps, we can teach them both a lesson in self-control."

Eden gives me a long look.

I squirm.

"Shay needs it," Eden replies. "Teach him to be silent. I've failed at that."

True but also...

"Hey." I give Eden a wounded look.

Eden's expression is stony, however, and he doesn't appear moved.

I should have paid more respect to the itinerary.

Never piss off a PA.

D'Angelo edges his hand from my throat around to the scruff of my neck.

Then he stands, dragging me up with him. "I don't intend to. Up."

I yelp, but my dick hardens.

A cock wants what a cock wants.

And right now, it wants the dominance that's radiating

from D'Angelo and promising a way to relax all of us, which is both heaven and hell.

I pretend to resist, but it's so unconvincing that D'Angelo actually rolls his eyes as he yanks me after him.

"What devilish things are you going to do to me?" I gasp, dramatically.

"You packed your ring, remember?" D'Angelo's eyes gleam. "You promised to show Robyn. You wouldn't want to disappoint her."

Eden carries Robyn in front of us, sliding open the door to the bedroom. He lays Robyn carefully on top of the bedding. Then he sprawls next to her.

D'Angelo, on the other hand, shoves me hard onto the other side of Robyn.

I laugh as I land.

It's exhilarating to be manhandled like that.

It's sort of like flying or being on the ice.

Exhilarated, I drag off my jeans and t-shirt, throwing them out of the sliding doors and not caring that they hit D'Angelo's legs.

D'Angelo's expression darkens. "Careful, cucciolo."

I smirk. "If I'm already screwed, I may as well be royally screwed."

"Does that make me the king who's doing the screwing?" D'Angelo kneels on the bed between my thighs.

He looks like a king now.

My breathing speeds up. My cock is already curving onto my stomach, and my balls ache.

"W-w-what?" Robyn's eyes flutter.

She sleepily turns toward Eden, kissing him.

Eden cups her cheek. "Wake up."

"Don't want to." Robyn cutely scrunches up her nose. I struggle not to laugh. "It's not morning yet."

"I'm going to make it worth your while," D'Angelo darkly promises. "I have a toy here for you to ride."

He rests his hand on my dick like he owns it. Except, he does…along with Robyn.

My breath hitches.

Robyn opens her eyes, focusing on Eden. Then she kisses him again, holding him by his hair.

Finally, she glances over her shoulder at D'Angelo, before scanning over me with a lazy enjoyment.

"When did we stop?" She asks.

"Just now," D'Angelo replies. "But you've been asleep for a while. We're parking by this store for the night. And since this one," he casually runs his hand up and down my dick, making my back arch, "has been incessantly talking all day, you'll need a lesson tonight. There could be anyone just outside. So, you'll both need to be quiet."

"Why will that be hard?"

She had to ask.

I groan. "Because these two will torment us, until we're out of our frustrated minds with pleasure. But we can't make a sound because—"

Robyn flushes and whispers, "Someone may hear us."

"You know me so well." D'Angelo looks smug. "Remember your safe words."

He turns to my bag, which Eden stowed to the side of the room earlier with the other bags. Then he rummages through it.

When Eden edges up Robyn's floral dress inch by inch, she's already struggling not to moan. He makes it harder for her by caressing her most sensitive places in circles, behind her knees, inner thighs, and hips.

He kisses down her neck.

Robyn's eyes are glazed by the time that he pulls down her panties.

How does D'Angelo make the act one of both domination and care?

Robyn is trembling.

"I gifted Shay this ring. It suits him." When D'Angelo holds up the cock ring with a flourish, my cheeks pink.

Robyn reaches to grasp my hand. "Does that go where I think it does?"

"Let me demonstrate," D'Angelo answers.

It does something to me the way that he talks about me to Robyn like I'm not even there or maybe, like I'm their possession.

D'Angelo pulls apart the silicon toy, fitting it snugly around my cock and balls, as well as pressing over my sensitive perineum.

He removes a condom from his pocket and slips it over my cock.

Then D'Angelo's eyes dance with wickedness. "But what he doesn't know is that I can flick this button…" He touches a hidden button on the side, and suddenly, pulsing vibrations start up all the way through the toy. "…and it vibrates."

"Fuck, fuck, fuck," I yell, as intense pleasure slams through me in waves.

D'Angelo slaps his palm over my mouth.

He leans over me. "Quiet, remember? Or are you eager for people to know that I'm wrecking you?"

I'm panting already, close to the edge.

I'd be coming, if not for the tightness of the cock ring holding me back, despite the fact that I'm now hard as steel.

"Cruel," I whisper.

My hair is damp with sweat.

I'm humping my hips, unable to stop myself.

"Your toy is ready for you." D'Angelo glances significantly down at my cock like it's a dildo.

When Robyn licks her lips, I can't imagine anything better than being enveloped by the warmth of her pussy.

Unless it was to be allowed to tongue it first.

"The cock ring will stimulate your clit with vibrations as well." D'Angelo draws a single finger over my balls. I bite my lip hard enough that I'm sure it's bleeding to stop myself crying out. "When you ride him, you'll both have earth shattering orgasms, cara mia. But this time, you won't scream. You'll gift me your silence."

"I'll try." Robyn looks determined.

Eden grabs Robyn by the waist, maneuvering her around, until she's straddling my hips.

My brother's arms are looped around Robyn. He kisses down her neck.

In turn, D'Angelo kisses me.

Yet he's looking at Eden, when he orders, "Fuck her."

I truly am the toy caught between the three of them.

Eden nods curtly, lifting Robyn onto me.

When I stuff my hand into my mouth to stifle my moan at the sensation of Robyn sinking onto my cock, D'Angelo tuts.

"Don't hurt yourself. Only I can hurt you." D'Angelo pulls my hand from my mouth, soothing over the bite marks with his thumb.

Something about *only I can hurt you* pushes me even closer to the edge.

I shiver, thrusting up to meet Robyn, as Eden lifts her up and down on me.

I can't see where I'm spearing her because of her long dress, which flows over me like I'm lying in a poppy field. The bedding around me is the sky.

In a daze, I realize that I'm the only one who is naked in this bed. But it doesn't feel wrong.

Robyn looks bloody beautiful with her hair tangling over her shoulders, and her head thrown back in ecstasy. D'Angelo is playing with her tits, thumbing across one and then the other.

She's blissed out, shaking from the effort of not making a sound, as much as I am.

"P-p-please," Robyn whimpers.

It's too much.

My hands clutch in the bedding. My knuckles are white.

I need to moan. Scream. *Fucking come.*

Robyn's gaze locks onto mine.

"Shay…" She whispers.

"Love." I smile, although there are tears on my cheeks.

"Come whenever you want to," D'Angelo says, softly. "*Silently*."

And I do.

I didn't think that it was possible while wearing the cock ring, but the vibrations drag it from me.

It's agonizing. Intense. *Incredible.*

Overwhelmed by sensation, I'm desperate to howl my pleasure.

But I can't.

Somehow, having to keep it inside because what we're doing is secret, forbidden, would otherwise be discovered by strangers, makes it a hundred…thousand…times stronger.

I throw my head back and see stars.

It's the longest orgasm of my bloody life.

It pulls Robyn into one above me.

Eden allows Robyn to fall forward onto me. She muffles her cry on my shoulder. I wrap my arms around her in support, as she shakes

For a long moment, I lie in shock.

Then my oversensitive dick begins to fucking hurt. "Turn it off. Bloody hell, turn it off."

D'Angelo chuckles. "That's hard, when you still have a woman attached to you."

"Sorry." Robyn scrambles off me, and Eden pulls her onto his chest. "Wow."

"How are you all? I'm certainly more relaxed." D'Angelo switches the button.

When the vibrations stop, I slump.

"I am now." I'm half-asleep, as Robyn reaches over and

plays with my hair.

I scooch closer to her, taking her hand in mine.

"That was amazing." Robyn smiles. "Can we do that again?"

"Perhaps not tonight, love." I yawn. "Unless you enjoy somnophilia. In which case, you have my permission to go for it."

Robyn closes her eyes. "I was the one sleeping in the first place."

"No sleeping, until you've done your teeth and are dressed for bed," Eden chides.

D'Angelo pulls the cock ring apart and carefully removes it, before taking the condom off me. "I'll dispose of the evidence."

When he stands, however, his phone vibrates.

He sighs. "Work never ends."

When D'Angelo takes out his phone and reads the message, however, he pales.

Worried, I snap awake, pushing myself up on my elbows. "What is it?"

"Another one of those messages." D'Angelo looks grim. "How did they get my new number?"

Dread churns in my guts.

Good bloody question.

"What does it say?" Robyn demands.

"It's a threat." D'Angelo taps on the screen three times in his anxiety. "It reads, *Truth: What's your greatest fear? Or Dare: Post a dance on social media, wearing the Bay Rebels logo. Play the game, then text me the evidence.*"

CHAPTER NINETEEN

Campsite, New Mexico

Eden

Why would anyone play truth or dare?

Isn't it choosing to make yourself vulnerable and humiliated?

It's handing a knife to a roomful of strangers and then offering your throat to them to be slit.

Do people play that as a *game*?

My brow furrows in confusion.

"Look at that sunset. It's as if the lake and mountains have been set on fire." Shay lies on his back. His face is soft with wonder. "I love this wilderness camping shit. New Mexico is bloody brilliant."

"Good pick for the campsite." Robyn smiles at me.

"It certainly is. Plus, this second day of driving was smooth with the route that you chose, Eden. The timings are working out." D'Angelo relaxes on a wooden log next to Shay.

D'Angelo's pride in me makes the flare of pain down my side from being unable to move around all day insignificant.

Pain is nothing. I can handle it.

But D'Angelo's approval is everything.

He's given me control over this journey. I never thought that a boss would believe in me.

I've spent my life in my brother's shadow, being scolded and punished because I wasn't as smart, talented, or socially capable as him by teachers, professionals, or coaches.

D'Angelo is different.

He sees and understands me.

He doesn't want me to change.

He praises me when I've earned it.

Now, I feel like I'm my own man.

D'Angelo is sharing his long, woolen coat against the cool of the evening with Robyn, who's perched next to him.

Robyn appears tired but as excited as Shay to be camping.

I'm sitting on the other side of the fire, which is surrounded by pine trees beside the lake.

The evening is filled with the gentle sounds of wildlife.

I feel most at home in the forest.

At peace.

Safe.

Tomorrow, we'll be returning to civilization and the overwhelming noise and crowds.

It's going to be tough to cope with.

I'll withdraw into myself.

But tonight, I can relax and enjoy being outside with the people who have become my family.

I wrinkle my nose at the smoky scent of the fire, which is made sweeter by the marshmallow that I'm roasting over it on a stick.

Robyn insisted that it was *traditional*.

Transfixed, I watch the embers dance.

It only takes a single, tiny spark to start a fire.

"Are we simply going to ignore the whole truth or dare thing?" Robyn's question jerks me away from the spell of the flames. "It's freaking me out. We've avoided the press successfully, and Dad called earlier to tell me that the other players and staff are doing fine. But those messages are…"

"A mindfuck." D'Angelo sighs. "The problem is that we all have enemies in our past who'd want to shake us up."

"Nemeses." Shay pillows his head on his arms. "It sounds like we should be saving the world or something."

"Perhaps, we should concentrate on saving our asses first." Robyn's lips thin. "Whoever they are could want to distract us before these games. So, I say that we don't give them the satisfaction."

"Agreed." I lean forward to turn and then remove the marshmallow from the fire, wincing as my ribs protest.

"Do you need your meds?" Robyn asks. "Cody will kick our asses, if we turn up with you at the arena in a worse state than we set out."

"I'm doing my exercises. I'm fine." I'm not ruining our first night camping with my shit.

Cody is the first person to want to talk to me and not my twin. I don't want him to be angry with me and take back his offer to show me the seals that bask near his cottage.

"You're not," Shay points out.

I ignore him. "Here."

I pass the first toasted marshmallow to Robyn. It's a gooey mess, but she claps her hands in delight.

It's my first attempt.

This is new to me but it feels right in a way that little does in my life.

I raise my eyebrow at D'Angelo.

He wrinkles his nose. "Not for me. I don't wear designer clothes in order to smear…" He watches in horror the way that Robyn is waving her gooey treat dangerously close to his coat. "…although, it may be a lost cause anyway."

"My clothes aren't worth fuck all," Shay says, cheerily. "So, load me up with melted sugar on a stick, until I'm sick."

"You can have two," I say, firmly, pushing the marshmallows onto a stick and then beginning to toast them over the fire.

Shay's happiness isn't dimmed. "I've always wanted to go camping. Thanks for this, bro."

I remember.

In our first year at high school, the whole class went on a camping trip, apart from Shay and me.

Shay begged our parents in tears to be allowed to go for an entire weekend.

But they couldn't afford it.

I sat in my room, glad that I couldn't speak because then I didn't need to tell them that *I* didn't want to go.

I couldn't.

The thought of being alone with all those new kids outside the classroom (kids who acted like I didn't exist), was enough to tip me into panic attack.

I swallow. My throat feels thick with guilt. My words are caught in it.

Silently, I hold out the sweet smelling toasted marshmallows to my brother.

Shay sits up, taking the stick from me. "This is fantastic. A campfire and marshmallows. All we need now are ghost stories."

"Ghost stories?" D'Angelo looks panicked.

Shay nibbles on his marshmallows. "That's what people do, isn't it? I mean, in the movies."

"In the horror movies, if they want to *die* screaming two minutes later," D'Angelo points out.

I ease my arm around my middle, settling back. I let the evening wash over me.

"I've never sat around like this." I can hear the longing in Shay's voice. "Couldn't I tell you a story from London?

Plus, there must be hundreds of spooky stories from Freedom."

"What a surprise that you want to scare us." D'Angelo quirks his brow.

"*Be* scared, darlin', " Shay counters.

"Oh, I have one." Robyn leans in closer to the fire. The light dances across her face. She looks fucking beautiful. "Who wants to hear the terrifying tale of Freedom's haunted road?"

"Pass." D'Angelo grimaces.

"Outvoted." Shay crawls closer to Robyn, sitting at her feet like an eager disciple. "What's the story, love?"

I watch the way that Robyn lays her hand on Shay's head.

She's telling this tale for his sake.

I love her for that…for giving him this.

What he missed.

"Be careful, if you drive your Harley on the coastal road that leads out of town," Robyn whispers, dramatically.

D'Angelo rolls his eyes.

Shay tips up his head, however, and his gaze is fixed intently on Robyn, drinking in every word that she says.

"Why?" Shay's breathing faster.

"Because of the old bridge." Robyn's gaze now sweeps to me with a wink. "You should avoid driving under it, unless…"

She lets the word hang there in the night.

My skin goosebumps.

"What?" D'Angelo demands.

My lips twitch.

He's as caught as Shay is in the story, despite himself.

"Unless you want to meet the dead who haunt it," Robyn replies in a hushed whisper. "Like the group of friends who took the risk one night and…"

"Yes?" Shay's eyes are wide.

"When they returned to town, they were half-crazed with wild stories of creatures with red eyes. Their car windows were fogged and covered in bizarre handprints."

Shay shudders. "As soon as we're back, I'm driving to that bridge."

Robyn sits back with a huff. "That's not the point of the story."

"If we told our little thrill seeker here that a mountain was the deadliest in the world, he'd still climb it," D'Angelo grumbles.

"It depends what was at the top." Shay grins. "Now, if it meant getting to any of you three, then of course I would."

"How reckless but romantic." Robyn exchanges a glance with D'Angelo, then they both snatch Shay by the shoulders and hold him still, as they kiss over his face, until they're all laughing.

This is what I wanted.

Hoped for.

My brother's happiness makes me happy. I could survive on it alone.

Shay turns his head to me, giggling. "Save me."

"I'm too comfortable." I relax further next to the warmth of the fire.

Perhaps, I could spend some weekends like this in the forest at Captain's Hall, sleeping beneath the open sky.

My wild squirrel, Puck, could sleep next to me.

Shay gasps in mock outrage. "So much for the Circle of Twins."

"You can escape our clutches by telling us a ghost story from London," Robyn offers.

"Deal." Shay struggles away from his kissing attackers to kneel by the fire. He looks set to act out his story for us. "How about I tell you one of London's darkest urban legends? Trust me, London has a lot, and fuck me, they're dark. In Epping Forest there's a pool. But it's no ordinary pool because this one murders people. Parents warn their kiddies, don't sneak out at night into the woods because the waters may swallow you."

"That's not real." D'Angelo is pale.

"It is," I reply.

No urban legend is *true*. But this one exists.

I love myths and legends. I've studied them.

And this one is fascinating.

Shay points at D'Angelo. "A doubter. Well, that's what the poor teenagers thought who ended up being drawn towards it and then drowned in its murky depths. You see, three hundred years ago a couple fell deeply in forbidden love and met to fuck at the side of this beautiful pond. But the woman's bastard of a dad found out and murdered her, right there. Then the bloke killed himself in despair."

"That's so sad," Robyn says. "Just because their dad didn't agree with the relationship."

D'Angelo looks away.

Shay pushes his hair back from his face. "The supernatural world must have thought so too because the water of that pool became inky black. The wildlife died. Look it up. Many people have been killed at its edges—"

D'Angelo claps his hands together once. "And that's enough trying to give your dom nightmares for a year. You're truly not scared of anything are you, cucciolo?"

Shay glances away. "Actually, I'm frightened of plenty."

"What's your greatest fear?" I blurt. "Your *nightmare*? Why would the person behind the text want you to face it?"

D'Angelo's piercing stare meets mine. "I don't know nor do I care. I don't hand psychos my own knife to gut me with. Why would I talk about something like that?"

I find it hard enough to make any words crawl from my throat.

But fears? Weaknesses?

My worst nightmares?

I understand why this is hard for D'Angelo.

"I trust you with all of myself." To my surprise, Robyn's expression becomes determined. "My greatest fear is that I'll lose the people who I love just like I did Mom."

"Cara mia." D'Angelo pulls Robyn closer against his side.

Instantly, Shay launches himself forward to wrap his arms around Robyn's legs. He rests his head on her lap, kissing her thigh in comfort.

Robyn cards her fingers through Shay's hair.

I study Robyn in confusion.

How did she simply voice it like that?

She made it look easy.

I clench my hands.

Nothing has happened. She's been surrounded by love and support. She's survived saying those words out loud.

I clear my throat, forcing myself to sit up.

The fire crackles loudly in the quiet. The smoke stings my eyes.

If Robyn can do it, then I can try.

"My greatest fear," I stare into the fire, hearing Shay's sharp intake of breath but focusing on the dancing flames, "is that Shay and I are still trapped in the Room. Or I died there. I'm not sure. And none of this is real. *I'm not.*"

Silence.

I don't dare to look up from the fire.

"Dee," Shay sounds shattered. "Please, look at me."

I can't.

Fuck.

I shouldn't have said it out loud.

I've kept it inside all these years.

I should have fucking known that it was a mistake to let it past my lips.

It's one of those things that you're not meant to say like how I don't feel human, I don't understand what people are feeling most of the time, or how often I fantasize about finding the couple who locked Shay and me up and burning them to ash.

What have I done?

"I didn't mean that," I say, hurriedly.

"Don't lie." Shay's voice is funny like he's crying.

"There's not a wrong way to feel. Sometimes, I have nightmares that I'm back in the Room too. One of the reasons that I don't sleep well is a fear that I won't wake up…here…but instead, back there."

This startles me enough to look up at my brother.

Robyn and D'Angelo both have their hands on Shay's shoulders in comfort.

Tears glimmer in Shay's eyes. Lit by the fire's light, they look like stars.

Perhaps, this is something that you *can* admit, if Shay can.

When I glance at Robyn, she gives me a reassuring smile.

It steels me, freeing my words further. "It's safer not to be seen because then you don't need to risk being rejected. But at college…" Shit, am I truly going to tell them this? Even Shay doesn't know about it. Shay stares at me, anguished. "In the first few weeks, I didn't want to let my brother down by being unable to make a single friend. But I didn't understand how to be…a real person. I wasn't sure that I was one. So, I studied a popular man on the hockey team who made it look easy."

My gaze slides away and up to the watchful night sky.

"You don't need to tell us this," D'Angelo says. "But you're surrounded by true friends now. People who love and care about you. I promise you this, Eden Prince, you're the most *real* person I know."

Shocked, my gaze shoots to D'Angelo's.

His expression is open and sincere.

It sparks a sensation inside me that I haven't experienced before, *of belonging*.

I'm no longer locked up. My words aren't caged. *I'm free.*

"I analyzed how this man smiled, made up nicknames for everyone on the team, even the designer socks that he wore for luck on game nights," I continue.

Shay's brow furrows. "Wait, I remember you saving for designer socks. They cost more than anything you owned. You were sort of obsessed about it. But then, after a couple of weeks, you threw them in the trash."

"When I was alone, I mimicked him in the mirror." The tips of my ears redden, but I force myself to tell the truth. "Then one day, I decided to risk it and copy him in public. I waited until Shay was talking to coach on the ice, then strolled up to the man's group of friends in the locker room." I shudder. So, this is what public humiliation feels like. Hot and sickening. I'd almost forgotten. "But instead of accepting me like they did him, they slammed me against the lockers. Later, I told Shay that I got the bruises from practice. They called me the *loser twin*. *They laughed at me.* They demanded to know *why I was smiling like a freak?*"

"Assholes," Robyn growls.

"I never tried to make a friend again. Because it was my own fault for thinking that I could be likable. I thought that if I only copied somebody, I could be. But that's when I realized people saw through it. It wasn't real. My emotions weren't. *I wasn't.*"

Shay crawls across the dirt to throw his arms around me.

He's shaking.

"Why didn't you tell me, Dee?" Shay whispers.

"You were having a good time at college. I didn't want to spoil it."

"I wasn't. I was with Blythe."

"Then why didn't you tell me about *her*?"

"We're both idiots," Shay says through his tears. "No more secrets."

I nod.

Then I yelp, when Shay yanks my hair. "Does that feel real enough? I can pinch your ass to prove it too."

"I'm convinced."

"I'll pinch it too," Robyn adds. "I'll do it every day, if I need to." That's not a deterrent coming from Robyn. "And I love your smile. I live for it. Don't listen to people who try to make you feel small, only because they are. You don't need to try and be like anyone else. The man who I see in front of me right now is talented, gorgeous, and not only likable but fucking *lovable*."

When Robyn says it, I feel like maybe it could be true.

When D'Angelo's phone vibrates, I stiffen at the same time as he does.

Shay disentangles himself from me, careful of my sling.

He sits next to me with his head on my shoulder like he used to do when we were younger.

"Don't look at the message," Robyn pleads.

"I can't ignore it, in case it's from coach." D'Angelo drags out his phone, reluctantly.

"What's it say?" Robyn chews on her nail.

"One word." D'Angelo's eyes flash. *"Choose."*

"And now we're in a *Ghostbusters* film." Shay glances around at the shadowy trees. "I better not be tempting fate, but unless there are hidden snipers, the bastard behind those texts can't force you."

"But what does it mean?" Robyn hugs her arms around herself.

"Nothing good." D'Angelo slips off his coat, draping it fully around Robyn.

Then he stands, shaking out his arms.

"What are you doing?" Robyn demands.

"They want a dancing hockey player, then they can have one." D'Angelo wrenches off his jacket, tossing it over the log. "I'm accepting the dare. We have no idea if this text harasser is Wilder, Melanie, Blythe, a journalist or any number of disgruntled friends, enemies, or players from our pasts. Right now, I don't give a fuck. You three are my priority. This is directed at me, and I won't risk it impacting on anyone else. I've made promises to keep you safe and I'm keeping them. If I need to look like a dancing dumbass online to do that, then so be it."

And that's why D'Angelo is my friend, boss, and fucking hero.

"This is a mistake," Robyn insists.

Yet D'Angelo holds up his phone and records live as evidence the most furious dance under the moonlight that I've ever seen or imagined.

Shay watches him, spellbound.

D'Angelo looks like a war god, celebrating a victory.

Then he switches off his phone; he's breathing hard. "There. Done. That's the end of it."

"It's not." I throw a stick onto the fire, and the flames flare up. "Now, you've told them that the game has just begun."

CHAPTER TWENTY

The Rose Palace, San Jose

obyn

My head's throbbing, and my nose feels stuffy. My throat is sore enough to make me wonder whether I've been drinking shattered glass, rather than water on the long journey from New Mexico to San Jose.

I can't go down with something now.

I have a feeling that the battle both on and off the ice is about to begin.

The PR Director who's holding up the shield can't also be holding up a tissue in front of their streaming nose, while bent over with a hacking cough.

In his typical captain of the motorhome manner, D'Angelo was determined to make it to San Jose in a single day. His goal was to give us Monday off, before the first game on Tuesday.

It's been an epic drive through the day and night into the early hours.

The only bright side has been Shay and Eden's excitement with every new state that we passed through. Watching the twins' faces, as they stared out of the windows at the mountains, lakes, and forests, has been a special and beautiful experience.

I understand D'Angelo's urge to provide the brothers with as many experiences like this as he can.

I simply want to make them feel loved.

And to help them believe that they can be.

Seeing their happiness, while Eden took photographs for the Bay Rebels social media account, was enough to make me forget Dad's warnings about his past.

But now, with my temples throbbing, it's all rushing back.

"What a shame that the hotel only has one room available," D'Angelo deadpans like any of us will believe that lie. How can he look immaculate in his pinstriped suit at 2 a.m. in the morning, while I'm a hot mess in a borrowed **LIFE IS BETTER WITH TEA, CATS, AND BOOKS** sweater from Eden and stained joggers? "We'll be forced to share. I signed us in under a false name."

I glance around the opulent corridor with white walls and high ceilings. "What?"

D'Angelo smirks. "Mr. R. Ebel."

"How could anybody crack that code? Leave the aliases to me next time." Shay almost topples over under the weight of our bags.

I take mine from him.

"Thanks, love." Shay shoots me a smile.

Eden trails behind us.

He's trying not to show it but he's stumbling with exhaustion. He's squinting in the light, which I know by now means that his head must be hurting as much as mine is.

"Luckily, The Rose Palace is run by a friend of a friend of a…you get the idea." D'Angelo leads us to an arched oak door. "The press won't find us in this oasis."

"Discrete, right?" Shay asks, lugging the bags under his arms.

"Do you know *everybody* through this kink network of yours?" I quirk my brow.

"Wouldn't you like to know?" D'Angelo whispers. "You'd be surprised how many celebrities and public people use the same *discretion* that I do."

I bounce on my toes, alight with curiosity. "I need names."

"And you're not getting them, principessa, because we protect each other. We don't share names, allow photographs of events, or talk about how people in the community identify. We care and look out for each other. Because nobody else is going to, and unfortunately, there are assholes out there who'd tear us apart simply for being who we were born to be."

I stroke the back of my hand down D'Angelo's sharp

cheekbone. "I hope that one day, I'll meet some of your trusted friends. I love that you've had people in your life to support you, when I wasn't there."

D'Angelo's expression gentles. "I'd like that to."

Then he twists away from me to face the door with a flourish, unlocking it with an old-fashioned, antique gold key on a tassel. "Who's ready for some pampering?"

"Fuck, yeah," I mutter.

Motorhomes sound fun, until you're stuck in a tiny space with Shay, the hyper puppy who bounces off the walls after sitting still for only a couple of minutes.

Try three days and nights...

D'Angelo pushes open the door and stalks inside.

Relieved to have finally reached an actual hotel room, I stumble into the brightly lit room after him, along with Shay and Eden.

Behind me, Shay whistles.

He spins on the spot, looking around himself in amazement.

I've been in a lot of luxury hotels. Wilder loved to travel in style, although I often felt as much a part of his baggage as his suitcases or hockey gear.

Yet this suite is staggeringly beautiful.

It's in Spanish Colonial Revival style with large, white pointed arches, high wooden columns, and a beamed oak ceiling.

The wooden columns are entwined with golden roses and thorns.

Dusky rose drapes are pulled open to reveal a stunning view over San Jose and rolling hills.

A four-poster bed in matching pink to the drapes has been covered in cushions that look like flowering roses. To the other side of the room are velvet couches and antique armchairs.

The elegant, claw-foot bath is open to the bedroom on a raised alcove through an archway.

"There's no way that Bay Rebels is footing the bill for this." I wander to a velvet, dusky pink couch and collapse onto it.

Shit, it's soft.

"They're not." D'Angelo adjusts his cufflinks three times. "I am."

Eden clutches his side as he slowly makes his way to join me on the couch.

He looks at me for a long moment. "Are you feeling okay?"

Hundred percent not.

"Fine and dandy." Why the hell did I say that?

I don't even believe it myself.

Eden gives me an even longer look.

I'm overly aware of the sweat beads glistening on my forehead.

Shay shakes his head. "This is too much. It's *literally* called a palace. Do you think that it looks like this in Buckingham Palace, Dee? Don't you reckon that we're true English princes now?"

Eden takes out his phone and begins to scroll through the photographs that he's taken on the trip.

Shay twists to D'Angelo, smiling. "Thanks, darlin'. I mean that. Robyn and you have made this whole trip incredible for us. I'm never going to forget it."

"Despite the broken television." D'Angelo narrows his eyes.

Shay doesn't look repentant. "Playing catch inside the RV wasn't my best decision, but you're the one who fumbled."

"Next time, give me more warning than yelling *catch*."

"Got it." Shay animatedly darts around the room, examining the floor to ceiling potted plants and complimentary fruit basket.

Feverish, I rub my hand across my head.

I'm sweating.

I swallow with difficulty.

Shit, my throat is sore.

My eyes feel gritty.

D'Angelo shrugs out of his jacket, throwing it over the end of the bed. "You deserve this treat. You've earned it after being stuck in the RV for such a long drive. We have one day and night to spend together, before tomorrow's game. We can relax and enjoy it."

As long as the truth or dare asshole leaves us alone.

I know that D'Angelo is deliberately not saying that.

Perhaps, D'Angelo's dance was enough to satisfy the jerk.

Except, I don't think so. Especially when I pull my phone out of my pocket and scan the social media and memes that I'm trying to protect D'Angelo from seeing.

Eden was right yesterday.

By playing along, D'Angelo showed that he was willing to engage.

Unfortunately, the strategy has already backfired.

Every time that a celebrity makes an appearance, or releases a photograph, post, or statement, it has a brand impact on them.

I've been working hard on improving all these men's image, since I started working at Bay Rebels.

It's effective.

Eden's photographs, for example, on the Bay Rebels' fan pages have humanized both Shay and D'Angelo.

I'm certain that the sun-drenched ones of them looking playful and beautiful (Shay), or commanding and determined (D'Angelo), as they make their way to the away games, will build the hype and fan base.

How can you not fall in love with the captain and star player, when you see them looking like that?

Except, the dance was a misstep.

One journalist ran with the headline: The Puck Off Dance from the Puck Boy.

From that moment, it became known to everybody as the *Puck Off Dance*.

There have been parodies by other teams and fans.

Worse are the comments from people who would never say such hateful things to someone's face but are emboldened behind a keyboard.

They're telling D'Angelo to never play ice hockey again, to harm himself, or even that they're going to kill him.

The security team are now having to work doubly hard to comb through the comments in case any are credible threats.

I never knew that a two second dance was a capital punishment worthy offense.

I wish that everybody online was forced to read their comments aloud to their victims' faces — just once.

Although, many of these haters are bots. How weird it is not to be able to tell how much of this rage and division online isn't real?

It's easier not to allow yourself to type angry responses back, when you remember that.

Eden is fucking real, however, and it's a huge step that he feels safe enough with us to open up.

I exchange a glance with Eden, as he notices the page that I'm on.

Eden's expression shutters. He glances at D'Angelo.

Then he looks back at me and shakes his head.

I understand, turning off my phone and slipping it into my pocket.

D'Angelo has driven the entire journey. He deserves this night off without knowing the dumpster fire that this whole situation has already become.

Shay continues to explore the room, ducking down to swing open a fridge. "Wow, look at this minibar. Can I raid it?"

Eden pushes his own phone back into his pocket. "It's too expensive."

"I'm paying. You can have anything you want from there." D'Angelo removes his cufflinks, laying them on the nightstand. "Room service too. Then can everyone calm down, so that we can get some sleep? I'm exhausted."

"Brilliant." Shay rummages in the fridge. "Shit, there's

everything in here. Beer, wine, crackers, nuts, and Michael would be over the moon, bloody hummus too."

"Is there any bottled water? I'd like…" I break off, as my wheezing turns into a coughing fit.

Startled, Eden wraps his arms around me.

D'Angelo strides across the room. "Are you unwell?"

I hold my hand across my mouth, coughing weakly.

My muscles ache. I suddenly feel very tired.

"I feel like hell," I admit.

Eden helps me to sit up, before resting his hand on my forehead. "She has a temperature."

"I'm calling a doctor." D'Angelo's jaw is clenched.

"I'm not dying," I protest.

Eden stiffens.

"Then I'm calling Mike," D'Angelo insists.

"Woah, hold up." I battle against the roar in my ears to focus on D'Angelo. "Mike *is* a doctor, one who should be sleeping at this time of night. One who only manages to grab a couple of hours of sleep each night as it is. Plus, if we wake him up with a phone call at this time, then he'll have a coronary, thinking that it's an emergency about Code. I don't want to do that to him, especially when this is the first time that those two have been apart since their wedding."

D'Angelo looks like he's going to battle with me over this being an *emergency*, before finally, he prowls back to the bed. He snatches up his jacket. "It's your choice. But don't expect us not to worry."

"You should have your minds on the game."

"You're more important than hockey."

My breath catches.

Before these men, I've lived surrounded by hockey and no one has put me above the game.

"Where are you going?" My chest tightens, as I watch D'Angelo make to the door like he intends to leave.

My eyes smart with tears.

Is he going to abandon me, until I'm well again?

"I'm going down to reception to order you chicken soup, also honey for your throat. Then I'll ask for directions to a twenty-four hour pharmacy to buy you whatever the best medicines are to help get that fever down." D'Angelo swings open the door. He glances over his shoulder. "And you're going to drink that water, then go to sleep and get some rest. I'll look after you, when I get back. I promise, you'll feel better soon."

Despite feeling like a furnace, I smile, as D'Angelo leaves.

Because I trust that he's coming back.

Shay grabs a bottle of water, before rushing across the room to the couch.

He kneels in front of me, holding the bottle to my forehead. It's coolness is like a balm.

I sigh, relaxing into its touch, before he rolls it across my face and then to my neck.

"What about if I run you a cool bath?" Shay offers. "It'd get your temperature down, while we wait for the medicine."

I nod.

It feels good to be surrounded by three men who are concentrated on making me feel better.

When I was married to Wilder, he hated it when I was sick.

He'd wrinkle up his nose in distaste, poking his nose in the bedroom to check how I was each morning but keeping his distance in case he caught anything.

I wouldn't see him apart from that because he said that he couldn't risk getting sick and missing games.

I became used to dragging myself through illness and injury.

Yet these men are only concerned with making sure that I feel better.

Shay exchanges a glance with Eden.

The twins are vibrating with worry.

Shay passes me the water and stands. He moves through the archway to the raised alcove. Then he turns on the taps, and water gushes into the claw-foot bath.

I bury my nose in my sweater, loving that it smells of Eden, sweetly vanilla.

Then I pull off the cap of the bottle and take a satisfying swig of the cool water.

When I finish drinking as much as I can, Eden takes the bottle from me and puts it down. Then he gently strips me, folding each item and putting it onto the floor.

I'm shivering, chilled.

Shit, I really am ill.

"She shouldn't take a cool bath in this state." Eden's brow furrows. "Make it lukewarm, then wet a sponge."

"You get our Robyn into bed. She looks half-asleep now." Shay leans over to grab one of the rose shaped sponges and dip it into the water.

Eden stands at the same time as me, holding me steady by the elbow.

My vision blurs.

Eden sweeps me up into his arms and carries me to the bed.

My teeth are chattering. My cheeks are flushed. My eyes are glassy.

Eden pulls a light sheet over me, which smells fragrant and floral. Shay bounds onto the bed and crawls next to me.

Two sets of matching beautiful gray eyes look down at me.

Someone grasps my hand.

The feel of the sponge, as it drags lightly over my forehead, then down my neck and collarbone, is like heaven.

"Robyn," a voice calls, fearfully.

Then everything fades to black.

CHAPTER TWENTY-ONE

The Rose Palace, San Jose

*hay*

I LIE next to Robyn on the luxurious bed in The Rose Palace hotel suite.

I'm exhausted but I don't look away from her still face. I haven't, since D'Angelo carried her here almost twelve hours ago.

A deep dread claws at my insides that if I do, then she'll die.

I can't bear to see her like this.

I need her brightness, laughter, *life*.

My hands shake, as I brush her hair.

I'm wearing the silk black pajamas that D'Angelo bought me. I wasn't going to change, but after a couple of hours, D'Angelo insisted that I did.

I was too hyped up and jittery to do it myself. I couldn't even undo the button on my jeans, my fingers were shaking so much.

D'Angelo calmly but firmly stripped me, therefore, and put these pajamas on me himself.

D'Angelo's still dressed in his suit, even if it's creased. His hair is a mess because he's run his fingers through it so many times.

I know that Robyn's only sleeping, unwell with fever.

The private doctor that D'Angelo hired checked her out.

This situation is a fucking trigger for me, however, and I can't control my reaction.

Eden is lying on the other side of Robyn.

He's sprawled on top of the dusky pink bedding in his joggers.

He hasn't slept either.

There are deep shadows underneath his eyes, and he grimaces like he's holding back showing just how much pain he's in.

When he catches my gaze, I can tell that he understands my anxiety.

Eden lays his palm on Robyn's chest over her heart. "It's still beating."

I drop the brush on the nightstand, avoiding his gaze.

Dee, Dee, don't close your eyes. What if you don't wake up and leave me alone with the monsters?

As kids, every time that Eden was hurt, ill, or starving and would pass out, I'd desperately shake him and say that.

For years, I could only sleep by lying with my head on his chest, listening to the rhythm of his heartbeat.

I had to know that he was still alive.

I glance at D'Angelo, who's leaning pensively against the wall next to the archway through to the bath, talking quietly to Cody.

Of course D'Angelo ignored Robyn and called Michael.

Despite being woken from deep sleep and initially panicking that Cody was either in hospital or jail, Michael calmed down and gave us some medical advice, as well as the name of a good private doctor in the area.

I wanted to take Robyn to hospital, but Michael said that it was better to let her rest and be cared for where she was.

After all, she had *three* private nurses.

Perhaps, we should have hired nurse outfits to wear as a nice surprise to cheer her up.

I'd love to see D'Angelo in one.

Actually, she has *four* nurses, since Michael called his husband, and Cody caught a taxi from across the city and the staff hotel immediately.

Cody looks as worried as the rest of us.

Suddenly, Robyn's eyelashes begin to flutter.

"She's waking up," I say, excitedly.

D'Angelo straightens.

Eden sits up, adjusting the sheet around Robyn.

Robyn's hair is damp. Sweat trickles down her neck.

Eden has changed her into one of his long t-shirts, which has the picture of a puffball of a kitten on the front under the words **FLUFF AND FIND OUT**, to keep her cool.

Robyn turns her head toward me like a wild flower searching out the sun.

When her wide, emerald eyes meet mine, my heart bloody melts.

"Shay...?" Robyn's voice is raspy.

"You're awake." I kiss her forehead. "You're cooler than you were."

"You didn't leave." Why does she sound surprised?

"Of course we bloody didn't. You need us," I whisper against her heated skin. "Don't worry, love, we'll always keep you safe."

She reaches out and takes my hand, entangling our fingers.

Shit, her touch feels brilliant.

Her life.

"Eden." Robyn turns to my brother, but a cough catches in her throat.

"Don't talk yet." D'Angelo's voice is guarded. "Your throat is still sore."

"Drink." Eden reaches for a warm honey tea that he's mixed the medicine into, which the doctor prescribed for us to give her, in order to make it taste less nasty. I smile, remembering that he'd do the same for me at college. "Medicine."

I assist Robyn to sit up.

Eden gently lifts the mug to Robyn's lips and helps her to drink.

Robyn looks weak but better than she has since we entered the hotel.

Cody bounds to sit cross-legged on the end of the bed. "It's good to see you awake, Ryn. I've been worried. Still, this hotel is luxurious. You should see the place that us staff have been stuffed into. FYI, I'm stealing your fruit basket for them." He tuts. "I can't leave you alone with these three for a single journey, huh?"

I freeze.

Guilt slams through me.

D'Angelo looks stricken, before his face smooths into a cold mask. "I should have taken better care of my principessa. Coach can bust my balls about that, when we see him. I pushed her too hard. Pushed everybody because I—"

"Woah, I was kidding." Cody glances between us. "Protective as I am of my sis, even I can't battle a virus. Mike says that he spoke with the doctor himself, and Ryn's fine. She'll be feeling okay in a couple of days."

"You called Mike." Robyn pushes away the medicine, staring accusingly at D'Angelo.

D'Angelo fiddles with his cufflinks. "Circumstances changed."

"Cheat."

"Creative thinker."

"Did Mike have a coronary?"

"Is this a list of things that begin with 'c'?" I ask. "In which case, *cock*."

Eden gives me a disapproving look.

"Mike better not have had *cock*, since I'm not with him," Cody chips in. "But he had as close to a coronary as it's possible for him to have, seeing as he never panics. He rang me up straight after to check on me. He gave this awesome romantic speech. He thought something terrible had happened to me. I have a feeling that I'm going to be showered with kisses and possessive love the moment that I return home."

"It's great that my illness has a silver lining for you." Robyn sniffs, loudly. "Now, what's wrong with me?"

"A virus," Cody explains. "You wouldn't feel so shit right now, if you'd used the scale that I gave Eden earlier, rather than pushing through your limits."

"Mean," Robyn mutters.

"Professional," Cody replies, "as well as caring brother. You have a virus, coupled with lack of sleep, and dehydration."

Robyn coughs. "Thanks for coming to be with me, Code."

"Hey, where else would I be, when you're sick?"

Eden places the mug back on the nightstand. "What matters is that she'll get better."

"It also matters how *you're* feeling." Cody looks at him, pointedly.

"I did the exercises." Eden meets Cody's gaze with a challenging air.

He sounds like he did at high school, when he was covering for reading his library books, rather than studying for a science test.

He's always been a terrible liar.

Cody hums, looking unconvinced. "What number are you?"

"Three," Eden replies in a determined way.

I know that he means: *This isn't about my shit, it's about Robyn, so I'll handle the pain.*

Cody settles closer to Robyn on the bed. "Tell me if you hit four."

I love the way that Cody sees through my brother's bullshit, ignores it, then insists that Eden cares for his own needs.

Robyn glances between us. "Have any of you slept?"

I quirk my brow. "No, but don't worry, insomniac here, love. Anyway, it gave me the chance to kick your brother's arse at Candy Crush."

Cody's eyes twinkle. "In your dreams."

Robyn's gaze becomes steely. "All of you in bed. Now."

Cody looks startled. "You're not well enough for an orgy, Ryn. I'd better call my husband. You're delirious and horny."

Robyn laughs, and fuck, it's incredible to hear that sound after her terrifying silence. "I meant to sleep. They have an important game tomorrow, and I'm not jeopardizing that. Imagine the headlines if they fall asleep on the ice."

"You're more important than a game, cara mia," D'Angelo replies, stubbornly.

"We can curl up in bed in a couple of hours." I stroke over Robyn's fingers. "We just want to know that you're getting better first, right?"

Eden lays the back of his hand across Robyn's forehead. "You're still too hot. The medicine should help bring down the fever in about half an hour." Eden catches Robyn's gaze, before his lips twitch. "Maybe you're an Omega going into heat."

D'Angelo snorts, but Robyn laughs.

"Is this my nest?" Robyn picks up a rose shaped cushion and weakly bats Eden with it.

I blink in confusion.

What is all this about Omegas, nests, and heats?

Sometimes, I think that Robyn and my twin have their own private language, which only they understand.

Eden and I had a secret way of communicating as kids.

I like that Eden has that with somebody else apart from me.

Yet does it mean that they have a deeper love than Robyn and I do? Will anyone truly love *me*, rather than simply want to use my body?

I'm grateful that someone as special as Robyn and D'Angelo want me to fit between them in their lives.

I can swallow the hurt that I know my own worth in the relationship. And it'll never be the same as my brother's.

"Help, where will I find an Alpha's knot in time…?" Robyn jokes.

I try not to show the pain the in-joke makes me feel.

Yet Eden's steady gaze sweeps over me, and I know that he notices.

Eden's an observer. He doesn't miss much, especially about me.

"Why don't we make a bet on these three away games?" Eden suggests.

My eyes widen at his sudden change of topic.

I know that it's for me. He's drawing me back into the conversation.

Cody rubs his hands together. "A bet. I'm listening. Also, as King of Bets, officiating."

Robyn shakes her head. "I'm out."

Eden tilts up his chin. "A bet between Shay and D'Angelo."

D'Angelo looks wary. "It depends. I'd never abuse my power, but this seems a good moment to remind you that I'm your boss."

Eden slicks back his hair. "*Boss*, the stakes are: Whoever scores the most goals, gets to choose their kink from our list once we're home."

Home.

It's powerful when Eden calls it that. I can see the way that it hits each of us.

"A kink contest rematch," I say, eagerly. "Every hockey team should use it for motivation. I'm in."

D'Angelo's shoulders finally relax, and his expression softens. "I accept. And I'm winning, cucciolo."

I smirk. "That's what you think, darlin'."

I have a kink on there that I really want to share with the others.

They have no idea how sexy I'd look in a bondage red corset with ribbons.

My smile widens at the image, at the same time that D'Angelo's smile becomes wicked like he's imagining a devilish scene.

Now, I don't know which of us I want to win.

I know what Eden is doing by raising this bet.

He's not merely letting me back into his private world with Robyn but he's distracting me — all of us — from worrying about Robyn.

But especially me.

Inside, I've been freaking out from the moment that Robyn became ill.

As kids, when Eden shivered with flu, wheezed because of bronchitis, or hurled from a concussion, his focus would still be on *me*.

He'd be checking was I okay? Sleeping? Being punished for school refusal because it terrified me to be apart from him, when he was ill?

Eden is the best brother in the bloody world.

But I know his secret.

He's just as freaked out as I am. He simply doesn't show it like I do.

But I can tell.

D'Angelo taps his thigh three times. "How are you feeling now, principessa?"

"My head hurts." Robyn scrunches up her nose. "So

does my throat and ears. But actually, better than I did before."

"Excellent."

When D'Angelo's phone rings, it's loud and breaks the peace that's woven like a cocoon around us.

D'Angelo frowns, pulling it out of his trouser pocket to answer. "What? Why are you phoning me? Well, that's because she's too sick to be answering her own phone, which is switched off. Take the hint."

"Who is it?" Robyn mouths.

D'Angelo's frown deepens. "Neve."

Perhaps, Neve and D'Angelo need to have an old-fashioned duel, possibly with dildos rather than swords, to get over their issues with each other.

Or possibly, it's a personality clash.

Asshole vs asshole.

That sounds either sexy or painful.

Robyn holds out her hand to D'Angelo.

D'Angelo stalks to the bed, sitting on the side next to Eden. Reluctantly, he passes over his phone to Robyn.

I lay my head on her shoulder, unrepentantly listening in on her conversation.

Robyn glances down at me, but I innocently look up at her through my lashes.

Robyn meets D'Angelo's glower. "Sorry about him, Neve, he turns into a Giant Grump, when I'm sick."

"Don't you mean Giant Dick?" Neve's tinny voice says on the other end.

I chuckle.

D'Angelo sends me a death glare, as if to ask what the joke is.

I don't share.

But still, *accurate*, as my poor arse can attest.

Robyn covers her mouth as she coughs. "He's been taking care of me. They all have."

"So, you're alive then," Neve says.

"Actually, you're talking to a ghost."

"D'Angelo drinks enough for this to be a spirit line," Neve replies. Now I'm glad that D'Angelo can't hear her. "What's up with your throat? You sound like you were over ambitious and attempted to deepthroat two of those giant dicks at the same time."

I stick my knuckles into my mouth to smother my laughter.

Robyn becomes even more flushed than she is with her fever. "My brother is just here."

"Say hi for me," Neve says, blithely.

"Neve says hi."

"Hi," Cody calls.

"Now, rest that sore throat of yours." Neve's voice softens. "Get well, RH. And the Bay Rebels had better kick ass in their game. I'm setting the television up in Merchant's Inn, so that everyone back here in Freedom can watch the game together."

"Thanks, Neve."

Robyn turns off the phone.

Her eyes look heavy.

"Do you want me to tuck you back to sleep, love?" I push a strand of hair away from her face.

She nods.

But then, the phone rings again.

Sighing, Robyn answers. "What do you want this time? To make another joke about blow jobs?"

There's a long silence.

Then a man's voice, which feels like it should be familiar to me but I can't place it, replies, "Actually, sweetheart, this isn't a joking matter."

"I'm s-sorry," Robyn blurts. "I thought that... I m-m-mean... Who is this?"

She slips the phone onto speakerphone.

"It's funny how people who are so important to you, don't even know who you are." The man's voice is tight with rage.

To my surprise, Cody scrambles to his knees.

He's pale, looking like he may vomit.

He gestures at D'Angelo like somehow D'Angelo is dominant enough to even bust the balls of a voice.

Instantly, D'Angelo is on the alert.

The man answers, "I'm Larry Gibbs, coach of—"

"The Ducks." Robyn's gaze shoots to Cody.

It feels like an entire conversation is passing between them in that look.

Why would a coach of another team be calling D'Angelo?

I glance at D'Angelo, but he shakes his head, as confused as I am.

He gestures for Robyn to take the call.

It's inappropriate for a coach of another team to be calling the captain of the Bay Rebels directly. Especially this close to a game.

It's not like they're friends outside hockey.

What the fuck does Gibbs want?

"As PR Director for the Bay Rebels, I take the players' calls," Robyn says, more diplomatically then I would have. "Or I could put you in touch with Mr. McKenna."

"Why would I want to talk to your *dad*," Gibbs' voice becomes low and dangerous. "The man who attacked me on the ice and ruined my career. The man who tried to kill me."

Cody and Robyn both hiss in a breath at the same time.

"That's it." D'Angelo tries to snatch the phone from Robyn, but she dodges, holding the phone more firmly against her ear.

I slip my arm around her shoulders in support.

Cody is trembling and trying not to show it.

Eden holds out his hand to Cody. "Come here."

Gratefully, Cody scrambles across Robyn to join us in the center of the bed. He grasps onto Eden's hand like it's a lifeline.

"Mr. Gibbs," Robyn says firmly, despite how croaky her voice is, "I know that my dad has a history with you. But that's in the past. Let's not add slander into the mix. Our teams are here to play each other. We need to be professional about it."

Gibb's laugh is bitter. "Was your dad professional, when he viciously attacked me on the ice?"

"It was an accident."

But there's doubt now in her voice.

Shit, is coach a violent man?

Eden is ashen now too. He lost his career just like this man did because of a concussion caused by other players attacking him on the ice.

They targeted Eden deliberately.

Stole his hockey career from him.

Could have killed him.

Was it the same for Gibbs?

Yet what makes true terror grip me is the thought that this means coach could have been violent off the ice as well.

I've always been haunted by the fear that my own anger issues on the ice would follow me off them as well.

Coach has been helping me with them. I don't mind that he's harsh and exacting with what he…or Colton… demand of me.

He's also given me therapy, as well as one-to-one time with himself to help me face my demons.

But has coach ever hurt Robyn?

I'd fucking kick his ass.

Eden would kill him.

I know that coach is tough. He's hard on me, and even harder on D'Angelo.

Yet he's good with Robyn, right?

But at the same time, not good at all with his son.

I glance at Cody.

Cody is staring intently down at where Eden's holding his hand.

I know that look.

I've worn it too many times, and so has my twin.

Fuck.

"It was deliberate, sweetheart." Gibbs sounds calmer now and more sure of himself. "It's taken me years to get over what happened and to try and bury it. But when Austin started up that team of misfit losers, it was like fucking salt in the wounds. When you began to actually *win*..." He takes a deep breath. "Then to find out that the captain, rising star, and his kids who he appears to spend so much time nurturing were on their way to play my own team... Well, let's just say that my therapist is on speed dial."

"That sucks." Robyn's voice hardens. "But it's only your slanderous opinion. It's not evidence. I still don't see what—"

"How do you think the press will react, if I go public with my side of the story? I haven't all these years. I have secrets about what happened. Do you think that your dad is a good man? He's not. The whole scandal will be dragged up again, your dad's reputation and legacy will be in the dirt, and your team's best season will be destroyed before it's even started. As the PR Director, are you prepared to be responsible for letting that happen to him, yourself, and the entire team? It's your choice if I go public with the coach's dark past or not."

Robyn's breathing too fast.

Trembling.

She's going to bloody pass out again.

I hold her more firmly by the shoulders.

"Jude..." I meet D'Angelo's gaze, helplessly.

D'Angelo growls, lunging for the phone.

This time, he manages to grab it from Robyn's weak grasp. "Listen here, asshole, you're not in control. We don't need to make any decisions because we're not going to play your game."

"But you already are." Gibbs sounds smug. "The only way that you can stop me telling the truth is to continue playing. *I dare you.*"

CHAPTER TWENTY-TWO

Rose Garden, San Jose

'Angelo

I STALK down the pathway in San Jose's Rose Garden park, as Gibbs instructed.

What a stunningly beautiful location to be blackmailed. But it doesn't make this any easier.

Fuck Gibbs.

Fuck his mind games.

And fuck his fucking truth or dare.

I clench my hands, letting out a deep breath. The sickly sweet scent of the roses invade me.

So, I may be rather angry about the way that a rival coach is making me dance for him.

I've been jerked around by journalists and other players for years. Hazing isn't new to me. Wilder's treatment of me was brutal at college.

I didn't suspect that a coach in the NHL, however, would be the one behind these texts. I hate that a man in a position of authority like Gibbs' can abuse it, forcing me to act like his puppet.

Yet I can't let Gibbs hurt Robyn.

He could be lying about what happened between coach and him on the ice.

No one but the two of them know the truth of what went down, and honestly, the press don't care about *the truth*.

It's all about the clickbait.

They'll print the most scandalous story, no matter who it destroys.

All I know is that Gibbs has only given me an hour to get to this location and I don't have time to come up with a way to counter him.

I'm not risking Robyn and Cody's past darkening their present.

I know how important it is to find a way to move on.

They both deserve to.

But I *will* find a way to destroy Gibbs.

I glance around at the miniature flower beds that are between rolling lawns. All different types of fragrant roses surround me, climbers and shrubs, in a dazzling array of colors.

Four pathways lead to a gushing, two-tiered fountain above a large reflection pool.

Couples stroll hand in hand in the hot, afternoon sunshine, tourists laugh, and moms push babies in strollers around the tinkling fountain.

Nobody recognizes me.

There are many unexpected upsides to wearing helmets on the rink, besides protecting your skull.

People rarely recognize me when I'm not in Freedom, unless I'm wearing my jersey, standing outside an arena, or being preyed on by paparazzi because I've been thrown out of a nightclub naked apart from flashing devil horns.

I adjust my sunglasses, tapping the sides three times.

It's also a celebrity secret that if you wear sunglasses, you magically can't be recognized.

At least, actors and rock stars use that trick.

I snap off the bloom of a hot pink rose as I pass, threading it through my suit buttonhole.

I'll fit the rose head into Robyn's hair, when I return to the hotel. She'll look beautiful.

At least one good thing will come out of this afternoon.

I reach the edge of the reflection pool as per Gibbs' orders, before scanning the crowds.

He has to be here.

A man who enjoys manipulating others, surely wouldn't miss out on the satisfaction of watching them obey.

Shit, I can't see Gibbs.

When my phone rings, I jump.

I wrench the phone out of my pocket to answer it.

"What?" I snarl.

"Are you in position?" Shay whispers.

I'll never admit to Shay that he made me jump.

I also should have known that he'd call.

Shay argued furiously about me coming here alone, despite that being part of Gibbs' dare. He swore that he could trail me as secretly as any skilled warrior.

Except, I knew that he would be more like the clumsy panda in *Kung Fu Panda*.

I blame Robyn for me knowing about animated martial arts films that teach about protecting yourself from adversaries by focusing on the here and now through the medium of a comedy panda. She watched the movie three times on the long journey here.

"Why are you making this sound like a spy movie?" I keep my back to the fountain, attempting to look casual. "Gibbs is not going to be passing me a secret briefcase. And why are you whispering, cucciolo? Your voice is echoing."

"I'm in the service stairwell," Shay replies.

"You're taking this Bond thing too far. Dare I ask why?"

"The medicine made Robyn groggy. Although she fought against it, she fell asleep. Colton called and yelled at Cody. So, he had to go back to the staff hotel and report for his duties. Eden is staying with Robyn to care for her. But I wanted to be on the other end of the phone for you. Is that bastard there now?"

I stealthily check out the garden again. "Not yet."

"We should have gone to the cops." Shay sounds anxious, but as furious as I am underneath. "That bloody arsehole shouldn't be able to order you about like this."

"I know." I gentle my tone to calm Shay. I don't want him to know how stressed I am. "It's not a big deal."

It is.

Shay doesn't need to know that.

I can't stop myself rhythmically rapping my fingers on my thigh in patterns of three.

I ruthlessly push my intrusive thoughts down.

I can't spiral right now.

I can't.

"It is," Shay insists like he's caught my own thought. "He's threatening all of us, and he's using those threats to push you into taking a dare. It won't be as innocent as a dance this time. You know that, right?"

"Gibbs will text me what it is, when he's ready. I learned long ago, however, that people can only humiliate you, if you feel shame." I cock my brow. "The discipline school operated on controlling and breaking you through both pain and humiliation. But the joke was on them because I learned that the only way to survive was to no longer feel shame."

"Darlin'," Shay sounds devastated, "that doesn't mean somebody should get away with—"

"He can hurt me less than he can the rest of you," I reply, firmly. "So, let the jerk think that he has. I'll style this out in the same way that I always do when I get caught doing things like fucking Seal, our mascot, in the locker room."

"You really did that?" Shay says, impressed. "Now I need to know what he looks like under the costume."

"I can neither confirm nor deny, but there's definitely photographic evidence from two years ago. And coach kicked both our asses, including Seal's, which I can tell you is biteable."

"I'll need to see that evidence to verify. Eden on the other hand, has been tracking down less sexy evidence. He's spent the last hour doing research on Gibbs." Shay sounds more worried. "Rumors are that Gibbs has radically improved the Ducks over the last year. He's considered one of the best coaches in the NHL. His nickname is Superpuck, while his team are called the Superducks in the press. Whereas the Bay Rebels are fighting to build a reputation as anything more than the outcasts, the Ducks are seen as the heroes."

"Ironic, when their coach is actually the villain." My brow furrows. "Look, Gibbs threatened to go public with his *side of the story* just before the game tomorrow, if we tell the cops. Plus, what would we even tell the cops to begin with? That someone wants to play truth or dare with us? We'd be laughed out of the station. Gibbs swore that he'd only give us three dares for the three games. I can suffer that for his petty revenge on coach."

"Then why isn't Gibbs getting coach to do the dares?"

Good point.

"Maybe because coach doesn't have to go out on the rink tomorrow and perform," I reply. "I'm the team captain, which makes me the best target. It's us that he wants to shake up."

Does that mean Shay will also be at risk?

My hand tightens around phone.

"Security will be mad that you're out there by yourself with nothing but the power of sunglasses to protect your secret identity."

"I left my superhero mask at home."

"Role play ideas. I like it. Why should the Ducks be the only ones who get to pretend that they're masked crusaders? We should be something edgier. I know, let's recreate *Batman vs Superman*. That way we'll bloody win. How about I be Robin to your Batman?"

My lips quirk. "Strange, when we have an actual Robyn in our team already. Okay, Robyn can be Catwoman. Although you do know that neither of those two are in the movie."

"I don't care. We can write our own story. Robyn would be fucking hot in a Catwoman PVC suit with a whip." Shay's voice, which had become breathy with desire on the idea of Robyn holding a whip, becomes serious again. "Be prepared for coach and the entire security team to bust your balls over this stunt."

"If that's the worst thing that happens to me as a result of this, then I can deal."

"Do you think coach actually did the shit that Gibbs is claiming?" Shay asks, tentatively. "Did he hurt someone on purpose? Eden's lost his whole career because of assholes like that."

I don't answer for a long moment.

The morning sunshine washes over me.

This park scene should be peaceful. The families and couples around me appear happy and relaxed.

For a moment, I envy them.

But then, who knows what's really going on in their lives? Behind closed doors?

"I don't know, cucciolo," I reply. "But coach has definitely been atoning for something with the Bay Rebels. It's why he believes in lost causes like me. He wants to give people second chances and an opportunity to redeem themselves. I have a sense that he knows what that feels like. But did he take that head shot on purpose? I hope not. I at least owe him the faith to believe that he didn't."

"Is that why you're doing this? For coach, as well as our Robyn?"

I stroke the soft petals of the rose in my buttonhole. "I'd do it for my principessa alone. But I'm also doing it for coach. He selected me and made me captain, when I was at my self-destructive lowest. He didn't let the fact that his daughter hated me back then color his judgment of me. He got me into therapy and kicked my ass when I needed it. He treated me more like family and a... just treated me more like I was family than anyone since my own disinherited me. I owe him far more than this."

He called me Jude.

No one but my sister called me Jude.

I'd been so fucking lonely, I'd ached with it. Then coach took me under his wing, mentored me, and called me by my first name.

I'd grown up with a large family. My name *Jude* would be called out often, said with teasing laughter or love.

I thought that I'd lost that side to myself.

That it had been burned and frozen, over and over, until it'd died.

Then coach called me *Jude*, and I allowed it to spring to life again.

Yeah, I owe coach.

"Then if he did all of that for you, I owe him the same for the sake of the man I love," Shay says, soft with an earnestness that makes me smile.

Hell, I wish that Shay was here, so that I could grab him by the scruff of the neck and bite, mark, and kiss his plush lips to reward him for being so fucking loyal.

All of a sudden, my phone vibrates with a text.

I stiffen. My heart speeds up.

"The text has come through." My pulse pounds, but I manage to keep my voice steady. "I have to go."

"Good luck. Call me the moment anything goes wrong or it's over," Shay whispers, urgently. "I'll be waiting."

I swipe off the call, then hesitate before checking the text.

I pull off my sunglasses, slipping them into my pocket.

Then I scan the crowds again, pushing myself onto my tiptoes to gain a better view over the flowerbeds.

Is Gibbs here?

I turn around, twisting at all angles to look down each path.

I can't see him.

I let out a frustrated breath, taking a step forward from the reflection pool.

At last, I force myself to read the text.

I know that it's from Gibbs because I saved him in my contacts on my phone under *Pucking Asshole*.

PUCKING ASSHOLE (16:23): Dare: Post on social media the story of your first kiss. I'll know if you lied.

I stare at the screen in shocked silence.

How can he know?

How can he *fucking know* my greatest fear? *Worst nightmare?*

I'm sweating. My clothes feel tight. My breathing is too shallow.

I'm tipping into panic attack in the middle of a public park and I can't allow myself that luxury because that would be front page news.

I crouch, resting my head in my hands. I force myself to take deep, slow breaths.

I count slowly, "One, two, three, four…"

My heartbeat slows. I draw enough oxygen into my lungs.

Relieved, I push myself to my feet. I smooth down my suit and hair.

Then I fix on a fake smile.

If I do this, then I'll do it with style.

No shame.

So what if exposing my most vulnerable moment that triggered a cascade of events, which tore me away from family, home, and self-worth, makes me want to flay my own skin?

Can I taste blood?

I lick my lip, as if I can taste the coppery tang where it split that day from my brother's punch.

I lift up my chin, clicking to my social media feed and turning it to live.

I take another step forward, staring at the phone in my shaking hands and refusing to look at the people around me who'll be able to hear me as much as the millions who may watch and share this video.

I swallow, refusing to let the tears fall.

I can't think about that.

That's for later.

Now, time to style this out.

If Gibbs wants to make me dance, then I'll fucking dance.

"A fan asked me today about my first kiss." I wink at the screen. Inside, I'm dying. "I was seventeen and I'd fallen for this gorgeous guy at school. I'd never dated a boy before. We were friends, but you know how it goes, I think he knew that it was more than that, before I did. I invited him over for a study *date*."

I pause dramatically, drawing out the word *date* in a knowing way.

I deliberately don't read the comments that are coming in faster and faster now underneath the video.

Most of them will be vile.

At least half of them will be slurs or calling me out as the play boy of the Bay Rebels.

I can't help myself, glancing down.

Then I wish that I hadn't, when I catch the word *puck boy* with a drool face emoji.

I hold back the shudder.

Rapidly, there's a flurry of comments underneath,

which are nothing but emojis — hot panting faces, eggplants, and bones.

What started as a sweet moment but became my most painful memory is nothing but jerking off material for strangers simply because I'm famous.

I snap.

I hold my arm out, twirling in a circle.

I declare, loudly, "Then I kissed a boy and I fucking liked it."

I furiously turn off the phone.

When I look up, my gaze meets my horrified parents' at the other side of the path.

I stop breathing.

This can't be real.

It fucking can't.

No, no, no.

I freeze.

It's not them.

They didn't just...not when I...

I drop my phone, and it shatters on the ground.

Mom and Dad stare at me in equally shocked silence, only they look…disgusted.

Dad is smaller than I remember.

He's wearing a smart brown suit with the same style of tan belt that he always used to. His black hair is slicked back. His bright blue eyes are so like mine that it's startling.

Mom is dressed in an elegant floral dress. Her brunette hair is swept back from her face. It's threaded with gray.

It didn't used to be.

She was famed for being a beauty. She worked as a model, before she married Dad.

But when did she become fragile looking?

How did I miss so much time with them?

None of us move.

A long moment passes in silence.

Yet a thousand words are spoken in it.

Childhood memories flash through my mind. I can't stop them.

The days spent in the kitchen helping Mom to cook her special lasagna, the scent of Sunday dinners with meatballs and sausages, the noise and chatter of large family gatherings at Easter, Maria helping me to learn the piano, or Dad tending the vegetables in our garden with me at weekends.

Then all of that shattered by one violent attack by my brother.

That moment lies heavy between us.

And what followed it: Mom and Dad's decision to have me kidnapped and imprisoned in hell for kissing a boy.

For not being the type of son that they'd dreamed of having.

They never fully saw *me*, only the fiction of a child that had never existed.

I guess that's why it was so easy for them to declare me to be dead to them.

I open my mouth to say all the things that I thought I'd say to them, if I ever saw them again.

The words that I've longed to say, have written in

letters in therapy, and raged at them, when I was locked up in the discipline school.

But the words fly out of my head.

Suddenly, these two people, grayer and more *normal* than I've been building them up to be in my mind for years, are just my parents.

The people who I still desperately want to love me.

And it's me who breaks first.

"Mom." My voice is unsteady.

I step over my broken phone toward them.

I hold out my hand, but Mom doesn't take it.

Instead, she drops her gaze. She looks away from me, resolutely grasping her hands in front of her.

I like to think that it's because she can still feel shame about what she's done and not simply because she's ashamed of *me*.

But then, that's delusion.

But delusion is better than the reality.

I'm left frozen with my hand outstretched.

My cheeks flush.

For the first time in a long time, I feel bone deep humiliation.

"Mom," I repeat in a whisper.

A single tear trails down my cheek.

This is too much.

Too fucking much.

"Don't," Dad says, brusquely.

I flinch, recognizing his tone even after so many years.

How could I forget that it's a warning?

He hasn't spoken to me since I was a teenager, and that's the first thing that he says to me?

Don't?

Dad grabs Mom by the elbow to tow her away from me.

I want to chase after her, force her to look at me — fucking see me for the man that I've grown into — at least once.

Yet I feel like I've been turned to ice.

"Don't talk to us." Dad shakes his head in disappointment. "You haven't changed, Jude."

CHAPTER TWENTY-THREE

SAP Center, San Jose

obyn

"Shoot, shoot, shoot," I chant under my breath.

D'Angelo shoots...and misses.

I groan.

He's seriously off his game.

It's Tuesday evening and the first game of the California road trip between the Bay Rebels and the San Jose Sharks.

I'm standing behind the glass in front of a cold metal bench in case I need to rest.

Noah perches on the bench, running his hand

anxiously through his curls. He's dressed in the medical staff nurse uniform with Bay Rebels logo.

Dad only cleared me to attend tonight, if Noah kept an eye on me. Of course, Eden is looking after me as well, standing close at my shoulder.

Eden looks gorgeous in a gray suit with light silver waistcoat. D'Angelo gifted him with a number of game night suits. The long woolen coat that Eden is wearing over it, exactly matches his eyes.

The suits make Eden look both dominant and more comfortable.

He appears to deal better with being around so many people, when he's dressed in them.

I'm bundled up more than normal in jeans, an emerald sweater, and thick, floor-length coat. Eden wound one of his gray scarves around my neck and pulled his fluffy gloves onto my hands.

The gloves are too large. But I love how it felt, when Eden put them on me.

I also love how looked after I feel to be wearing them.

I squint through the bright lights, which make my head throb.

I can't smell anything because of my stuffy nose.

The atmosphere in the arena, however, is electric. The crowds are noisy with joy.

Unfortunately, the excitement is one-sided from the fans for the home team.

This is a nightmare start for the Bay Rebels.

My heart is beating too fast. I feel lightheaded.

I shouldn't be out of bed yet. Michael made his views

on that *very* clear in his best stern voice, when I insisted that I wasn't missing this game.

My guys need my support.

Eden should be here, and I know that if I stayed away, then he would as well in order to be with me.

Except, now I wish that I *was* back in the hotel room.

Then I could hide from Dad.

My gaze darts to Dad, who is standing further along from me in a huddle with the other staff and coaches, watching the game like a glowering hawk. Both Colton and him appear ready to swoop onto the ice and tear their team apart with their talons.

The Bay Rebels are already being slaughtered by the rival team.

On the other hand, how would Dad feel if he knew the reason behind why D'Angelo is putting on the worst performance of his life?

If he knew that it was because D'Angelo is trying to save Dad's reputation?

But by doing so, he's destroyed himself.

Yesterday afternoon, D'Angelo stumbled back to the hotel room like he'd seen a ghost.

He didn't tell us anything.

Instead, he started to tidy.

And clean.

Fold everything in each of our suitcases.

Then refold.

Then tidy some more.

He was caught in the grasp of his OCD, worse than I've seen it.

It was evening, before D'Angelo was able to tell us simply that he'd *seen his parents.*

It broke my heart.

I wanted to call Dad and break Gibbs' secret hold over us.

Gibbs set up the man who I love to face his worse fear, and I wanted to call a stop to this.

Yet D'Angelo insisted, "Just two more dares, cara mia. Seeing…those people…today made me realize that I know what it feels like for your life to implode. To lose your family. I'd do anything to stop that happening to you. *Anything.*"

Except, D'Angelo is falling apart tonight with the whole world watching.

Helplessly, I clench my hands.

I wish that I could help him.

I don't look away from the rink for a moment.

Shay appears to feel the same as me, attempting to skate closer to D'Angelo.

The Sharks are an outstanding team, however, and scenting blood, they've been working on separating the flow between the two players.

They've been blocking Shay, stopping him from creating chances.

Shay should be scoring more than this.

A hulking winger closes in on Shay. He's a head taller and twice as wide as Shay.

Eden's piercing gaze is focused on the ice.

"Concentrate," Eden mutters.

Shay, however, isn't looking at the winger. He's hyper focused on D'Angelo, as concerned about him as I am.

Normally, Shay and D'Angelo's close connection is a strength. But now, it's a serious weakness.

Shay is skating into position to score, only D'Angelo is too distracted to notice.

This is a disaster.

Suddenly, from the side, the winger crashes into Shay, slamming him into the boards.

Shay hits his hip and shoulder hard.

I wince.

Then he's slapped down to the ice.

Is he going to fight?

I hold my breath.

I'm proud, however, when Shay struggles to his feet, blanking the winger.

Next to me, Eden stiffens.

Throughout the game, I've been intensely aware of Eden standing so close that our shoulders touch. Also, the way that he grabs my elbow to steady me, whenever I feel dizzy.

I wish that I could hold his hand.

The way that I notice his fingers twitching, I think that he's resisting the urge the same as I am.

I drag my handkerchief out of my pocket, which I borrowed (stole) from D'Angelo. I only have paper tissue ones, but D'Angelo has an impressive collection of fancy silk handkerchiefs to match his suits.

He now has one less.

I blow my nose noisily into it, giving a weak cough.

Yeah, D'Angelo won't want this one back.

I stuff the handkerchief back into my coat pocket.

"Would you like some water?" Noah stands and holds out an opened water bottle to me.

I wrest my attention away from the ice.

"Thanks." I take the bottle from Noah and take a deep swig. "Sorry you have to act as my nurse tonight."

"Literally my job." Noah pushes his wild hair out of his eyes. "Your dad made it clear that I'm your on call medical staff member from now on. He told me that I'd better make sure that you don't faint or anything in front of the cameras." Then he drops his voice to a whisper. "And he scares me."

Eden's lips twitch. "I'll protect you."

"My hero." Noah smiles, shyly. "Actually, Jude text me. He asked me to look after you as well, as a favor. I care a lot more about not disappointing him, than I do about getting my butt kicked by coach."

I know the feeling.

D'Angelo has the ability to inspire that type of loyalty.

Even now, when he's struggling so much, the entire team is attempting to rally around him.

It should be a frozen bloodbath, but the score is still **4 — 1** to the Sharks.

The Bay Rebels could come back from a three-goal deficit.

Maybe.

If Shay wasn't being targeted as a tactic by the Sharks, then he'd have scored at least one more goal already.

Grayson is taking up the slack on the left wing and trying to cover for D'Angelo.

Atlas and Lucas have been blocking and making smart decisions. Their defense has been fucking dogged.

Plus, D'Angelo owes Zach, our goalie, a beer for the number of practically unhinged dives he's done to save shots on goal.

The score should be closer to **9 — 1.**

Noah isn't the only one who's loyal to the captain. D'Angelo's team are proving it with their sweat and bruises on the ice now.

Except, it's not enough.

They need their captain as well, only D'Angelo looks to be in a daze.

He's not present right now.

I hate that I have a good idea where he's trapped, and it's the moment that his asshole brother came home and found him kissing his friend.

Or possibly, the moment that he saw his parents out of the blue for the first time in ten years.

Only for them to reject him all over again.

When Colton sharply gestures at Noah like he's a servant who can be summoned, Noah sighs.

"And there's someone who scares me even more. I'd better see what Stick No Carrot wants." Unexpectedly, Noah becomes briskly professional. "Keep drinking. There are bananas, oranges, and yogurts for you in my bag under the bench, which will all be good for you, if you're hungry. If you feel faint, like your temperature is rising, or just feel worse in any way, come get me at once.

You're my number one priority tonight, no matter what Mr. Colton thinks."

"I'll watch her," Eden promises. "I won't let anything happen to Robyn."

"I believe you." Noah's shoulders hunch, as he turns away and trudges toward Colton.

When I glance up at Eden, his stormy gray eyes are sweeping over my face.

He brushes his knuckles over my forehead, checking my temperature.

I think that he's using it as an excuse to touch me.

He needs it.

But then, so do I.

"They're going to lose." Eden's gaze darts back to the rink.

What can I say?

"It looks like it." I frown. "Statistically, no one wins all three of these road games. Neither the board nor the press will expect it. But we must win at least one of them. The problem is that this first game is meant to be the easiest to win because our team is at its freshest. The games will only get harder from here on out. If we lose this one, then each game will become more and more difficult to win."

My throat is sore simply from talking.

I cough, taking another drink. Then I place the water bottle down on the bench.

With trepidation, I look back at the rink.

My heart speeds up, as D'Angelo loses focus yet again.

His emotions are going wild.

The real competition is always inside yourself.

Right now, D'Angelo is losing.

I think that he's winning, however, for even putting on his skates, after the mindfuck Gibbs has put him through.

D'Angelo makes another unforced error, losing the puck to the rival center.

Dad reddens, yelling at him.

"I'm going to burn Gibbs alive," Eden says with a calm certainty.

It's eerily like he means it.

"How about you don't discuss your murder plans in public and in front of the cameras, Dexter?" I swing Eden by his good arm to face me.

Eden's brow furrows in confusion. "He hurt Jude. He made his worst fear come true."

My chest feels tight. And this time, it's not because of the virus.

"I know," I murmur. "It was fucking cruel. Why would Gibbs go to the trouble of organizing for Jude's parents to be in the same place? If he merely wanted us to lose these games, he could have done anything. But he's psychologically torturing D'Angelo. Why does he want to…?"

"This is personal." Eden's expression is grim. "It's Gibbs' revenge, but I'm not convinced that we know what it's for."

Surprised, I tilt my head. "You think that it's about more than that one incident on the ice."

"I want to know what the chirps were from Gibbs that made coach attack him in the first place."

Hell, that's a good point.

"They were about Mom." I lick my dry lips. "I remember Dad telling me that."

Eden looks thoughtful. "If somebody talked shit about *you* on the ice, Shay would punch them."

But Dad didn't merely punch Gibbs.

"Still, how did he know about all that stuff? The kiss? D'Angelo's parents?" I shove my gloved hands into my pockets.

"Could we be under surveillance again?"

I shake my head. "Security are hot on that now after last time. Dad vets them closely. It's unlikely."

"How would he know our private…?"

"A Trojan horse." I gasp.

Why didn't I think of it earlier?

Shit, it's the staple of shady journalists everywhere; part of their *dark arts*.

"Did we accept a gift from an enemy?" Eden asks.

"In a way." My eyes flash with anger. "It means that we've been infected with a different type of virus to the one that's making my voice hoarse. It's a Trojan horse virus. Certain jerk journalists use them to break into celebrities' computers. All you need to do is click onto a link, then it gives them access to everything on your email, phone, *fucking everything*. Except, we all know not to click on links, so…"

Eden adjusts the scarf at my neck, but I know that it's an excuse to get closer to me.

"Robyn, I'm sorry." He looks stricken.

"Why?" I ask.

Fuck, I know that look.

He clicked on a link.

"I don't understand emojis," Eden bursts out in a mix of guilt and frustration. "I got this weird email from Shay, when I was busy on D'Angelo's computer for work. It was this long string of emojis, ending with a wink face, then: *look at this!* But the link underneath didn't lead to anything. I thought my brother had just messed it up. I'm a fucking idiot."

"Hey, you're not." I force him to meet my gaze. "We're going to sort this."

"Jude will hate me." Eden's voice is low like he's struggling to force out the words. "He won't want to be my friend anymore. It's my fault that he had to see his parents again. It would kill me, if I saw my biological ones. I did that."

"You didn't," I reply, willing him to believe me. "This is Gibbs' fault and no one else's."

"I let him down as his PA." Eden's expression is stoic, as if he's bracing himself for punishment. "He should fire me."

"He isn't going to fire you for clicking on one link. These assholes are good at what they do — tricking people. Gibbs must have hired them. And when are you going to realize that D'Angelo is more than your friend? He's your family now."

Eden's shoulders relax but he still looks tense.

Finally, he nods.

I'm not sure that he fully understands what I said.

Perhaps, he *wants* to but is still struggling to accept it deep within his soul.

"Plus, it's good that we at least know what's happened," I continue, hoping to make him feel better. But then, dread makes my guts roil. "Except, if it's the type of virus I think it is, then it will have given Gibbs access to every email and computer in D'Angelo's friends list, as well as every phone, including Shay's and mine. *And any therapy notes sent out to them.*"

Horror stricken, Eden and I stare at each other.

Behind us, the Shark fans roar, as their team score again.

My knees buckle. I sit down heavily on the bench.

The Bay Rebels have lost to the San Jose Sharks.

D'Angelo has lost.

And we've lost this first game to Gibbs.

CHAPTER TWENTY-FOUR

Park, Kern County

hay

I GLANCE out of the parked window of our motorhome at the farm.

Ducks waddle through the barns and groves of trees.

Eden's definitely going to get out and pet those ducks.

It's bloody weird how peaceful it is here. It's jarring after the noise and commotion that followed one of the worst games of my life yesterday.

We've stopped for lunch on the way to Los Angeles and our next game tomorrow.

I grimace, stretching my legs up onto the plush silver couch and massaging my calves.

Everything fucking hurts.

My muscles are so sore, I feel that I've been used as a punching bag.

In the game against the Sharks, I pretty much was.

Although, if we'd won, it would have been worth it for the tender way that Robyn stripped me in our hotel room and then rubbed arnica cream into the bruises on my hip and shoulder.

I tried to convince Robyn that there were bruises on my balls.

I failed.

Sunlight streams through the RV's window, making the silver accents gleam against the wood.

I'm dressed in casual jeans and red t-shirt. My feet are bare. It's the only reason that I'm allowed to put my feet up onto the couch.

D'Angelo has a lot of strict rules like not putting booted feet on the furniture.

He'd have hated how I lived at college.

I'm going to keep quiet about the way I'd wear whatever I picked up off the floor, used an old pizza box as a plate, and had a work desk that could be described as *controlled chaos*.

Robyn and I have a lot in common that way.

Robyn and D'Angelo sit on stools on one side of the table, which is behind the curved couch. The table's blue cover is almost hidden by piles of sandwiches, salads, and an array of cream cakes.

Trust my brother to be able to create a feast even in this small space.

The table is also covered by a mountain of papers, displaying hockey strategy and plays.

Coach gave them to D'Angelo last night or more like, threw them in his face, insisting that he study them before the next game.

I waited outside the locker room, when the rest of the team had left, listening to coach yelling at D'Angelo.

Coach busted D'Angelo's balls for over an hour.

I shook, as I heard how coach threatened to take D'Angelo off the ice and even take away his captaincy, if he turned up to a game so distracted again.

Yet D'Angelo is suffering because of coach.

I know what it's like to be triggered just before a game.

It happened to me with a flashback of Blythe refusing to respect my safe word.

I tried to support D'Angelo like he helped me, but the Sharks were a good enough team to work out that tactic and block me.

I pressed my face against the door, desperate to support D'Angelo but unable to.

"Are you drinking again?" Coach barked, furious.

I flinched.

That was low.

There was a long silence.

"Think what you want," D'Angelo replied.

His voice sounded level, but I could hear the strain beneath it.

"I think that you fucked up the game."

"I know, coach. I'm owning it."

"The rest of the team stepped up. They damn well carried your ass, but at this level, that's not going to be enough. This season means everything for Bay Rebels. Both our legacies. But how you acted on the ice tonight makes me think that you've slipped back to acting the playboy who only cares about himself. I thought that you'd changed."

Now, D'Angelo's voice wavered. "Perhaps, I can't change."

Now, my gaze slides to Robyn, who looks as beautiful as she always does in a cotton green dress. She's a little too flushed still.

She seems a lot better than she did.

She gave us a bloody scare.

How can you make sure someone is never ill?

I wish that you could guard against that. But then, I also haven't been able to stop Eden being hurt.

I glance uneasily at Eden's arm, which rests in his sling.

Eden's standing in the gleaming kitchenette in leather trousers and gray hoodie, stirring a bowl of steaming chicken soup.

He carries the soup to the table, placing it in front of Robyn. "Eat."

"I'm starting to see the upside of being sick," Robyn says. "I get pampered."

I narrow my eyes. "We can fuss over you all the time. No wishing yourself sick, love. It may cancel out *our* wishes for you to be well."

Robyn nods, picking up her spoon.

Eden sits on the stool next to her. In the small space, their thighs touch. He leans over and blows on the soup to cool it for her.

Their gazes meet.

She smiles, as she starts to eat.

I glance at D'Angelo, who is too intent on his homework from coach to eat lunch.

I've never seen D'Angelo so disheveled before. I'd find it sexy, if I didn't know that it was because he was distressed and refusing to speak about it.

He's not wearing his suit jacket or tie. And his shirt is creased.

For D'Angelo that's practically being a hot mess.

I push myself up from the couch and wander to join them at the table.

I press a kiss to the warm top of Robyn's head as I pass, then I rest my hand on D'Angelo's tense shoulder.

"How about a sandwich? Or an apple?" I offer.

D'Angelo shakes his head.

I catch Eden's eye.

He's watching us both intently. Why does he look guilty?

"Starving yourself won't help anyone." I wrap my arms around D'Angelo's neck, resting my head against his check.

"I'm busy," D'Angelo replies, curtly.

"Colton caught me in the corridor, while I was waiting for you. He was bloody furious about the game. He chewed out my ass."

"He did what?" D'Angelo snarls.

A laugh bubbles up in my throat. "Calm down, possessive bear. It's not as sexy as I made it sound. You're the only one who eats out my ass."

I never thought that something like *that* could make me see stars.

I'm an astrophysicist but I'm learning all sorts of new kinky things, since coming to America.

"Neither of you should have been *chewed out*." Robyn slams down her spoon. "Dad had no right to yell at you. Why don't we tell him…?"

"We can't." D'Angelo finally looks up from his mountain of papers. "Gibbs made that clear. What was the point of me facing the worst…something that I've been avoiding for a long time…if we back out now?"

"Because Gibbs is getting what he wants," Robyn replies. "He's traumatizing you. How could you have been expected to play well after that? He's ruining this season."

When D'Angelo flushes, I kiss his cheek, before straightening.

I run my fingers through his hair to tidy it into the style that he loves.

"He's not," I reply, firmly. "Gibbs fucked up a single game. But *our captain* is bloody fantastic. The whole team is dedicated. We could have lost by a large margin but we didn't. We simply take it as a lesson learned and then we win one of the other games. We can do it."

I hope D'Angelo knows that I'm talking to him.

I smooth down his shirt for him.

D'Angelo straightens his shoulders. His eyes blaze.

That's the D'Angelo I know and would give my last fucking breath for.

"We can." D'Angelo sweeps the papers off the table. "And we do it my way."

"Rebel against the system." I kick the papers for good measure.

Then I stumble, as D'Angelo turns and grabs me by the arm.

His expression is darkly dangerous.

He raises what I call his *dom-brow*. "And I'm starting by relaxing us both. Why don't you crawl under the table and keep that busy mouth of yours quiet, and at the same time, keep my cock warm?"

I stare at him in shock.

Then a slow smile spreads across my face.

It'll settle the nerves vibrating through me, the exhaustion and aches from the games, and the echo of Colton and coach's insults that are ricocheting through my mind.

How does D'Angelo know what I need before I voice it?

I need D'Angelo's cock in my mouth.

Although, I think that he needs this as much as I do.

Robyn catches my eye with a smirk.

Her cheeks are pink.

She's excited to watch this.

I smirk back, allowing my gaze to become heated for her sake, before I drop to my knees and crawl underneath the table between D'Angelo's thighs.

It's cramped underneath here and dark.

D'Angelo spreads his legs to give me room.

Then I hear him reach for an apple and take a crisp bite, ignoring me.

I smile, relieved that this has got D'Angelo eating.

Already feeling relaxed, I reach forward and undo his suit trousers. I reach into his underwear and pull out his dick.

I stroke it reverentially for a moment.

I'm beginning to fucking love this dick.

It's large and starting to harden.

But this isn't about making D'Angelo come.

At the moment, he seems more concerned about devouring his apple.

I shuffle forward, unable to resist kissing the head of D'Angelo's cock.

D'Angelo stiffens.

Finally, I take the cock in my mouth, stretching my lips around it.

Then I place my hands on my lap.

Saliva is already building in my mouth. I work my tongue around, trying to find a way to accommodate D'Angelo's dick.

D'Angelo rests his hand on my head, stroking my hair. "Only soft sucking. No licking. And don't speak. Your only job is to warm my cock like the toy you are."

His words make my own cock harden but also help to calm my racing thoughts.

This isn't a BJ.

I don't need to do anything.

D'Angelo's not even fully hard.

"I've been looking through the press response to the

game throughout the journey," Robyn says like I'm not underneath the table. It does something to me that she's talking about business, while I'm being used. I fall further into my headspace. "It's negative but also, confused. No one knows what to make of such a bad performance, when within it, there was still good gameplay. We can turn this around."

"Statistically, that should have been the easiest game to win," D'Angelo replies, evenly. You'd never guess that I was between his thighs, even if his cock twitches. I know that this is helping him as much as it's helping me. "Almost no away team wins the middle game and even less win a final game against the Ducks."

"With optimism like that, why I am worried?" Robyn teases. "Sure, they're tougher games. But we know Gibbs better now. Even if he tries to fuck with us before them, then we'll be better prepared. We only need to win *one* of these games to save our head from the chopping block. Plus, I have some ideas to keep the fans on board."

"I have the photographs," Eden points out.

"Look, they're going viral." Robyn passes something to D'Angelo above me. "Bay Rebels has dedicated superfans now. *You* do. Support like that, which is based on authenticity, can't be bought. So, you can have an off day. You're not robots. You're human."

I'm only half listening.

My main focus is on the heat, feel, and weight of D'Angelo's gorgeous cock in my mouth.

My whole world is narrowed to serving D'Angelo.

To being his good boy.

D'Angelo reaches down, tracing with his thumb over where my lips are stretched around his cock.

When I whine, he taps me sharply on the head.

I settle down again, and he pets me.

My shoulders relax. I struggle not to move.

I fall fast into a blissful, meditative space.

I breathe through my nose, allowing myself to feel safe, fuzzy, and calm.

Even when I hear Robyn mention my name, I don't move. D'Angelo rewards me by caressing behind my ear. My eyelashes flutter in pleasure.

"I've created a headline on Shay's page and his social media that the fans like," Robyn declares. *"A day without Shay is a day without sunshine."*

"It's true," Eden says.

"It is." D'Angelo's voice is soft. His cock twitches. "But I can't ignore the question that's more important than the press reaction or coach kicking my ass. How did Gibbs know my pain point? How did he know what would trigger me?"

There's a long silence.

I freeze. My eyes snap wide open.

"We figured out that he must have used a Trojan horse virus that would then have given him access to our computers and phones," Robyn finally replies. "Unfortunately, this means that he'll have access to any files stored on them, including things sent to you like past records and therapy notes that have been shared with you."

Paling, I violently pull off D'Angelo's cock. "Bloody hell."

Someone has every sext, private text to Eden, and my most private emails and notes from my therapist…?

I'm going to hurl.

I'm breathing too fast. My heart's pounding.

My eyes are burning.

I never even wanted to talk about…those things.

I hate therapy.

But now a bastard who's trying to wreck us has access to my most intimate and private secrets.

My skin crawls.

He'll know what trash I am. What's been done to Eden and me.

Where we come from.

Fuck, fuck, fuck.

I'm shocked out of my thoughts by D'Angelo threading his fingers through my hair, as if he can sense my horror, and guiding me back to his cock.

He's calm but firm.

It's reassuring.

"Be my good boy and get back to your job. Open your mouth," D'Angelo commands.

It's easy to follow orders and not need to think right now.

I can process my panic later.

I open my mouth, allowing D'Angelo to feed his cock into my mouth, where it lies on my tongue.

I don't move, simply letting my mouth be used like I'm an object. It helps me to calm again.

"Who would let a virus like that onto our system,

principessa?" D'Angelo demands. "You'd need to be dumb enough to—"

"It doesn't matter," Robyn says, hurriedly. "The important thing is that we work out a way to beat—"

"I did it," Eden blurts. "I resign."

Shit.

I ball my hands into fists on my lap.

My twin can't resign. This job is all he has. He needs it.

Without it, we won't be able to remain together.

Without it, Eden won't be able to attend my games.

Without it, my brother won't have any money. It means the world to him to be independent and to be able to send money back to Mom and Dad.

Without it, he'll probably need to return to England.

That'd kill us both.

I slap D'Angelo's thigh.

I'm not allowed to talk but I think he gets the message.

Immediately, D'Angelo responds by dropping his hand to my hair, tugging on it painfully hard.

Worth it.

"I don't accept your resignation," D'Angelo drawls. "Who else would understand my filing system? Color code my scheduling? Pack those delicious BLT sandwiches for me?"

"You don't…?" Eden sounds unsure and like he's struggling to get out his words. I remember a time when he could only speak a single word at a time, and we celebrated with cake, when he managed two. "You're not…?"

"What I am, is signing you up for an online IT course.

Let's call it staff development. Would you prefer that to an in person group course?"

"Yes, Jude." Eden sounds so bloody relieved that my chest tightens.

I adore that I've found a lover who understands my twin.

One who includes him in our family, taking the time to think about what he needs without making it a big deal.

D'Angelo could have blamed Eden for this but then, that would have made him a hypocrite.

Everybody's human, right?

And this bloody fantastic human is getting a reward.

I don't care if he punishes me for disobeying, I suck D'Angelo's cock to show my gratitude.

D'Angelo hisses a sharp breath.

His dick hardens satisfyingly fast in my mouth.

"Behave." D'Angelo gives my hair another warning tug.

"So, Gibbs has all the dirt that he could possibly want on us," D'Angelo says. "You do realize that means he'll have worked out about our relationship, Shay's sexuality, *everything*."

I'm glad that I have D'Angelo's cock in my mouth or else, I'd be struggling to hold back my cussing.

Eden doesn't.

"Fuck," he snarls.

He sounds like he's about to rip someone's head off.

Gibb's.

"Then why isn't he using those secrets?" Robyn's voice sounds small and fearful. It makes my soul ache. "He could ruin our lives. Tear down everything that we care about and have built."

"Except, this is about hockey." Eden stands up. I hear his footfalls, as he prowls to the window. "Gibbs doesn't care about the other shit. He's obsessed with bringing down coach."

"So, he's only using what he can to bring you down on the ice?" Robyn asks.

"This has to be about more than what happened in that one incident." D'Angelo tightens his hold on my hair. "This level of planning and hate is personal. Gibbs didn't act, until your dad challenged him by becoming a coach. In fact, when he turned up in the news again. Perhaps, coach's success started to piss off Gibbs and opened old wounds. Maybe this road trip simply gave him the opportunity to humiliate coach. And he took it."

"What old wounds?"

"That's what we need to find out. Don't we all have them? Isn't that's what he's proving with these dares?"

Unexpectedly, my phone vibrates with a text in my pocket.

I ignore it.

Until my phone vibrates again.

D'Angelo yanks on my hair. "That could be coach. You know what a hard-ass he becomes, if you don't answer him. You can stop being my cock warmer. Apart from one act of rebellion, you've done an excellent job, cucciolo."

I glow at his praise.

And I don't regret my rebellion.

D'Angelo lets go of my hair with a final stroke, before I

reluctantly let go of his cock. I place a final cheeky kiss to the head of his dick that makes his breath hitch, then I crawl out from beneath the table.

I blink in the light, as my eyes adjust.

"Hey." Robyn smiles down at me.

It feels weird to be acknowledged.

"Hey," I reply. "A day without Shay is a day without sunshine…?"

"It's cold and dark, when I don't see you."

I grin widely.

I sit cross-legged on the floor next to Robyn. "I thought that you liked gazing at the stars at night with me, love."

Robyn's smile becomes softer. "Only because I have the sun with me, even then."

Warmth fills me.

I lean forward and rest my head on her lap. "I feel happy and fuzzy, love, but now I have to open a mean text from your dad."

"The life of a pro hockey player, huh? I bet the fans will never guess the truth."

My phone vibrates again. "Cock warming followed by chewing out via text: The secret life of a player."

When my phone vibrates yet again (just how impatient is coach?), I wriggle my hand into my pocket and pull it out.

When I turn it on, however, I stare in shock at the screen.

My pulse roars in my ears.

The texts aren't from coach.

UNKNOWN NUMBER (12:42): Truth or dare.

I swallow. My mouth is suddenly dry.

I force myself to look at the next one.

I don't want to but I don't have a choice.

Shit, is this how D'Angelo felt?

I understand now.

It's so much more violating when it's on your own phone.

When Gibbs is talking to you.

I love horror movies. I don't scare easily. I thought that I was desensitized.

But living through one feels bloody different.

UNKNOWN NUMBER (12:43): Don't ignore me.

I force myself to read the next ones, two in a row.

I think the others are calling to me, worried about how ashen I've become.

I can't answer them.

I'm glued to the screen and Gibbs' texts.

I know that it's him.

And I know that he's going to mindfuck me next in the same way that he did D'Angelo.

He said three dares.

Yet at the same time, I'm glad that D'Angelo isn't the target. Whatever this is, then I'll take it to protect my boyfriend.

I spent two weeks wishing that I could take Eden's place, when we were locked up as kids.

I'd do anything to take on the pain for the people I love to make up for that time.

I know D'Angelo will hate that. But he'll have to suck it up.

Sometimes, people can save him too.

UNKNOWN NUMBER (12:45): McKenna's rising star. D'Angelo's mentee. Bay Rebel's top scorer…

I take a deep breath, before I read the final text.

UNKNOWN NUMBER (12:46): I'm sending you a location. Be there within three hours. Dare: Remain inside the haunted house alone for one hour.

CHAPTER TWENTY-FIVE

Haunted House, Los Angeles

hay

Despite the hot Los Angeles sunshine bathing the courtyard, I shiver.

Robyn slips her arms around my shoulders.

I stare up at the wide steps that lead to a grand front door, which is flanked by gray columns.

Above it, swings a banner in spooky writing: **HAUNTED HOUSE**.

In case we miss that this is the right location for the dare.

D'Angelo stomps through an overgrown flowerbed,

hissing as he catches his hand on a bramble. His suit jacket rips.

I wince.

The suit is one of D'Angelo's favorites. Yet another reason to kick Gibbs' arse.

Eden is standing unnaturally still. He's glaring at the mansion like he's imagining it exploding into flames.

D'Angelo attempts to peer through a window. "The drapes are pulled. I can't see inside."

"I didn't think that it'd be as easy as that." I shrug. "Why don't you all go and wait in the motorhome? Eden can make you some tea or something. No sense you waiting out here in the sun."

"Nice try." Robyn draws away from me, only so that she can kiss me instead. "We're waiting just here…"

"So that we can run inside and save your ass, if we hear screaming," D'Angelo drawls.

"I'm not Scooby-Doo," I say, disgruntled. "Anyway, this place is so large that I doubt you'll be able to hear me scream."

"Of course you're not Scooby. You're Shaggy." D'Angelo disentangles himself from the brambles, stumbling out of the flowerbed toward us. He grimaces, stroking over the tears in his suit. "Shit."

"I can fix those." Eden's gaze darts to the damaged suit, before settling back on me again.

D'Angelo rests his hand on my lower back, and I lean into his touch. "I don't know about this, cucciolo. This place is giving off serial killer vibes."

"Isn't that the point of a haunted house?" Excitement

rushes through me, as well as fear. I fucking love this type of thrill. "Whatever Gibbs thinks he has in there that will freak me out, he's made a mistake. I was babysat by late night horror movies. I never thought that being desensitized would end up saving me."

"You're only desensitized to moving lights on a screen," Robyn points out. "Real life isn't the same thing."

"And this isn't England," D'Angelo raises his hand to the back of my neck, squeezing in the way that makes me melt back against his chest, "where all the criminals are armed with is a harsh word."

"Have you seen the size of the zombie knives in London?" I huff.

"Have you seen the size of the guns in LA?" D'Angelo shakes me.

Robyn holds up her phone. "I have the cops and our security team on speed dial. Gibbs said that you needed to be in there alone for one hour. A single minute longer, and we'll rush in to find you. If anything goes wrong, we're calling them and…"

She breaks off, hugging her arms around herself.

"Hey, nothing will go wrong because the bastard picked the wrong bloke for this dare." I give a bright smile. "I'm the horror fanatic, right? The one time that my parents took me to the fair, there was this brilliant haunted house with a man dressed up with a chainsaw. He chased you and shit. I went on the ride three times, until my money ran out. Do you remember, bro?"

Eden's lips tighten. He doesn't answer.

Concerned, I squirm out of D'Angelo's grip. "It'll be fine. I like being scared."

Eden's eyes narrow.

When I take a step toward the door, however, he deliberately blocks my path.

"You're not going in." Eden tilts up his chin.

I know that look.

Eden has spent his life giving in to me on anything that will make me happy. He's more dominant than I am but he's never used that to push me around, only look out for me.

It's what he thinks he's doing now.

He's more scared than I am.

Throughout our lives, Eden has done anything to make sure that he's the one suffering the pain, rather than me. But he doesn't understand that watching someone you love suffer instead of you, is worse.

It hurts more than anything in the fucking world.

I rush to my brother, resting our foreheads together. I give him a one-armed hug.

Eden never takes his intense gaze off my face.

"We both adore our Robyn," I whisper. "And this man could destroy her family. She loves her dad. I don't know what's behind this shit Gibbs is talking about but I won't risk screwing this up for coach or the Bay Rebels. I know you wouldn't want Robyn to be hurt in the crossfire. Just one short hour, yeah?"

"We're twins." Eden's eyes are stormy. "I'll take your place. Gibbs won't know. It doesn't matter what happens to me."

Something sick twists inside me.

Not again.

He can't expect me to watch him do that for me *again*.

"No, Dee," I hiss. "And it fucking does matter." I take a deep, steadying breath. Then I say, louder, "I need you to wait out here and guard Robyn for me. I can't trust Jude. He may fall into more brambles like a himbo Prince Charming."

"I heard that," D'Angelo says, icily.

"I know." I grin, drawing away from Eden.

Then before Eden can protest that he should pull some twin switching place trick because he's more expendable than me or other bullshit that'll make me want to knee him in the balls, I bound up the steps.

I stare up at the intimidating door with the banner swinging above it.

Is this Gibb' mansion, or has he simply hired it?

He's truly planned this.

He's been careful to make sure that this place is secluded at the bottom of a long driveway.

Yep, serial killer vibes.

"Anybody home? Ghosts? Vampires? Psycho coaches?" I knock on the door.

No reply.

When I push on the door, it swings open.

And that makes me shiver more than anything in the haunted house back in Guildford managed.

There's something freaky about stepping into someone else's home uninvited, especially when it's the type of multi-million dollar mansion that your mum cleans for a living.

"Leave the door open," D'Angelo calls.

I rip off my t-shirt and bundle it into a ball like I would when I played soccer with my mates in the schoolyard and needed something to use as a goal.

I shove the t-shirt onto the floor, using it as a wedge to keep the front door wide open.

Light streams in through the door, otherwise the entrance hall would have been pitch black.

"Wow." I stare around at the giant ghosts that are hung in shadowy sheets from the ceiling.

I bounce on my toes.

It's like a film set.

I'd have walked straight into the ghosts, if I hadn't propped open the door to allow in the light.

Gibbs may expect me to be fearful and on the alert. But if this is the level that the game is going to be played at, then I'm not going to lose it.

I bat the swinging ghosts, pushing them aside.

My feet are loud on the marble floor. The further that I walk from the front door, the darker it becomes.

Anxiety itches under my skin that the further I move into the mansion, the less likely my lovers are to be able to hear me, even if I do scream.

I wrinkle my nose against the smoky stench.

What's that smell underneath it? Something rotting?

I tense up.

I didn't expect to be this hyped. Yet this doesn't feel at all like it did in the fair.

Robyn is right.

Real life truly isn't the same as watching the movies or false frights for entertainment.

I know that some bloke with a grudge has set this up. It's easy for thrills to turn into genuine terror.

Then they don't become as fun.

I strain to listen.

Shit, is that someone else's footfall?

Is somebody else inside here with me?

Or am I hearing the other's moving around outside?

It's disorientating.

My heart hammers hard in my chest.

I lick my dry lips, shoving through the ghosts to the back of the mansion.

I move into a room, which is deep in the haunted house.

It's completely dark now.

I strain to listen.

Is someone breathing close to my ear?

Hot breath gusts against my neck.

My skin goosebumps.

I twirl in a panic, flailing out my arms.

My pulse roars in my ears.

But I touch nothing but empty air.

"Who's there?" I yell.

Silence.

For a long moment, I don't move.

Did I imagine it?

Slowly, I force myself to turn around. Then I hold my hands out in front of myself, edging forward slowly.

All of a sudden, something falls down on top of me.

"Fuck right…absolutely…off." I rip at the person…thing…I don't even know.

I swipe with my arms, as my heart leaps into my throat.

I slip my hand into my pocket and pull out my phone. I use its small light to see in front of me.

It's a giant, grotesque skeleton.

I stare at it for a long time, as my heart slows.

Then I give a relieved laugh. "Bloody hell, D'Angelo is never learning about this."

I push at the skeleton, feeling my way into the next room.

Something sticky wraps across my face and chest.

I scrub furiously at my skin, but when I take another step, my cheeks are covered again in what feels like spiderwebs.

I drop my phone to the side in shock.

My eyes widen.

"Fuck." I stumble forward, frantically breaking through the webs.

My skin is crawling like I'm covered in spiders.

Could I be?

I'll kill Gibbs, if I am.

"Only silly string," I chant to myself. "Only silly string."

I raise my phone and check myself.

My chest and hair are covered in pretend spiderwebs and silly string.

Nothing else.

Relieved, I collapse against the wall.

It's fake like the ghosts and the skeletons.

Perhaps, there's no one else in here with me.

Gibbs is relying on my imagination playing tricks on me.

After everything that I've been through in my life, if he thinks that Hollywood nightmares can put me off my game, then he's the one who's dreaming.

If anything, I'm feeling energized.

Defiantly, I stride forward like the lights are on.

How long have I been wandering around in here?

It feels like hours, but I bet that it's only been minutes. I can't see my watch, how am I meant to know?

When I reach what must be the wall, however, I notice a sign stuck on the wall above a door.

ENTER HERE, IF YOU DARE

I laugh. "Cute."

I push the heavy wooden door open and swagger into the room.

Immediately, I fall over something soft.

I drop my phone.

I feel around, and to surprise, realize that it's a thin mattress.

I wrinkle my nose at the stink of musty mold.

All of a sudden, I hear fast footfalls behind me.

Horrified, I push myself to my feet.

Someone *is* in here.

"Who…?" I demand.

Then the door slams shut.

My guts churn with dread.

I throw myself at the door, feeling for its handle.

There isn't one.

My stomach drops.

That's not good.

I shove on the door, but it doesn't budge.

"Hey." I bang furiously on the door. "Open up right bloody now. Let me out. *Let me out...*"

My head feels like it'll burst. I'm sweating.

Suddenly, I feel young and out of control.

Claustrophobic, I'm trapped.

This is familiar. The smells, darkness, and the sensation of the wood beneath the fingers.

Banging on the door and demanding, let me out.

I stagger back, falling onto the mattress, which I realize with revulsion is familiar too. "He wouldn't. He hasn't. I'm not back there. This isn't the same. I escaped."

Bile rises up the back of my throat. I choke.

Putting my head between my knees, I spit up.

My breathing is too fast.

I'm trembling.

This is the Room.

The bloody Room.

My nightmare.

And my worst fear, which is the same as my brother's, that I never escaped from here.

My thoughts are spiraling. Sitting in the dark, I'm shaking apart.

I'm slipping back to that time.

I can't let myself.

I hit my head hard with the heel of my fist to ground myself. I mustn't fall into a flashback.

It's not a proper mental health technique, but it's all that I have right now.

"I'm not back there," I mutter because in the darkness, hearing my voice is the only thing that I have to hold onto. "I'm a grown man. Dee saved us. This is just my past haunting me."

Believe it, believe it, believe...

Except, tears still well in my eyes.

When Eden and I were kids and had been sold by our biological parents to the other couple, I begged them each night to choose me to *play* with.

Except, they always chose Eden.

The bastards had a contest going to see who could get him to speak first.

Neither of them won that bet.

I've had to live my entire life, however, with the guilt that they *didn't want me*, and sick as that sounds, I did everything to try to get them to choose me instead of my twin. Because then Eden wouldn't have been beaten so hard and repeatedly that now he can't play hockey.

Being locked up in the room next door, listening to my twin being hurt through the wall, while I banged and screamed, until I lost my voice, is my hell.

Only, it really happened.

And Gibbs has recreated it.

"Dee is safe." I draw my knees up to my chest and hug my arms around them. "He's outside the house."

I have my phone.

I could call for Robyn or D'Angelo.

They'd rescue me. Stop this. Free me in a way that my brother and I had no one to call to help us back then.

I'm lucky to have found two people who I trust will always come to save me from the monsters.

Yet I promised that I'd stand up and be the one to face the danger this time.

Eden spent weeks facing the monsters alone, when he was only a kid.

What would it look like, if I'm the one who backs out now?

I can't let Robyn down.

I'm bloody crazy over that woman.

Plus, D'Angelo had to face his past. Aren't I merely doing the same thing?

I can handle this.

It's nothing more than a dark room, right?

I take a steadying breath. "Dee's safe…he's not next door…he's safe."

Memories force themselves into my mind.

Eden carried into the Room, bruised and bloodied and not moving. Sitting with him for hours afterwards, desperate and holding him in my arms. Having no idea whether my brother was dead or alive.

The fear, when his eyes would finally flutter open.

Dee, Dee, don't close your eyes. What if you don't wake up and leave me alone with the monsters?

Unexpectedly, something loud thumps against the wall in the room next door.

I jump.

It sounds like someone being thrown against the wall.

A kid.

The noise is followed by a slap, punch, and…

"No," I shout.

I can't help it.

I hold my hands over my ears but I can still hear it.

Sobbing, I scrabble back against the wall. "Stop it."

The sounds continue.

I'm back there.

They have my brother.

They're hurting my brother.

I shake my head from side to side. Dazed, I'm lost in a maelstrom of emotions.

"Dee." I can't see through the blur of tears but I stagger to my feet, falling against the thick door.

I claw at where the handle should have been in my desperation. My nails snap off, but I hardly feel the pain.

"Let me out," I scream. I bang on the door with my bloodied hands. "Stop hurting my brother. Dee! Let me out. *Dee!*"

CHAPTER TWENTY-SIX

Crypto.com Arena, Los Angeles

Shay

Dee, Dee, don't close your eyes. What if you don't wake up and leave me alone with the monsters?

I rapidly blink my eyes, forcing away the echoing voice in my mind.

It's not real.

I'm not back there.

I'm on the ice. This is the evening of the game between the Bay Rebels and the Los Angeles Kings.

It's a tough game, which the pundits are predicting us to lose.

I've promised D'Angelo that I'm not going to fall apart, during the game. I won't be distracted like he was after his dare.

I can't be.

We *have* to win tonight.

The rest of the team is relying on me to score.

What's there to be scared of? It was only smoke and mirrors in that haunted house. A musty room with a mattress and no light with sound recordings set up next door to freak me out based on what I'd told my therapist.

It wasn't real.

And I'm free now.

But it bloody doesn't feel like it.

I force myself to concentrate.

I can't hear the crowds. I can barely see the rest of the players,

Everything is narrowed down to my stick, the puck in front of me, and the *white, white, white* all around.

The world is blurred like there are still tears in my eyes.

There aren't.

Yesterday, in that room, I cried until my eyes were dry again and swollen.

I'm glad that my face is hidden underneath this helmet.

I skate like there's wind beneath me, as if I'm flying.

Fleeing.

Perhaps, I'm faster on the ice than anyone else because they're not running away from monsters like I am.

I skate toward the goal as fast as I ran out of Gibbs' mansion, once the hour was up and the door swung open.

Ran and flung my arms around Eden, refusing to let go.

Ran from my haunted past.

Thumps, smacks, a kid's desperate sobs...

All of a sudden, a LA Kings' defenseman swerves in front of me.

I'm too lost in my head to see him, until it's too late.

But my mind clears, snapped into sharp focus at the challenge.

I don't bloody think so, Your Majesty.

Adrenaline rushes through me, as I don't drop my speed, but instead, fake going wide.

Then immediately, I take a quick glance at the goal.

A lot of blokes shoot the puck at the net. But I shoot to bloody score.

And I do.

Suddenly, it's like the lights and sound have been turned on in the arena.

I stagger from the sound of the crowd exploding with joy. I squint against the bright lights.

My teammates are offering each other fist bumps in celebration.

I don't raise my stick, however, or even smile.

Everyone is watching me.

Suddenly, I feel lost.

"Dee," I mutter.

I stare down at my hands in my gloves, confused.

They don't feel like they belong to me. This uniform

with its pads, tight socks, and polyester jersey feels too constricting.

I'm trapped.

I need to escape.

I begin to pull at the strap on my helmet, but then someone wraps their arms around me in a celebratory hug.

"Deep breaths," a calming, familiar voice whispers. "I've got you."

I raise my hands, clutching onto the man's strong shoulders. I take deep breaths of his masculine scent.

"That's it." D'Angelo — it's my captain — continues. I know that he has to let go of me now with the whole arena and everyone watching but I don't want him to. "You should enjoy this moment. You've been lighting up the lamp all evening. Both teams have three goals. We need one more, and I bet that'll be enough to win. This has been hard on you, but I'm with you. You're not alone. We'll kick these Kings' asses and show them who the true ice royalty are. We can do this together, right?"

He pulls back, giving me a piercing look.

I struggle to meet his frosty gaze, nodding.

He gives a curt nod, skating away to the face-off zone.

I glance to the side of the rink.

Robyn and Eden are standing together on the other side of the glass.

Robyn catches my gaze, grinning.

She's wrapped up in a long coat, as well as Eden's gray scarf and gloves. Also, a woolen hat that Eden insisted on going out to buy for her, which makes her look like an elf.

Her hair still splays around her like tentacles, when she jumps up and down in excitement.

She waves at me.

I force myself to raise my stick in answer.

Guilt slams through me, however, when my gaze darts to Eden standing at Robyn's side.

Eden's shoulders are hunched in a way that tells me that his ribs are hurting.

He's been pushing himself too hard. The long hours in the RV are bad for his recovery. I better make sure that he's truly giving himself enough time for his physiotherapy exercises.

Yet he's doing this trip to support me.

He's taken every step of his life to stay with me.

My shadow.

Shakily, I turn away from them both.

I didn't think that anyone could accept or understand me in the way that my brother does, but then Robyn burst like a klutzy angel into my life.

I don't deserve either of them.

I let them both down yesterday.

My stomach twists.

I didn't tell Robyn. I couldn't.

How could I admit that I tried to escape the Room? I'd have run from the haunted house before the hour was up, if the door hadn't been locked, failing the dare.

Shit, I'd have been the bastard who wrecked *her* family.

It's the same way that I let down my own brother by not being able to protect him, when we were kids.

That eats me up.

I spent our entire childhoods trying to make up for it, but no matter what I do, it's never going to be enough.

After that long hour trapped in the dark with only my demons, I see that fucking clearly now.

My heart beats faster.

I slowly skate to line up to face the Kings in a circle.

One more goal...

My hands are sweaty, slipping on my stick. I clutch it tighter, white knuckled.

Finally, the referee drops the puck between D'Angelo and the Kings' center. They battle for it, and D'Angelo wins.

I turn quickly, making for the goal and working to get myself in a position that he can pass to me.

We're good at this.

D'Angelo and I have an intuitive understanding of each other's play. It gives us the edge.

For the first time, my normal thrill at playing rushes through me. I smile, glancing at the net. I find open space to the side and a brilliant position, from which to shoot.

D'Angelo has set me up on the perfect goal.

He raises his stick and passes the puck to me.

To my shock, all six feet six solid muscle of Minchew, the Kings' left defenseman, barrels into me. He's hardly even pretending that he's going for the puck.

Minchew elbows me in the stomach with the butt end of his stick.

I wheeze, unable to breath.

Bent over, I suck in desperate gasps of air.

I don't know where the puck's gone.

I've lost it.

When Minchew slams me back against the boards, my back protests.

"B-b-bastard," I gasp out.

But for a moment, I revel in the pain.

Since the moment that door slammed shut in the haunted house, and I realized that I was back in the Room, this is what I've needed: The clear, simplicity of physical pain.

It hurts less than emotional pain.

It blocks memories and spiraling thoughts from my mind.

I clasp my bruised stomach, peering up at Minchew, who's still casually caging me.

I hate that I'm the shortest player on the rink.

Minchew's long, auburn hair flows out of his helmet, matching his stubbly beard.

"Some kind of fucking hero, huh?" Minchew leans closer. "You're a newbie who doesn't know shit. You just got lucky. So, don't go thinking that you deserve to win, sunshine."

He starts to turn away.

I should let him.

Minchew's only venting because he's pissed at how well the Bay Rebels are playing. He's reached the playoffs three times already, but I've been schooling him this game.

Fucking hero?

My chest is tight. The sound of thumps and slaps echo around my mind.

I drop my stick, holding my hands over my ears.

Minchew twists back to me, narrowing his eyes at me in confusion.

Suddenly, I'm desperate for more pain — *anything* — to make the memories in my head quieten.

"If I'm lucky, then *your* bad luck in this game must be karma for being such an arsehole," I spit my chirp at him like a challenge.

Hit me.

I may as well have yelled it.

Minchew stares at me in surprise. "What?"

"Or is it that you're too old to win, grandpa?" I tilt up my chin. "Do the nurses know that you left the care home? Wait, does your coach even know that you're out here?"

I used this trick at high school.

When I needed pain to block out everything that I couldn't face, I'd allow the class bully to corner me. Then I'd talk back with as much sass as possible.

It wasn't difficult for me to be a brat.

I never dared use the same trick with Blythe. She hurt me enough, even when I was trying to be good.

I can't suppress this urge to get what I *deserve*.

D'Angelo is too good a man to treat me like this. No matter how much I screw up, break the rules, or brat, he's never harmed me.

I don't understand why.

And Eden would cut off his own hands, before he laid one on me.

Minchew slowly and deliberately pulls off his gloves, followed by his helmet. He throws them onto the ice.

He looks at me expectantly like he expects me to follow suit and join in the fight.

I don't.

This isn't a fight.

It's a beating.

"Shay," I hear D'Angelo's desperate call from behind Minchew.

But it's too late.

Minchew shrugs like he doesn't care that this is one-sided. "It looks like I need to teach this newbie a lesson about what happens to mouthy shits."

When Minchew punches me in my bruised stomach, I double over in agony. I wrap my arms around myself, but it's no protection from the flurry of blows to my chest.

I close my eyes. Submitting to it. Falling into the pain.

I force my arms to drop to my sides, no longer protecting myself.

I'm a sacrificial offering.

I'm sorry, Robyn. I'm sorry, Dee.

CHAPTER TWENTY-SEVEN

Ocean Hotel, Anaheim

Eden

RAGE SWEEPS THROUGH ME, burning the words in my throat to ash.

If I tried to speak, nothing would come out but smoke.

Last night, when I'd been forced to helplessly watch from the other side of the glass, while Minchew beat on my brother, I wouldn't have been breathing smoke.

I'd have been roaring fire like a fucking dragon.

I wanted to burn down the entire arena.

Yet it wasn't Minchew, with whom I was angry. It was

my twin, who'd stood there, with his arms at his side, *allowing* himself to be pummeled.

I know why I've lost my voice this morning.

It's because I know that I'm really angry at myself.

I should burn myself to ash for being unable to protect Shay.

I can feel every line of my phoenix tattoo on my back and remember each second of the pain, as it was inked.

A pain that at the time meant freedom and reclamation of my body.

If I'd been on the ice with Shay like I used to be, then I'd have stopped Minchew.

I should have tried harder to stop Shay from entering that haunted house.

I concentrate on rubbing arnica cream into Shay's bare back in circles. It helps to hide that my hand is shaking.

Shay doesn't also need to worry about my shit.

Shay and I have rubbed arnica into each other since we started playing hockey. It's a physical game. This is part of our routine.

But this time is different.

Because I know that Shay deliberately got himself hit.

Concentrating on tasks has helped to hide my turmoil this morning. I focused on packing up alongside Robyn from the Los Angeles hotel, getting us into the motorhome, then the short drive to Anaheim, which is the final leg of the road trip.

Exhausted, I grimace, as my shoulder aches.

The Ocean Hotel is bright and modern with a balcony and views over a beautiful pool.

Shay is sitting in a cool bath with his knees pulled up to his chest. He's staring with glassy eyes at a random point on the far wall of the bathroom.

He's not snapped out of this half dazed state since the end of the game yesterday.

I expected coach to bust Shay's balls after the game, but for the first time, D'Angelo squared off to coach. He insisted that Shay skip the debriefing. Instead, he guided him gently back to the hotel.

D'Angelo spoke to Shay more softly than I've heard him talk to him before, wrapping him in a blanket and stroking his hair. Then he asked me to raid the minibar for chocolate and a Gatorade.

Robyn spooned close on the other side of Shay on the bed.

Shay didn't speak.

It was like he'd switched places with me.

I watched them in confusion, awkward and unsure. My skin itched.

D'Angelo appeared to know what to do.

I wanted to hit something.

Maybe myself.

The bathroom is large with navy blue walls and driftwood floors.

There has been an attempt to make the room feel like the seaside with wooden bowls filled with shell shaped soap and seaweed shampoo.

Potted palms lean beside the window, which looks out over the park. A gleaming luxury corner shower would dominant the bathroom, if there wasn't also a sunken bath.

It's a calming oasis.

Shay isn't calm, however, even laid out like a merman in the most indulgent bath that either of us have been in. He's not enjoying it like he should be, however, and I know that he'd normally be happily talking about how he's never been in a bathroom this big, lain in a sunken bath, or whether if he uses that shampoo, his hair will transform into seaweed.

I need his sunshine back.

How can I jolt him out of this state?

I take a deep breath of the delicious white tea fragrance, which washes through the room.

I like this hotel the best.

This is why D'Angelo is such a good boss. I bet he chose it for me because he knew that it was tea scented.

Are there hotels that also come with complimentary cats?

I'll ask D'Angelo.

I'm stripped to my joggers in order to not get wet. I shuffle on my knees, glancing to get a better look at my brother's face.

He doesn't notice.

His expression is still blank like his typical easy smile is trapped inside.

When I look up, Robyn meets my gaze. Her expression is sad.

She's sitting on the other side of the bath with the

sleeves of her ivory shirt rolled up. Her pants are soaked, but she doesn't appear to care.

Robyn is grasping Shay's hand and examining his fingernails with a frown. "These are torn and... What the hell happened? Sorry, you don't need to tell me. Once you're out, I'll give you a mini manicure and sort them out, okay?"

Shay doesn't reply.

Robyn continues to examine the bloody tips of his fingers.

I narrow my eyes, before washing the cream off my hand and gripping Shay by the chin.

For the first time, he focuses on me. "Dee?"

He blinks, rapidly.

I try to force out what I want to say, but my throat is too dry with ash.

Instead, I forcibly turn Shay's head to make him face Robyn.

"Your fingernails." Robyn places his hand down on the side, tracing over it. "You must have hurt them. I can sort them out and then paint them for you."

"Thanks, love." Shay sounds far away.

Robyn meets my gaze over his head, as lost as I am.

Then she puts on a determinedly bright smile. "Your brother bought chocolate chip muffins as a treat for breakfast."

She reaches behind her and drags out the basket of muffins, which I went out myself this morning to a bakery down the street to hunt out.

Few things put Shay in a better mood than pastries.

I bought them myself.

Shay may have new lovers in his life who have much more money than I ever will, but I'm still his twin.

I can take care of him.

"And one more thing." Robyn dangles a bottle of beer in front of Shay like it's candy.

I expect him to snatch it. He always does.

Instead, he turns away his head. "I'm not thirsty."

When my brother and I were in high school, sometimes I'd find him like this — beaten and bloodied in a corridor with the same glassy eyed expression.

I didn't understand it then.

I thought it may be that he simply felt emotions more strongly than I did. Happiness and pain were intense highs and lows to Shay, whereas to me, they were numbed.

Shit happens. You live with it.

Shay experiences things differently.

I wish that D'Angelo was here, but he's off meeting with his PI, Garcia.

Last night, in a deadly cold voice, D'Angelo declared that we were no longer taking any more of Gibbs' dares and that he was finding a way to end this.

D'Angelo and I stayed up all night, while Robyn and Shay slept curled in our arms. I wasn't allowing either of them out of my sight for a moment.

Together, D'Angelo and I brainstormed, made emergency calls, and listed everyone within the NHL who owed him favors.

The primary of those being the captain of the Anaheim Ducks.

I ease myself back from the bath to give Shay space.

But all of a sudden, words are freed from my throat.

Shit, they're not the ones that I intended to say.

"I'm angry with you," I blurt.

Silence.

Robyn shoots me a dirty look.

"I'm angry with me too." Shay's wet hair hangs over his face.

My lips pinch.

I'm talking about him allowing himself to be hurt on the ice.

"We're not talking about the same thing," I say.

I think.

I'm never sure about shit like that.

Shay clutches his arms tighter around his knees. "I'm sorry that I let you down."

Robyn slowly places the beer beside the muffin basket. "You didn't. It was a draw last night. No one expected us to be able to achieve a win. So—"

"In the dare." Shay's voice is so soft that I need to lean closer to hear him. "I freaked out and would have failed it. I only didn't because I was locked in."

"After this, do you think that I give a fuck about the dare?" Robyn looks like an Amazonian warrior with the way that her eyes flash. I believe that she'd stand up to any one to battle for my brother. "You're what matters."

Shay shakes his head like he's struggling to truly take in her words. "You're not angry? I deserve—"

"To be loved." Robyn kneels up, kissing Shay on the forehead. His gaze snaps to hers. "To believe that you deserve only the best things in this world and always have. To know that I'd never put you at risk. If you hadn't consented to do the dare, then I wouldn't have been okay with it. Hell, I was never okay with it anyway. The moment that you wanted to leave that house, you were no longer consenting. I wouldn't ever be angry about that. Fuck, the asshole actually locked you up…? But the front door was open all the time. We didn't hear any noise from inside. You were meant to call us, if there was a problem."

Shay shivers. "I guess that it was soundproofed."

"What was?"

"The Room."

I become ashen.

Memories of a stained mattress, darkness, bruises and pain and Shay sobbing flood through me.

I can't stop them.

Abruptly, I push myself to my feet, backing off to the wall.

My expression is shuttered, but inside, I'm a mess.

Except, it was in the room *next door* to the Room that I died and was reborn into a phoenix, as I flew through the air over and over.

I know that Robyn only heard the *room*, without a capitalized 'r'.

I wish that I did.

Then I wouldn't have to know that someone forced my brother back to the worst two weeks of his life.

I brace myself against the wall. I wish that I was alone with Shay so that I could hug him.

Luckily, Robyn's here to lean up and kiss Shay, tenderly.

When she draws back, she cups his cheek. "I'm sorry that you were trapped inside, and we didn't know. Shit, is that why your fingernails are…? I swear, we'll help you through this. Just tell me what you need."

For the first time, Shay's expression brightens. "You, love."

"Lucky you have me then." Robyn kisses him again. Then she entangles their hands, raising them to show his ring on her thumb. "Four stars, one to represent each of us in this relationship. We're equals; it doesn't work without every single one of us. Dad, the Bay Rebels, and the terror of my past being opened again are all important, but nothing will ever be as important to me as you three."

She sounds like she means it.

I watch with an intent gaze, as Robyn brushes my brother's hair out of his face. Then she reluctantly lets go of his hand and stands up.

She grabs a fluffy white towel from the rack and holds it up. "Come on, no prunes allowed."

Shay smiles for the first time. "Yes, ma'am."

Robyn chuckles. "Are you trying to make me wet?"

"In both ways." When Shay splashes her deliberately, as he pulls himself out of the bath and his muscles bunch, she squawks in outrage.

Robyn attempts to retaliate, but Shay dances away.

Robyn snaps the towel at his ass, and he yelps. Then he catches the towel with his hand, yanking her closer into his arms.

Shay's eyes are dancing.

His wet body is pressed to hers, as they kiss.

Then together, they…inefficiently…dry him, before he wraps the towel around his waist. His chest is still glistening with water droplets, but he's now grinning.

I'm happy to see Shay coming out of that trapped place, which frightens me.

But I've fallen into a dark place of my own.

"I'm going to kill Gibbs." My words are calm.

A statement.

Inevitable.

Shay's smile fades.

"Good sentiment. I believe you. But I have a better idea," D'Angelo drawls from the doorway.

Relieved, I glance over at him.

D'Angelo's dressed immaculately in a light navy suit and waistcoat, whereas the rest of us are half naked and wet.

He eyes the disaster zone that's the bathroom for a moment. "I can't leave you alone for a couple of hours, can I?"

Robyn snorts. "Says the playboy infamous for trashing hotel rooms by holding wild orgies with cake fights."

"Fair. But those hotels agreed beforehand because I tip exceptionally well."

Then D'Angelo's gaze slides to Shay. His eyes darken with rage as he takes in the expanse of bruises over almost every inch of Shay' chest and abs, as well as wrapping around his kidneys.

Minchew truly worked him over.

"How are you feeling?" D'Angelo's voice is tight.

Shay plays with the towel at his waist, anxiously. "As shit as I deserve to. Are you disappointed in me?"

Surprise flashes across D'Angelo's face. "I'm *proud*, cucciolo. You scored three goals in yesterday's game. Who could ask more than that? I only scored one. So, we drew the game. It only means that we'll have to kick the Ducks' asses tomorrow. And don't think that I won't be trying my hardest because right now, you're winning the kink contest. I'm not losing to you."

Robyn grins. "See, healthy competition because of kink."

Shay licks his dry lips. "But I freaked out."

"You didn't." D'Angelo's voice becomes harder. "You made a decision to throw chirps at a brutal jerk like Minchew. Or do you want to pretend that you didn't know how he'd react?"

Shay reddens and doesn't answer.

D'Angelo is looking at Shay severely, not allowing him to drop his gaze. "Whatever is going on, you need to tell me. I'm your dom. Communication is the most important thing for me to be able to keep you safe. You don't get to punish yourself. And you know what you truly don't get to do? Incite someone else to do it for you."

Shay wraps his arms around himself. "I don't know if I can stop."

"You can. Because I'm adding it to the rules." D'Angelo

cocks his head. "When we're back home, we need to renegotiate the contract to add: No harming yourself or using others to deliberately harm you. What do you think?"

"It's a good rule," Shay whispers.

Robyn gently lays her hand on Shay's arm. "It sounds a good idea for all of us. I know how you feel about therapy, but at least talk to us if you can."

"And if you ever feel that desperate need to be punished," D'Angelo appears pained, and I realize that he doesn't want to add this but he is for Shay's sake, "then you come to me. I'm responsible for you. I'll find a way to help you with this that won't harm you, I promise."

Shay is looking at him with wonder. "Why would you bother with my shit?"

D'Angelo's expression finally gentles. "Because I love you, cucciolo. And I'll tell you that as many times as you need to hear it. I'll do whatever I need to do to prove it to you."

D'Angelo marches across the wooden floor to Shay. He pulls Shay against his chest, ignoring the way that his dampness is ruining his suit, at the same time as Robyn slips her arms around Shay's waist from the back.

Shay is caught safely between them both.

I stay back, in the shadows.

Watching.

My brother has found two people who understand him and can keep him safe.

As kids, he only needed me.

Once, I always wanted to be the one to protect him.

Now, I know that he needs more than that.

Since I met Robyn, I know that *I* do as well.

I need her.

"If I have to make you wear your cock ring every day," D'Angelo growls into Shay's ear, "to remind you that you're secure, owned, and loved, then I will."

Shay's smile is finally relaxed. "Promises, promises."

Robyn smothers her laugh against Shay's shoulder.

"How do we stop Gibbs?" I clench my fists. "I can kill him."

I repeat that end part, in case they didn't believe me the first time that I offered.

Seeing the three of them together and happy again, I know that I'd do anything for them.

"Firstly, I already heard you on the whole killing thing." D'Angelo pulls back from Shay to shoot me an assessing glance. "Secondly, surprising as this may sound, murder isn't always the answer. This man is a sadistic asshole who's revenge obsessed. In order to get that, he's been going after *my* family as well as me. Did you think that I ever intended to let him win? I'm going to fucking destroy him."

Robyn stares at D'Angelo. "Wait, you've only been playing along…?"

D'Angelo gives a devilish smile. "I needed the time to dig enough dirt on him in order to go on the offensive."

"We were up last night, calling final contacts and putting things into place," I comment.

I don't say that my idea is still better.

It is.

"This morning, I missed the bathtime fun in order to

meet with Garcia and put together the final pieces of the puzzle." D'Angelo pulls at his cufflinks. "Gibbs is meant to be Superpuck. He's not branded only as an outstanding coach but he's built his entire career on his reputation as an outstanding family man."

"Why does that help us?" Robyn demands. "Gibbs is well known in the press to be a good guy. I've been researching him since this began, and anyone would be envious of his golden reputation."

"Except, it's bullshit." Why is D'Angelo studying Robyn with a regretful expression, as he continues, "People sometimes aren't who you expect. Even the dead."

"What do you…?"

"This guy is more like Lex Luthor in secret, a cocky womanizer who indulges in misogyny. And that's not to mention the sexual harassment of female staff members, which he's managed to keep quiet through NDAs."

"Shit." Robyn clings tighter to Shay. "If he has enough power to keep this quiet all these years, how did you manage to find it out?"

"Garcia is good at his job, principessa, partly because I pay him so much." D'Angelo looks unsettled. "Plus, the thing about bullying sadists, who can play games as smoothly as Gibbs has with us, is that they've been playing them for decades. Gibbs is a coach. I knew that he must have treated his own players in the same way. So, I hit up my contacts in his past teams and even amongst the current Ducks. Some were too scared to speak but others, once they knew in vague terms that their coach was hurting young players on my team, as well as *me*, were willing to help, off the record. Most of the players in the NHL have each other's backs, when we can. We're brothers."

"He hurts them like he's hurt us?" My jaw is clenched.

"Some worse," D'Angelo replies. "He hacks their records and monitors them. It's why I decided to return the favor. He finds out their pain points, then he presses and presses, until he breaks them. He's like Colton but a hundred times worse. He has to hold the control."

"Then we take it back," Robyn says.

"No more dares." I step forward, determined.

D'Angelo shakes his head. "There's going to be a dare. But it'll be *ours*. He wanted three, right?"

Shay's eyes are bright and excited again. "I never could play defense."

D'Angelo slips his phone out of his pocket.

Then he reads out the text as he types it, "Dare: Meet us alone in the Ducks' locker room four hours before the game tomorrow."

CHAPTER TWENTY-EIGHT

Honda Center, Anaheim

obyn

"This is dangerously like trying to lure a wildcat, while on enemy territory." My heart beats fast in my chest. "Why did we choose the Ducks' own locker room?"

Anxiety skyrockets through me.

I wipe my sweating palms down the front of my woolen coat.

"Because an ambush is more effective, when the prey thinks that they're safe. Anyway, I happen to be good at taming wild cats." D'Angelo snags Shay by his team tie and yanks him closer, while possessively wrapping his arm around me. "A pride of them."

"Two," I correct. "And you have the ringmaster's outfit to prove it."

"It's unfair that you haven't shown me that yet, darlin'." Shay catches my gaze, and we smile at each other, conspiratorially. "Lions need to be tamed together, you know."

I shiver at the thought of D'Angelo dressed in his ringmaster outfit, holding his riding crop, while both Shay and I are tamed as his pets.

I'm adding that to our list of role plays.

Both D'Angelo and Shay are dressed in matching navy suits with arctic blue waistcoats.

They look stunning like this: dramatic opposites who fit together.

Eden is seated on a bench at the side of the locker room, focused on his phone. His brow is furrowed with concentration, as he continues to work on the plan for D'Angelo.

Even though it's within his role as PA, I know that Eden's really doing this for me.

When was the last time that he slept?

He's wearing a black suit with a gray waistcoat that matches his eyes. He looks gorgeous but dangerous.

The Honda Center's locker room is at the end of a long, white corridor, past a state-of-the-art gym. The walls are lined with stalls above orange, padded benches. The players' equipment is hung up on each stall: pads, helmets, skates, and jerseys.

The walls are emblazoned with motivational words like **CONSISTENT** and **COMPETE**.

My nose wrinkles at the chemical scent of rubber mixed with sweat, along with the mildew stench of hockey equipment.

"Is it all set up?" D'Angelo demands.

Eden nods.

I bite my lip.

These could be our last moments alone. I must grab them.

"This is our first road trip." I glance at each of my men in turn. "Despite everything, it's been special to me. I won't let some pathetic man, who can only live in the past, steal that from us."

"Too right." Shay grins. "I know that I've found some things difficult. But most of this holiday has been bloody brilliant. Hasn't it, Dee?"

Finally, Eden looks up from his phone and straight at me.

He nods again.

"My brother and I got to see some of America for the first time, as well as having our first experience of traveling in a motorhome." When Shay happily counts off his first experiences on his fingers, D'Angelo tightens his hold on Shay's tie like he's frightened of losing him or wants to be certain that he's now his. "Camping was fantastic. I'm going to want more of those roasted marshmallows on our next holiday together."

Our next holiday.

He says it so naturally. He doesn't appear to have realized what he's said.

Does that mean he's starting to accept that D'Angelo and I are in this relationship with his twin and him long term?

D'Angelo smiles, meeting my eye.

He's thinking the same as I am.

"Done." D'Angelo moves his hand from Shay's tie to his shoulder. "But next time, no smearing that gooey muck down my suit."

"I make no promises."

"Do you know what else I enjoyed about the trip?" Shay nudges D'Angelo cheekily. "Teasing you over the radio channel. I've seen that in the movies but never had the chance to torment anyone that way, since my parents don't have a car."

"I'm glad to be of service," D'Angelo says, dryly.

"My favorite memory was the vibrating cock ring." I smile, dreamily.

"The hotel that smells of tea," Eden adds.

"Simply being able to spend time with all of you together." D'Angelo's cheeks flush. "Being allowed to spoil you."

Shay looks at D'Angelo through his eyelashes. "Permission to always spoil us."

"You can't take that back now, cucciolo. Remember that."

"I never knew that being spoiled could be a threat."

"I'm creative, remember?"

"I just want you to know how proud I am." I look

down. "Dad sent us alone on this trip because he didn't trust you. But ironically, it's *his* past that's screwed things up." I glance at Eden. "The itinerary, which I have finally — maybe — read has kept us perfectly on time. You've coped with the new and busy social situations. I know that's been tough. Your efficiency is mind-blowing."

Eden places down his phone, looking like he doesn't know how to respond to the praise.

"It's especially mind-blowing," D'Angelo agrees, "considering I'm one of the most demanding and micromanaging bosses in existence."

"You're not." Eden crosses his arms. "You're the best boss."

D'Angelo's eyes widen.

I struggle not to laugh, when I see that he's equally unsure how to respond to praise.

Shay, on the other hand, simply claps his hands together. "A mutual appreciation society. The best boss gets the best PA. And Dee and I should know whether you're a good boss or not. Do you remember that time at college, when you had a summer cleaning job, and your boss kept making you illegally work double shifts? You were working sixteen hour days without a break for months."

"I earned more money." Eden stands up, picking up his phone and pushing it into his pocket. "I could buy you the new stick you needed."

"Not the point."

"And that's why you have a proper contract," D'Angelo's voice is tight, "which protects you from working conditions like that. Talk to me, if you need anything. I won't be like Colton who overworks his staff. But it's men like Gibbs who truly give bosses a bad name."

Gibbs.

I wish that I could forget that we're here because of him.

My pulse races.

Will Gibbs truly show up? And if he does, what will happen?

I touch the glistening hockey jersey pendant at my neck.

Facing the past demons that have haunted my childhood is one of the hardest things that I have done, as frightening as leaving Wilder and starting my life independently again.

Yet I managed that.

I survived.

Now, I have a career that I love. A home. And a new relationship where I'm loved for who I truly am.

I'm seen.

I won't allow these childhood fears to control me any longer.

I definitely won't allow it to haunt Cody.

When the locker room door swings open, I jump.

"Why do you need to see me, Eden?" Cody rushes into the room. "Your text, confusing as they often are, sounded urgent. But you pulled me from a staff meeting. Colton will kick my…"

He stops and stares at us in surprise.

Cody's wearing the Bay Rebels staff uniform and looking unusually smart.

I pull away from D'Angelo to wave weakly at him.

"Why are you having a cuddle, possibly the prelude to an orgy, in the rival team's locker room?" Cody puts his hands on his hips.

I can't stop myself. I run to Cody, hugging him tightly.

All the stress and fear that Gibbs has put me through washes over me.

I shudder.

Immediately, Cody hugs me back. "Hey, what's this all about? Ryn, you're scaring me. It's okay. I'm here."

"I'm sorry." Eden sounds nervous. "Did I get you in trouble?"

"Pfft, Colton can go shove a stick up his bullying ass." Cody strokes my hair. "If you guys need me here, then I'm all in."

"Excellent." D'Angelo tugs Shay by the hand closer to Cody. "Then here's the short version: Gibbs has been playing a twisted version of truth or dare with us, since we started on the road. He threatened to tell the world that your dad deliberately attacked him on the ice, if we didn't play along. He'd tell that *truth*, if we didn't take the *dares*. I did one, then Shay. They hurt us, badly."

"So, that's why you sucked in your games," Cody exclaims.

D'Angelo glares at him.

I pull back from Cody, wiping at my eyes. "Way to go with the diplomacy, Code."

Cody gives an apologetic shrug. "I mean, why you were *distracted*."

Shay squeezes D'Angelo's hand. "You could say that."

"Now, Gibbs wants a third dare," D'Angelo explains. "But I won't allow him to target Eden or my principessa. So, we have a plan to stop him."

Cody's eyes widen, before he pulls me into a hug again. "This is the truth or dare that you were talking about in Merchant's Inn. Fuck, Ryn, why didn't you tell me that it had become more serious?"

"I wanted to keep you safe."

Cody draws back, looking at me searchingly. "You spent your life trying to keep me safe from Dad. It's not your job. I have to look out for myself sometime."

"It's not a job," I reply, stubbornly. "You're my younger brother. Looking out for you isn't something that just ends when you turn eighteen. Plus, you've always been just as protective of me."

"Michael is going to…" Cody tilts his head. "Well, probably give you a patented stern and disappointed look. I'm the one who'll be in trouble for not stopping this."

"I didn't want to involve you but I thought that you deserved to be here this evening. You've had to deal with Dad's shit because of what happened on the ice between Gibbs and Dad."

Cody looks worried. "Don't you remember that my husband warned how dangerous these games were?"

"We've learned that lesson." Eden's expression is stony.

When the door slams open, Cody shoves me behind him.

"It looks like the family are all here," a deep but smarmy voice says. "*Almost* all."

A tall, handsome man in his late fifties saunters into the locker room. He's wearing a scarlet suit, which makes his fiery red hair gleam brighter. His eyes are a pale blue.

He has the air of a golf pro who'd sleep with your partner.

Instantly, my skin crawls at his fake smile.

All three of my men prowl to stand next to Cody, blocking his view of me.

Cody's expression is fierce. "Hey, asshole, why the hell have you been screwing with my family and friends?"

"Because your dad screwed with me, sweetheart," Gibbs replies.

"You made the decision to turn up. So, you can follow orders, as well as give them," D'Angelo says, icily.

Gibbs' fake smile dies. "And you definitely know how to follow them, don't you? You dance, confess your sins, and sob on cue. Highly entertaining."

"To a psychopath," Eden says.

"Or a sadist," Shay adds.

Gibbs ignores them, leaning against the wall. "It was fascinating seeing how far I could push you for Austin. I never thought that you'd suffer your worst fears for that bastard. My boys wouldn't suffer a paper cut for me. I don't mind admitting that those snowflakes couldn't endure what you have."

"You won't mind if we're not flattered," D'Angelo drawls.

Gibbs shrugs. "Do you think that I care what you think

or feel? It was when I fully read your texts that I knew the real reason you were doing everything. You're friends with the asshole's son and in love with his daughter. All of you. You have filthy minds, by the way. The things people text to each other nowadays."

"Sorry to have shocked you." D'Angelo takes a step forward. "Can you get to the point?"

Rage flashes across Gibb's face. "The point is that then I knew you'd do anything to protect her. That's your pain point. Your weakness." He gives a bitter laugh. "I understand that drive. When you're so obsessed that you'd give up anything to keep and own a woman."

My stomach turns.

I want to hurl.

Eden launches himself at Gibbs, taking him by surprise.

Eden looks coldly deadly like this. His face is impassive, but his eyes are blazing.

"Dee," Shay calls. "Don't. It's what he wants."

Eden ignores him, however, slamming Gibbs back against the wall. Gibbs lets out a pained sound, scrabbling at Eden's hand, which is wrapped around his throat.

Eden may have one arm in a sling, but right now, he's furious enough to still be deadly.

I notice that D'Angelo doesn't move to stop Eden.

This isn't part of the plan, right?

Anxiously, I shift from foot to foot. My heart is hammering in my chest. My pulse roars in my ears.

What the hell should I do?

Gibbs chokes.

"Robyn isn't property." Eden tightens his hold on Gibbs' neck. "Nobody owns her. *She isn't a slave.*"

"Get in here," Gibbs wheezes, slamming his palm repeatedly against the wall.

What does he mean?

Cody glances back at me, confused.

The Anaheim Ducks team start to stream into the locker room. They surround us, backing us into a tight group, until we're forced against the wall.

Cody backs towards me. "Hold onto me."

I grasp onto his shoulders.

"Nobody had better fucking touch Ms. McKenna," D'Angelo commands.

Isn't the captain, Folkes, D'Angelo's friend? Weren't they in on this ambush?

Or did they betray us because they're more afraid of whatever their coach is holding over them?

Shit.

"Get. Him. Off. Me," Gibbs rasps.

A couple of large hockey players grab Eden by the waist. When he still doesn't let go, one of them snatches hold of his bad arm and begins to drag it out of his sling.

Eden howls, letting go of Gibbs.

My chest is tight. "Stop it."

Gibbs takes deep gulps of oxygen, massaging his throat.

Eden is shoved to his knees.

He's biting his lip hard enough to make it bleed now to stop himself from showing his pain again.

His whole body is tight from it, however, as his arm is twisted behind his back.

They're going to fuck up his shoulder.

"He's recovering from a serious injury, which he received on the ice," Cody yells. "I'm in charge of his medical care. You have to stop twisting that arm. As players, don't you have any respect? Fucking cowards."

"Bastards." Shay wildly punches at the men in front of him who stand a head taller.

They shove him back, but he barrels through them again.

He struggles to get through to his brother like he's possessed, desperate and shaking at the same time that he fights like he used to on the ice.

Shocked at his savagery, the Ducks allow Shay through to Eden's side. But then, two of them violently shove Shay to his knees.

Gibbs watches smugly, as Shay's arms are also yanked behind his back.

"It's going to be okay." Shay rests his forehead against his brother's. "I'm here now, bro."

Eden meets his brother's gaze but can't answer. He's working too hard on not making any sound from the agony.

"Folkes," D'Angelo addresses the captain who is standing guard over us with such iciness that I'm amazed he doesn't freeze him. "If your teammates don't let go of my friends, I am going to make it my personal mission to destroy you. And that includes no more invites to any type of party. Do you understand?"

What does he mean? *Party?*

Is that the exclusive kind that D'Angelo told me about, where you need to be vetted and wait for an invitation?

Folkes is a powerfully built player with blond curls and a scar across his bottom lip.

Folkes' eyes widen.

"Sorry, D'Angelo. No one was meant to be hurt." Then Folkes orders, "Back off, guys. *Now.*"

The rival players let go of both brothers.

Shay hisses in relief, swinging his arms forward and rubbing them.

Eden doesn't move.

Shay looks Eden over, before gently taking hold of his arm.

"Bite my shoulder, if you need to," he says, quietly.

Eden nods, hiding his face on Shay's shoulder.

Eden's scream is muffled, as Shay brings his arm forward and carefully fits it back into the sling.

"He needs pain meds and to ice that shoulder. I should check it." Cody looks worriedly at Eden.

Eden shakes his head. "I'm fine."

"Pain scale."

Eden doesn't answer.

I know why.

He's so high on the pain scale that he's probably off it. But he doesn't want to lie.

D'Angelo looks as ashen, as I bet I do. "What now?"

Gibbs adjusts his tie, trying to look in control again. "You broke the rules. There was only one dare to go. Why wouldn't you follow through? I'm giving you one more chance, before the only option is truth. And you won't like me to tell you every detail of that."

"Pass."

Gibbs gestures around at the crowd of men surrounding us. "Not an option. Your only choice is who plays the dare."

"Me," Cody says, quickly.

"Obvious. Me." Eden's kneeling but he doesn't look weak.

Gibbs steps away from the twins and weaves through the Ducks to stand in front of D'Angelo.

Then he points behind D'Angelo and Cody at *me*.

My mouth is dry.

I clutch more tightly to Cody's waist.

"But she's the one who you've all been standing in front of," Gibbs says. "So, since you don't agree on who plays, I'm picking her."

"Fuck off," Shay snarls.

"Hot tempered, isn't he?" And there's Gibbs' fake smile again.

"Actually, he's usually a ray of sunshine," I reply. "But you bring the thunder out of him. Soon, maybe even the lightning."

"Sassy, I like that." The way Gibbs is peering over Cody's shoulder at me is making me sick. "You're as pretty as your mom was, sweetheart."

"Don't talk about my mom." I tremble with rage.

"Why not? She's why we're here." Gibbs glances at Cody and me. "So, my pretty as her dead mom, here's your dare: slap the person in this group of family or *friends* who you love *least*."

I draw in a sharp breath.

Both the twins have become very still.

The asshole.

The cruel asshole.

Gibbs knows how much we love each other.

If I pick just one person, single them out and humiliate them — slap and hurt them in order to do it — then I'll destroy our poly relationship.

I'll wreck this new life that I've been forging in Freedom.

This is my worse fear.

Eden pushes himself stiffly to his feet. "It's fine, Robyn. Let's get it done."

I stare at Eden in shock.

He's standing there patiently like he believes it's a foregone conclusion that I'll choose him.

Like there could be no other choice for the least lovable.

In his life, he's always come last.

Not anymore.

"I'm not choosing you." My eyes smart with tears. "Do you know how important you are to me, my phoenix?"

Eden's gaze snaps to mine in shock.

"Phoenix?" He repeats, pleased and shocked.

His lips twitch into an almost smile.

"A slap? That's all?" D'Angelo asks, evenly.

"All?" I let go of Cody. I'm shaking. "I'd never slap any of you. Never."

"I'm cocky, grumpy, and draw smutty stickmen in the Guide." D'Angelo turns to face me. His gaze is soft in a way that it rarely is, and I suddenly realize that he's giving me permission to choose him, which will take away this pressure from me and the others thinking that they may be chosen. D'Angelo knows that he never could be. I hope. "*Green.*"

How can D'Angelo turn something that's meant to be a humiliation into an intimate moment between us?

A show of love, rather than hate?

I work my way around Cody to stand in front of D'Angelo.

"You are cocky, grumpy, and do draw a lot of smut." I take a deep breath.

Then I slap D'Angelo gently on the cheek.

D'Angelo's head doesn't even move, the slap was so light.

His pupils dilate, however, and his gaze dips to my lips like he wishes that he could kiss me.

I'm acutely aware of how many people are watching us.

Fuck, that makes me wet.

By the way that D'Angelo pushes closer to me to hide how hard he is in his pants, he's as turned on by that fact as I am.

So, face slapping.

Something to add to my kink list.

Gibbs, however, crows with delight. "Poor captain. A lesson to learn there, Folkes, don't be a cocky loser like D'Angelo or nobody will ever—"

"Thanks for keeping Gibbs here for me, until I could

arrive." Dad strides into the locker room. Then his gaze sweeps across the way that Shay is kneeling on the floor and Eden is cradling his arm. "Although I didn't say anything about roughing them up."

"They fought back," Folkes says, defensively.

Dad looks proud. "Of course they did. I don't allow anyone soft onto my team."

Shay stands up, helping his brother to his feet.

Dad is dressed in the same matching game night suit as D'Angelo and Shay are.

Cody stares at Dad, confused. "What are you doing here?"

"Saving your asses by the look of it," Dad barks.

So, that was what Eden was arranging this morning.

This is the ambush.

D'Angelo nods at Folkes, who gestures at his teammates.

"Come on, guys. Time to practice on the ice," Folkes calls.

"What the hell do you think you're doing?" Gibbs scrambles through the players, who are pushing past him like he doesn't exist. Fuck, that's satisfying to see. "Get your useless asses back here. I *own* you. I know every secret about you. Do you want me to leak to the press…" He points from player to player. "Your illegitimate child? Or your debts? Or how your Mom used to…"

Folkes grabs Gibbs' finger, bending it back.

Gibbs cringes, rather than fights.

He's only brave, when he's threatening other people from a distance.

"Listen here," Folkes leans over Gibbs, "you're never going to threaten me or my teammates again. You don't own shit."

Then he knees Gibbs so hard in the balls that I think they may pop out of his mouth.

I wince at the same time that inside I'm cheering.

Shay actually *does* whoop.

Gibbs drops to the ground with a groan.

Folkes steps over him with a wink at D'Angelo, before he leaves and shuts the locker room door.

It's suddenly quiet in the locker room, apart from Gibbs' quiet gasps.

Dad glowers at Cody. "You should have told me what was going on. You endangered your sister."

Cody stiffens.

"He didn't know, until today," I rush to explain. "It's me who kept it quiet."

"And me, coach. You knew about the original text," D'Angelo adds, tapping a rhythm of three on his thigh. "But to be fair, we couldn't tell you what happened after that because it was a provision of the threats that Gibbs here set for us. We couldn't inform you, or he'd immediately go to the press with the truth about you."

"The truth...?" Dad marches to Gibbs, dragging him to his feet by the front of his shirt. "And what's that then, Larry?"

"You tried to kill me."

Dad's startled enough to let go of Gibbs' shirt. "Is that how you see it? You're wrong. I own that I lost my temper.

I screwed up. And you paid for that. But I never meant to injure you like I did."

"You never even spoke to me after it happened." Gibbs' voice is softer.

Caught off guard, I stare at the two men.

What actually went on back then?

What *is* the truth?

Dad looks awkward. "My lawyers advised me not to. That was a mistake. So, I'll say it now. I'm sorry."

"You're apologizing?" D'Angelo bursts out. "This man has put us through hell."

"Shut up, D'Angelo," Dad orders. "That's now, and I'm talking about the past. Wouldn't you expect the men who ended Eden's career to apologize? I've spent all the years since, looking for ways to somehow redeem myself. Helping players who need second chances and support through the Bay Rebels is part of that. But that doesn't mean I've forgotten what you're doing *now* to my kids and players, Larry."

Gibbs shrugs. "It caught your attention, didn't it?"

My eyes widen. "You're kidding me. That's what this was about?"

Gibbs runs his hand through his hair. "To start with it was rage, when I saw your team performing well. Then when I read the emails and texts…" To my shock, Gibbs pushes closer into Dad's space, and Dad lets him. "Do you remember the truth or dare game that we played the first night we three met?"

Truth or dare game?

All of a sudden, my stomach is churning.

I know that I'm not going to want to hear this, but at the same time, that I need to.

Cody moves closer to me. His hand slips into mine.

"Ancient history." Dad glances at Cody and me, anguished. "If you wanted to beat my ass, then you should have fought me like a man. These games are a kid's tantrum. We're not at college anymore."

"Because if we were," Gibbs shoves Dad, "you'd remember that was the night you first kissed Beth. But then, I did too."

Cody and I both gasp at the same time.

Beth.

Our mom's name.

D'Angelo darts a concerned glance at me.

"And you wouldn't have forgotten," Gibbs continues, resolutely, "that she loved us *both*, refusing to choose between us. That we shared her. It was tough because I loved her so fucking much. I coped, however, because you and I were friends and I'd have done anything for her. Those were my happiest times: Beth watching us play hockey, studying in dorm together, and joining the boxing team because you had. We were a force."

Eden clenches his hands. "Why didn't you like us being with Robyn, coach?"

My throat tightens.

Dad accepted my polyamorous relationship but not easily. He's been on the guys' backs about it.

Yet he was in a similar relationship at college.

Except, is that the reason? He was in an unhealthy dynamic, or one that went wrong?

"Because I hated being in that type of relationship," Dad replies. Gibbs makes a wounded sound. "You appear to be wearing rose tinted glasses, Larry. It wasn't a poly relationship. It was Beth being torn between me and you — an obsessed jerk."

Gibbs' expression transforms with rage.

Before he can attack Dad, however, Cody, D'Angelo, and I step to stand at Dad's shoulder.

Shay and Eden block Gibbs in on the other side.

Gibbs looks around himself. "You're only saying that because you can't bear to face that Beth loved me."

"But she chose *me*." Dad's eyes are hard. "She married me. You never respected her decision."

Shay is watching D'Angelo and me closely.

Eden stands, until his shoulder is touching his brother's in support.

What if the twins think that this is what will happen to them? I'll use them, until I choose D'Angelo to marry?

I never would.

Except, Mom did.

That hurts my heart.

Whatever Dad says now, Mom was in a relationship with Gibbs throughout college.

Gibbs *did* love her.

Okay, he was also an obsessed jerk who acted like he owned her.

He didn't deserve Mom's love.

But still, he had no idea that he'd be cut out.

I understand now what the chirps on the ice must have been about.

How can I prove to my men that what Mom and Dad did in the past won't be repeated?

In my head, Mom is wrapped in the golden light of grief. She's an angel, from before everything went to shit in my life.

It's hard to see that she was human and flawed as well.

Cody looks as shaken as I am.

D'Angelo doesn't appear as surprised by these revelations as the rest of us are.

He must have suspected it already. He tried to spare me.

Secrets come out eventually, however, and that terrifies me about my own relationship.

Gibbs' pale blue eyes are watery with tears. "Fuck you, Austin. You both abandoned me. I'm going to play truth now in the press."

"Go for it." Dad arches his brow. "Desecrate the memory of the woman who you claim to have loved. See how many people believe you, when you try to say that it was a murder attempt, even though you've waited years after the fact. You'll look crazy. And you know what? Too many people already know what you're like behind the scenes."

"What do you mean? I'm a family man. You're the one who's a washed up loser with anger issues."

I've never seen two coaches fight like this before.

They're squaring off like two old stags.

D'Angelo turns to Cody and me, winking.

Then he coughs, before sauntering forward like he's about to put on his greatest performance.

"Really?" D'Angelo can't quite keep the satisfaction out of his voice. "I have it on record from scores of past and present players that you're a bully and a blackmailer, Gibbs. After this game, your team and staff are going to the board to have you removed as coach. I also hear that you're about to be sued for sexual harassment, while your affairs that are about to be revealed will literally make the journalists orgasm. Now, if anything that you discovered from the information you hacked illegally from my computer is leaked or used against me, then I will sue you for everything that you've got."

Gibbs gapes at him, paling. "You can't…I mean…this isn't…"

Joy surges through me.

Confident now, I stride to join D'Angelo. "You've just been played."

Shay laughs, and I love how sunny it sounds.

"This is your last game as a coach, even in the minor leagues." I look Gibbs straight in the eyes. "I hope you enjoy it because the Bay Rebels are going to kick your fucking ass."

CHAPTER TWENTY-NINE

Honda Center, Anaheim

Eden

I'm not skating on the rink with D'Angelo and Shay tonight but I feel like I'm flying.

Phoenix.

My phoenix!

My shoulder and arm are in agony, but it's my back that feels like it's on fire.

No one has given me a nickname before.

Dummy, loser twin, freak.

I've been called those.

But not an actual nickname like I've read friends give to each other.

Plus, this is even better because it's a pet name like D'Angelo has for Robyn and Shay.

A phoenix is beautiful, representing hope and renewal. *Life after death.*

Robyn doesn't want only part of me, but the dark as well as the light. She knows about the fire, which led to the ash. And she wants to be part of the rebirth that comes afterward.

Happiness bubbles through me.

Is this how Shay feels most of the time?

It's overwhelming. Almost too much.

But I don't hide from it.

It's as good as an anesthetic for the throbbing through my shoulder, which is lucky, since the meds that Cody gave me aren't coming close to touching the pain.

Back in the locker room, when the Ducks players twisted my arm out of its sling and then behind my back, I was a full ten on the pain scale.

My lips twitch at the memory of Cody dramatically overacting that ten by rolling around on the floor like an electrocuted worm, when he first showed me the scale as my physical therapist.

But I don't need to bother others with my shit.

I hadn't been able to hold back yelling out though.

I feel like a bastard for worrying the others.

My lip is sore from where I bit it through, holding back any further sounds. I learned that trick in the Room.

I know that I didn't con my brother this time.

After Robyn iced my shoulder, I swore that it was feeling much better. It's the only reason she agreed that I could come to the arena, rather than return to the hotel with Noah to have my shoulder properly sorted.

I couldn't miss this game.

"Pass the puck!" Robyn chants under her breath.

She's hopping up and down, gesturing wildly like she does when she's caught up in a game. She appears to think that she has an invisible stick in her hand.

Her hair bounces on each hop.

She's definitely at her cutest like this.

Although, she's also cute when she's snuggled in the nest that I make of blankets for her, during our book club.

Or when she's wearing one of my cat t-shirts.

She has a lot of cute moments.

She looked beautiful and fearsome, on the other hand, standing up to Gibbs.

I cock my head in thought.

My brother fought for me. The scheme that I planned with D'Angelo, beside the damage to my arm, worked perfectly.

Our family came together to save each other.

I side-eye Robyn.

This woman didn't choose to slap me.

"Pass, pass, pass." Robyn swipes even more energetically with her arm.

I dodge to avoid accidentally being slapped this time in her enthusiasm.

To the other side of Robyn, coach huffs in amusement.

I give him a hard look.

About ten minutes into the game, coach joined Robyn and me beside the glass to watch the game. He hasn't done that before.

I don't know why he has tonight.

I hope that this doesn't become a regular thing.

This time with Robyn is special to me. And coach makes my throat close up.

I clench my jaw.

Only three minutes of the game between the Bay Rebels to go.

Only three minutes before the last game of the road trip.

But it's a draw, **4 — 4.**

Shay has been setting D'Angelo up to score all evening.

I know my brother's play. I've been on the ice with him, since we both learned hockey as kids.

He could have taken the shots himself. He could have made himself tonight's star.

Yet he's been working to make sure that D'Angelo is the one who shines.

He's been restoring D'Angelo's reputation, even if it dims his own light.

He loves that man.

My brother makes fun of himself, hiding his smartness and how kind he is.

Not many people are unselfish enough to give up their place in the spotlight.

I shove my hand into the pocket of the long woolen coat that I'm wearing over my suit.

"Fucking score," I mutter.

I hold my breath, as Shay dodges a defensemen, glancing to check whether D'Angelo is free.

The atmosphere in the arena is electric.

It's loud standing here close to the glass. It makes my head ache to be surrounded by so many people.

Too much hyped up emotions whirl around me. I don't understand them.

But the happiness inside me is new. I want to understand that.

The players are skating, as if they're flying on a cloud of ice.

My chest is rapidly rising and falling. I take a moment to draw in a deep breath.

In this final game, the Anaheim Ducks have been tough and aggressive. Their strategy has been to exhaust our team, which has worked because it's the last leg of the road trip.

It's why away teams rarely win this third game.

Yet our defensemen and goalie have shown the same courage as they did in the earlier game to rally behind their captain and stop the Ducks from scoring too many goals.

At the same time, despite the fact that D'Angelo hasn't slept for as many days as me, he's on fucking fire.

How is he managing that?

My legs feel like buckling. But D'Angelo is playing hockey against one of the best teams, as if he's rested.

Playing like a fiend.

Shay is matching D'Angelo's fire.

It's incredible to watch.

The crowd, even the Duck's own fans, are going wild for it.

It's inspiring to see the whole team's connection.

Like they're a family.

"They're going to score. I can feel it," Robyn says. "They're playing the best that they ever have."

In her excitement, Robyn turns to me, as if to grab my arm. But then, remembering that we're in public, she stops herself.

Robyn glances around at coach. Her expression becomes wary.

Before tonight, I haven't seen her look at her dad like that.

Robyn bites her lip. "Dad, can I ask you something?"

"There are less than three minutes left of the game." Coach watches the rink with piercing eyes. "Get your ass in gear, Grayson. Hell, Colton needs to work these spoiled, lazy players harder."

"They're not spoiled or lazy." I surprise myself, when the words burst from me.

Coach doesn't look around at me. "*You* weren't. You were the most dedicated player on the team. But don't tell me my business. I know that I'm a hard-ass but I get results."

I bite the inside of my cheek not to answer.

"Dad," Robyn tries again.

"Damn it, two minutes left. What the fuck does Lucas think he's doing?" Coach barks. "Talk to me after the game."

"Why are you standing with me?" Robyn demands. "You never do."

Coach's gaze finally darts to Robyn. "After what happened in the locker room, I needed to see with my own eyes that you were okay. I don't do emotions but allow me this. I'm still your dad."

"What about seeing that Cody's okay?"

Coach looks at the rink again, turning his back on Robyn. "Your brother has work to do. Now, you've had several questions, let me concentrate."

Robyn's cheek twitches. "What I wanted to ask was whether Mom really loved…that guy?"

I stiffen.

Robyn can't say Gibbs' name, in case one of the press or public picks up on what we're talking about.

I've learned since coming to America that fame is shit.

Everything that you give up, including the right to privacy, being openly in a relationship with the people who you love, to the protection from being a public punching bag, is only worth it if you have a talent that you love more than anything else.

Playing a sport, singing, or acting.

A driving passion that it'd kill you not to pursue.

Fame itself is poison.

When coach's expression darkens, I stand straighter, despite the pain lancing through me.

Coach holds too much power over our lives.

Robyn loves him, however, so she forgives him because she's kind and sweet.

But she appears to think that he hasn't hurt her.

I know better.

"I'm not talking about that, Robyn." Coach lowers his voice further. "End of discussion."

"Did she love him?" I repeat, harder.

I won't let Robyn be silenced. Plus, I need to know for Shay and my own sake.

How easy is it for the least loved people within a relationship to be discarded?

When Robyn slapped D'Angelo, it was consensual.

The slap was like a kiss.

Intimate.

Her way of showing who she loved the most and not the least.

Coach shakes his head. "I don't know. Not as much as *he* loved *her*."

My chest is tight.

I stare steadily at the ice.

I'll deal, if Robyn can't love me, as much as I adore her. I never expected her to.

If she decides that she doesn't want me anymore, then it'll break my heart, but I don't own her.

I'll accept it.

It would fucking wreck Shay, however, to be thrown away like trash again. He doesn't only adore Robyn. He's given her everything of himself.

It's who he is. There's no point trying to warn him of the danger.

I've managed to start trusting Robyn with my body. But it's harder, when it means risking the twin who I've spent a lifetime protecting.

As if she can hear my thoughts, Robyn turns to me. "I'm not like her."

"I didn't say you were."

"You don't need to. I'll prove it."

My gaze flicks to Robyn's face. I wish that I was better at reading expressions.

My brow furrows.

Is Robyn angry? Disappointed? Determined?

I want to believe her.

"Forget about it," coach advises, before continuing with an effort to keep things vague, in case we're overheard, "We were silly college kids. He called us *friends*. Bullshit. Maybe in his deluded head. I tolerated the jerk for your mom's sake. Everybody goes through phases of experimenting. It's all that it was. But he took it more seriously. You're not the same that we were back then. I've seen you together and even I can tell that. It's why I accepted...you know. I only want you to have what you need and to be happy, Robyn."

"Thanks, Dad." It's me that Robyn offers a secret smile to, however, brushing her fingers against mine.

My skin sparks, where our fingers touch.

My breath hitches.

Our relationship isn't the same as her mom's was with coach and Gibbs.

Robyn won't abandon Shay and me.

I hope.

"One minute left," Robyn whispers.

She presses a hand against the trembling glass.

I notice the way that D'Angelo glances urgently at Shay.

They can do this.

Excitement sweeps through both the crowd and me.

"If they win," coach mutters, "the Bay Rebels will have achieved something that they have never have before. More than anyone will expect from the newest team in the NHL."

"And if they draw? Robyn asks.

"I'll still be proud. But the board will have questions."

I wince.

My pulse is pounding.

We must win.

Just one more goal.

One more.

Thirty seconds…

Shay makes a break for the goal. His skating is breathtaking.

The crowd are on their feet. The noise is so loud that I fight the urge to put my hands over my ears.

I watch with wide eyes, hardly daring to breathe.

The pass to D'Angelo is laser sharp.

Twenty seconds…

D'Angelo hits top speed, blowing past Folkes toward the goal.

Ten seconds…

My heart is hammering in my chest.

Please…

D'Angelo raises his stick, aiming at the goal. Then he slickly backhands the puck through the legs of the goalie.

He scores.

"Fuck, yeah!" Robyn leaps into the air with a whoop.

"They damn well did it." Coach grins, running his fingers through his hair in relief.

The arena goes into a frenzy.

I don't look away from the rink, where the team are raising their sticks with D'Angelo leading them.

Shay waves over at Robyn and me, however, with a wide smile.

My heart soars.

Shay plays for all of us in the same way that he *loves* us all.

It doesn't matter what happens to him, or how much he's hurt.

It's not able to darken his soul.

We've fucking won.

We've survived this road trip and beaten Gibbs, as well as the Bay Rebels board.

Robyn didn't reject or choose us as the least loved. She's promised that she'll never abandon us to settle down with D'Angelo.

She's wearing our rings.

Perhaps, we haven't only found a place where we're accepted.

A family and home.

We've found somewhere where we're safe.

Tonight, I'm going to make certain that we celebrate.

D'Angelo may have won the kink bet, but we've all won Robyn.

CHAPTER THIRTY

Ocean Hotel, Anaheim

'Angelo

I LET Shay's excited chatter wash over me, as he relives the game goal by goal in exuberant detail.

I'll never admit how much I love watching him, when he's on a high after a game.

I'm perched next to him, resting against the headboard of the bed, which is carved out of driftwood. The bed has navy sheets and pillows. The matching navy drapes are pulled against the night.

The room's walls and furniture are white but with an opalescent sheen like the inside of a shell.

I take a deep breath of the white tea that fragrances this hotel.

I chose this place for Eden.

I hope that the tea fanatic liked it.

"So, my heart is in my throat, but I know that our captain can do it. *Ten seconds.* There's only ten bloody seconds left, but Jude raises his stick and…" Shay gestures with his champagne glass to illustrate, and I wince as the bubbling champagne sloshes to the rim.

I steady his hand just in time.

"Cucciolo," I warn, "these are one thousand dollar sheets."

Shay pales. "Then what the fuck are we doing sitting in bed drinking champagne and eating sticky chocolates?"

"We're celebrating on our last night, before we make the long drive back to Captain's Hall." I reach over to the nightstand and pick up two more glasses.

I'm wearing my black silk pajamas. Eden is dressed in casual gray joggers.

Shay and Robyn, however, are both naked, which is just how I like them to be.

Before the next home games start, I should negotiate at least a weekend a month where they shouldn't be allowed clothes.

They could be called Naked Weekends.

Shay would be delighted.

Eden pulls Robyn more firmly onto his chest on the other side of Shay, before handfeeding her a heart shaped truffle from the box, which is balanced on these luxury sheets.

It's worth the inevitable bill tomorrow from the hotel, however, when Robyn's eyelashes flutter in a distracting way, as she chews the chocolate.

Then she sucks on Eden's fingers, cleaning them.

Eden's eyes darken.

He leans down and kisses Robyn, in turn kissing the smeared chocolate from her lips.

Perhaps, they're both trying to save me the bill.

It's both sexy and efficient.

Robyn reaches up, cupping Eden's cheek.

When she draws back, Eden searches out her lips again like he can't bear to be parted from them.

"All I've wanted this entire trip," Eden rumbles against her mouth, "morning and night, and every time that I see you, is to kiss you."

I study the two of them together.

I have to admit that they're good for each other.

Eden has already changed a lot.

I rarely get to see these quiet moments between them.

I'm possessive, but it's excellent to see how deeply they love each other.

Shay becomes still. "How are you better at romance than me?"

"Maybe you should take tips from your brother." I struggle to keep my face straight. "Your idea of romance is to torment your lover by changing their ringtone to something obnoxious."

Robyn laughs.

It hadn't been funny, when my phone had burst into

The Lonely Island's "I Just Had Sex" in the middle of a briefing with coach and the entire team.

Well, *they'd* found it funny.

Lucas and Grayson in particular, who'd crowded around me afterwards, patting me on the shoulder.

"Good job on the having sex, bro." Lucas nudged Grayson.

"Yeah," Grayson added. "We should have a beer together to celebrate you finally popping your cherry after only twenty-seven years."

I'm going to find a way to prank Shay back.

"Torment *you*." Shay grins. "But I worship Robyn. I could live in her kisses."

"See, you are romantic." Robyn smiles at each of the twins in turn. "You both are."

Both brothers blush.

"Here." I pass Robyn a glass of champagne. Then I pull an apologetic face, as I hand over an apple juice to Eden. "Sorry, non-alcoholic only because of your meds. Doctor Michael's orders. I put it in a champagne glass, if that makes you feel better."

"It doesn't." Eden takes his glass, sipping the juice.

"I propose a toast," Robyn says.

I pick up the final glass, smelling the fruity scent. "I'm scared but listening."

"To winning the final game against the Ducks!"

We clink our glasses and drink.

The champagne tastes velvety but crisp and dry. It's the best that the hotel has.

Shay chokes. "Can I have a beer instead?"

"Sacrilege." I arch my brow. "Of course, it leaves more for me."

Shay raises his glass. "My turn. To kicking Gibbs in the ass!"

Our glasses clink again.

"To all of us." Eden holds aloft his apple juice.

We clink and drink.

I smirk. "To me scoring the highest in the games, which means that I win the kink contest."

I clink my glass with Shay's, before draining it and placing it on the nightstand. Then I snatch Shay's from him and drain it too.

It's a crime to waste a bottle of champagne that costs more than these sheets.

I'm not telling Shay that. He'd probably have some type of crisis over it, and I'm trying to spoil him.

He's not easy to spoil.

But I have several other cards up my sleeve.

Shay's face falls. "Huh, how could I have forgotten about that? I guess being blackmailed into taking terrifying dares will do that to a bloke." Then he looks eager again. "What are you plotting?"

"We can't do it tonight. There isn't enough space."

"Now I'm intrigued." Robyn leans over to place her empty glass on the nightstand closest to her, along with Eden's.

When I flick a switch on the wall, the music system that's embedded into the room's wall bursts into life. The White Stripe's infectious alternative rock "Fell in Love with a Girl" hits us with waves of rhythm guitar and a high-speed beat.

This is how I spoil my cucciolo.

Shay bounces on the bed like he's battling to restrain himself from a bout of air guitar.

I bet that he spent his college years in his dorm pretending that air guitar was a real instrument.

My lips quirk. "How can we not listen to your favorite songs and share your passions on a night like this?"

Shay's smile is wide.

I can't even pretend that it doesn't make me want to spend a lifetime making him look like that. "Thanks, darlin'. Getting to share the music that I love with all of you is better than expensive champagne or chocolates."

Robyn twirls a strand of hair around her finger. "I'm trying to work out why you can't also claim your reward tonight. Something that you need space for…? Is swinging from the chandeliers a literal thing?"

I chuckle. "It could be. But I'm thinking of something outside. We'd need to talk about it more and negotiate once we're back at Captain's Hall, but would you like to know now? Anticipation adds to the thrill. You'll have days of frustration, waiting until we're home."

Home.

I said it so easily.

It hits me like a punch to the gut.

"Yes, Sir." Shay is already breathing faster.

I reach to bury my hand in his hair, yanking him closer.

His breath hisses out, but his cock hardens.

"Look at you, already being a good boy for me." I tug on Shay's hair again, and his pupils dilate.

When I raise my eyebrow in question at Robyn, she nods.

"Lie our principessa down," I command.

Eden twists until he's kneeling over Robyn, then he pushes her down against the pillows. He uses his free hand to pin her hands above her head.

"Keep them there." Eden takes his hand away, but she doesn't move her hands from where he put them.

Robyn's chest is rapidly rising and falling, as Eden traces his hand down her neck to her collarbone.

He caresses circles on her skin.

Without warning, I drag Shay closer by his hair, resting my teeth against his pounding jugular.

Shay lets out a panicked sound, which goes straight to my cock.

When I lightly graze him with my teeth, he humps against me.

"I am the predator," I growl, sinking my teeth in slightly deeper, before licking over the teeth marks. "And I love to hunt willing prey."

"Oh, I'm willing." Shay bears his neck further. "Bloody willing."

This time, I kiss the bite mark.

I don't want Shay pushed fully into subspace, before we can talk this through.

I let go of Shay's hair with a gentle stroke.

He looks wrecked already.

I knew that he'd love this kink.

But I wanted to be sure.

I glance to check the other two.

Robyn's eyes are glazing already, as she lies beneath Eden. He looks natural in the dominant role.

I sit back, straightening my pajamas. Shay remains where he is sprawled beneath me.

"I'm choosing primal kink as my reward," I explain. "When we wrote our innermost desires into the Guide, I included as one of my fantasies a role play in the forest behind Captain's Hall. I'd like to act it out. None of you marked primal kink as a limit on our contract. But I understand, if it's not your thing."

"It is," Shay breathes. "I spend most of my life trying to piss you off enough to hunt me."

"You say that like I don't already know."

Robyn's tongue darts out to wet her lips. "I've been dreaming about what your secret fantasies are, which you've hidden in the Guide. Fuck, I'd love to act one out."

Eden's brow furrows. "I don't know what it is. But I trust you."

Warmth unfurls through me that he *trusts* me.

From Eden, knowing what he's survived, that means a lot.

Until Robyn, Eden was a virgin. She was his first kiss.

Unlike his twin, he has no kinky experience. With us, he's having a true sexual awakening, as well as discovering his dynamic.

It's clear to me that he's a caretaker dom.

He's one of the most natural doms that I've come across. But I don't want to push him. He's on his own journey, and although I can guide him, he needs to find what works for him.

I push my curls back from my face, thinking about how best to explain it to Eden. "People like primal kink for different reasons. You can be primal like a wolf and just forget the world and nothing but sensation. As a dom, I can be an unashamed predator, chasing down my prey. When I was in the discipline school, I was repressed by so many fucking rules. You couldn't smile or cry or… anything. Primal kink was one of the things that helped me access my raw emotions — my dominance — in an intense but pleasurable way. In those moments, I don't feel controlled by anything. I'm free."

Eden looks serious. "Free?"

"Plus, it's a fucking thrill like being on the ice, hunting down that goal. Your pulse pounds. You're focused. Adrenaline spikes."

Eden sits straighter, looking interested. "What happens when you catch the prey?"

Now, both Robyn and Shay perk up.

"You pin them down like we just were," I growl. "Then you can bite, lick, pull their hair, or fuck them until they see stars. But you mark and claim them as *yours*."

"I'm the prey," Shay says, quickly like I'm about to take back the treat.

"Predator." Eden taps his powerful chest.

We all look at Robyn.

She squirms. "I feel like the prey with you looking at me hungrily like that."

"You are, cara mia." I reach over and stroke down her

calf, making her shiver. "As always, we'll use safe words. The forest behind Captain's Hall will be perfect to hunt both my pets."

Now, both Shay and Robyn shiver.

"Stop saying things like that, darlin'," Shay pleads, "or you're going to make me come all over these expensive sheets."

"You'd better not." I grab him by the base of his cock and squeeze. He whines. "I need this cock very soon to pleasure our Robyn."

Robyn's face lights up. "Will vibrations be involved?"

"Not this time. But how do you feel about two dicks?"

"Two dicks are better than one." Robyn waggles her eyebrows. "But three are a party."

"I'm happy that you think that way, principessa." I smile, wickedly. "Because we've tested negative. I've kept the printouts in the Guide. And you're on the pill. I'm only pointing this out because if we make this a double vaginal penetration tonight, then we can't use condoms. The friction of our two cocks rubbing against each other inside your pussy would break them."

"Rubbing against each other *inside her*?" The idea appears to short circuit Shay's mind, before his cock twitches in my hand.

He's as turned on by the idea, as Robyn is.

Robyn is flushed, clutching her hands in the bedding.

"Do you want that?" Eden checks in.

"I'm committed to this relationship with all of you." Robyn glances between us. *She's fucking beautiful.* "I want the feel of you — all of you — inside me at once. I need you. Why have double, when I'm fucking lucky enough to have triple?"

She reaches to grip Eden's hand.

Shay tilts his head. "I'm not sure that we'll all fit, love, unless that's a burn about us having small dicks. Have you forgotten how large D'Angelo is? Every time that he smothers me with that monster, I reckon I should receive a medal for valor afterward."

I preen.

A man can't help enjoying having his dick size praised.

It makes me want to facefuck my pet right now and make him earn another medal.

"I have a mouth as well," Robyn points out.

Eden leans down to kiss her. "This is already mine tonight. Can you use my mouth, instead of my cock?"

I wondered if that would be too far for Eden, especially after the day that he's had and his pain level.

It's why I suggested Shay and I do the dick work.

Dick heavy lifting.

But I'm impressed.

Eden's voiced what he needs like he's worthy of receiving that.

He's becoming better at that too.

Robyn's expression softens. "Of course."

Eden's shoulders relax. "I also have talented fingers."

He slips his fingers to Robyn's clit, tracing circles.

Robyn groans but she doesn't move. She's trapped by Eden's steady stare.

See, he's a natural.

He's preparing her for me, getting her wet.

I reach over to the nightstand, pushing aside the champagne bottle to get to the tube of lube behind it.

Shay sits up. His eyes are dancing with excitement.

I slip off my pajama bottoms, folding them and putting them on the pillow.

Then I rub the lube down my cock generously because this will only work with lots…and lots…of lube.

I hiss with pleasure on each, slow stroke.

Shay watches me intently.

When he reaches to touch his own cock, however, I stop him with a pointed stare.

"Don't you dare," I say, frostily. "Your cock belongs to me. Only I touch it."

Shay moves his hand shakily away. "Yes, Sir."

"Come here."

Shay crawls to the side of the bed in front of me.

I hold Shay's gaze, as my heart beats faster in the intimacy of the moment — the depth of his submission — while he holds still, not touching himself. Instead, he allows me to run the lube up and down his cock, preparing him to fuck the woman who we both love.

We're going to give Robyn the best orgasm of her life.

This is the ultimate celebration and end to our road trip.

I grimace at the sensation of the lube on my hands, wiping them dry on my pajamas.

Then I toss the lube to Eden.

Eden wets his fingers with lube and slips them into Robyn's pussy, scissoring in and out.

"Fuck," Robyn gasps, arching her back.

I want her teetering on the edge of orgasm but not falling over.

It'll make this easier.

When Robyn's breathing becomes labored, and her hair is damp against her sweaty forehead, I climb back onto the bed.

"Stop," I command.

Robyn looks at me, devastated. "W-w-w-hat? I'm just about to…a little m-m-more…please…"

"No." I turn to Shay. "Lie on your back with your legs off the end."

Shay throws himself back dramatically like he's about to be debauched.

He is, but then, so is Robyn.

I crawl to join Shay, running my hand down his chest and tweaking his nipples. I tease him, until his cock is hard and weeping pre-cum onto his stomach.

Then I prowl to my feet and stand between his thighs.

I give Eden a conspiratorial look. We're already the predators in this bed.

Playing with our prey tonight is fun.

"Bring my good girl over here and lay her on top of our pet." I revel in the way that Robyn and Shay both flush at the same time.

Eden helps Robyn to crawl across the bed and lie on Shay's chest.

I grasp Robyn's hips and widen her thighs, raising them high on either side of me.

Her pupils dilate.

Robyn's falling into the right headspace by being so exposed.

Shay slides his hands around either side of her to both anchor her in place and play with her breasts.

Her nipples peak.

"I've got you, love," Shay murmurs against her neck.

Eden kneels beside Robyn's head, stroking her hair.

"Okay?" I check in.

Robyn nods, staring down at both our cocks. "Will they fit?"

"You can take them for me. Color?"

"Green."

I stare at Shay's cock and balls, as well as his strong thighs that are splayed either side of me. Then how Robyn's soft pussy is directly above it.

I've never seen such a delicious sight.

They were made to fit together.

Both are mine.

I growl, surging forward.

I need to fuck Robyn.

But I force myself to take this slow. It's the first time doing this for every one in this bed but me.

I gasp Shay's cock, guiding it toward Robyn's pussy. When I allow it to nudge against her several times, she moans.

"Slowly, pet," I order. "Rock into our principessa. Make her feel how much you love her. Stretch her out ready for me."

Shay obeys.

Inch by inch, he pushes into Robyn. He gives her time

to adjust, before he begins to move.

"How does that feel?" Shay asks.

"Like I never want you to stop," Robyn replies.

I love seeing the way that Shay is spearing into her.

I love his cock.

I love her pussy.

Together, they're glorious.

I bite my lip, forcing myself not to come too soon, as I line up my cock against Shay's.

"Fuck, that feels…" Shay goes still. "It's like you're electrocuting me."

My lips quirk. "Wait until we're moving against each other."

Then I start to slowly thrust.

Robyn's so tight with both of our dicks inside her.

She whines.

"That's right, principessa, relax for me," I gently coax. "Let me in. Don't worry, we're taking care of you. You're being so good for us. Look at you, taking our cocks."

Robyn's eyes are blown wide.

She doesn't look away from me.

Fucking her like this, being able to see every shift in her expression, is incredible.

She's allowing herself to be open.

She's showing that she belongs to all three of us, but only because we belong to each other.

Plus, the sensation of my cock rubbing against Shay's is electric.

It sparks through me, until I'm gasping and flying apart.

It's intense.

I'm already close to coming.

"I c-c-an't." Shay's balls are tight. His thighs are quivering. "P-p-please…"

I pound harder.

Our cocks rub against each other, while we fuck the same woman.

It's like we're frotting but inside the pussy of the woman who holds our hearts.

Eden leans over Robyn, kissing her passionately.

Her kisses her, until he steals her breath.

She trembles.

"I love you," Eden whispers against her lips.

I need to feel both Robyn and Shay come at the same time.

I need to feel Shay's cum spill over mine inside Robyn.

"Now," I command. "*Come.*"

When I flick Robyn's clit, I set off a chain reaction.

Robyn comes with a scream, which makes her pussy tighten.

The sensation is like heaven.

It pushes Shay's cock even closer against mine. The pressure is almost painful. It milks our orgasms from us at the same time in a way that makes me stagger.

I can feel Shay's cock pulse, as his cum spurts, mingling with mine.

Ecstasy slams through me.

This moment is what the entire road trip has been about.

We're together. United. And now we're going home.

CHAPTER THIRTY-ONE

Captain Forest, Freedom

obyn

I RUN THROUGH CAPTAIN FOREST, along the trail that's part of the estate. I catch my boots on the thick undergrowth.

My heart is beating wildly. My hair is plastered over my forehead. I can hardly catch my breath.

I'm a hot mess being chased through a forest, even though I've only been back from the road trip since this morning.

But I feel free.

D'Angelo deserves this reward. We all do.

He opened the Guide to let us read his primal kink fantasy, and fuck, he should write smut, as well as draw it.

Perhaps, it's his secret career.

It'll give him something to do, when he retires from hockey.

The midday sun spears through the branches of the tall pines and oaks. I wrinkle my nose at the sweet scent.

The birds chatter in the low branches.

I grin, scrabbling over a moss covered log, which is a more dangerous maneuver than you'd think.

I could be scratched somewhere that should *never* be scratched.

Normally, in action movies the heroines aren't escaping from the villain naked.

Apart from a short, red cloak.

Well, unless it's the type of porn that Neve watches.

I gasp, clutching onto the nearest oak in the clearing in time to stop myself from falling over.

I hold my hand over the stitch in my side, attempting to catch my breath.

I should really go on some more morning runs with Shay, if this type of play is going to become a regular thing.

I know that I'm the prey, but playing this with professional sportsmen doesn't feel fair.

Behind me, I can hear Shay crashing through the forest at least three times as loudly as I have been.

I smile.

You'd almost think that Shay *wanted* to be caught.

I pull the cloak around myself, luxuriating in its softness.

The sensations of being outside, surrounded by nature, but naked apart from this one piece of cloth, are amplified.

The sun feels hotter on my face, the scents of the forest are sharper, and the birdsong sounds brighter.

I feel attuned to the world around me.

For the last few weeks, my dark past, shadows, and anxious fears have haunted me.

But now, I'm fully in the present.

It feels like a luxury that I haven't been able to indulge in…ever.

When D'Angelo said that he was going to spoil us, I didn't know just how creative he could be.

Earlier, after Shay and I had stripped in the entrance hall, only wearing sturdy boots to protect our feet and ankles since we'd be outside, D'Angelo threw the scarlet, velvet cloak at me.

I held it up and studied it in confusion. "What's this?" When D'Angelo opened his mouth, I quickly added, "And don't say a cloak." I narrowed my eyes. I knew that look in his eye. "Or a red cloak."

"A red, *velvet* cloak."

Jerk.

D'Angelo and Eden were dressed in matching designer gray suits. I was discovering how intimidating that could feel, when you were naked in an entrance hall and were about to become their prey.

Also, how much I loved the flutter of anticipation mixed with fear that made me feel.

D'Angelo fastened the cloak around my neck, adjusting it elaborately several times. "This scene between us is *Little Red Riding Hood* themed, principessa. I rather fancy being the big, bad wolf."

I shivered.

"You look gorgeous, love." Shay strolled toward me, tracing down my cheekbone. He pressed his hard, naked chest against mine. "I could drop to my knees and eat you up right now."

Yes, please.

"Except, you're not the wolf." D'Angelo flashed a smile that revealed sharp, white canines. "You're Little Red Riding Hood's younger brother. And *I'm* going to eat *you*."

Eden tossed a second cloak at Shay.

Shay looked disgruntled but he still pulled on the cloak.

Then he met D'Angelo's eye like a challenge. "Only if you catch me, darlin'."

"A predator always catches his prey."

Shay twirled.

The cloak was so short that it revealed *everything*.

Perfect.

Shay didn't appear to think so. "My arse is hanging out of this thing."

When D'Angelo stalked toward Shay, his eyes widened like a trapped rabbit.

D'Angelo had that effect without trying.

Was it a dom thing?

I bit my lip. I was wet already.

D'Angelo snatched Shay by the arm, turning him around to reveal that *arse*.

Then he smacked it crisply.

Shay gasped, but his gaze instantly became half-hooded.

I admired the crimson outline of D'Angelo's handprint that matched the color of our cloaks.

D'Angelo yanked Shay closer and murmured, "The better to spank you, my dear."

I laughed, before running my hand suspiciously over my soft cloak. "We've only been back a couple of hours and we've spent those unpacking, reading your fantasy in the Guide, and finishing negotiations about the scene. When did you get these?"

D'Angelo crossed his arms. "I already had them."

"Kinky." Shay clearly wanted to be bitten *a lot* today. "Have you been imagining us in them, while you jerk off? Or are they for a roleplay with Eden and me as English princes?"

"That's one of your fantasies, isn't it?" I asked, eagerly.

How could I encourage D'Angelo to let me read the rest of the fantasies in the Guide?

"Don't say that I wouldn't make a gorgeous prince, love." Shay struck a princely pose with his hand on an imaginary sword hilt at his waist.

His *other* sword was already up and ready for action.

D'Angelo snorted. "You'd make a pretty princess. These cloaks are left over from a twisted fairy tale themed Halloween party that I held at my mansion. I had a good friend — one who I hope to introduce you to soon — search them out and drop them off earlier."

My brow furrowed.

Who was this friend?

I loved that D'Angelo had a close friendship group in Freedom.

After the way that his parents treated him and then abandoned him, along with the extreme hazing that he was subjected to in college, I was happy that he hadn't suffered alone for the last six years.

I couldn't wait to meet the people who'd supported him, when I hadn't been around

I wanted to know more about his life. He was still mysterious about sides of it.

"What were you at the party?" I asked. "Wait, don't tell me. Jack Frost, right?" D'Angelo glared at me, icily enough to turn me into a snowflake. "You're making me cold with a single look. I bet you that you won the costume contest."

Shay sidled closer to me, wrapping his arm around my waist.

Then he glanced back at D'Angelo from underneath his eyelashes. "Wrong fairy tale, love. He of course went as the Beast."

D'Angelo's eyes flashed. He prowled towards us.

Uh-oh.

Shay and I stumbled backward towards the door.

"*Run*," D'Angelo growled.

Now, I rub my aching legs, scanning the forest.

I can still hear Shay close behind me.

It worries me that I can't hear either Eden or D'Angelo.

D'Angelo, as the savage but grumpy wolf, is invisible somewhere in the wilderness.

How is he so good at stalking people? Is that a thing that all handsome billionaires learn as a skill?

I strain to quieten my own breathing and listen.

I can't hear anything but Shay's cussing, as he trips over a log, and a squirrel scampering overhead.

Eden is still injured and can't run fast. But then, neither can I.

He's also stealthy.

I've caught glimpses of Eden's golden hair and gleaming eyes through the trees, but he's kept his distance.

He reminds me more of a big cat: silent, watchful, and dangerous.

A delightful shiver runs down my back.

It's only because I feel safe that fear becomes pleasure.

It's a fucking thrill.

I give myself over to it.

I turn and jog deeper into the forest. Panting, I clutch onto the edges of the cloak. Twigs crack and crunch under my boots.

Unexpectedly, I stagger into the middle of a small clearing.

I twirl around.

This looks familiar.

Hell, have I been here before?

Have I just been running in fucking circles?

I stand still, wiping my hand over my face.

When I look up, however, I'm shocked to meet Eden's steady gaze from the other side of the clearing.

He's slouched against a tree with his hands in his pockets.

My eyes widen.

Is this an ambush?

Has Eden been waiting for me here without needing to bother to run anywhere, knowing that I was circling back to him?

We share a long look.

My breathing speeds up.

Like I've summoned him, rather than have been hunted by him, Eden slinks towards me.

He doesn't drop his gaze. I feel mesmerized.

My chest is tight.

I know that I should run.

But I can't.

When Eden whistles, I blink in confusion, until D'Angelo prowls from the trees behind him.

Shit, this is a double ambush.

Clearly, doms hunt in pairs.

Now, I back up until I hit the trunk of an oak.

I flinch.

Eden continues to advance.

Shay sprints into the clearing after me. "Did you just whistle, love…?"

"*I* didn't." I gesture wildly at the two men across the clearing.

Shay's mouth drops open. "Shit."

He turns to escape, but D'Angelo is too fast.

And honestly, Shay doesn't truly *want* to escape.

He's been waiting to be caught from the moment that he bounded into the forest.

D'Angelo wraps his arm around Shay's throat. "Where are you going, little prey?"

Shay's eyelashes flutter, and his dick hardens. "Grandma's house."

D'Angelo snarls, roughly grabbing Shay by the hair and dragging him backward by it.

Shay hisses in pain, struggling to break free. D'Angelo merely throws him to the floor, before turning Shay onto his stomach and pinning him down.

It's fucking hot how much they're both enjoying the play-fight.

My breath hitches, when Eden reaches me.

When he towers over me like this, allowing himself free of his inhibitions, it's breathtaking.

Eden lowers his mouth to my neck, nuzzling and licking, while keeping me pinned against the tree with his hand to my shoulder.

I feel overpowered but safe.

Then Eden snatches me by the hair, and I gasp. He manhandles me down to lie on my stomach on the floor of the clearing. He's far gentler with me than D'Angelo was with Shay.

I turn my head, watching as D'Angelo pulls up Shay's cloak, bunching it at his throat. He licks over the pale canvas of Shay's shoulders, looking for a part that isn't already marked with bruises.

Then he bites — *hard*.

Shay screams.

But it's the *pleasurepain* one, which I've come to recognize with him.

"Again," Shay hisses.

D'Angelo noses down Shay's back, alternating licks and bites to each unblemished inch of skin, until Shay looks close to coming from the sensation alone.

He's shaking.

But then, so I am.

This is intense but in the best fucking way.

Eden nips at my ear.

"You're not allowed to run from me," he rumbles.

Don't leave me — *us*, is what I hear.

My heart clenches.

Eden lets go of me to crouch down, peering into my face like he's looking into my soul.

"You've caught me, phoenix." I can smell Eden's sweet vanilla scent, as it mingles with the earthy smell of the forest floor.

I need him to understand that his scent makes me feel protected.

I trust him.

And I hope that soon he can trust I want him and his twin to be by my side for the rest of my life.

To my surprise, when I call him *phoenix*, Eden's face brightens with a genuine smile.

It's so unexpected that it floors me.

It's like he's caught on fire but this time, he's not burning to ash.

Eden nuzzles me, wrapping his arm around me.

Then he pushes himself up and straddles me. He pushes my thighs apart, before working my clit with his fingers and thumb.

I gasp, writhing beneath him.

I'm being pushed to the edge faster than normal. My thighs shake. I scrabble at the leaves with my hands.

My mind whites.

Next to me, I hear Shay's cock being jerked just as ruthlessly between his splayed thighs by D'Angelo.

"I love you, pet," D'Angelo growls, but there's a softer edge to his voice now. "I fucking love all of you. Now, you're both going to come for us like the good little prey that you are."

When I come with a scream at the same as Shay, it feels nothing like I expected it would.

I'm floating, and smiling, and blissed out.

After this road trip, we needed this moment of happiness together alone in the woods.

Away of the noise, pressures, and demands of both the press and life in the hockey world.

We could have lost everything on this trip.

Yet together, we dared to face the truth.

Whatever struggles are ahead, and no matter who tries to rip us apart or tear us down for being rejected or broken, we'll always have each other.

Because we love each other.

I'm making it my mission to protect these men from the press. They make it their mission to protect me.

Except, the season is far from over.

There are many dangers to our careers, along with the increasing difficulty of keeping our love secret.

I know now how hard we'll fight for this relationship because it'd break our hearts to lose it.

Yet now Shay will be under more pressure from the bullying Colton, as well as being under intense press scrutiny.

Eden will need to work even harder to recover from his injuries.

D'Angelo must captain a team, which includes his secret lover, without pissing off a hostile board and a coach who's warned that it's his responsibility alone to get the Bay Rebels to the playoffs.

But I'm the PR Director who'll do anything to support my men.

The press may want to see them as beautiful disasters. The world may be obsessed with the Bay Rebels as the youngest team in the NHL.

Yet I'll protect my men from that obsession.

How dangerous can it be?

Want to know what happens to Robyn and her men next?
Continue the Bay Rebels adventure by clicking HERE now for PUCKING OBSESSED and find out what happens as the season continues!

https://rosemaryajohns.com

Thanks for reading **PUCKING ROAD TRIP**! If you enjoyed reading this book, **please consider leaving a review on Amazon.** Your support is really important to us authors. Plus, I love hearing from my readers! Thanks, you're awesome!
Rosemary A Johns

Click now to sign up to Rosemary A Johns' Rebel Newsletter and receive these special perks: promotions, exclusive teasers and art about the Pack Bonds world, and hot releases before anyone else.

PUCKING OBSESSED

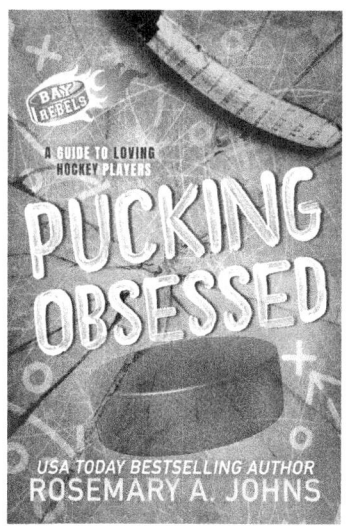

WHAT TO READ NEXT: PUCKING OBSESSED BAY REBELS!

Rooming with three members of the same hockey team as their live-in PR Director could be a nightmare. But when they offer to fulfill my fantasies? Sign me up.

The captain, D'Angelo, is my perfect man. Best friend, protector, and so hot it should be illegal, he's been obsessively in love with me since college. Shay has a rock star swagger and winter-gray eyes that are enough to make me melt. Sweet, intense, and tattooed, Shay's twin, Eden, is the heart of my new found family.

Together we face our team's toughest test this season. This is our final chance to prove ourselves, and nothing can stand in our way.

But when these hockey gods discover how bad my ex was in bed, they spoil me. Sparks fly, leading to the wildest nights of our lives.

Can I learn to let go of the past? Can we all escape the monsters whose dangerous obsessions would destroy our futures?

PUCKING OBSESSED is a STANDALONE why choose hockey romance by USA Today bestselling author, Rosemary A Johns.

TROPES:
- Pro Hockey Romance
- Why Choose
- Forced Proximity
- Second Chance
- Found Family
- Men obsessed
- Forbidden

ONE-CLICK TO READ WHAT HAPPENS TO ROBYN AND HER GUYS IN THEIR MOST IMPORTANT HOCKEY SEASON!

ICE HOCKEY ROMANCE, PACK BONDS

YOUR NEXT WHY CHOOSE ICE HOCKEY ROMANCE WITH AN OMEGAVERSE TWIST, PUCK AND HER BLADES!

An Omega reject. Alpha hockey players, the Blades. A pack bond that changes everything.

"Alpha!" I writhe in the nest, which is built out of sweet smelling hockey jerseys.

If I don't bond with the NHL star players, then I won't survive the night.

"I've got you, good Omega." The captain's voice is deep and rumbling. He kisses me passionately. He's the most handsome man in the sporting world with broad shoulders and raven hair. "We'll cherish and protect you."

"We…?" I gasp.

Then I notice the Beta with golden hair and the male Omega with pretty violet eyes. These men have given up everything — even their dreams — to be with me now.

I shiver, desperate for their touch and love…*but it's forbidden.*

A Why Choose Contemporary Omegaverse

- Ice Hockey Romance
- Dominant Alpha
- Found Family
- Reject Figure Skater Omega
- Scent matching
- Omega with Chronic Pain
- Nesting
- Knotting
- Men who worship and protect their woman
- Sweet & Steamy

- MM
- Plenty of purring!

CLICK HERE FOR YOUR NEXT ICE HOCKEY ROMANCE, PUCK AND HER BLADES, PACK BONDS!

ABOUT THE AUTHOR

ROSEMARY A JOHNS is a USA Today bestselling and award-winning romance, omegaverse, and fantasy romance author. She writes sexy shifters and immortals, swoonworthy book boyfriends, and addictive romance.

Winner of the Silver Award in the National Wishing Shelf Book Awards. Finalist in the IAN Book of the Year Awards. Winner in the Best Indie Book of the Year Awards. Runner-up in the Best Fantasy Book of the Year, Reality Bites Book Awards. Honorable Mention in the Readers' Favorite Book Awards. Shortlisted in the International Rubery Book Awards.

Rosemary is also a traditionally published short story writer. She studied history at Oxford University and ran her own theater company. She's always been a rebel…

Thanks for leaving a review. You're awesome!

Want to read more and stay up to date on Rosemary's newest releases? **Sign up for her *VIP* Rebel Newsletter and get FREE novellas!**

Have you read Rosemary A Johns' Contemporary Romance?
Elite
One Secret Rule
Darling Madness
Being Pucked, Bay Rebels
<u>**Secretly Pucking, Bay Rebels**</u>
Pucking Road Trip, Bay Rebels
Pucking Obsessed, Bay Rebels
Rebel & Her Knights
Ember & Her Marshals
Angel & Her Champions
Jewel & Her Kings
Puck & Her Blades
Mercy & Her Devils
Candy & Her Saints
Juliet & Her Romeos

Have you read all the series in the Rebel Verse by Rosemary A Johns?

Rebel Demons
Rebel Academy
Rebel Gods
Rebel Werewolves

Rebel: House of Fae
Rebel Angels
Shadowmates
Rebel Vampires
Rebel Legends

Have you read all the series in the Oxford Verse?

Biting Mr. Darcy
Hexing Merlin
A Familiar Murder
A Familiar Curse
A Familiar Hex
A Familiar Brew
A Familiar Ghost
A Familiar Spell
A Familiar Yule
A Familiar Bride

Read More from Rosemary A Johns
Website
Merchandise
Facebook
Instagram
TikTok
Bookbub
Twitter: @RosemaryAJohns

Become a Rebel here today by joining Rosemary's Rebels Group on Facebook!

APPENDIX ONE: BAY REBELS MEMBERS

PLAYERS
Jude D'Angelo, Captain, Center
Shay Prince, Right Wing
Grayson, Left Wing
Atlas, Right Defenseman
Lucas, Left Defenseman
Zach, Goaltender

COACHES
Austin McKenna, Head Coach
Colton, Assistant Coach
Goalie Coach
Strength and Conditioning Coach

TEAM SUPPORT AND OPERATIONS/MANAGEMENT
Robyn McKenna, Austin's daughter, PR Director
Eden Prince, Shay's twin, D'Angelo's PA

Operations Manager, Felix
Finance Manager, Silas Anderson
Senior Board Member, William Bronwyn
Equipment Manager, Kay

MEDICAL SUPPORT

Cody McKenna, Austin's son, Director of Physical Therapy

Noah Anderson, Team Nurse

Team Doctor

Sports Therapist

Nutritionist

Psychologist

Massage Therapist

Mental Skills Coach

APPENDIX TWO: FRIENDS, FAMILY, OR ENEMIES

Doctor Michael Gaines, Cody's husband, Doctor at Freedom Heart Hospital

Neve, owner of Merchant's Inn

Tom, bartender in Merchant's Inn

Larry Gibbs, coach of Anaheim Ducks

Folkes, captain of Anaheim Ducks

Minchew, LA Kings player

Blythe, Shay's ex-Domme

Melanie Helt, journalist at Peninsula Daily News

Wilder Talon, Robyn's ex-husband, Pittsburgh Penguins player

Beth McKenna, Robyn and Cody's mother

Maria, D'Angelo's sister

Bruno, D'Angelo's brother

Mr. and Mrs. D'Angelo, Jude D'Angelo's parents

Mr. and Mrs. Prince, Shay and Eden's adoptive parents

Garcia, D'Angelo's friend and PI

SHAY'S TEN FAVORITE SONGS PLAYLIST

The Strokes — "You Only Live Once"
White Stripes — "Fell in Love With a Girl."
Arctic Monkeys — "R U Mine?"
Kasabian — "Days Are Forgotten"
FOALS — "Mountain at My Gates"
Blur — "Song 2"
The Lumineers — "Ophelia"
Yeah, Yeah, Yeahs — "Maps"
The Smiths — "Heaven Knows I'm Miserable Now"
Pulp — "Common People"

Printed in Great Britain
by Amazon